WINNER OF THE

1998 ████████████

for Best Regency, J█████████████████ been
nominated for twelve ████████████████

PRAISE FOR JEAN ROSS EWING'S

Illusion

"Wonderful! Trust me on this. If you like Regency historicals that are sexy, complex, and darkly dramatic, you'll like this one."
—Jo Beverley

". . . *Illusion* seethes with passion. Ewing's characters are distinctive and complex, her settings carefully crafted. Her prose is mature and as smooth as the Indian silks that Frances wears."
—*Valley Times* (Pleasanton, CA)

"Jean Ross Ewing explodes on the historical romance scene with a simply splendid romantic adventure in which nothing is as it seems. Ms. Ewing's highly complex hero is absolutely mesmerizing . . . he stands at the center of an intricate, brilliantly developed plot. Pure reading magic." —*Romantic Times*

"One of the best novels of the decade, *Illusion* makes no pretense at being sweet. Its visceral approach to the boundaries of sensuality marks it as a passionate encounter of the best kind. Not since Dorothy Dunnett . . . has an author come close to creating a hero so cogent and forceful as Rivaulx."
—*Romance Communications*

"A bold and exciting story . . . thick with hidden intrigues and dangers, and the suspense is a killer!" —*Affaire de Coeur*

"Ewing has written an erotic and dark historical romance with characters as complex and intriguing as the plot." —*Booklist*

"A classy historical romance that will leave readers salivating for more stories from this talented newcomer."
—Harriet Klausner

"Wow! An absolutely glorious book! There's a powerful wisdom that threads its way all through *Illusion* . . . intricate plot, strong suspense, extremely likable characters of great depth and complexity, wonderful sensuality, and that mesmerizing romance at the very heart of it all."
—Mary Balogh, bestselling author of *Irresistible*

PRAISE FOR JEAN ROSS EWING'S

Flowers Under Ice

"Jean Ross Ewing is rapidly becoming the mistress of lush, dramatic romance. A passionate love story rivetingly well told in language to take the breath away. Don't miss it." —Jo Beverley

"In *Flowers Under Ice*, Jean Ross Ewing stakes her claim as one of the most powerful voices in historical romance. Beautifully written and richly evocative of the Scottish Highlands, *Flowers Under Ice* is the story of Dominic and Catriona, star-crossed lovers who come together in passion and lies, and must triumph over devastating enemies before they can forge a lasting love."
—Mary Jo Putney

Flowers Under Ice

JEAN ROSS EWING

BERKLEY BOOKS, NEW YORK

FLOWERS UNDER ICE

A Berkley Book / published by arrangement with
the author

PRINTING HISTORY
Berkley edition / September 1999

ISBN: 0-425-17036-5

BERKLEY®
Berkley Books are published by The Berkley Publishing Group,
a division of Penguin Putnam Inc.,
375 Hudson Street, New York, New York 10014.
BERKLEY and the "B" logo are trademarks belonging to
Penguin Putnam Inc.

PRINTED IN THE UNITED STATES OF AMERICA

10 9 8 7 6 5 4 3 2 1

Acknowledgments

I OWE VERY special thanks to the generous scholars at the library in Inverness and at the School of Scottish Studies in Edinburgh, who enthusiastically shared their time and their knowledge. Sincerest thanks are also owed to my family and to all those Gaelic speakers who gave me their help. Any errors in this book are mine alone.

Flowers Under Ice

One

London
Early June, 1816

HE HUNG SUSPENDED in emptiness, caught neatly between heaven and hell.

Major the Honorable Dominic Wyndham, brother and heir to the Earl of Windrush, was reputed to be a man of very wicked tastes. He had never yet refused a challenge. But this was a little excessive, even for him.

Dominic clung to the iron spike at the top of the church spire, leaned his forehead against cold, hard metal, and laughed.

Night air chilled his naked back. Far beneath him, the chimneys of Mayfair jutted in the glow of the gaslights. The Canal in St. James's Park reflected the moon and the huge wheeling arc of stars above his head. Away to the east, the Tower bulked against the gleaming ribbon of the Thames, a fire of some kind burning near it. The rest of London slept beneath rooftops faintly silvered with moonlight, ignorant of the mayhem far above their heads.

How many of those roofs sheltered women he knew? Mirth bubbled in him in crazy defiance. Too damned many!

"I can't do it," gasped a voice somewhere in the blackness below him. "For God's sake! I shall fall!"

Dominic lifted his head and peered down. The steep roof plunged away far too precipitously for comfort. With a kind of frantic desperation, he controlled the errant laughter.

"You can, sir," he said. "I shall help you. Here, hold on to this!"

He had earlier pulled off his cravat and shirt, and with the help of the small knife attached to his pocket pistol cut them into strips, now braided together into a short rope. He tied one end to the spike and dropped the other away into the void. The linen shone white against the dark slope of the roof.

"Now do it, Stansted." It was the tone he might use for a reluctant horse, combining reassurance with authority. "Tie the rope to your wrist, grasp the fretwork, and don't look down."

The disembodied voice floated up to him. "I'm going to be sick."

Dominic hooked his elbow around the iron spike. His bare feet were wedged firmly into carved loops of stone—secure enough, had the stone not been rotten with age. He allowed nothing of this judgment into his voice. "My dear sir, it's only the drink. Put one foot after the other and come up. The view is wonderful."

A weight pulled the rope taut. Lord Stansted's white face emerged from the gloom, his red hair darkened to umber in the moonlight. He had the linen wrapped around one hand. "It's not the drink, believe me. Claret would never upset my innards."

"No, I suppose not," Dominic replied. "When wine refuses to settle in your belly like a gentle old dame dropping into her armchair is when we shall see wonders. But if you're not too foxed, sir, you have no excuse. Come on. This is the easy part." He reached down a hand. "You're almost there."

Gloved fingers reached up and the men's hands locked together.

As Dominic took his weight Stansted lurched, his feet slipping with a dreadful clatter. A broken piece of stone careened away into the darkness. Losing the rope,

Stansted's other hand slid across the slates. "By God! Dominic!"

Strain burned across his shoulders and back as Dominic braced against the iron spike. Pray God it wasn't rotten, too! "You would have been advised, sir," he said, allowing himself the ghost of a smile, "to have left off your damned boots."

The spike held. Dominic pulled steadily. Lord Stansted arrived at the top of the steeple. "By God, I almost went to meet my Maker that time." His voice shook. "How the devil do we get back down?"

Dominic ignored him. He pulled Stansted's handkerchief from its pocket and tied it to the spike. It was a deliciously precarious moment, to take both hands from their grip and balance on his toes, his knees braced against the roof, while he tied the knots. An odd, breathless irony scintillated about the moment—to be this close to death now, for God's sake, after surviving so much—when he could have been safely entertaining some eager lady in her bed. There were unquestionably easier ways for a half-pay officer to support himself, besides risking his worthless life in absurd wagers.

But he was not quite ready to die.

Though Stansted had no idea of it, this gamble was a stone dropped in a pool. While the shock waves filled his empty purse and the splash might bring Stansted his heart's desire, the small ripples embodied the one reason Dominic had to live.

With wry gratitude, he returned one hand to the iron spike. "Do you know, I don't believe I was ever in a more peaceful spot. It soothes my troubled soul to be so close to the heavens—like a medieval anchorite finding a place of repose in the chaos of the times." He looked up and studied the stars. "Do you think I am destined for heaven? A matter for some debate, perhaps?"

Stansted clung to him, shaking his head. "Don't make me laugh. By God, you're the very devil, Wyndham! Get me down to the street in one piece, or they'll swing you at Newgate for murdering a duke's only son."

Dominic grinned at him as he untied the linen cord. " 'If

he be not born to be hanged, our case is miserable.' Here.
Use the rope. Keep one end tied to the fretwork and the
other about your wrist. Go down in stages. I'll come behind
to release and retie it for you each time.''

Stansted's white face wavered as a cloud drifted in front
of the moon. ''What about you?''

''I shan't fail you. Now, are you ready?''

The duke's son smiled wanly at Dominic for a moment,
then the men inched their way down the spire, leaving Lord
Stansted's handkerchief flying high above the city like a
flag.

The crowd waiting at the church steps burst into applause.
Hands thumped heavily on Stansted's back and grasped at
Dominic, trying to shake him by the hand or buffet his
shoulder. Mirth ran freely as wine passed from hand to
hand. Dominic began to laugh with the rest. It was done.
Hope—however vain—was renewed. And besides, the
pavement felt so charmingly solid beneath his feet. Gold
clinked into a hat. Some men scrawled promissory notes.

The fellow passing the hat made an exaggerated grimace.
''Devil take it if I thought you could win, Wyndham! We'll
all be washed up, sir! How the hell did you get him to do
it?''

''We supported each other.'' Dominic leaned back
against the church door and pulled on his stockings and
boots, catching his breath between gasps of laughter. ''Like
two fishwives carrying a basket: first one hauls, then the
other, and the entire enterprise stinks.''

Amid the renewed burst of merriment he looked up and
the laughter died in his throat. A carriage had pulled up at
the curb. He recognized the horses, the coachman, and his
family's crest on the panel. Shadowed by a black bonnet,
a woman's face gazed from the open coach window.

It was as if reality shifted on its moorings and time became transparent. As if the intemperate crowd were not
there. As if there were sudden silence instead of bedlam.

As if a clear wind blew into these raucous streets from some unknown wild place. Dominic knew in his soul something had happened to shatter his life.

Yet he had never seen the woman before.

The coach rocked as his brother stepped down, the Windrush crest bobbing with the movement.

Dominic shook himself. He must be damnably foxed. "Alas, we have company," he said. "Our little wager is about to be witnessed by my brother, the puissant Earl of Windrush. Sadly, Jack has a severely deficient sense of humor. We little fish are about to be roasted, gentlemen— stripped of our scales, basted with butter, wrapped in pastry, and roasted."

Jack thrust through the crowd. He elbowed aside a dandy in a pink cutaway coat, rapping him sharply in the ribs with his cane, and pushed past an indignant viscount.

The woman remained in the carriage—a vision of disapproval, lips pressed together, brows drawn into a frown. Not a pretty face. Yet there was something remarkable in the very turn of her head, a grace like a roe deer. As their eyes met he felt the force of her gaze like a sudden drench of water, the candor in it piercing to the bone.

Ignoring her, ignoring the persistent warning in the back of his mind, he waited quietly until Jack stopped in front of him. Dominic spoke first. "Good evening, my lord. We were talking of fish. Come for a bite?"

The earl frowned. "What the hell tomfoolery is this? You are half-naked."

"A steeplechase." Dominic shrugged into his coat, the lining cool against his skin. He was damned if he'd tell Jack his real purpose. "My shirt has been sacrificed, alas, to the cause. After all, when life has no meaning, it must offer amusement. Pray stand aside. Lord Stansted is unwell. The piscine scent of the trouble you bring with you, perhaps?"

As Dominic spoke the duke's son made a face, then stumbled away from the dandies to dispose of his supper in a corner.

His brother's frown intensified. "By God, what the devil do you mean: a steeplechase?"

The viscount who had been so ungraciously thrust aside gazed at the earl through his quizzing glass. "We wagered, Lord Windrush, that your brother couldn't get Stansted's handkerchief tied to the top of the steeple, but damme if he didn't do it."

Dominic leaned back against the church door and folded his arms across his chest. "A new-sprung form of a favorite sport, vertical instead of horizontal for a little added spice, and without the horses. The evidence of success now flies above London, and I am the richer by some two thousand guineas."

The earl's brow contracted into yet deeper furrows. He had begun to resemble one of the choicer gargoyles Dominic had passed on his climb up the steeple. "You mean these gentlemen wagered there was any daredevil thing you would *not* do?"

"Not at all. No one would bet against my idiocy, of course. The wager was that I could not get Stansted up there with me." Dominic's voice had become cool. His brother often had that effect on him. Jack was nine years older and three stone heavier. No question at all where power lay in the Wyndham family.

"What is this? Some desperate attempt to recapture the excitement of the war?"

It struck deep, but he couldn't concentrate on his brother. Everything in him was aware of the woman. No, not pretty exactly, but intense, striking, with a stunning purity of bone—not a face to forget. Her gaze didn't waver. Absurdly, it pressed on him. Damn her! Couldn't she look away? His reply was biting. "The war? If you recall, I missed Waterloo because I was locked in a cellar in Paris. Excitement isn't exactly the word I would choose to describe the experience."

"Then it's boredom? Contempt? What, for God's sake?"

He forced his attention back to Jack and smiled. "There was a certain symmetry to the event which appealed to my sense of the ridiculous. After all, I was married in this church. And, like me, Stansted has a spouse who ran away to Scotland.''

"By God, Dominic, you are mad!''

"Am I?'' he replied innocently. "Why? I have just won a great deal of money.''

His brother glared at him. "But you have just lost your wife. I'm sure you think it fair trade. Harriet died in Edinburgh last week, while you caroused away your days in St. James's.''

It was a shock like a misfiring cannon—or like the loss of a limb on the battlefield—almost too absolute to be believed. Dominic looked away, fighting the need to react. He wasn't sure what he might do if he did. Laugh? Weep? Break something?

How could Harriet be dead? He had been going to win her back. There had been all the time in the world. How could it have collapsed into nonexistence? The pain was intense, as if his heart were flayed and held above flames, which was where absurdity reached its peak. In spite of what he had just achieved, Harriet would never have come back to him, would she? And now she was dead.

The crowd stood silent, shuffling with a vague embarrassment—a fear they might witness some indecorous emotion? Dominic willed himself to show nothing of the kind. He made himself smile. "Not my *days,* Jack. My nights. I carouse away my nights. Sin is better suited to the dark.''

The earl's features seemed to melt. "Is that all you can say when you receive such news?''

"Of course not.'' He was almost blind with distress, but he was still burningly aware of the woman in the black bonnet. "I can remind you of your manners. Who is that doxy scowling at me from your carriage? Won't you introduce us?''

His brother glanced at her with indifference. "Miss Catriona Sinclair. Harriet's companion, who brought us the report from Edinburgh. If you are interested, she can tell you the details.''

Catriona. The Scots Catherine. Ca-*tree*-ona, the emphasis on the second syllable. So his instinct had been right—

this unknown woman had shattered his life. And now he knew where he had seen such a gaze before: on the face of Highland soldiers going into battle, roused by the tumult of the bagpipes, fixed on destiny. Even in the uncertain light, he knew her eyes were blue—a bright blue embroidered with gold, like bittersweet or forget-me-not—the eyes of the Far North, where flowers grow under ice.

"Oh, dear." He was dimly conscious of the faces of the crowd and most importantly, that of Lord Stansted, white-faced, hanging on his every word. The duke's son, whose wife had taken Harriet away to Scotland. Another poor soul who foolishly thought a rogue like Dominic Wyndham could teach him something about women. Stansted had no idea of that rogue's noble efforts on his behalf—now shattered and made meaningless.

Summoning the last ounce of his self-control, he gave Catriona Sinclair a short bow, horribly aware it would seem merely callous and insulting, and let his voice show nothing but irony.

"Good evening, Miss Sinclair. You find me sadly bereft of both spouse and shirt. How very unfortunate."

Two

CATRIONA TWISTED HER gloves in her lap and stared back. Her heart thumped in an odd rhythm, too hard and fast. All these men belonged to a race she despised, a race whose vain, idle ways had corrupted the pure, ancient habits of the north. Not that she had known many English aristocrats in her twenty-five years. But she knew *of* them, or at least, she knew of this one, Dominic Wyndham, the man she had come to seek. She cursed softly in Gaelic, or if it was not a curse, it was the very name for iniquity: *Diabhal*. Lucifer. About to be bearded in his den. But with a fine Highland courtesy, of course.

His eyes met hers boldly, yet there was something disconcertingly shuttered about his expression. He was tall, dominating the crowd. Red-blond hair tumbled over his forehead. The rest blurred into an impression of strength, ease, and indifference—something rugged and untamed, something she hadn't expected in an Englishman. He had no cravat or shirt beneath his jacket, just naked flesh, mitered with muscle. His unbuttoned coat framed and emphasized it, this masculine nakedness.

She had heard every word of his exchange with the earl. *Sin is better suited to the dark.*

And then he smiled at her and bowed, after calling her a doxy. His smile was charming, sending a deep dimple

into each cheek. Yet his eyes remained guarded, dark, like
moss under a waterfall and hiding as many secrets. What
on earth was she going to do now?

He gave her an immediate answer. She scrambled for the
far side of the carriage as he strode up and swung himself
inside, his brother at his heels. Then Catriona sat silent as
Dominic Wyndham, poor Harriet's husband, callously be-
littled the awful news and made a sarcastic play, brilliant
but soulless, out of the entire situation. He ignored her and
asked his brother questions, then mocked the answers with
a quicksilver wit. His every word betrayed him to be heartless, corrupt, and immoral—and without doubt as drunk as
a laird at a wake. She was not surprised.

The carriage rolled up to the earl's imposing town house,
where she had arrived from Edinburgh with her news barely
an hour before. Catriona was handed down, then led inside
by a footman. Dominic Wyndham instantly disappeared.
She watched him stride away down a corridor and heard a
door slam. The earl winced, but he would not apologize to
a female of her presumed station for a nobleman's behavior.

"We shall offer you a bed for the night, of course, Miss
Sinclair," he said with a distracted frown. "And any further assistance you may require."

Jack Wyndham was stockier than his brother, with straw
hair and something of the bulldog in his face—like a rough
draft, a model blocked out of clay, before the artist per-
fected his idea and cast Dominic Wyndham in gold.

Catriona glanced away from the earl at the grand entryway, at the gilt pillars and rich paintings, the opulent display of English wealth, and remembered her purpose. "I
am most grateful for your offer, Lord Windrush," she said
quietly. "Your lordship is most kind."

The earl waved to a servant. Catriona was swept away
and taken upstairs to a bedroom. She had to carry her small
case herself.

Lord Windrush walked into his study. His brother stood at
the cold fireplace leaning his yellow head on his hands, his

long fingers locked on the mantelpiece, the knuckles white. The earl was vaguely aware that his own hands were clenched into fists.

"Good God, Dominic!" he began. "If you cannot behave like a gentleman—"

"Don't start!" The tall, lithe body turned and Dominic faced him. His skin was white, the green eyes blazing. "If you think for one moment this is the time for an unctuous sermon, I shall knock you down. I am aware you find my every action reprehensible, my friends tawdry, my activities dissolute. Harriet no doubt cursed me on her deathbed and cried to heaven to punish me for my wickedness. Yet her death has been a shock, nonetheless. You could have shown something more of decorum in broaching the news."

"Decorum! When I find you drunk and half-naked, profaning a church! How dare you, sir!"

"Yet you thought it an appropriate enough time and place to tell me of the death of my wife—God help me if I ever develop such a fine sense of etiquette! And to drag that Scottish girl with you! Since you know me so well, you might have predicted just how ugly it would be. There was no need at all for her to witness it."

"What difference does that make?" Lord Windrush glared at him, bewildered. "What impression can you make on any decent female, except the one you made on Harriet?"

"I don't care what impression Miss Sinclair may have formed of me. By God, how could anything be more irrelevant? But didn't you see her face? She had just traveled from Edinburgh, alone and very possibly frightened. Her clothes are threadbare, her shoes cracked. She obviously has no money, and she probably felt real affection for Harriet. Oh, devil take it! What can it matter? You will see she is provided for, of course. And now I am very tired. You will not object if I stay the night in my old room?"

With a control remarkable in a man who a short hour before had taken part in a besotted wager to climb a church steeple, he stalked away and closed the door softly behind him.

The earl stared after his brother. He had never understood
him. There were too many years between them and too
much time apart. Once there had been a golden-haired little
boy, obscurely a nuisance, underfoot too much, who had
somehow survived when all the intervening babies had
died, one after another. Now there was a man of secrets, a
man who had played some vital hidden role in the war, a
man who had plunged the family into the scandal of the
age. Anyone else would have exiled himself permanently,
yet Dominic had come back after Napoleon's final defeat
and stayed, accepted nowhere, except by the wild youth of
London, men without conscience, and by women, so rumor
had it, privately.

Yet as Dominic had passed the candles, his hair gilt and
the rugged bones of his face stark with shadows, the wavering flame had reflected on eyelashes suspiciously bright
with moisture. Lord Windrush dismissed the thought. A
trick of the light, perhaps. There was no possibility at all
that his reprobate brother, the hardened rake, would shed
tears over the death of his estranged wife.

Dominic stopped at the top of the stairs and ground his
fingers over his mouth, choking back his pain, barely aware
of the bite of his rings against his lips. Harriet. His pretty,
confused blonde wife. Gone to her greater reward. The
enormity of his failure lived in him still, a daily ache. The
panic. The recriminations. The final humiliation of her sobbing hysteria. In the years since she had run away, had
Harriet given one thought or one prayer to the husband she
had left behind in England?

And now it was too late. Forever. Forever too late.

He looked up as a footman padded past, carrying a small
tray. A door opened farther down the corridor and Miss
Catriona Sinclair stepped out. The footman bowed and retreated, but she stood in the doorway of the room, the tray
in her hands, and stared at Dominic. The wavering light
cast a halo about her hair, like a severe Madonna in a

fresco. He knew, for he had seen them in the carriage, that those staring eyes were as blue as the Virgin's robe.

He dropped his hand, disconcerted at what she might have seen.

She set down the tray on a table by the door and folded her hands, still fixing him with that intense harebell gaze. Her figure was outlined by the candles behind her. A slender female body, strong-boned, ripe, yet with that wild, natural grace. Desire stirred in him, crazily. An obstinate, senseless male reaction, to be ignored.

"Major Wyndham," she said softly. "I should like a few words in private, if I may."

"Now?"

She nodded.

He wasn't sure if he could trust himself. Control was stretching like a rope running through his hands, becoming taut enough to snap. He had seen it in soldiers after battle, the untamed barbarity of shock, something better dealt with in private. Whatever she wanted, it would have to wait. He walked up to her, planning to brush by with a denial.

She was a head shorter than he. Her hair was fine and dark, dressed in intricate plaits wound into a bun at the back of her neck. She had the look of a governess, or an impoverished gentlewoman, typical of some kind of paid companion. Yet in spite of her severity she wasn't tame enough, as if those blue eyes remembered warrior kings and Norsemen streaming over the water in ships with a dragon's head at the prow.

The harebell gaze did not waver. "I must catch the stage from the Golden Goose at five this morning. The maid will awaken me. I was afraid you would not be up." As if audacity came in a rush, she looked up at him with chilling directness. "I cannot leave until we have spoken together."

It would help if he didn't feel so remote, like a changeling moving through a charade of his own life. He definitely didn't want to sneer, but he knew it would sound like one. "To bring me some last words of remorse from my late wife? Don't bother."

She had the grace to blush. The color began as a spot in

each cheek and spread over her austere bones up to her brow and down her neck. Her skin was remarkably fair for a dark-haired woman—fine, northern skin, unused to much sun. Her features might be too grave to be pretty, but her complexion was perfect. He wanted to touch her.

"No, I'm very sorry," she said stiffly. "She had no affection for you. There is something else, of the utmost urgency. Where may we be private?"

Footsteps sounded on the stair. Jack coming to bed, no doubt. Suddenly Dominic wanted very badly to hear Miss Sinclair and he didn't want his brother taking part. Grasping her elbow, he thrust her back into the bedroom and closed the door behind them.

"We can talk here, if you feel that a lady of such upright probity has anything to say to a rake. What the devil do you wish to tell me?"

∽

Catriona looked about, at the mahogany wardrobe and brocade-covered bed. Though there were chairs and other furniture, it was unquestionably a bedchamber, and he was standing very close, still holding her arm. Her nerves prickled with awareness, of the long fingers on her sleeve, of the intensity flowing from him like the Falls of Conan roaring in spate below Loch Luichart.

At the shock of it, she drew back.

He strode across the room and carried the chair at the writing desk to join its fellow beside the fireplace. "It's not proper, of course. But for heaven's sake, try not to look so much like a schoolmarm confronted with a mad dog. You may spend a quarter of an hour with me without being deflowered—unless you wish it, of course."

She stood stock-still, gripping her hands together until they hurt, watching the lithe movements and the unquestioning certainty of his manner, as if he deployed troops and commanded obedience. "That is not what I have been led to believe."

He turned to her with an ironic twist at the corner of his

mouth. It was a firm mouth, the bottom lip curved above his chin with a hint of derision. She had not thought he would be quite so attractive. How incredibly foolish!

"Really? And what do you believe? No, don't tell me. I can imagine. Here, sit down."

She went to the chair and sat. "Thank you."

Dominic took the tray and brought it to her. "And your meal? Don't let me disturb you while you break your fast. Pray, eat first, then give me your message."

Catriona looked down at the tray. She felt very hungry and a little faint. "Very well." She bit into a thin slice of beef on a piece of bread, the meat richly flavored with wine and herbs. Her last meal had been a slab of cheap rye bread and some cheese, the day before. She nibbled at a slice of apple. The simple fruit tasted like ambrosia. Deliberately she made herself chew slowly, but he noticed, of course.

He dropped into the chair opposite hers and watched her in silence.

Catriona broke some more white bread into small pieces, spread them with butter, and chewed them. English food, soft, sweet, and decadent, like all this wealth, the hangings and the carpet. Only one thing in the room was inflexible and vigilant: the man sitting in front of her. He had unbuttoned his jacket. It made her feel impossibly self-conscious to eat like this in front of him—far too intimate.

Candlelight limned his cheeks and burnished the gold of his hair. He was disturbingly athletic, with the look of an Athenian discus thrower, cut cleanly from stone and concentrated forever on a target. Yet there was also a ruggedness to him, as if the stone had been weathered by years of storm. Pray her plan was not as imprudent as it seemed, a net of duplicity designed to weave a trap about this one vital man!

She gathered her courage, buttressing it with censure. "There is something I have to tell you, sir. You must come to Edinburgh."

The firm skin at his waist flexed as he stretched out his legs. The green gaze locked on her face. "*Must* I? Good God, why? Surely you don't wish for my companionship?"

"Indeed, I do not!"

"Am I so accursed?" He smiled as if she had paid him a compliment. "In the past I have been compared, Miss Sinclair, to the Archangel Michael, but only by a lady of the night, of course, and no doubt the angel is fallen, his wings tarnished by villainy. If I offended your sensibilities in my brother's carriage, I am sorry. I wish very dearly you had not been there. There is nothing else I can say. You are from the Highlands?"

There was no reason for the question to surprise her, but it did. "How did you know?"

"The purity of your accent betrays you: the way you say 'food' as if the vowels were beloved, and remember the 'h' in 'where.' " His voice was quiet, but there was humor there and something else she could not identify. "I have known some Highlanders."

Was this mockery? She bridled. "If you insist on knowing, I am from Glen Reulach, north of Inverness." She had been surprised into the truth. Instantly she tried to cover for it. "I met your late wife when I came to Edinburgh for work." Not knowing quite how to cope any longer, she set the tray aside. She was determined to outwit him, but she wasn't sure how much he knew of Edinburgh. "She hired me, and—"

"And filled your virtuous—but curious—ears with tales of the very, very naughty man who was her husband."

Relieved, Catriona met his eyes without flinching. "Och! She told me what I might find if I met you. I have no desire to further an acquaintance with a Don Juan of your notoriety."

He had the insolence to grin at her, this man who claimed kinship with archangels. "I suppose not. But being so notorious is bloody hard work. You might at least give me credit for that."

It annoyed her, that he could be flippant. "Sir, I believe you are wicked. Nevertheless, you must come back with me."

"Wicked?" He turned his head to look up at the mantel. A faint pulse beat at the edge of his jaw, as if anger underlay his ridicule. Well, let him be angry! She cared nothing for his feelings. "I am certainly an infamous rake, mired in scandal. If we travel together to Scotland, your reputation will be annihilated. And since I am such an unholy rogue, your virtue will doubtless be lost into the bargain, a sweet enough thought, but not, perhaps, what you had in mind?"

The threat of it sang in her blood. Harriet had warned her. "We do not need to travel together. I have a seat on the public stage. I assume you have a carriage?"

The muscle at the corner of his mouth tightened, as if the anger deepened to rage. "Of course. But I shall certainly not come under such conditions. If you require me in Scotland, Miss Sinclair, then you must travel with me." He looked back at her, his grin sending a deep dimple into his cheeks. "And thus my immodest presence will both tarnish and tempt you. Affection is not required to discover temptation. No, if you want me, you will travel with me like a loose woman. I give you my word, madam: there is no other way I shall leave London."

The blush heated her cheeks and fired her resentment. She clasped her hands hard in her lap. "There is something you don't understand. This is not an idle whim. Harriet asked me on her deathbed to let you know. There is a child."

His chair clattered into the wall as he leaped to his feet. Letting the chair fall, he stalked away, back rigid. "By God, what child?"

"Your son, Major Wyndham."

He spun to face her, his expression stark. *"My son?"*

For a moment his obvious distress unnerved her. But it had to work. No man cared much about babies, but if he believed her—then, surely, surely he would come? Harriet had said Dominic Wyndham was in Edinburgh two years before. So it *could* be his child. "Harriet had a child. He is fifteen months old. You must come to Scotland and take him into your care, so he may claim his rightful name and place."

To Catriona's dismay, quite helplessly Dominic Wyndham began to laugh. He leaned his head into a corner post of the bed while his shoulders shook with uncontrolled mirth. "Dear God! What a night for news! When for these last years I have had my sins thrown into my face, and the horror of what I demanded from my innocent wife sniggered over in drawing rooms, now I learn she had a child. Fifteen months ago, which would put me in her bed—when?—the summer of 1814?" He turned to her, his face lit with hilarity. "I'm sorry, Miss Sinclair. I shall not come to Edinburgh. In fact I have nothing left to say."

Catriona fixed her eyes on his knees, not daring to look into his face because of what her own might reveal. "But the bairn, sir! Surely you cannot abandon your own lad?"

"There is not much I am sure of in this world, madam, but I am certain of one thing: any child of Harriet's is not mine." His voice was scathing. "For God's sake, don't you know why she left me? Haven't the scurrilous rumors reached Scotland?"

Appalled at her mistake, she dropped her eyes to his boots. They were expensive and very black—a quality of leather the clansmen knew only in book bindings. "I don't know. There were hints—"

The shining boots strode across the room to stand in front of her. "Hints! My wife left me within hours of our wedding night, Miss Sinclair, protesting, weeping to her parents. Society was rallied to the cause."

Catriona raised her head. His eyes were dark as sin and filled with self-mockery. "She said nothing of that to me."

"For God's sake! Her father threatened to horsewhip me for imposing my unnatural appetites on his spotless daughter, and took her back into his own household. When he died, she left with Lady Stansted to do good works in Edinburgh. That was three years ago. It is simply not possible I am the father of this boy. Why the devil should I care what becomes of him?"

Catriona took a deep breath. He must come! So she must tell more falsehoods. "Then he is left without anyone in the world. I must immediately take up another post, in Stirling. I cannot take the child with me. It was your wife's dying wish. I thought you would provide for him, at least. Will you see him given to the parish and raised to dig ditches? I beg you, Major Wyndham. Please come to Edinburgh.'' She rubbed both hands over her cheeks. "If you disown him, no one knows his father! I will do whatever it takes to save him. I will travel with you, if you wish."

"Will you?" His voice mocked. He caught her by the chin and lifted her face, so she was forced to look into his eyes. They were filled with a sharp intelligence, as if he saw right through her deceptions. "Like a loose woman, Miss Sinclair?"

"My virtue is in no danger from you whatsoever."

A grass-green flame, devouring, hungry, his gaze ran over her. It was as if restraint shredded in him, as if he was flooded with wildness. His lip curled. "Is that a wager? I'm not sure it's one you could win. If you were Harriet's friend, were you also a member of the Souls of Charity, that charming sisterhood devoted—or so I have been led to believe—to probity, piety, and chastity, like a flock of damned nuns? What if a rogue like me required the ultimate sacrifice for the sake of this orphaned babe?"

She felt hot and uncomfortable, but she clung stubbornly to her plan. "I will do whatever is necessary. Harriet warned me you were entirely without conscience. I do not expect you to behave with honor, but I won't see the child abandoned."

"At the price of your virtue?"

Did he think to test her mettle? He would find she was made of harder steel than her own knife blade. "If you are wicked enough to require it."

"But you know I am wicked, Miss Sinclair. You have said so. Show me your legs."

Shock stiffened her spine. "What?"

"The lower limbs, madam. Ankles, calves, knees, thighs. You have just agreed to travel as my mistress. I should like to see what's being offered."

A tremble began deep inside. Her face felt red and flushed. He would make her pull up her skirts and sit exposed before him? "Very well," she said, not moving. "I have two. They carry me quite well from place to place. Which do you want first?''

"Oh, your right ankle, I think." His fingers trailed up the side of her neck, touching below her ear, moving delicately into her hair, a man's fingers, strong and sure. "Your slender calf in its white stocking. Your knee, dimpled no doubt like a dumpling. Your naked thigh, soft with promise . . . your body, Miss Sinclair . . . surrendered for my pleasure . . . and yours.''

His caress brought a betrayal, prickly flashes of seductive sensuality warming her skin, firing into her blood. Her breath was ragged, but so was his. His smile concentrated in his eyes, like a hunting wildcat's. Catriona sat mesmerized, staring at him as he began to undo her buttons one at a time, opening the front of her dress.

"You have lovely skin, pure as white silk . . . so fine your veins shine pearl and blue like tiny fish below water. How they dart and flash as your heart beats faster! Do you offer these pearls to a swine like me for the sake of Harriet's bastard? Is the silk even softer below? Are the veins on your breasts as delicate?''

Swallowing hard, she tried to still the pounding in her blood. Her gaze stayed locked onto his. His breath was sweet with wine, dangerous with desire, the seductive curve of his lips only inches away. Insolently she pulled at her unbuttoned dress, tugging it down off her shoulders so the swell of her breasts glimmered above her shift.

"Here," she said. "Look for yourself."

His hand slipped down her throat, his thumb brushing her jaw. "Dear God," he said quietly. "I believe you really mean it."

She could not look away. "I give you my word, right now, that I do."

"Pride and defiance." His fingers lay still, his thumb moving slowly in an entrancing measure over her skin. "Highland virtues or Highland vices? But I don't want a mistress rigid with contempt and dignity, Miss Sinclair. If you want me so badly, you must at least pretend to be willing."

Blood pounded in fury, melting resolution in the flush of impotent rage. "If I am proud," she said, "it is because I know my own honor, and that your own means nothing to you."

"Honor?" He laughed softly. "I have nothing to lose in this world. I am very foxed. Why the devil should I care about honor?" He caught her hands and pulled her upright. Would he force her, here, in his brother's house? Were it not for the child, she would rather thrust her dirk into his hard belly. "How much do you love this boy of Harriet's? Enough to kiss me of your own volition?"

She looked up at the curve of his lip. He still held her fingers pinioned in his. "I cannot," she said. "You are too tall."

He moved his hands out to the sides, an open gesture of submission—but false, like the grin of a lion. "Ah, yes, you can. Reach up, pull down my mouth, and kiss my lips with yours."

The handle of her dirk pressed into her side, asking, begging, to be drawn. She could wipe the arrogant smile from his face before she wiped his blood from her blade, and gladly, gladly be hanged for it. But there was a child and everything that child meant. She touched his jacket. Without a word, he moved her fingers to his naked chest. Beneath the smooth, firm skin, his heart beat steadily. He stood perfectly still, the hard muscles moving with his breathing, and gazed down at her, his eyes black.

She reached her other hand to his neck. It was corded, strong. He bent his head a little, enough to allow her fingers to touch his shining hair, softer than she expected, enough to bring that sarcastic mouth within inches of her own. What was a kiss? Or even a tumble on the bed and the clumsy thrusting of a man into her body? Nothing. Catriona opened her lips. As a cold contempt chilled into her bones she prepared herself to kiss him.

He smiled, expertly seductive, unsettling her. The dimple indented his cheek. He caught her waist in one arm. She stood melded against him, her breasts crushed against his body, her palm slipping over his smooth flesh. Gently, entrancingly, his thumb traced her upper lip. A dulcet heat warmed her skin. For a moment it threatened to flare, like sheet lightning flashing about dark summer clouds, threatening to melt the snow in the corries, threatening a downpour to flood through the heather.

His nostrils flared as his hand slid down her neck and over the fabric of her dress. His fingers brushed her breast. Instantly her nipple rose to meet his touch. Pleasure coursed, throbbing into her belly. Desire flooded in a mad rush, sweeping defiance and confusion before it. She wanted to open her mouth, open her thighs, and let him in. *A Dhia,* did she want him?

But his thumb stilled.

"By God!" He spun her away and let her go. "Don't offer yourself to a rake unless you mean it, or I *shall* take you—here and now—on that bed, though I'm damned if I want to couple with Sacrifice dressed as Nobility. Is this child worth a virgin immolation?"

She dropped onto the chair. *If he had kissed her?* Mary, Mother of God, help her! To hide the shaking, she crossed her arms over her breast. "How can you know what I am, or what I value?"

He turned away, his boots scraping on the floor. While she sat pinned in place, he strode to the bed and stared down at the covers. "I can't, of course. Yet I wish—I wish to God you truly were wanton." He glanced at her, insolent in his male power, the blond hair sparking gold, and grinned. "I don't know what you are, Catriona Sinclair, but I know you are not that."

In surprise she looked down, knowing her cheeks burned while her soul quailed. She couldn't begin to understand her own feelings. For with her body she did want him, and she was too honest to deny it. Her heart hammered and pounded—*did she have honor, to do this, to trap him like this? Wouldn't she deserve whatever revenge he would take?* Tension hung between them, like the weight of unreleased thunder.

"There is a child," she said doggedly. "Only you can save him. Nothing else matters." That at least was true.

Hand on hip, he pushed aside his jacket. Framed by the fabric, the hard muscles over his ribs flexed as he moved. Strong veins tracked the back of his hand. A man's body, beautiful, glorious, like the warrior Archangel Michael. No wonder women came to him. No wonder his wife had left. She would think it fine enough to be such a man's mistress if she were really a servant, but she was not—and her purpose caught hard at her heart.

He looked up. "Then let us go to Scotland and rescue this poor infant."

"You will come?"

His grin seemed merely dissolute. "Apart from anything else, I'm devilish curious to find out who the father is. There is only one problem."

Catriona could still feel the touch of his fingers and the throb where her thighs met. "Which is?"

He rubbed his mouth with his thumb. "You see what I am. However we travel, the respectable family from Stirling will believe you a lost woman. Link your name with mine, even loosely, and you'll never work again. You cannot afford that, can you?"

She took a deep breath. "I don't mind."

"You still offer yourself, devil take your commitment in Stirling?"

"I have said that I do. I shall not go back on my word."

He laughed. "Neither shall I. I swore I wouldn't come unless we traveled together, so we're stuck with it. You willingly sacrifice your reputation? For how can you save it when I insist on such conditions?" His gaze was speculative, as if he rapidly calculated the answer to a problem. "Shall we make this a secret journey, Miss Sinclair? Creep into Scotland like mice into the wainscoting? You must put yourself entirely at my disposal, to make whatever arrangements I see fit. Then you may keep your reputation intact."

The entire future hung in the balance, poised in this one moment. She didn't try to hide her surprise. "I did not expect you to be generous. What is your price?"

He moved casually, running his hand over the carved wood of the bedpost. "Your virtue, of course. Your virtue is the price—but when you really mean it, tenderly, with a woman's open welcome. I shall not force you. Does that seem too easy?''

She stared at him.

"I don't want dishonesty from you, Catriona, or a confused, desperate pretense at love. I will come to Edinburgh. I will take care of the child. But these are my terms: to risk not only your virtue, but your heart—and to put up with my brackish temper. Do you agree?''

I will take care of the child. Relief came in a torrent, like a summer storm. Catriona nodded, blind, lifting her palm to brush away the gathering moisture. "I agree."

His boots struck hard on the floorboards. Firm fingers took her hand and supplied her with a handkerchief. He gave her a half smile, the trace of disbelief in his voice.

"These are tears of happiness?" he asked softly. "Don't be too sure. I give you notice right now: you will be under attack. You will want to surrender. Every day you will be besieged by a man who has a great deal more experience in the game than you do. I shall seduce you. You will fall in love and I shall break your heart. I guarantee it. What say you to that?''

Catriona met his eyes with all the disdain she could muster. "That you are an arrogant man. I can withstand you, Major Wyndham."

"Oh, no, my dear, you cannot. This is a game women lose. And what if every lurid tale they tell about me is true?" It was impossible to read his voice. Irony was there, and mischief, but the undertones might still prove dangerous. "Where is the child now?"

"With his nurse. Mrs. Mackay promised to keep him for the month."

"Then we had better go immediately. What is this estimable nurse's address?" Catriona told him, though he didn't seem to pay it much attention. The rapid voice went on, as if entranced by its own flexibility. "We shall not tell Lord Windrush. My brother would be hideously likely to try to interfere, but it would not be to rescue the child. Anyway, he leaves for the country in the morning. Thus if he is allowed his cue, he will be out of our play for the next several acts. Get some sleep. We'll leave at dawn." He raised her hand to his lips and kissed it. "To our journey, madam—and your seduction."

Catriona watched him walk away. He moved well, like a wolfhound. At the door he paused and turned to grin at her. "By the way," he said, "I am very foxed. In the morning I'll have the devil of a headache and the temper of a cornered badger. You'll have to put up with that, as well. What's the name of this child?"

"Andrew," she replied, closing her eyes for a moment. "Thank you, Major Wyndham."

"You think this some uncharacteristic act of charity? No, Miss Sinclair. Whether I'm his father or not, as Harriet's husband any child of hers is mine. Whatever my reputation, the law will thrust this innocent into my keeping. You knew that, didn't you? You just wanted to intervene, before a little boy was sent willy-nilly into the arms of depravity. Well, you may have your wish, but you may have to pay more than you bargained for it."

He bowed once and left.

Catriona stared at the heavy oak panels for several minutes. The impression of his firm fingers lingered on her palm and the faint trace of his lips burned across her knuckles. Had she hoped, against all the evidence, for a noble champion to help her in her quest? To share the burden she had taken up? For a savior?

She stood up and looked at herself in the mirror over the fireplace. Her face was flushed, her eyes too bright. She pulled the pins from her hair and untied it, shaking it free, as no man had ever seen it. It rioted darkly over her shoulders. Her dress still lay open. She unbuttoned it all the way down the front. Then she untied the ribbons in her shift and dropped the linen away from her breasts. They were round and white. She looked at them critically. The veins did dart blue beneath the skin, moving with her breathing. Tiny fish? It was ridiculous. But as she gazed into the glass, her nipples puckered in the cool air as if remembering the touch of his thumb. *This is a game women lose.*

Damn him! She was a fool. She needed a hero. Instead she had a rake, insolent with drink, but attractive in spite of it. Indeed. Indeed. Physically, an attractive man. But she wouldn't give two eggs for his soul.

Three

DOMINIC LEANED HIS head back against the wall. Candle-light wavered in the quiet corridor, throwing mysterious shadows into the corners. What the devil . . . What the *devil* had possessed him to do that? The aftermath of shock had left him oddly disoriented, dangerously vulnerable, so he had struck out instead and entangled himself like a dog in a thicket. He would go to Scotland with this Highland woman and rescue the child—of course, of course, he would rescue the child—but how would he cope with all that cold ferocity? And how dared she throw her precon-ceptions so brutally into his face?

Yet a memory of the weight of her breast, lush and soft, ached in his hand. Her lips had fired hot and red, ready for his. He had wanted to kiss her. He had wanted to keep loosing those buttons and free her nipples to his mouth. She would have gone as far as he'd asked. Should he have asked for more and kept asking?

His laugh held a bitterness he could no longer hide, even from himself. For a man with the reputation of a sinner, he had just behaved like a damned saint. *Catriona.* It was a name like a song. There was ancient music in her blood, waiting to be played. She would have let him assuage his grief and his rage in her body, there in that bed with the four posts. She would have done it hating him.

He did not want, ever, to have another woman hate him.

Instead, since he had come back from the war, there had been all those ladies of the beau monde, whose white thighs opened to him because they wanted to know—to find out with their inquisitive, yielding bodies—what it was like to bed a rogue. He had tried not to disappoint, but for four years he had never really pursued a seduction.

Yet Catriona Sinclair had accepted his mad challenge: *I am very foxed. You will have to put up with that, as well.* Was his insanity due to drink, or had all those years as a spy corrupted his thinking, making him look for complexity where it didn't exist, convincing him nothing was ever as it seemed? For he was sure she'd lied to him, though he didn't know how. She was prepared to give anything for his cooperation over this child, even falsehoods, even her virginity. Why? For God's sake, why would a servant sacrifice so much for another woman's bastard?

A candle guttered and went out.

Andrew, Harriet's child. An unknown little boy, left among strangers. At fifteen months old, would he be toddling on unsteady, fat little legs? Was he blond and blue-eyed, with smiles like rainbows, like the son he had once thought to have with his wife?

Distant clocks ticked into the silence, then in a random scattering of chimes and gongs began to strike the quarter hour. It would soon be morning.

Time to fulfill the first part of this fantastic bargain, and make sure her reputation survived unsullied, whatever suspicions he might have about her honesty.

He went to his room—Jack always kept it ready for him, though he had his own flat in St. James's—washed in cold water, and found a clean shirt. Stopping only for another swallow of his brother's brandy, he dressed again and left the house. Rapidly he walked along the hushed pavements to a set of rooms in Ryder Street. He went up the stairs and knocked for some time at the door to a top flat. He was acting purely on instinct now.

At last a sleepy servant opened to him.

"Wake Lord Stansted and tell him Major Wyndham is here."

The servant scratched at his wig, hastily donned over his nightcap. "Lor', guv! His lordship's fast asleep, and a wench with him, and all!"

With easy authority Dominic stepped past him. "Make some coffee, light the lamps, and give the hussy her shilling. Your master would wish to see me, were it the dawn of Ragnarok and the sun turned to blood in the heavens."

The servant looked blank for a moment, but he bowed to such a vastly superior knowledge of Norse mythology and ran to obey.

Ten minutes later Dominic sat opposite Lord Stansted. The duke's son grinned sleepily at him over a silver coffee urn.

"You are tufted with silk, like a bloody Eastern potentate," Dominic said. "I suggest you dress in something more suitable than a blue-and-gold dressing gown if we are to go out."

Stansted ran his fingers over his head. His hair stuck up in red tufts. "Out? For God's sake, it's almost morning. Where?"

"Drinking, gaming, wenching, and making more public mayhem."

"Damn it all!" Stansted groaned. "Not another bloody wager!"

"Not exactly. There is a babe in need of succor."

"A babe?" Comprehension dawned over the freckled face like a sunrise. "You have a byblow?"

"Not me. Harriet. She left a little bastard behind her in Edinburgh. The child has no one else. Devilish, isn't it?"

Stansted seemed entirely blank for a moment. "A bastard? Harriet had a child? *Harriet?* The child isn't yours?"

"No, sadly it's not. But it's splendidly ironic, don't you think? Harriet managed to keep this secret, until now, after she's dead."

The duke's son poured himself more coffee and drank it. His hand shook. "*Harriet?* By God! What do you mean—succor?"

"I shall rescue the boy from the Souls of Charity—dear God, what an asinine name! I can talk to Rosemary, take her a message, if you like."

"I haven't seen her since we were there two years ago, when Father made me go. His grace wants a grandson, so when I'm Duke of Rutley in my turn, our noble line won't end with me. It's bloody useless. Rosemary won't come back, any more than Harriet would. But why the hell go to Scotland? Can't you send for the child?"

It was barbaric enough that little Andrew had been abandoned, let alone that he should be packed up like a parcel in brown paper and shipped to a strange country. Even if this child weren't his own flesh and blood, he was a baby, innocent of the crimes of his parents. And Catriona Sinclair loved him, loved him enough to sacrifice her virginity, if necessary.

Dominic looked up. "So you don't think I should turn up soberly in Edinburgh, filled with responsibility and serious purpose?"

Stansted watched him for a moment. "It'd look devilish odd!"

"Exactly. And if I don't want to let half the beau monde know by breakfast that I go to Edinburgh after Harriet's child, I must leave secretly, at least. So I want your help. I would like you to give the impression for as long as possible that I'm still in London."

A brandy decanter sat next to the coffee urn. Reflections of red hair bloomed in the glass and silver like tiny flames. "This is some damned crazy scheme of yours, isn't it? Why drag me into it?"

Not even the coffee could counteract the anguish running in his veins. For the child, Andrew? This unknown little boy? Or for his own unknown baby son? The son he had hoped to see grow into manhood. The son he had buried in a coffin smaller than a writing case.

Dominic set down his cup. "Who else? You and I will

go from here to a very public debauch, then tomorrow you can put it about that I am suffering the aftereffects in my rooms. My man will defend my door with his life against curious sympathizers. After a few days there can be delicious rumors. By the time I reach Scotland's capital, my presence there can be seen to be random and ideally somewhat depraved. No one will know my real purpose.''

"Are you mad?''

"Yes, yes. I am mad.'' Dominic grinned. Had he just told the truth? Why did this matter so much? "I shall spring upon Auld Reekie like a Lord of Misrule.''

Stansted poured himself some brandy. "Oh, God! Don't tell me there's a woman in it?''

Dominic rose to his feet. "Isn't there always? But this time it's a douce Highland lass, replete with virtue and repressed emotions.''

"The girl in the coach?''

"Sad to say, she is stoutly impregnable to all my wicked ways—fortified with upright Highland values and buttressed with dire suspicions. Yet we shall travel together to Scotland. Unchaperoned. Indiscreet of me, isn't it? Nevertheless, I wish to save her reputation.''

There was silence for a moment as Stansted gulped again at some coffee.

"Why, Dominic?'' he asked suddenly, caught between the brandy and the coffee in a rare moment of candor. "Wouldn't it be easier to find a willing doxy?''

Oh, God. Oh, God. His life had been nothing but willing doxies. He longed suddenly, fiercely, for oblivion. "Easier, but less interesting. When respectable ladies shrink from me as if I were Lucifer, I must be allowed some kind of recompense.'' He pulled on his gloves. "Don't worry, the lady will be ruined, but—if you will lend me your assistance—privately, at least. Now, for God's sake, get dressed.''

∞

They reeled from gaming hell to bawdy house, the rowdiest, most decadent places Dominic could find. Stansted was weaving, his face lead white beneath his red hair, like window putty in a rusted frame. Dominic dragged him on with inexorable purpose. They had roared through a muddle of streets, drinking, gaming, being noticed, as the night died around them. Now the dandies, like vampires, were crawling back to their homes before the sun came up. Would any of them cast a reflection in a mirror? Would they all shrink and scream at the sight of a cross? Was he a vampire, too? Would sunlight dissolve him?

But he had not melted away at the scent of garlic.

For the first time in his life Dominic had paid money to a woman for sex, a blowsy whore, a woman he would normally have brushed aside with a kindly refusal and the gift of a halfpenny. Instead this time he had given her two shillings, and agreed to take her up against the wall in her own noisome alley. As the drink clamored in his head he had been rock hard for her, raging with a mad caricature of desire.

Stansted, collapsed against a coal hatch, had watched them go with open astonishment.

The whore had taken his coins and his arm, swinging her hips against him as they walked to the alley, the garlic strong on her breath.

"Steady, guv," she had said. "Steady now. What's a fine lord like you doing with the likes o' me, then, eh? I'd give it to you for nothing, just for the sake of your handsome face, didn't I have five chicks at home wanting their bread."

The rage had died. He'd had a sudden vision of ice-blue eyes, as blue as the sky blazing between clouds, and as distant. He had found himself staring into the harlot's rouged, honest face. She had been a pretty girl once. Her lips were stained carmine, like blood, but the smile over the spoiled teeth was genuine.

"Come, now, guv," she had said kindly. "Do you want a fumble, or not? What is it, then? Tell Mary what your trouble is."

I am drunk, he wanted to say. *I am damned. I have just*

lost my wife. Three and a half years ago I had to bury my son.

And at last, in her filthy alley, he had wept against her generous bosom, sobbing out his grief in a paroxysm he could no longer control. Was it sorrow for Harriet? Or for the death of a dream and the final end of innocence?

He had given her a guinea, no doubt the easiest money she had ever earned, and felt like a damned fool.

Dominic turned, half supporting Stansted, into St. James's Street. As the dandies disappeared, honest citizens emerged like dormice from hibernation. Some time ago a flock of geese had waddled by, herded into the city on tarred feet. The goose girl had grinned at him, though she looked tired enough to drop, so he had given her a shilling.

Yet the gentleman now gazing at him through his quizzing glass was not grinning and he was not honest. Rufous as a fox, he was up early with his manservant to stalk the streets for his health. It was slightly inconvenient under the circumstances. Two miserable, besotted wretches—like errant schoolboys caught stealing apples—were face-to-face with the Duke of Rutley, an eminently respectable peer of the realm and Stansted's father. Dominic laughed. Why the hell was he floating in this absurdity of thoughts, as if his mind ran loose from its bearings?

The duke stared at him from yellow goat's eyes, his skin pale beneath his red hair. He glanced once at his son before stepping closer.

Dominic bowed, amazed he could keep his balance. "Your grace."

"My son seeks the company he is worth, I see," the duke said without flinching. "Do you drown your sorrows, Major Wyndham, or celebrate your good fortune?"

"Neither," Dominic said. "It is merely the excess of youth."

"Indeed? Of course, Harriet's death leaves you free to wed again. I would the same were true for my son."

Free to wed again. Dear God! He hadn't even thought of it. "Alas, your grace," he replied. "If a Soul of Charity must die before her time, do you openly admit you would rather it were your own daughter-in-law, Rosemary, Lady Stansted?"

Rutley wore a faint trace of powder, but he was still fit and hard for a man of his age. He had no more sons and only a single daughter. It made him dangerous.

"If she does not come to her senses and do her duty, I would." He grinned then, displaying aging teeth. "But perhaps Rosemary isn't fecund? Or perhaps it's my son who cannot keep up with your supposed example, however hard he tries. And yes," the duke said, "that is a pun. Good day, sir."

"Good day, your grace."

The duke nodded to his manservant and walked away.

"Oh, God," said Stansted, staggering and pale. "I *am* going to be sick now. I'm terrified of him. He wants me to produce heirs for the bloody line. How can I, when my wife lives in Scotland like a nun? At least you don't have a devil of a father to answer to."

Dominic stared at the white face, the freckles stark, and felt a sudden pang of regret. Why *had* he dragged poor Stansted into this? Because it was Rosemary, Stansted's wife, who had taken Harriet to Scotland? If the glamour of good works and the company of a duke's daughter-in-law had been too much for her, it was hardly Stansted's fault.

And neither was it Catriona Sinclair's.

He would not—whatever the temptation—ruin her, of course. But he would certainly plague her a little, for her damned judgmental attitude and for whatever she wasn't telling him, if for nothing else. After all, now life really had no meaning, mustn't it indeed offer entertainment? Yet she had seemed desperate, and desperation was never amusing. He would like to make the severe lines of her mouth relax into ripeness, assuage whatever sorrow made her so grave, and see her happy, if only for a moment. He would like to see her laugh.

"*Will* you marry again?" the duke's son asked.

"Don't talk balderdash," Dominic replied. "It's out of the question. Here, let me get you home."

∞

Catriona was woken early by a maid. A drift of noise seeped in from outside. Exhausted from lack of sleep, she rapidly repacked her small case. After carefully tying the strings on the unfamiliar English bonnet, she went softly down the stairs and waited in the imposing hallway.

Dominic Wyndham came striding into the hall five minutes later. He looked brittle and ferocious. He wore a shirt, at least. Indeed, he was correctly turned out in high collar and cravat, but his clothes seemed slovenly and the skin beneath his eyes was smudged with dark shadows. She felt the simple aesthetic impact of it, the golden looks marred by dissipation, as if a work of art had been wantonly vandalized.

He stopped and bowed to her.

"Your carriage awaits, madam. Let us to horse and the merry high road."

The slightly slurred speech betrayed him. He must be soaked with drink.

"Have you been out?" she asked.

"All night, Miss Sinclair, forging sins in the devil's workshops. What have you been doing?"

"I left a note," she said stiffly, "for your brother. I felt I owed the earl that much, at least."

Debauching away the night had not improved his temper. "For God's sake, why? Let Jack slumber on in fitful ignorance. He won't care in the least what has happened to either of us, nor question it."

She refused to look down. "In spite of your wishes, I believe I must inform Lord Windrush that we leave together."

He seized her by the arm. "In surety for my good behavior? Do not, Miss Sinclair. His lordship may seem to have prettier manners, but he has a more choleric humor. Do not forget the knowledge that brought you here: the

child is legally mine. Not even my brother can dictate what
is done with him. And Jack will not want the child befriended, believe me. When he learns of this, he will do his
damnedest to see him disappear—the son of a stranger,
foisted on the Wyndhams? Jack has no children yet. Unless
he is admitted a bastard, this child is potentially an heir to
the earldom. If you have dreams that little Andrew may be
raised in some dignity and comfort as befits a gentleman,
I am your only hope. Cruel, but true. Where the devil is
the note?''

Without waiting for her reply, he crossed to the silver
tray on the hall table, where a piece of paper lay folded
and sealed with wax. He flicked it open, scanned the few
lines, and tore it to shreds.

''Now,'' he said. ''Let us to Scotland.''

She bit her lip and followed him from the house. Whatever this man might be, it was vital he offer Andrew his
protection. Once he discovered the truth, surely he would
immediately lose interest? Meanwhile, only he could
achieve what must be done, and only he had the power and
standing to make sure the evidence could not be over-
looked. What other chance could the child have—or Glen
Reulach and the souls who hung in the balance? If the price
was putting up with a rake's dangerous, reckless company
on the journey, then she would, gladly.

A chaise and four stood waiting. Catriona stopped for a
moment and looked at it, the brilliance of the varnish and
the elegant lines. It appeared new and expensive, and very
respectable, not the usual carriage of a man-about-town.
The matched bays shifted a little and were efficiently corrected by a coachman in livery. Dominic gave her an
amused glance.

''You are surprised, Miss Sinclair? What did you expect?
A high-perch phaeton and the wind tearing at your bonnet,
while the fey storms of summer soak us both to the skin?''

''I thought we were to travel secretly.''

''We are. No one of my acquaintance would ever asso-
ciate this carriage with me. What would you choose? That
we should dress as gypsies and be smuggled out in wagons?

I prefer both more discretion and more ease. It is more than four hundred miles to Edinburgh. If we go sixty miles every day, it will still take us a full week. We may as well be comfortable.''

"Seven days?'' she said in dismay, glancing up at him. "But the stage—''

"Traveled also at night. I see no need to rampage through the dark without recourse to a feather bed and a coverlet of sweet dreams. Why not seven days? You told me the child was safe for a month, and I have sent a message, with gold and promises, in case Mrs. Mackay needs reassurance. After all, seven is a magical number—seven league boots, seven dwarfs, and seven deadly sins. We shall have twenty-four hours for each of them.''

She felt the threat of it. If nothing else, for his rapid dance through the language, a language she knew fluently, but was not her mother tongue. "I don't understand.''

He grinned with pure devilry. "The deadly sins? The first is pride, which is your sin. The others are covetousness, lust, anger, gluttony, envy, and sloth, which are mine. We shall dedicate the seven days of our journey to each sin in turn.''

She hadn't meant she didn't know the seven deadly sins. But she couldn't follow his mood or his thinking. She suspected suddenly that he was teasing her, but that nothing he said was entirely frivolous. "You are being absurd.''

"Am I? Because apart from pride, you suffer from none of these causes of spiritual death, do you? But they are all my daily companions, and we shall explore each one to while away our time. Pride for today, covetousness for tomorrow, and lust for Friday. Then you will be angry—and gluttony, envy, and sloth will seem mild in comparison.''

She felt lost. "I am not used to pleasantries, Major Wyndham, nor banter. I grew up far from the artifice of an English drawing room. Our Highland songs are of wild things, the sea, and the heather. We don't joke about sin.''

"Oh, neither do I. I'm very serious about sin. Yet they say pride is the worst of them all.'' He took her bag and tossed it into the carriage. The effects of the previous night

showed in his movements and the veiled look in his eyes.
"Perhaps you could unbend and show a little less of it?
Pray, climb into the chaise and let us be off."

She did so, bemused. His obvious determination to maintain control showed an odd vulnerability. She had seen
drink turn men into puppies or into beasts. But this was
something else—almost as if he weren't foxed very often,
or if in spite of his debauchery he abhorred total abandonment—because of his own pride?

The coach rocked as the horses started forward.

Of course, pride was the essence and first breath of the
Highlander, who wore it as naturally as his bonnet and
plaid: the essential, necessary core of his courage. She had
never thought about it—was that a sin?

He settled into the seat beside her and leaned his head
back against the squabs, closing his eyes. Catriona looked
at him thoughtfully. A proud man. It sat in the very turn
of his nostril and the cavalier manner. He would not be
easy to outwit. *You may have to pay more than you bargained.* But she had already wagered everything of importance. She would not hesitate to break his pride if it was
necessary.

"Perhaps you confuse pride with dignity," she said at
last.

He moved nothing but his lips. "Do I? I don't know.
Pride is a sin of the spirit, and dignity a gift of grace, yet
each combines reticence and self-confidence, so perhaps
they are not so far apart. You seem very confident, Miss
Sinclair, so certain of your probity. I don't know if that's
strength, or just that you have never really been tempted."

"And you have?" she asked.

"Oh, yes," he replied softly. "I think so. Too much, too
long, and too often, and I'm really very tired of it."

The rising sun gilded the streets and filled the air with
warm vapors: of coal fires, and bakeries, and fresh dung.
London was coming awake, and stretching, and asking for
its breakfast. A shaft of light poured through the window,
illuminating his hands lying loosely in his lap, the long,
cleanly molded fingers curled a little, glazed with gold dust:

beautiful hands. With a shock of pleasure she remembered those fingers at her breast, opening her buttons—hands which had touched her skin and teased her nipple in a sensual promise. But that was easy. It wasn't hard to rouse the body.

The coach turned at a cross street. The sun fell across his jacket, lighting the fineness of the weave and sending shadows into the creases at waist and elbow. The clothing hid a frame she could picture clearly, neatly muscled, sleek, and unshakably strong. Catriona raised her eyes and studied his face. The taut, spoiled lines were softening as he relaxed, his hair resplendent above the glorious bones. *The Archangel Michael.*

How could such a man avoid sin? And how will I keep to my true path in his company?

And then she realized he had fallen asleep.

The coach was very well sprung, rocking rhythmically to the cadence of the horses' hooves. The seats were clean and smelled faintly of freshly cut wood. Like the man beside her, Catriona had missed sleep the previous night, and for the days before that let herself get worn down with perilous ventures. The squabs against her cheek faded gently away.

She dreamed of the hills above Loch Reulach and the keep of Dunachan. The eagles soared over Ben Wyvis. Heather ran purple down to the water like the folds of a cardinal's robe gathered into an edging of silver. With the cries of lost children, seagulls followed the plows, and curlews called their lonely lament across moor and quavering peat bog. *"Cha till mi tuilleadh,"* a voice said in Gaelic, "I shall return no more," but the whisper was lost in the sound of the wind wailing and the smell of smoke drifting over the glens.

There was warmth under her cheek. She put her hand there
and felt hard muscle beneath cloth. At the same instant she
became aware of gentle fingers moving the hair away from
her brow, a soft, delicious caress, devoid of anything but
tenderness.

"Hush," said a masculine voice. "It's all right. You
slept. Like I did. I must admit I feel a damn sight better
for it. Curled together like two puppies, we have innocently
and chastely nuzzled a little. Here, let me help you sit up."

She felt dizzy and disoriented for a moment as she
opened her eyes. The coach rocked. Dominic Wyndham
still sat in the corner of the seat, but she was nestled against
him, her face turned comfortably into his shoulder. One
hand cradled her head, while the fingers of the other stroked
rhythmically, moving strands away from her forehead. His
fingertips brushed softly from cheek, over temple and ear,
to run wantonly over her hair at each stroke. The temptation
to succumb, to surrender to delicious sensation, shook
her to the soul. She struggled to extricate herself. He
dropped his hands and took hers, steadying her.

Her bonnet lay, with its ribbons trailing like wrung-out
stockings, on the opposite seat.

"It was damned uncomfortable and jabbed hideously
into my chin." He nodded ruefully at the English hat. "I
hope you don't mind."

She put her hands to her head, confused in that moment
between sleep and waking. "Don't!" she began, glancing
up at him. "I did not mean any familiarity—"

"Don't be silly." His smile was touched with affront.
"There's no need to protest, or apologize for using me as
a pillow. As an indiscretion, it's pretty minor, and as a sin,
it's negligible. Anyway, I have already exacted payment."

She lifted her chin and her hair tumbled through her fingers.

"What have you done?" Dark hair webbed into the buttons of his coat and wound in a fine skein over his golden
hands, trapping her like the princess tied to the rock in the
fairy tale. She tugged at it.

His voice warmed with mischief. "Taken out your plaits.

You have lovely hair. It's as thick as thieves and as fine as a summer's day, with all the colors of brandy and night, shot through with moonlight and shadows like a blackbird's wing. If you stood up, it would fall to your waist like a Nereid's in a woodland pool. It was the devil of a task to untie it all with one hand.''

"*A Mhuire!* You are a thief!'' She gathered her hair and wrapped it around her fists. The riot of misplaced similes she couldn't begin to match.

"A thief steals, a one-way transaction. I traded. My pleasure in playing with your hair, for your pleasure in the feel of it. It was pleasurable, wasn't it?''

She bridled. "It was an unpardonable invasion.''

He grinned, the dimple shadowing his cheek. "Yes, it was, wasn't it? But that's not what I asked. If we are to abandon pride, then we must tell each other the truth, unvarnished and naked. There is no sin in pleasure.''

"Och, and if there is not?'' She remembered her breasts in the mirror and her flushed face surrounded by hair, as no man had ever seen her. Honesty asserted itself, honesty honed by indignation. "So the body has its own betrayal. What of it? What does that have to do with what you have just done? You are a robber. You have stolen my right to take down my hair for you, if I wished it.''

He gazed at her with incredulity. "*Did* you wish it?''

"I did not, but if I did, it was mine to give, not yours to take.'' She bent quickly and wrapped her hair in a knot, using her handkerchief as a snood. "Would you have undressed me and touched my body without my knowing?''

"Perhaps. You agreed to travel as my mistress. If it were true, you would welcome my touch, and waking, reach for me.''

"If it were true, I would. I don't deny you are a bonny man, Major Wyndham. Do you think I am a prude? We Highlanders don't put so much value on chastity. To give myself freely to the man I loved would be no affront to my honor. But it won't be you, sir, and if you steal from me, you will make me hate you.''

He looked thoughtful, his profile cut clean as he gazed

from the window, and his voice hardened. "Hate, they say, is the closest thing to love. Soon I shall undress you and you will welcome it. What did you think our bargain meant? That you would be safe? Some places respond to touch with physical delight. If you allow it, you will be tempted."

"I do not wish to be tempted."

He turned and grinned at her. There was the devil in it. "That does not sound like the truth. But we agreed to dedicate this day to losing our pride, and tomorrow to exploring covetousness. We aren't going to worry about lust until Friday, remember? We have plenty of time to discover temptation. Or do you wish to cancel our bargain?"

Her hair was heavy and hot. She pushed at it fiercely. *Temptation.* Everything about this man's body was a temptation. "I cannot. There is the child."

He kicked his feet onto the opposite seat and closed his eyes. "Tell me about him."

She sighed with relief at the respite. "He throws tantrums and squalls when he can't get his way, and frowns like a black-browed kelpie. Yet he could charm the berries off the rowan with his smile when he's happy. Sleeping, he looks like a wee dark-haired angel. He is an ordinary enough bairn."

"Dark-haired? But Harriet was all milk and cream. So his father is dark?"

What made his good looks so much more? Was it in the shape of nostril and jaw? The sensuous mouth? The golden sheen to him? Or was it in that heady mixture of intensity and abandonment? She replied absently. "He was dark and blue-eyed with it. He was a grand man."

He opened one eye, his glance keen with intelligence and cynicism, his voice sharp. "You know that?"

She had slipped! *If you disown him, no one knows his father!* Would he remember what she had said? Surely not, surely not. Had he not been soaked with drink?

"How could I?" she said quickly. "But he must be, surely."

It hit him with an unexpected rage and an odd despair. *He was dark and blue-eyed with it.* So this was it: she *had* known the child's father. Dominic knew it now with certainty, as he realized he had unconsciously known from the beginning, when his instincts had told him this Highland girl was deceiving him. The child couldn't be Harriet's. It was inconceivable his wife could have changed so much. Harriet would never have taken a lover. Catriona had lied to him, cruelly.

But if Andrew weren't Harriet's child, whose was he? The answer had just become obvious. Catriona must have compelling motives for protecting the boy. Why else would she risk so much? Why else agree to this outrageous journey? Why else would she have been prepared to kiss him— even bed him? She had told him she put little value on chastity. She had known the child's father—no doubt in the biblical sense. It came to him in a flash of certainty: the child was her own.

Catriona Sinclair might not be wanton, but she was experienced. So she was a hypocrite, like all the rest. Pursuing him for her own purposes. But why insist he come to Scotland? Probably to entangle him in some scheme for her child's support. Dear God, then why the devil shouldn't she pay for it?

Doubts scattered like leaves in the wind. If he had begun this as some kind of game, it had just turned deadly earnest. The thought came to him with a ruthless delight, overlaying his moment of despair: he would hunt down her weaknesses and ruin her. Success was as inevitable as breathing. He would court her until she was enticed, beguiled, willing— any of his friends would lay money on her willingness— and give her one night she would never forget. He would steal her heart and then he would leave her.

He had been hanging on to restraint by a thread. A thread which had been unraveling ever since he'd heard of Harriet's death. He had tried against all provocation to hang on—and now it had snapped. Why the hell show Catriona any more mercy than she had shown him? To tell him Harriet had borne another man's child! Damn her! Damn her! He would make her pay for it with her lush body—a prospect filled with nothing but enchantment.

The coach had been traveling along the turnpike. The hard rattle softened as the wheels rolled onto the dirt of a side road. High hedgerows ran down both sides of the lane, staining the air with dampness and green. Dominic stretched deliberately and sat up.

"Ah," he said. "We're almost there."

She moved to look from the window. Folds of handkerchief lay against the sensitive skin of her neck, imprisoning her hair. His fingertips burned with a memory of that soft darkness loose in his hands. He wanted to peel away the handkerchief, peel away her dress, and her shift, and her stockings. He would watch her arch naked beneath him, offering her white breasts, her dark hair free over her fine skin. He would take her, he would ruin her, he would leave her sobbing for him.

"Where?"

He smiled at her. "Ralingcourt—where we sleep tonight."

There was no alarm in the ice-blue gaze, only that passionate determination. "There is an inn here?"

Dear God, he wanted her so fiercely it ached. "Not exactly."

"But rooms?"

Rage mixed very oddly with desire, but both burned in him, wickedly.

"You are traveling as my mistress. And we still have pride to demolish." His voice filled with wantonness. Dominic heard it without shame, as if something had broken in him that moved him beyond shame and beyond conscience. "So not 'rooms.' One room. Obviously, we shall share it."

Four

REFLECTIONS OF THE coach rippled in a series of polished windows as they pulled up before the front door. Catriona knew a trickle of fear. This was no public hostel. He had brought her to a private country house.

"Whose place is this?" she asked.

The dimples chased into his cheek. "I should have explained. Ralingcourt is one of the minor properties belonging to the Windrush estates."

"It is not yours?"

The grin widened. "Nothing is mine. As the eldest, my brother inherited everything, but he leased me this house when I married Harriet. We spent our honeymoon here."

Her breath sucked raggedly in her throat. "You have no mercy, have you?"

The front door opened and a footman let down the carriage steps.

"Mercy?"

"On either of us."

She stepped down and followed the footman inside. Dominic shadowed close behind. She was painfully aware of him, of his height, his vitality.

Servants took their coats and carried in their cases. Obviously they were expected. He must have sent word ahead. Yet the hall felt disused, slightly damp, though everything was polished and clean. He led her into a drawing room on the west of the house. The dying sun cast a red glow over gilt furniture and inlaid tables, dainty and delicate. Faintly sentimental paintings hung on the walls, of rustic cottages idealized into prettiness. Unsure how to cope any longer, Catriona crossed the room to the window to stare out at the trees and the rolling fields.

"Do you think you are safer there?" he asked dryly. "Close to nature?"

She whirled about. He was lighting candles. While she stood in her cracked shoes, awkward and apprehensive, he strode about the room with a taper. Branch after branch of white wax leaped into flame, chasing shadows across the wallpaper and sparking gold in the carved backs of chairs.

"This is a damned uncomfortable house, but Harriet liked it." He doused the taper and turned to grin at her. Gilt blazed on his rich hair and the sensuous lines of his mouth. "Relax, Miss Sinclair. You aren't about to be ravished. But we shall share a bedroom."

"That is absurd." She was spikingly aware of the contrast—this golden man in the dazzling room and the darkly rustling green outside. "Why insist on it?"

He tossed the taper into the grate. "Because the idea adds an element of interest to this evening I don't want to miss. Possibilities are like spice. A small sprinkling of them enhances experience. A tiny edge of fear lets us know we are truly alive. We have this journey, you and I—a few days out of a lifetime—to share. These days can't be lived again. Why not make each moment as vivid as possible?"

"Are you afraid?"

He dropped onto a brocade sofa, flinging one arm along the back, and looked up at her from moss-green eyes. "A little, yes. I shan't force you. So in a way, I have more to lose than you. What if I fail? What if you refuse to be tempted? Then I am left with nothing, while you celebrate your triumph over a foolish man with as much smugness as you wish."

Catriona crossed the room and sat down in an ornate chair opposite him. "You are being honest!"

"Of course. How else do we demolish pride? I offer you mine to trample as you wish. That was part of our bargain. Pride is today's deadly sin. By all means, let us annihilate it."

If we are to abandon pride, then we must tell each other the truth, unvarnished and naked. "Then I shall give you back this truth: I am afraid. And I know clearly at this moment that I am alive. But it isn't from fear of you. I am afraid of my own weakness and you distract me from my purpose. There is a bairn whose happiness depends on us. What good does it do him, this silly game you want to play?"

"And what harm? None!" A fleeting pain crossed his features as he looked away. "Don't think I have forgotten him, or his smiles that charm the berries off the mountain ash." He glanced back at her and she saw that he would indeed—ruthlessly—risk everything on one throw. "Did you know Harriet miscarried my son?"

Her heart leaped in shock. "Is that why she left you?"

The vulnerability was instantly veiled and he laughed. "God, no! She left me long before that, because I offended her in every way conceivable. The result was my first major lesson in sacrificing pride—so it's an appropriate enough tale for today."

In spite of her reservations, she was curious. This was not what she'd expected. He wasn't flirting or offering compliments, though his glance was seductive enough. Instead, he was offering himself and there was an undeniable fascination to it. "How?"

Humor flashed in his eyes. "What a price in humility I'm obliged to pay, aren't I? We had been married a day when Harriet called for the carriage, drove to London at breakneck speed, and burst into a social affair held by her mother, Lady Arnham. The flower of the beau monde was there, dressed variously in diamonds and gold. In tragic contrast, Harriet was disheveled and hysterical."

"Hysterical? Why?"

"She announced to the company that I had forced her into unspeakable acts—things too degrading ever to be described—that she was forever dishonored and ruined. I arrived, a little disheveled myself, just in time to witness it. Every person in the room turned to stare at me as if I'd grown horns. Some of the ladies fainted. As Harriet sobbed in her mother's arms Lord Arnham had his footmen throw me bodily from the house. I was foolish enough to resist. The result was neither elegant nor decorous, as I'm sure you can imagine.''

''Why you are telling me this?''

''Why not? It's public knowledge in London. I think you should know what you're dealing with.''

She looked away, burning with uncertainty. ''That you are a man of unsavory tastes?''

He laughed. ''Certainly a man who knows how a vicious dog feels, but then dogs have no pride. You must see I have very little left.''

''Which only makes such dogs the more dangerous. *Are* you vicious?''

He kicked up his feet to lie back on the sofa and crossed his hands behind his head. ''I don't think so, but Lord Arnham would happily have brought out the spiked collar and the muzzle.''

''What happened next?''

''It was suggested we annul the marriage, but she was found to be with child.''

''It *was* your child?''

He seemed merely cavalier now, throwing out the words with clear defiance. ''Oh, yes, definitely, which made annulment impossible, of course. I was asked for a public apology, which I gave. I was asked to send notice of my insensitivity to the newspapers, which I did. I was asked to make a financial settlement, which I paid, though I couldn't afford it. Alas, all that humiliation availed me nothing. I was not allowed to see my own wife. Six months later Lord Arnham had an attack of apoplexy. It killed him. I had spent some months with Wellington and had just come home from the Peninsula when it happened. At the news of my return, Harriet threw herself down the stairs and miscarried.''

Catriona sat silent, appalled. It was essential he believe Andrew to be Harriet's child—but, *a Mhuire,* wouldn't her courage have faltered, if she'd known of this? Her heart quailed. "When did she go to Scotland?"

"As soon as she recovered. Harriet went to Edinburgh with Lady Stansted. I was obliged to return to the war. I was a soldier by profession."

She glanced at the blaze of candles, the sheer excess of it. How did he afford all this on a soldier's salary? "Harriet told me you still provided for her."

His voice was wry. "I'm sure she did."

She felt lost. He had told her a story with more gaps than substance. But he could hardly have stated the essential elements more baldly: a son, born dead. A wife fleeing in fear. And a man filled with bitterness, and rage, and bravado.

The scent of hot wax filled the room. A multitude of tiny flames chased away every shadow. A clock ticked into the loud silence. "So now you hate women?"

"What? Oh, no. I like women. I even liked Harriet. Though our disaster was generally seen in Society to have been my fault, which resulted in a great many closed doors and a universal cut direct." He glanced at the clock and swung his feet to the floor. "Come, it's time to eat. Do you mind if we don't change?"

Did he guess she had no formal gowns with her? Or did he assume she possessed no such garments at all? Either way, it was tempting to see it as a small kindness, that he hadn't taken the chance to humiliate her by suggesting they both dress for dinner. Or did he guess she cared nothing about such things? Dominic Wyndham seemed to have an almost uncanny perception. So had he told her this story only to disarm her? She didn't know, but she knew sympathy was hazardous.

He led her into the dining room, to a table set with silver and crystal. They were served elaborately and well, course after course: sole, veal *à la daube,* sorrel sauce; baked almond pudding, codling tarts, country cheeses; the finest wines. Food designed to seduce. With a careful, almost delicate wit, he asked her questions too subtle for flattery, yet flattering nonetheless. She turned them aside unanswered. She could easily outwit him in that. Yet why tell her so much of himself and so little? It left her hungry for more, and not at all hungry for this feast of English food.

Obviously he valued all this luxury and saw no sin in waste, yet there was still something strangely direct and sparse in him. As the cloth was removed she challenged him directly, needing to understand. "You said you had known some Highlanders."

He leaned back, idly playing with the stem of his glass, and glanced up under his lashes. "I would rather talk about you."

His gaze promised something wicked and delicious. A tiny flush heated her cheeks. "Do not turn me aside. Tell me how you met them."

"In the Peninsula," he replied. "Your countrymen are rare soldiers."

"We are a fighting people. But few enough of those soldiers went willingly into the service of King George."

"They still fought like demons. And more: the Highland regiments have a natural discipline. Flogging's essentially unheard of among them." The dimples deepened as he grinned. "A proud race."

"And a practical one. Many a laird raised his regiment by threatening a young man's family. But once a Highlander has given his word, he'd not disgrace his kin nor his homeland by inviting the degradation of a flogging or offering less than his best."

"Whatever the reason, I never saw soldiers with more courage nor more dignity. Many of the men didn't speak enough English for me to have learned much firsthand from them. But the officers—"

He set down his wineglass and spread his right hand flat upon the table, as if studying it.

"—are the laird's brothers and cousins, and gentlemen," Catriona finished for him. "With the Latin and Greek along with their French and Italian and English. What of them? Were you surprised to find such learning and so many languages among men from such a barbarian land?''

"The officers became my friends." His voice was stark with sincerity. "I did not find them barbarians. I know something of how they felt—how you must feel—about your country."

Her heart bounded as if he'd touched it. Why had she thought this topic safe? To be with this man was a violent enough ride, plunged in and out of a sea of emotions. He had made her feel that flash of sympathy. Now he was treading closer and closer to the core of her passions and her very being. She clenched her fists in her lap.

"How can you understand anything about the Highlands?"

He watched his own fingers moving slowly over the polished wood as if he had suddenly forgotten her. The light outlined his clean profile, the seductive lashes. "Only what I was told, of course. But I knew an officer from your home—Glen Reulach. We were trapped together once behind French lines, with nothing to do but exchange stories. He told me of the homesteads clustered in the strath, the merrymaking, the poetry: never a task, however humble, without its song. The singing as the hooves of the black cattle clicked and sucked when they were driven up into the Ross-shire hills in summer. The singing of the women in their homes. I felt rain running down my neck. I heard fish leap in the lochs. I saw red deer tread like dancers."

Her pulse ran and leaped and danced. "Don't," she said fiercely. "Don't tell me any more!"

A shadow sprang along his jaw. "And deny someone who gave me both trust and friendship? Why? He had words like music. I could never forget. There was a cave where he'd hide as a boy to watch the eagles soaring— spread out before him the shine of flowers, an intensity of summer life. Perhaps you know it?"

She sat silent, willing him to stop, the emotion choking, clutching like a steel band about her chest. Yet lost in remembrance, not watching her, he went on without mercy.

"One afternoon great flakes of snow fell from a blue sky, to sparkle on the harebells and mosses and gentian.

Shadows ran over the turf as sun vied with snow, half melting as it drifted. Ice coated the flowers, turning each into a jewel. It was so clear to me as he described it. That is how I have pictured the Highlands ever since.'' His hand stopped as he glanced up at her. ''His name was Calum MacNorrin—a captain. I don't know what became of him.''

Did hearts truly break, rent apart like a hare in the talons of an eagle? Her heart tore. ''Och, you diabolical man! Why do you tell me this? What if I know this man and this story?''

She pushed back her chair and stumbled toward the doorway.

Instantly he came after her. ''What is it, Catriona? *Did* you know him?''

The pain stabbed. She looked up at him through a red mist of anger and hurt as he caught her by the arms. ''You know that I did. How could I not know the cave and not know Calum MacNorrin? Do you pretend you cared for him? He died at Waterloo in one of those brave regiments you admire so much.''

''Oh, dear God.'' His voice was ragged. ''Dear God. I had no idea.''

His hands tugged, pulling her against his chest, holding her encircled in his warmth. She would not weep. She had cried out those tears long ago. Yet the ashes of her grief filled her throat and choked her. So she buried her face in the coat of a man she despised and clung to the strength offered by his arms.

Dominic held her steadily, caught in the doorway. Her grief was palpable. She was shaking with it, like a harebell assaulted by snow.

Part of what pinned him, holding this woman to his heart, was his own anger and sorrow, the pain of loss and regret. Calum MacNorrin had died at Waterloo, while he lay imprisoned in a cellar in Paris, and he hadn't known. Dominic had refused to look at the lists of killed and wounded when he came home. He had just wanted to believe all the men he had cared for were alive. How could MacNorrin, in his red-and-blue plaid, with his vitality and outrageous humor, have died? Why the hell had the Fates taken the life of the better man and left Dominic Wyndham to uselessly live on?

And Catriona had known him.

Yet her torment was for more than just a man from her homeland; it was for a man she had loved.

He was a grand man.

The thought struck hard: had Calum MacNorrin been Andrew's father? He had shared Catriona's Highland looks, the blue eyes and black hair. He would have gone home in the Victory Summer of 1814, when Andrew must have been conceived. Perhaps they had planned marriage and not waited. If so, Calum's death had left her abandoned, grasping at straws, even prepared to use an English rake for the sake of their child.

And now that rake, ruthlessly, had told her a tale to remind her of her lover. And he had not stopped, even when her eyes had begged him, until it was too late.

I had no idea. Weak words to express a soul torn open in sympathy.

Carefully, he moved his fingers to her cheek and chin. Carefully, gently, as if she were fragile china. Grief for all the folly of his days caught at his heart, an intense sorrow. He tipped her face up to his.

"Catriona," he said, his own voice broken in his ears. "I'm a bloody bastard, but I hadn't known, truly."

She glared up at him, her breath coming fast and her face flushed. Her eyes shone like blue steel, yet she clung to him fiercely. "No better man ever lived."

"Yes." He cradled her jaw, her hair soft on his fingertips. "That is true."

Her lips trembled. Behind the blue steel dwelled an infinity of sadness. He meant only sympathy—a gesture of atonement and comfort, perhaps—when, without thinking, he bent his head and kissed her.

Her mouth blazed under his, opening.

Shock fused with a surge of white-hot desire. He kissed deeper.

She pressed herself against him and welcomed it.

Control shredded as Dominic groaned, pulling her closer. She ran her hands into his hair and sought his tongue with her own, vibrant, questing. Her breath burned in his mouth. Her breasts crushed against his chest. Her scent maddened his nostrils. Shivers of fire sparked an intense jolt of craving. He was instantly erect, wanting desperately, without subtlety. In reckless need, he suckled her pliant, flaming lips. Blindly he searched and tasted, exploring every corner, scorching without restraint.

With the same passionate fire, she kissed back, melded as if they were metals poured from the same crucible. She clung to his neck, ravishing his tongue with sweetness, her fingers so tight in his hair that it hurt. The throb of longing inflamed his blood, firing, making him rock hard for her. His entire being pooled in his groin.

As the pulse of desire overwhelmed him he attacked her buttons, opening her dress, until her naked skin flamed under his palm. Beneath her shift her nipples stiffened, taut for him. Urgently he touched, devoured by need, rolling the hard peaks with his fingertips. A fierce delight spiked—in the weight of her breasts, their softness and life. His cock throbbed. Enraged at the ribbons in the way of his hands, he tore fabric, consumed in the moment, wanting her more than life, and nothing else mattered.

Still kissing, he dropped one hand to her skirts, bunching the drab fabric, tugging it up, wanting her here and now in the doorway, wanting to bury his passionate need in her hot female flesh. And she welcomed him! Surprise shook him to his soul. She welcomed him!

He broke the kiss, burying his mouth in the curve of her neck, tasting woman and honey. The satin of her naked thigh burned beneath his palm. Desperate, his groin flaming with pleasure, he groaned aloud, half laughing. Her flank curved like a shell. Her soft buttocks slipped under his fingers. In seconds he could have his own buttons undone and release his cock for her. He traced over her beckoning belly to brush curls and a hint of moisture, and thought he might burst.

A splintering crash boxed his ears. As if a limb had just been sheared off, she tore herself away. He stared at her helplessly, his erection throbbing and his blood on fire. She was flushed, panting, her pupils huge, her back pressed into the doorjamb. She was exquisite, exciting, captivating, her lips bruised.

"I didn't know," she said bitterly. "I didn't know that was how it was done. *Diabhal—!*" She broke off and looked over her shoulder. "We have frightened your servants."

He glanced into the hallway. A tray lay upended on the carpet, glasses shattered on a spreading stain.

"Oh, God. My man bringing brandy."

Then, madly, he began to laugh.

Catriona tugged down her skirt. Her fingers shook on her buttons. Her nipples thrust hard against the front of her dress. "I didn't know what was meant by 'ruthless' until I met you. I thought you would try to entice me with flirtation. But you're more clever than that, aren't you?"

"Clever?" The blood thundered in his ears, in shock, in aborted desire. "I should think I've just made a bloody fool of myself."

"Pitiless, then, even to yourself. Everything you offered me this evening, everything you told me, was genuine. Deliberately you wrung my soul. Yet it was all done in a calculated play, like moves on a chessboard. I didn't know you would seduce me by touching my heart and playing with my feelings like toys. I didn't know you would use anything—even horror, even grief—without scruple, to gain your ends. Will you tell me that isn't true?"

He caught himself before he should be tempted to deny it. His erection died. "Yes, it's true. Or I think it is."

Running one hand over his swollen mouth, he strode into the hall. He was drained, shattered. What the hell was true? Only that he wanted her. He knelt and picked up the tray, the fragile shards of glass. Moisture shone on them like dew, the crystal transformed into worthless debris in a moment.

"It almost worked," Catriona said. "If it hadn't been for that footman, you could have taken me, like a doxy, up against the wall."

The image was too apt. He saw again a rouged face and the poor, spoiled teeth. Another woman he had almost taken for all the wrong reasons. "No," he said. "Not like a doxy. Believe whatever else you like, but believe that, at least."

"I was willing," she said. "With sadness for your poor dead bairn and your tale of a man I loved, you could have taken me easily. So you have broken my pride, as you set out to do. Do you think you have won?"

"Won?" He rocked to his haunches, willing himself to shed the taste of her mouth and the memory of her body beneath his hands. The air was heady with brandy fumes, rich in his nostrils. "How the hell can you claim that? I have humbled myself, offered myself—deliberately, yes. Believe it was only manipulation if you like, but it was done, it was real. What the devil have you given in return? You have lied to me, refused me, revealed nothing of yourself or your true purposes. Even now you won't tell me, will you? You loved him, that can't be denied, but what place had Calum MacNorrin in your life?"

"You are right," she said. "I won't tell you. What is it to you?"

He traced his fingers over the wet carpet. If he had thought to also shed shame, it came back now threefold. *If it hadn't been for that footman*—He recalled his rage in the carriage and the ruthlessness he had felt. How, when had that changed? Or was there still a bright anger in him, too deep to quench? An anger that forced him into honesty?

The carpet breathed brandy vapor. Liquor stained his fingers. "I will give you the truth, as well as I am able. I began this evening determined to get you into my bed. I would still like that. Perhaps I told you about Harriet because I wanted you to understand something of my side of our story, as well as to engage your sympathy and your interest. I am not—" He took a deep breath. "Whatever she told you, I am not a monster. I don't know why I told you the rest. You brought up Scotland."

"I didn't know where you would take it and keep taking it, even after I asked you to stop." Her tone cursed him.

He offered candor, even if it damned him. "Perhaps I hoped if I conjured thoughts of your homeland, you would open, tell me about yourself, soften to me. If it was manipulative, I'm sorry. But Calum was my friend. I didn't know he was dead. I would not deliberately have used him against you. I loved him."

"Love? The word is soiled in your mouth."

He glanced up. She was rigid, her fists clenched at her sides and her eyes blazing. "It's a mouth you just kissed in a damned good imitation of passion."

"You tricked me into it."

He had thought her striking. Now he knew why she wasn't pretty. She was beautiful.

"I'm not sure who tricks whom. Listen, Catriona: I know you're using me. I'm not sure I care, yet to enjoy your body seemed a fair enough exchange. For God's sake, you offered yourself to me in London. But I have never, in spite of my reputation, in spite of everything I've told you, been deliberately cruel to a woman—any woman, even a whore."

"You are mad."

He no longer cared how she might react. Honesty seemed the only path left. "Perhaps my desire for you is a kind of lunacy. I can't remember ever feeling such need. And knowing you were using me, I would have tried damn near anything to win you. I don't think I cared if it was honorable or not." He found a last shard of glass just before it cut him—it would be far too melodramatic to bleed—and set it carefully on the tray. "Yet I know what love is and respect it."

"Don't talk about love!"

He wiped his hands on his handkerchief. "I don't offer love, for God's sake. I offered you a game, thinking we both knew what we were about and that as intelligent adults we could enjoy it. Why not indulge the body? Why not take a moment of pleasure wherever we can find it?"

"You are a liar," she said. "And you are lying to your-self more than me."

Dominic leaned his head against the wall and closed his eyes. She was right. Though a merciless seduction was completely foreign to him, he had wanted to break her heart. It was the most dishonorable thought he had ever entertained. His code had been simple and clear-cut, until now. Once he had even offered a duel to a friend he had thought too ruthless with a lover. Why was he moving in this madness with this one woman?

He didn't know any other way out except the truth. "Ly-ing to myself? Right now I'm being so bloody honest it hurts. You demanded this journey for a purpose of your own. I agreed on one condition. I was angry when I made that condition, yes. But you didn't show much mercy to me—bringing me the news of Harriet's death like a harpy. As it happens, I was in love with her. Is that laughable to you?"

Her voice snapped. "What do you expect me to say? *Is minig a bha an donas dàicheil*—Often has the devil been handsome and his words can be smooth as a priest's. I cannot let it matter what you felt about Harriet. I cannot even let it matter if Calum offered you friendship. I only care about the bairn. Only his fate is important—much more important than you or me. I cannot tell you why. There! Is that enough?"

Why? Why the hell was it so important that Dominic Wyndham rescue Calum MacNorrin's child—if, indeed, that's who Andrew was—from the Souls of Charity?

He opened his eyes. The turn of her neck beneath the heavy dark plaits took away his breath—that tender, vul-nerable, female grace. Her mouth was still swollen from his kisses. "Can you give me no credit that I am prepared to go through all this for the sake of a baby that isn't mine? I could have turned you away, sent for the child, and dealt with the consequences in London."

"I concede that." Her color was still high, her beauty wild, streaming like a sunset. "What do we do now?"

"That's easy." He stood up and faced her, the stained carpet damp beneath his boots, his hands sticky with brandy. "We go to bed together. How the hell else will we dissipate this tension between us? In sex sometimes there's comfort, even between strangers, even between enemies."

The harebell eyes widened into darkness. "Never!"

"You can't deny what just happened. I can still taste you."

She blushed, furiously, like a virgin. "I demand a room of my own."

He stood still, stubborn, glad to his soul she was experienced. She'd borne a child; he didn't have to prevaricate. "The servants have gone to bed. Only one bedroom has been prepared. We shall share it."

"How can you insist on it, after what I have said?"

His cock stirred again, the wanting fierce. After the passion she had shown him, he was sure she couldn't really refuse. "You agreed to let me make all the arrangements. This is one of them. I don't think either of us should be alone tonight."

Her hands twisted together. "I would be private."

He longed to take her fingers and soothe them, open them, kiss her palms. "We desire each other. It doesn't need to go any further than that. Hearts aren't involved, but a little kindness wouldn't come amiss. God knows, I have shown you little enough yet. Allow me to atone for it."

"A Dhia!" She struck her hands together, hard. "Stop! I am tempted. I think you a bonny man. But I won't sleep with you. There, that is enough!"

"I will be kind, Catriona." He grinned. His arousal throbbed. "Your body will be a temple for my worship. Take me any way you like. I surrender completely."

"I will not!"

The absurdity welled up deep inside. He was begging. He would get on bended knee and beg her? A man women had pursued, and entreated, and made love to with abandon? Dear God, he had lived hard and fought hard. He had courted the Tsar of All the Russias to help bring about Napoleon's defeat. He had once taken for a lover the most devious female spy in Europe. He had known pain and glory in the service of his country. Men he respected had trusted his honor and his loyalty. And he would beg this demon woman from the Far North to open her legs?

She was right. It was enough. He no longer wanted to hurt her, the woman Calum MacNorrin had loved. He wanted to heal her, if not in his bed, then out of it. Though he would rather—if she would only agree from her own free will—it be in his bed. He laughed.

"The deal is made, Catriona, and you can't back out now. It's only a game. But we share a room. Will you walk to it willingly, or shall I carry you? Don't think for one moment I won't do it."

As if she caught his change of mood, she looked uncertain. "You cannot make me share your bed."

He knew he was grinning like an idiot. Perhaps all that brandy vapor had gone to his head. His erection pulsed in his breeches, the one part of him that couldn't understand his finer scruples. "Of course not. Oh, for God's sake, let's go upstairs and sleep. And if you can't see the funny side of all this, then I can."

She glanced away and nodded. Then to his immense surprise, she smiled. It broke over her face like a flower opening, as if she, too, welcomed the release from that heady tension.

"Very well," she said. "I will share your one room, and we shall see who laughs in the morning."

Five

∞

AS HE HAD done downstairs, he lit candles. The taper in his hand danced from mantel to bedside like a will-o'-the-wisp over the marshes. Candlelight flared over rich velvet hangings and fine china washbasins, a brass carriage clock and two paintings of spaniels. The silver patterns on the fitted carpet were echoed in the covers of the chairs and long sofa. Had he shared this very bedroom with Harriet? Was it from this chamber that his wife had run sobbing to her parents? Was that why he filled it with brightness?

"Why so many candles?" she asked. "Are you afraid of the dark?"

He turned from the last sconce and smiled at her. "No, but I think you and I need as much light as possible. Perhaps it will dispel all the damned obscurity between us." With one hand he tugged at the knots in his cravat, unwrapped it, and tossed it aside. "Ah, that's better." He opened his shirt at the neck.

"I see there is a couch," she said, indicating it. "As well as a bed."

"You may have the bed, of course." He shrugged out of his jacket and carried it to hang in the wardrobe. His waistcoat followed.

"I would rather take the couch." Her voice sounded stiff.

He glanced at her over his shoulder. "And deny me the chance to act the gallant, and make up for my shameful behavior thus far?"

"I will not lie in that bed, with you in the room."

He tugged his shirt over his head. "You think I shall creep in upon you in the night and ravish you, like the Sleeping Beauty? I could do it just as well on the couch."

His naked back was a play of mitered muscle and bone, shadows and lithe golden gleam. A spike of treacherous heat moved in her. "Take the bed. I shall not lie down at all."

The bootjack sat next to the wardrobe. He hooked it with one heel and began to work off his boots. "But, my dear, I could as easily ravish you standing up. I thought we had proved that?"

It burst from her: "You will undress, completely, in front of me?"

He looked around. "Why not? I usually sleep naked. Look away if you wish."

"I will not!" she said stubbornly. "If you will shame yourself, on your own head be it!"

He began to undo the buttons at his waist. "I have nothing shameful to hide."

It was as if she were rooted there, on the blue-and-silver carpet, as the dancing light caressed his muscles, his strong forearms gilded with crisp hair, his back smooth as bronze. He dropped his breeches and draped them over a chair. Then he set each foot in turn on the seat and peeled off his stockings. He bent to fold them neatly, as a soldier does, his white linen underdrawers stretched over curved buttocks and down his long thighs.

It was like panic, like the blind foolishness that overtakes a mob. It made her head spin and her heart thunder. A weakness. If she weren't careful, she would be gasping for breath as if she had run over the naked peaks of Ben Wyvis.

Catriona folded her hands, though the pulse throbbed in her palms. "You think I will blush and turn away? You think I will hide my face? Go ahead. A man's body is an ordinary enough thing. There are many millions of them in this world.''

''True enough.'' He untied the laces on his undergarment and flicked open the three buttons at the front of the waistband, his back still to her. ''But of course, each one is different. Or at least, I have found that each woman's body—'' As he stretched and yawned, his underwear slipped down a little over his loins. Shadows lovingly draped over whiteness. ''Each woman's body is entirely unique. It's a great part of the charm of being a rake, to explore that.''

A weakness. That he was so lovely and that she was so burningly aware of it. That he was a rake and knew how to explore women's bodies. His shoulders flexed as he stepped out of his underwear. Her heart raced like a stream in spate. ''You will not turn around,'' she said. ''Even you cannot have so much effrontery.''

''Oh, yes,'' he said, turning. ''I can.''

Her hands moved involuntarily. Heat seared her cheeks. Yet she stood still, refusing to move, or look away, or flinch. His eyes met hers, that fathomless, secret green, and she locked her gaze on his. As if defying her, he strode casually around the room snuffing candles. Each flame died, leaving its scent of burned wick. She would not do anything so ignominious as to glance down. She would not look to see if he was as aroused as she, or if his hair at the groin was as golden as the hair on his head. *She would not.*

Mercifully the room was steadily plunging into darkness. His body became more shadowy and indistinct. It was not until he reached the bed and pulled back the covers that he moved back into the light of the one remaining candle. Helplessly her gaze wavered. Hot, filled with shame, she let her eyes slip down, over his spine, over tooled muscle and bone. By the flicker of that single flame, she saw around his waist—no doubt snatched from the washstand— a beige towel. The towel was tented in front, but it covered him.

She looked up, blushing. Laughter shone in his eyes, but there was more—something that surprised her, but she couldn't mistake it—a recognition of his own absurdity, an invitation to share the joke, and joke it was. He was teasing her!

"Take whatever bedcovers you wish from that chest," he said. "Princess of Pride. You are safe. In spite of what happened downstairs, I can control my male appetites. Unless you fling yourself into my arms, I'll no doubt survive my frustration." He glanced up, smiling. "After all, I've done it before, upon occasion."

"Och, no doubt you have." She bit her lip as she looked away, not wanting him to see the laughter threatening to bubble up in her, too. "And thus you have won. I am defeated—pride abandoned—fair and square. But you cannot blame any of this madness on me." She choked back the heady giggles. "You were wholly mad and half-naked when I met you."

"Half-mad and wholly naked is preferable." He slid between the sheets, pulling the covers over his chest and tossing the towel to the floor. "As I am now. Are you sure you don't want the bed?"

"I am certain." Catriona turned, threw open the chest, and found blankets and pillows. *"Fhuair mi m' fheumalachd,"* she said absently.

"What?"

She hesitated for a moment, surprised she should have spoken to him in Gaelic and aware of the double meaning to it. "I have what serves my purpose," she translated hastily. *My purpose.* She had his promise to come to Edinburgh. It was enough. Nothing else mattered. "Thank you for the lesson in humility."

"No," he said. "Don't be humble. It wouldn't suit you."

Making her selection, she carried enough bedding to the sofa and arranged it. "We are all enjoined to be humble. *'Bheir mise suaimhneas dhuibh—'* " Once more she caught herself and began again in English, the words from the Bible. " 'I will give you rest—' "

He instantly took up the quote. " 'Take my yoke upon

you and learn of me, for I am meek and lowly in heart,
and ye shall find rest unto your souls.' ''

It arrested her, in surprise and something dangerously
close to pleasure. "I did not know I would find spiritual
guidance in the games of a rake."

"You did not." From the corner of her eye she saw a
long, muscular arm reach out. He snuffed the candle.
"There is no guidance or succor to be learned from me.
Sleep well."

Entirely in the dark, she slipped out of her dress and
shoes, and into her makeshift bed on the sofa.

Lord Stansted was uncomfortable. In fact, now he came to
think about it, he was downright miserable. He was made
to stand, like a schoolboy, while his father gazed at him
with those unfathomable yellow eyes. He never knew what
Rutley was thinking. Of course the duke was disappointed
in him, but he generally left him alone, especially this late
at night. Stansted had startled like a partridge when he received this summons, and now he stood, a little drunk, on
the rich Turkish wool—a rug an ancestor had brought back
from his Grand Tour—and wondered if the papers on his
father's desk had anything to do with him.

Rutley pushed back his chair, his white fingers splayed
on the edge of the carved walnut in front of him. "You
seek ruin alone tonight?"

"Oh, not more—" Stansted cleared his throat. "Not
more than usual, your grace."

"Major Wyndham is not with you?"

He remembered in a slightly foggy way what he had
promised Dominic. "He's in his rooms."

"Is he?" The duke's yellow gaze did not waver. "Why
do I think you do not tell me the truth, sir?"

Stansted blushed scarlet, hating himself for the betraying
color. "He's ill. Drank too much. His man's telling everyone."

"So I have been informed. However, Dominic Wyndham

does not, I would imagine, possess a constitution given to
vague maladies, and certainly not those engendered by an
excess of wine. In fact, I do not believe he generally in-
dulges as deep as he would have us all believe. A drunkard
could not have achieved what he did against Napoleon.''
He stared thoughtfully at a mirror which hung over the
mantelpiece. Stansted glanced at it, but nothing was reflected there except his own red head. The silence stretched.

"May I go?" Stansted asked nervously.

The duke waved his hand dismissively. Eyes pinned to
the Turkish carpet, his son turned toward the door.

"There is one thing," the duke said.

Stansted spun about. "Sir?"

"The Scots girl, the one in Lord Windrush's carriage.
What became of her?" The yellow goat's eyes narrowed.
"Come, sir. Any of a dozen witnesses saw her there."

A wave of panic ran up Stansted's spine. "I don't know,
your grace. I'm sure I don't!" In a sudden flash of inspiration, he blurted out: "Perhaps she's why—perhaps she's
with Wyndham in his rooms?"

And then realized as he escaped down the great marble
stairway that Dominic might not agree that his inspiration
was so brilliant, after all.

Dominic woke up certain this present scheme was as far
from brilliant as chalk is from cheese. He looked immediately at the couch. What a bloody telling metaphor—the
shock of dry dust in the mouth instead of the nutty smooth
tang of good Cheddar!

*If you want me, you will travel with me like a loose
woman. I give you my word, madam: there is no other way
I shall leave London.* He had, obviously, been out of his
wits, the worst bloody inspiration he had ever had.

Catriona was gone.

He had been unconsciously aware of her all night, the
soft female presence in the room, designed—like the fruit
of Tantalus—only to torment. But she had left, and he

hadn't woken. He threw back the covers and strode across to the couch. She had put away her blankets and neatly folded her sheets. His fingers lingered on them for a moment, then he lifted the pillow to his face. It was still faintly warm, with the scent of her hair, so she had not been gone long.

Shrugging into a black silk dressing gown, he crossed to the window and gazed out. It was very early. Mist wreathed about the lawns and shrubbery, beading the gardens with moisture. An effulgence of birdsong rose from the bushes, little birds singing out their hearts. Indefatigable, like Catriona Sinclair. He knew without question she was out there in the garden, among the mist and the birds, and realized of course she had not run away. Without him, she had no way to get to Edinburgh and the child.

He rang the bell and ordered hot water.

Why had he brought her here? Had he thought her stubborn Highland presence would dilute memories of Harriet? How damned foolish even to *have* memories of Harriet! Dominic jerked tight the knot in the sash of his dressing gown and went deliberately down the hall.

The door opened silently on well-oiled hinges and memories billowed like cream silk to engulf him. Immediately before their disaster, Harriet had sat there, in her ivory nightdress. Her hair had shone gold against the cream velvet hangings on the bed. She had been lovely enough to die for. And he would have done it, laid down his life for her, for her favor, for her smiles.

Before the wedding, Jack had refitted the room and Harriet had chosen the decor, all blue white and cream, like a snowbank in sunshine. Like an idiot, Dominic had leased the house for five years. Like an idiot, he had left it as Harriet liked, in case she ever wanted to come back.

He tugged at the bellpull. In a few minutes a maid appeared.

"Sir?"

"Tell the housekeeper I wish this room redecorated. Fetch some of the other girls and get rid of all this white velvet, for a start."

The maid gaped at him. "Sir?"

"You may share the fabric among you. Go, do it!"

She curtsied and ducked from the room.

Dominic walked back to the guest bedroom. Although he had ordered all his clothes and personal things moved there, it was a bedroom he had never used before. He knew with an instinct honed by years of intrigue that trouble awaited him.

Catriona breathed the morning deep into her lungs. The air was heavy with English scents, damp smells of earth and woodland. There was no tang of the sea in it. No hint of the saltings, the watery expanses that lured the winging geese. No hills rose beckoning beyond the trees. No mountain peaks loured against the sky. It was all strath and glen—all valley—this England, with nothing in it for the soul.

Did he love this place?

The lawn cooled, rich and deep, beneath her feet as a frenzy of birdsong rang in her ears. She bent and touched the soft, loamy soil, the grass springing strongly.

Did he love this land he didn't own, that he leased from his brother? Or did he belong nowhere?

How could a man have a soul if he didn't have a home? If he didn't love one spot on God's earth with all his heart? Where else did honor come from, if it did not come from that certain knowledge of one's place and one's identity, rooted in homeland as a rowan tree roots itself under rocks by falling water?

This Englishman was too strange for her to fathom.

Yet last night she had known the meaning of desire and could only despise herself for it. In Glen Reulach she had been courted. She might have wed more than once. Yet she had never before felt this heat, this hunger. Her body craved him. Indeed, indeed. What he had said last night was true. It would not be any dishonesty to act on such a desire— purely for the body—and thus purge it and burn it away.

In that, she believed him. Hearts need not be involved. They could go on more cleanly afterward, two adults, freed from this obsession.

But the child awaited them in Edinburgh. She was driven by her desperate purpose. And she could allow neither herself nor Dominic Wyndham the satisfaction of such a thing.

∞

Dark, with the bowed chest and sloping shoulders of a hawk, the man had the look of an organ grinder holding out a hat, greedy and expectant. He had been kept waiting in an antechamber, secretly. The Duke of Rutley knew a slight shudder of distaste. The man was efficient and knew his business. But his grace felt no obligation to embrace such tools too closely.

"What can you tell me about my interest, sir?"

Yarrow Fletcher took a deep breath, visibly expanding the hawk chest, and bowed. "As you surmised, your grace, the woman who calls herself Catriona Sinclair is not what she appears."

The duke narrowed his eyes, leaning back. "And?"

"She is indeed involved with your grace's concern in Scotland."

The duke deliberately remained impassive. "You interviewed the understairs maid at the Earl of Windrush's residence?"

"I did, your grace. The Highland woman left early yesterday morning with Dominic Wyndham."

The duke let silence stretch for a moment as the clock ticked. There were times when one's distaste came close to repugnance. Fletcher seemed too eager, like a dog slavering at its chain. But His Grace of Rutley could not let that turn him aside. The results of this touched too deep. However it might appear, he cared for his son, Lord Stansted, and even more fiercely that his line continue. He would allow nothing to diminish—however slightly—anyone of his blood.

"Major Wyndham is known to you?" he asked at last.

"From Peninsular days, your grace."

"I do not wish them to reach Edinburgh before you," the duke said after another pause. "See to it."

Yarrow Fletcher bowed. "Your grace."

The duke nodded and the man left the room. Rutley closed his eyes for a moment, pinching the narrow bridge of his nose between thumb and forefinger. The pet that grovels is often the same cur that later springs for the jugular. Something had vibrated in Yarrow Fletcher at the mention of Wyndham's name, something implying a personal antagonism. If the matter were not already so far under way, he would dismiss the man and find someone else. But Fletcher was discreet and efficient. He knew his business. There was no better instrument for the Scottish affair.

Dominic hesitated for only a moment before turning the doorknob to the guest bedroom. Trouble had never turned him from his purpose. In her black dress, Catriona stood before the hearth. Her face was flushed like a rose, the tip of her nose bright red. Beads of moisture sparkled on her braided hair.

She looked angry. "I have been waiting. Would you sleep all day?"

In front of her on the hearth rug stood a copper tub filled with steaming water, a brass bucket, and towels set before the fire to warm.

Dominic closed the door behind him and kept his voice gentle. "You should have woken me."

"I thought to allow you privacy, but I come back and you are not even dressed. It is time to go."

"You have bare feet."

She glanced down. Her toes, as rosy as her cheeks, peeked beneath the hem of her skirt. "I have been outside."

Deliberately, he let his incredulity show. "In *bare feet*?"

She seemed matter-of-fact. "Had I worn shoes, they would have gotten wet with the dew. It is not healthy to wear wet shoes and stockings. I will put them on when we go.''

"Good God. You only have one pair of shoes?"

"I have everything I need."

He ignored her obvious impatience. "What did you find outside?"

Tiny beads of moisture winked like dying stars in her hair. "I don't know. You care nothing for this place, do you?"

"I prefer town. I like the theater and politics and the buzz of a gentleman's club. I like the meetings on science and the latest explorations in Africa. I like the women. What the hell would I do out here in the country?"

Her eyes flashed blue beneath her lashes, cobalt silk and black lace. "So why are you wasting time? We must leave.''

He grinned and crossed his arms, leaning back against the door panels. "I am not bathed yet."

"Then wash yourself and have done."

Dominic pushed away from the door. The water steamed gently. "A mistress would offer to assist me."

"Very well, if it is necessary to get us started on our journey. I believe I can do it quite well, though I'm not as expert, I am sure, as your regular lovers."

He couldn't read her at all. Surely she couldn't be serious? He had expected her to demur and leave the room. Her harebell eyes were shuttered, her cheeks and toes innocent as a cherub's. Pleasure spread from his groin. Not surprisingly, at the very thought of her sponging him, he'd become hard for her. It was becoming, he thought ruefully, a regular occurrence.

"Catriona, I can bathe myself. As it happens, the servants here aren't used to my wishes. I usually shower."

"In that contraption in the dressing room?" She leaned forward and dipped the bucket into the hot water, before balancing it on the edge of the tub. "That copper on four legs? I did wonder why a pan should be so full of holes. But it looked like a lonely enough device to me, when you have a woman ready to serve you instead."

"You have it all wrong." Still grinning, he walked up to the tub, his erection brushing the silk of his dressing gown. He didn't care if she noticed. "My mistress is always the first in hot water."

He reached for the bucket.

Without warning, she dumped the contents over his head. Water streamed off his hair and face, blinding him. His hands closed on air. Stumbling against the tub rim, he slipped on the wet floor. In instinctive capitulation he turned as he fell, so his back hit the warm water. It rose in a wave, splashing out onto the carpet. Dominic leaned his head onto the metal surface behind him and choked back helpless laughter as he let himself sink, in billows of black silk, into the flood. He opened his eyes under the water and watched air bubbles rise and burst.

Distorted by water, her face wavered. He couldn't tell if she was laughing or frowning as he tugged at the knot in his sash. He came up gasping, his dressing gown in one hand, and dumped it onto the sodden carpet, a glistening pile of dark silk. As water ran in long tendrils over the floor, she retreated.

"All right!" He leaned forward, swallowing the laughter as he wiped water from his eyes. "Come here and start scrubbing."

She moved fast, a wet swishing of skirts. "*Och-òn,* you will put me in the water with you." Her voice gurgled.

He opened one eye and looked at her. "You're already wet." Her face was lit like a lamp, both hands over her mouth. He had never seen her laugh like this. Helpless female giggles. He liked it.

She stepped back, farther out of reach, beginning to hiccup. "It . . . it will dry."

Water sloshed as he leaned back. "Haven't you another dress?"

Catriona took a towel and rubbed at the moisture on her skirts. "I have, but this one will do."

"No, it won't. Today is our day for covetousness, remember? A sin so deadly it's one of the Ten Commandments. 'Thou shalt not covet thy neighbor's house, thou shalt not covet thy neighbor's wife, nor his manservant, nor his maidservant, nor his ox, nor his ass, nor anything that is thy neighbor's.' "

"Thy neighbor's house?" Her fragile nape shone white as she bent and wiped her hem. It caught his heart. "There is water on the floor of this one."

Dominic watched the rivulets running into the cracks between the floorboards. He stretched for the soap. "Very possibly it will bring down the ceiling downstairs."

She shrugged, straightening. "It is your ceiling."

"No, it is Jack's ceiling. When I married Harriet, I signed a lease on the house for five years. The bloody thing precludes subletting and he won't break the terms. The upkeep and cost of a house I don't use has been damnable, so I believe Jack's ceiling can go to the devil."

Her laughter died. "Your own brother—he holds you to such a thing?"

"It doesn't matter. I can pay." He wallowed back in the water, soaping his chin. "Would you please do me the kindness to pass me my razor?"

She found the razor and a small mirror, and gave them to him. Then she watched as if fascinated by the sight of the blade scraping his chin. "You told me you inherited nothing. How can you afford so much?"

"I gamble. And I have some funds invested."

She couldn't hide her curiosity. But since her interest in him was undoubtedly entirely mercenary, that wasn't surprising. "How is that?"

"Very early in the war I had the good fortune to be on a ship which captured a French vessel. Loath to ignore easy gain, I performed some incautious actions that gave me a large cut of the prize money—enough to make me sufficient match for Lord Arnham's youngest daughter, at least. That income pays for this house. I need covet nothing."

He stretched his chin and scraped the blade over the underside of his jaw, watching his distorted expressions in the mirror.

"But the Commandments talk about people, as well,"

she said. "Do you not covet thy neighbor's wife, or his manservant, or his maidservant?"

He glanced up directly into her eyes and was serious, not caring if she knew it. "Oh, yes. The man in question isn't exactly a neighbor. He lives north of here. In a day or two you can meet him. It isn't his servants I covet."

"Then you desire his wife?" She seemed caught between her laughter and her sensitivity to his sudden change of tone. "Who is he?"

"The Marquess of Rivaulx. An old comrade. It's an ancient Norman name, with an 'x' that's not pronounced. And yes, I covet his wife." Then he ducked beneath the water so he couldn't hear her answer.

Catriona wasn't sure why it bothered her. Of course he desired other men's wives. But there was something in the way he'd said it—almost a wistfulness—that made her think this was something more.

She watched his head, slick as a seal's, rise above the water again. She had not been surprised by his arousal. *A Dhia,* she had seen enough horses and cattle on the farm. But a man—? She looked away, unconsciously striking her hands together. Anyway, he wanted this other lady—the Marchioness of Rivaulx. And no, that did not bother her at all. It only strengthened her resolve to resist him.

He rose from the tub, rubbing vigorously at his head with a towel. If she had thought she could remain unmoved by him—by his animal grace, by his golden body—*och-òn,* she was wrong. She was moved to her soul. Yet it changed nothing. It changed nothing that he created laughter from her impulsive attack with the bucket of water. It changed nothing that he made her laugh, too, in spite of herself. Nothing mattered but Andrew, and that they reach Edinburgh soon.

He kept his back to her as he dried himself, then went to the clothespress. He flung open the doors to reveal shelves packed with linen, enough clothes to last a township for a lifetime. With exaggerated care he began to select a shirt, stockings, underclothes. He slipped into them as neatly as Roane, the Merman, slipped into his sealskin. A pair of beige pantaloons followed, then a blue waistcoat.

In his shirtsleeves, he stood at the mirror arranging his hair. There was a piercing intimacy to it—to all of this. To share a room with a man and witness such small personal attentions, the details of grooming. Was this why he had made her stay in his bedroom? He began to tie his cravat. It was a display, she realized suddenly, like a peacock spreading its tail. Was she so easily mesmerized by the shimmer and rattle of shaking feathers?

"You are very careful with your clothes," she said at last.

"Indeed." He tossed the crumpled cravat aside and reached for another, raising his chin as he tied it, the line of his jaw strong and pure, outlined against the dark wardrobe behind.

"You are a fop."

The dimple shot into his cheek as he grinned. "Very likely. It is all designed to attract, of course." He reached out a hand and tugged at the bellpull. "I trust you are attracted?"

She lifted her chin and looked away. He did not need clothes to attract!

A servant opened the door and Dominic nodded to him. "Clear up this mess, Linton, and bring the things I ordered."

The man bowed. He came back into the room with a tail of menservants. The tub was removed, the wet towels picked up, the floor mopped. Then a train of maids appeared, bearing packages. One after another they set them on the bed.

As soon as the servants left, Dominic propped himself on a corner of the dresser. The line of jacket and trousers was precise, compelling. An enhancement of what lay beneath.

He indicated the packages. "Open them."

"Why?"

"Today's deadly sin. I want to see you indulge in covetousness for a moment. It is all for you. Take what you want."

Unsure, still in her bare feet she walked to the bed and untied a parcel. Brown paper fell open in her hands to reveal blue silk. She opened another. This one was muslin, in ivory and rose. As she discarded the wrappings fabric bloomed on the bed like a riot of bright flowers. Dresses. He had bought her dresses. Panic leaped into her throat. Angry, she tore into more paper. Shawls, gloves, stockings—a cornucopia of English fashions, silk heaped on satin, muslin on sarcenet.

"What is all this?" she asked, breathing hard.

"Gifts. For you."

"Why? I don't want them!"

He slid from the dresser and came closer. "They are beautiful." His lean hands tossed the paper aside and shook out the rich fabrics: walking dresses, gowns, a pelisse lined in fur. "Feel this. It's lovely." He held up a silk shawl and touched her cheek with it.

Catriona flinched away. "Why did you do this? All this extravagance?"

"A gentleman always gives presents to his mistress."

She pressed her hands together. "Where did they come from?"

"London. I ordered them to be sent here before we left." He stood looking down at the bounty of textiles. "I thought it would please you."

"It does not please me at all." Her voice rang with anguish. She could not contain it.

He looked hurt, a small contraction crossing his features. She thought for one moment he really *was* hurt and her heart turned over. But he glanced up and grinned. "Gifts are a traditional part of seduction."

Catriona slumped to the bed, pushing aside the clothes. "You wanted me to feel sinful desire, to covet worldly goods?" A crazy laughter threatened to bubble up her throat. *Och-òn,* but she was touched! Foolishly, foolishly, like a lass with a lover. She felt overwhelmed by his excess, but hardly flooded with avarice. It was not clothes she coveted. "Och, the things are lovely, indeed." She waved her hand over the profusion of fabric. "But I do not desire such stuff."

"Good God!" He looked closely at her. "You mean it. You really don't care about clothes. Do you care for nothing?"

"Why should my cares mean anything to you?"

He stood still for a moment, the shawl in his hands, then he dropped his face into its soft folds. "You know none of the sins?"

"Covetousness, never. I don't care for possessions. But I have known anger and envy and sloth."

He looked up, any vestige of hurt apparently gone, buried in irony. "You have left out my favorite—lust—and rampage wantonly through the sins like a goat in a garden. Sin must be savored, or there's no point to it at all. Are you totally impervious, Catriona Sinclair, to all my fatal lures?"

"I am to this one." She touched the silk as it slid from his hands, moving sensuously in ripe folds onto her lap. "What would I do with such stuff in Glen Reulach?"

"Wear it to the assemblies in Inverness. Turn heads. Feel your own beauty enhanced. Enjoy loveliness for its own sake."

"At home, I have dresses for Inverness." She let her hands drift on the shawl. Was the disappointment in his voice genuine? Had he really meant to please her? It was generous. Whatever his motives, it was generous. "I am not impervious to loveliness."

"Then you admit desire?"

She glanced up and their eyes met. Silence stretched for a moment as Catriona sat pinned, unable to look away. She did not care about possessions. She never had. But she knew desire. His nostrils flared as he smiled and the dimple deepened in his cheek. She could hear his breathing. His clean masculine scent enveloped her. His mouth beckoned, as sensuous as the shawl, and far more enticing. Heat spread through her limbs like sunshine over snow, melting.

"Not for this." She touched the clothing piled on the bed.

"For this, then?" He leaned forward and brushed her mouth lightly with his. A brief touch, feathered on her lips, then gone.

Her fingers involuntarily touched her mouth, as if to capture the sensation of that brief kiss and hold it.

"Whether you accept the silks or not, I shall seduce you," he said.

"Because I did not turn away in maidenly outrage? You do not seduce me."

"No, that will happen tomorrow when the day's sin is lust."

Catriona stood up and brushed past him, suppressing the clamor of need he created in her. "When I know all your attention for a deceit and a manipulation? I can resist you. So how will you cope when I refuse lust, just as I refused covetousness?"

"I don't know," he said, laughing suddenly. "And that's God's honest truth."

Six

∞

THEY WERE TRAVELING fast and at times not on the turn-pike, though always north. The carriage rocked steadily. Catriona had not taken the dresses, nor the soft kid gloves. She would not be so indebted to him. Yet the silk shawl was around her shoulders. If she turned her head, she could feel its sensuous caress on her cheek. He had insisted, with that charming persistence, teasing until she agreed to wear it. To have done otherwise would have been merely petty. And she would not be petty just to spite him.

She was trying to read in the corner of the carriage, but she was aware of him, as a squirrel is aware of the stoat that lies hidden on the forest floor. He lounged casually on his seat and watched her. His eyes held a veiled intensity, promising secret desires. His hands lay clean-knuckled and strong, where if she glanced at them she would lose her breath. She knew his lip curled, as if with sarcasm.

But she would not look at him.

If she did, that suffocating longing would become over-whelming. She would want to let him run his clever mouth and his long-fingered hands wherever he would. She would feel again that urgency to surrender, to give her body to his expertise. Of course, he would be expert. This man who had befriended Calum and driven away his own wife. This man who had bedded myriad women and loved none.

The book blurred. She glanced out of the window. *A Dhia!* It had been a madness to agree to this journey!

It had rained, a drenching rain with a hint of thunder behind it. The trees sparkled with moisture. Heavy clouds still hung in the sky, darkening the late afternoon into an early twilight.

"Will you leave me with nothing?" he asked suddenly.

Catriona tensed. "What?"

She could hear the smile in his voice, tinged with a seriousness designed to disarm. She knew he did not mean it.

"It would be a politeness, don't you think," he said lightly, "if we conversed. I do not expect you to reveal anything of yourself or your life, or even the real purpose of this bloody journey. You may nod your head or make small sounds—even an occasional comment, if you wish— in all the right places. If you insist, you may ignore me and not even do that, but for God's sake, can't we talk?"

She set her book aside and looked at him. "I will give you common courtesy, certainly."

His pupils glimmered beneath half-lowered lids. "I have never known a woman who did not desire pretty things, who was not envious of her friends' new wardrobes, who did not crave fashion and beauty."

So his feelings *had* been hurt when she refused his gifts. She could not afford to let it disturb her. The happiness of hundreds of souls depended on her steadfastness. "Then for all your prowess, you have not known many women."

He glanced from the carriage window. "Harriet delighted in such things, even after she had gone to Edinburgh."

"How do you know?"

His profile cut clean against the bright light from the window. "A life of chastity did not apparently put a damper on a fashionable appearance. The bills kept coming—from her mantua-maker, the glovers, the milliners."

"Why not? She had not seen you for over a year."

"She did not wish to see me, Catriona. Pray, don't hold that absence against me."

The cover of the book was a rich red leather, soft under her hand. "I do not. She hated you."

"Yes," he said dryly, glancing back at her. "Of course."

Deliberately Catriona picked up her book, shutting him out. He would wear her down, weaken her, exhaust her. And then she would surrender. All day he had offered her odd glimpses of himself, some charming, some intriguing. And now this—*the bills kept coming*—a reminder that he had been forced to win wagers to buy trinkets for Harriet. She bit her lip and felt tears burn suddenly. Devil take him! It was so unfair.

"You are holding the book," he said with a hint of humor, "upside down. Perhaps you are hungry?"

She jerked and dropped the book. "Hungry?"

His grin was infuriating. "For food. We can picnic."

He rapped on the panel and the coach stopped. Dominic leaned from the window and exchanged a few words with their driver. Within half an hour they stopped again. Catriona glanced from the window. Sunlight slanted low over a small clearing beside a brook. The grass sparkled with moisture.

"I must get out and walk," she said, fighting that odd strangling panic.

Without thinking she leaned down and stripped off her shoes and stockings, climbing barefoot from the carriage and onto the wet grass. As their coachman spread an oilskin and blankets on the ground, then produced a hamper, Catriona walked rapidly down to the water. It swirled lazily under overhanging willows. She crouched down and splashed a little water over her face. If it were only the brattling waters of a Highland *sruthan,* dancing downhill over its stone bed to the loch! If only she had not had to make this journey at all!

Dominic dropped onto the blankets and waited for her. She came back and ate in silence, unable to face him any longer. Yet he served her with courtesy, as the coachman sat, impervious, on the box and drank ale.

As soon as they finished the meal Catriona stood up.

"You cannot get back into the carriage like that," Dominic said.

"What?" She stared down at him.

"You have mud, dear Catriona, on your beautiful feet. Here, let me wash them for you."

Before she could react, he leaped to his feet and caught her, swinging her into his arms with a strong hand at her shoulder and one behind her knees. Holding her close to his chest, he carried her down to the sluggish English brook and deposited her on the low-sprawling limb of a willow. She clutched at another branch for support, her feet dangling over the water.

"I am waiting," he said merrily, "for you to wax indignant."

"Mach as m' fhianais!" she spat. "Leave me alone!"

"Alone?" He waded into the brook, ignoring the water swirling around his polished boots, and bent, taking her right foot in his hand. "I am here only because you demanded my company. I am your obedient servant, ma'am. You cannot expect me, however, to allow you to dirty my carriage with muddy feet."

She sat stiff as he splashed water from the brook over her toes, his hands rubbing at the sensitive instep, the cold water raising goose bumps on her legs.

"You should not," she gasped at last. "You should not humble yourself."

He grinned up at her. He had now, extravagantly, dropped to one knee in the brook. Water eddied about his thigh. "Oh, I don't," he said. "I'm enjoying myself."

She could not pull away her foot without falling back into the water. So Catriona turned her face to her shoulder and closed her eyes. His touch was tender—cool water and warm hands—soothing, delicious. Tomorrow's sin was lust, today's only covetousness. Yet this was what she coveted: to be taken care of, for just a moment, before she took up all the burdens of the world once again—and to feel his hands on her skin.

With a great splash he stood and swung her into his arms.

With her head on his shoulder, he carried her back to the carriage and set her inside.

"Now it is you," she said. "You are streaming water. You have ruined your boots. Why must you be so imprudent?"

He looked down at himself, at the beige trousers and brown boots, the clothes he had taken such care over that morning. He laughed. "I don't know. Perhaps I'm in love."

Her heart turned over. "Stop it! Do not do this any longer! I cannot bear it. What do you want? This journey is not about me. It is only about the bairn, wee Andrew! Do not punish me because he needs you."

"I don't wish to punish you. I like you, though I'm aware of a certain madness in your company. It feels very close to being in love. You should try it."

She hit out, without thinking. "Are you driven to this wildness because you failed your first baby? He died because of you. Did you even care? You only play games. You never even saw your own bairn."

He was rigid for a moment, his face terrible. Then he spoke slowly and carefully, as if consciously holding on to control. All the humor and irony were gone. "I did see him. He was tiny, like a wax doll. His eyes were closed. He had perfect little fingers. I thought he was smiling, though his mouth was blue. Lady Arnham sent me his body for burial."

Appalled, silent in heartbreaking shock, she stared at him—the water pooling about his feet, the cress stains on his pantaloons.

He gave the ghost of a smile. "But no doubt you are right. It was my return to England made Harriet miscarry. My son died because of me. I don't know if that's what drives me. It doesn't matter much now, does it?"

"I am sorry," she said brokenly.

"No, I deserved it." He looked up at her. "Catriona, life goes on. My life goes on. So I play games with the devil. I have tried to make Lucifer sing a little for his trouble, that's all. I have nothing to hide. Why are you hiding from me? What's your secret?"

"I have no secret. I only want you to claim Andrew—for his sake."

"You are lying. Who the devil is Andrew's real mother?"

"Harriet," she said stubbornly.

"No, it is not. My dead son was my wife's first and last child. You are using me and I'm damned if I know the reason. If it's for money, ask for it."

"It is not for money," she said. "I will not tell you more."

"Then why the hell do you think you deserve mercy from me?"

He swung into the carriage opposite her. Catriona turned away and closed her eyes, drawing the silk shawl up over her hair. She could not risk telling him, and she did not want him to see her tears.

∽

The sudden lurch threw her violently forward. Her head thudded into the edge of the door. Noise cracked sharply outside. Catriona staggered awake, unaware she had slept at all, as the coach shuddered to a stop. But the view from the carriage window was only of trees. Dense trees, a thick woodland. It was almost dark.

Dominic was braced back against his seat, a pistol in his hand, his hair silver in the half-light.

"What is it?" she whispered.

His hands moved rapidly, reloading. So he had just fired, too. "Highwaymen—apparently."

"Apparently?"

"We are in Sherwood Forest, or what's left of it, on a back road. We left Nottingham an hour ago. But our assailant is not Robin Hood's band of merry men." With a click, he set the pistol to full cock. "They seem strikingly reluctant to identify themselves—"

Another shot rang outside and the coach lurched again.

"Damnation! Who the *hell*—" Dominic leaned his wrist

on the open windowsill, the pistol's barrel pointing into the dense gloaming. "Stay down."

The next shot rattled out above their heads—Coachman's blunderbuss. Totally alert now, she crouched on the floor of the carriage against Dominic's damp, stained boots. The old refrain ran through her head: *your money or your life*. A horse neighed. She imagined the animal's panicked eye and alert ears, and Coachman struggling to reload his weapon.

Dominic fired. Noise boomed in the close confines of the carriage. Her nostrils filled with acrid black smoke. A man cried out.

More shots exploded from the road. Something thumped heavily to the ground. The coach lurched, rocking violently, then their team plunged forward. In three strides they were galloping full tilt. In a thunder of hooves, more horses followed. Catriona struggled back to the seat. The entire exchange of gunfire had happened with no one outside speaking a word.

Dominic was reloading again, rapidly pouring powder and ramming the ball, his feet braced against the swaying carriage. She knew he had killed one of the highwaymen.

"Do you have another pistol?" she asked.

He glanced at her. "No, why?"

"I could shoot it. I know how."

He looked grim. "Then shoot this one." Without hesitation he handed it to her, with the powder horn and bullets. "I must reach the box. The bloody bastards have murdered our coachman."

So the horses ran unguided into the oncoming night, with pursuit hot on their trail. There was no time for fear. Catriona braced the loaded pistol on her windowsill. Dominic threw open the opposite carriage door and clutched at the swaying roof.

He hung there for a moment as his voice dropped back to her. "Aim to kill. These are no ordinary highwaymen."

Moments later he had wrenched himself up, clawing for hand and footholds. As he disappeared a masked horseman drew level and raised his gun. Without hesitation, Catriona fired. The man cursed and fell forward, clutching his arm, and dropped his reins. The horse stumbled over the looping leather, throwing the rider to the ground.

Another man had come up on the other side. She heard a crack. Dominic must be on the box. She saw the long carriage whip flick through the gloom, lashing into this second rider. He cursed and pulled up his horse, blood springing from a cut across his face.

There were at least two more horsemen, perhaps three or four. Desperately she worked to reload—powder, ball, flashpan, half-cock, touchhole, prime, tap. She fully cocked the pistol and fired at a rider who streamed past the window. She missed. But the whip coiled about the man's wrist and his pistol flew away to land on the road. Reload again. In an agony of frustration, she rammed the ball, risking the dirty touchhole, fumbling the priming. The fourth rider took aim at Dominic. She fired just as his pistol went off, with a flash and explosion of powder, but the man swore and fell back as her ball found its mark.

The carriage careened wildly, swaying on and off the narrow road. With a great crack, the open swinging door ripped off against a branch. A shower of debris from the tree rained down. The horses were running blindly now, flecks of foam flying past the windows. It was almost impossible to reload. Twice she spilled powder on her skirts.

A hoarse shout made her glance up. The rider Dominic had disarmed was galloping level with them. He looked at her once full in the face, before he leaped up onto the carriage.

She heard Dominic's voice, clear, cold, even slightly amused. "Good God! What the devil are you doing in Sherwood?"

There was no reply, only a deadly thumping and scraping. Obviously, the men wrestled. Something snapped behind her. Catriona turned in time to see another man launch himself from his horse and through the open doorway into the carriage. Her knife slid like an old friend into her hand. She did not blink or hesitate as he lunged at her.

At the same instant the man fighting Dominic slipped,

yelling obscenities, from the carriage roof. She saw him hit the soft turf at the side of the road and roll. Moments later Dominic swung back in through the doorway.

"Dear God," he said lightly. "A corpse. Are you all right?"

Catriona nodded. She felt odd, as if she were numbed by a blow. "You are bleeding," she said.

A red stripe marked his cheek, a graze across the bone.

"A scratch, nothing to worry about." He bent and heaved the body out onto the road. The carriage rocked violently, ever faster.

She tried to speak normally. "The horses?"

He leaned back on the seat, holding his handkerchief to his face. "Run unguided, alas. The reins are destroyed; they have half a birch tree across their backs; branches are caught in the harness. Don't worry. They'll get tired."

"Unless they wreck the carriage first."

"Should I attempt some feat of derring-do?" He reached out and took her left hand. Catriona stared at his strong fingers holding hers. "Failure—sadly the most likely outcome—would leave you alone in a runaway carriage, as well as my mangled remains on the road. Not worth the risk." Still clutching her hand, he glanced at the blood smeared across the carriage floor. "Where the hell did you learn to kill a man with a knife?" His voice was surprisingly gentle.

There were red stains on the handkerchief, but his wound had stopped bleeding. Fantastically, it accented his lean cheek. "Calum taught me."

"But you never put his teaching into practice before today, did you?"

She shook her head. She felt remote, as if her soul were leaving her body.

His voice was composed, careful. "Let me have your weapon. I'll clean it."

She hadn't realized the knife was still in her hand. As she looked at it nausea rose in her throat. She began to shiver.

Dominic took the blade from her limp fingers and

wrapped an arm about her shoulders. "It's all right. You had no other choice. This is just shock."

"I shall be sick," she said.

"The feeling will pass. Drop your head to my lap."

She did, because she was shaking. He held her firmly, stroking her hair, his fingers a warm balm, easing the fine strands from her neck and cheek.

"It's not so easy to kill," he said slowly. "After I killed my first man, I was sick to my soul. I hadn't expected to like it, but I wasn't prepared for so profound a revulsion. Yet it was necessary. I have done it many times since. War involves killing. It never gets much better, but there's some comfort in knowing you had the courage and the skill, and that your cause was just."

She turned her face against his thigh, holding on to him fiercely now with both arms about his waist. "I would not have done it for myself. But there is Andrew—"

His fingers feathered away the moisture on her cheek. "Hush, now. Yes, you would have done it for yourself. And so you should." His voice was steady, reassuring. "There is nothing noble about sacrificing your own life for a criminal's, especially when he's trying to hurt you. Feeling better?"

She struggled to sit up, but the thunderclap cracked immediately beneath her. The carriage tilted violently, throwing her back against Dominic. Immediately he drew her close to his chest, shielding her head with his hands.

"Hold on to me," he said. "We've shattered a wheel."

The axle scraped, screaming metal and splintering wood, but the breakneck speed lessened. The horses dropped to a canter, then a trot, and finally a walk. Leather snapped. The coach tipped entirely. In seconds there was complete stillness and a dreadful silence, but for the blowing and jangling of four winded animals. Catriona had tumbled over Dominic. Gently he extricated himself, until they sat side by side on the overturned seat back.

"We are alive," she said.

"And unhurt." Dominic took her head in both hands.

His eyes searched her face. "Don't demur," he said, and pressed his lips over hers.

She kissed back, hungrily. His tongue was hot and alive. They were both *alive*. The sensation was like a straight shot of whisky, lifting the top off her head, making her gasp for joy.

He pulled away, panting, then placed kisses gently on her forehead and each cheek. "Let's get out of this bloody coach."

With his help, Catriona climbed from the wreckage. The horses hung their heads and trembled. One of the wheelers was bleeding freely from an injury to the shoulder. He must have run lame, for the leg beneath the bullet wound was mangled where it had beaten against broken chains and traces.

Dominic set Catriona carefully against a tree. "You're sure you're not hurt?"

She nodded.

He went to the horses and began to cut away the harness, using her murderous knife.

"Poor fellows. Poor fellows," he said gently, turning each exhausted horse away to graze. The horse with the wounded shoulder stumbled.

"Will you shoot him?" she whispered.

"No. Let him have his chance at life. It might not be that serious an injury. But none of these poor creatures is going anywhere tonight."

The horse took another hesitant step, but he put a little more weight on the injured leg. Catriona watched him and whispered a silent prayer.

Dominic looked up, listening like a hound. There was noise on the road.

"What is it?" she said, although she knew. A thundering of hooves.

"Alas," he replied. "Our pursuit. They must have had extra nags and regrouped. Catriona, unless we can fade into the forest like a band of merry men, I'm afraid we're about to be accosted once again. Can you run?"

"We don't have coats of Lincoln green. And we cannot outrun men on horseback."

He took her hand, raised it to his lips, and kissed her knuckles. Then he gave her the knife, cleaned now where he had wiped it in the grass. She took it without flinching. "We can give it a damned good try."

They raced through the trees, dodging shadowy undergrowth and thickets of young birches, Catriona half dragged behind Dominic. Her legs were on fire. The horses crashed behind them. In a few more minutes they would burst into view.

Dominic stopped suddenly and pulled her against his chest, whispering. "We must hide. Now."

He was looking at the clear black surface of water. A small lake, thick with reeds, shone in the darkening forest like an eye.

"The lochan?" she asked.

He was already stripping off his coat and shirt, and jerking off his boots. She pulled off her silk shawl and dragged away one petticoat, tearing it as she kicked off her shoes. There was no time to unbutton her dress. Without speaking again, Dominic thrust their removed clothes under a fallen tree trunk—a huge oak, uprooted in the forest—and taking her hand again, ran with her to the water.

They slid into its chill embrace, dissolving in blackness. As she waded Catriona cut reeds with her knife and gave one to Dominic. She didn't have to explain. She knew without asking he would know this old trick, one Calum had shown her many years before, one they had practiced as children, for a game. She had never dreamed she might one day have to use it in earnest.

As they reached water of the right depth Dominic grinned at her.

" 'Shall we give o'er, and drown?' " he quoted softly. " 'Have you a mind to sink?' "

" 'I would fain die a dry death,' " she quoted back.

He grinned again before placing the hollow tube in his mouth and sinking beneath the surface, leaving only the tip of the reed above water. She did the same, breathing through the tube, knowing nothing would reveal them among the reeds. Their pursuers would see only the silent black lake among the ghostly trees.

The vibration of hoofbeats shuddered through the water as the highwaymen rode up to the lochan and thundered around it. It was a sensation, only barely a sound, but it beat loudly in her ears. Cold seeped into her. Her skirts were clinging around her legs. Ignoring the discomfort, quietly, calmly, she breathed.

The horses trampled. There were muffled voices.

Her fingers were still trapped in Dominic's. She held his hand steadily, an odd solace. In twenty-five years she had never killed. In twenty-five years she had never met anyone who wanted to take her life. The terror of it began to erode her courage. Did those men want to murder her? Why?

And then she remembered—his voice, ripe with sarcasm: *Good God! What the devil are you doing in Sherwood?* Dominic had recognized one of their assailants. He had not seemed surprised when the man attacked him. *A Dhia,* what an irony! He had enemies who wished to murder him? Had she forced this man into her adventure, only to bring fatal danger to her own cause?

Something pulled at her hand. Water splashed. Gasping, Catriona thrust her head out of the lake.

"They're gone," Dominic said. She thought he smiled. "Come, if we don't get dry, we'll freeze to death."

It was the deepest end to twilight, the day faded to a faint bruise beyond the trees to the west. The early-summer darkness was not really cold, but the air bit like needle teeth though her wet clothes. Cold water ran from her hair over her soaked shoulders. Her legs were numb. She had no feeling left in her fingers.

Water rippling away, he led her from the lake, his bare back lithe in the glimmer of the almost dead day. Catriona was shivering, an involuntary shaking, chattering her teeth. She stumbled.

" 'And think'st it much to tread the ooze of the salt deep, to run upon the sharp wind of the north,' " he quoted,

supporting her with one strong arm. There was a laugh
buried in his voice.

She was too cold to answer, but she knew the reference.
Prospero, Duke of Milan, to the sprite Ariel, reminding him
of his recent exploits—and his indebtedness.

At the fallen oak, Dominic bent and retrieved their dry
clothes. Where the roots had torn away from the ground,
the base of the tree formed a little cave, black like the
mouth of a kelpie. Under the forest canopy, velvety darkness streamed and embraced. He began to unhook her buttons. She stood like a child as he stripped away her wet
dress, then sat her on a low branch snaking from the fallen
tree and knelt to take off her shoes. Modesty seemed absurd.

"It's n—" His teeth clattered together. She saw the flash
of them as he grinned, and started again. "It's not healthy
to wear wet shoes and stockings."

"You, t-t-too," she replied. "You must t-t-take off
yours, too."

"Very well." He bent and tugged off his ruined pantaloons and underwear. "Thank God you brought that
damned shawl."

Rapidly he dried himself on the silk. Naked, gleaming in
the shimmering, dying twilight, he turned to her and put
his hands under her armpits, making her stand up. He
seemed carved from marble, smoothed by the hands of a
master, lovely in the ebbing light. Apollo, stripped of the
sun's blaze and washed by moonlight, his man's organs
contracted with cold like those of a statue. She dropped her
face, biting her lip as he unlaced her frigid corset, then
raising her arms as he pulled her shift over her head, until
she stood nude before him.

He moved behind her and began to rub her chilled flesh.
Her head, her arms, down the length of her legs. Rubbing,
chafing away the cold, drying her. The silk massaged over
her back, over her buttocks and thighs, warming, comforting.

In a strange, lost daze, Catriona let him do it. *To run
upon the sharp wind of the north.*

Once, long ago, her old nurse had dried her like this after her bath before the winter fire, while her nightdress hung to warm beside the hearth. She had been tucked into heated sheets, while Magaidh sang in Gaelic. Lonely, sad songs of lost bairns. Lost among the lochs and the bens. Songs of mothers who traced the trail of the swan and the deer to find them. *Och-òn,* but they never did! The children remained lost forever and the mothers remained forever weeping. Poor bairns, stolen by the wee folk!

Yet she had been cared for, enfolded in love, and safe. Why was that remembered warmth pierced always by poignancy and plangent loss?

Still standing behind her, he reached around and dried her legs, rubbing up over her knees and thighs. Then he began to rub her breasts and belly, wrapping her in his arms, holding her close. His chilled stomach was against her back, yet warmth began to run from his flesh, like a flame across dry heath.

Gently he dried each breast, careful and tentative. The silk dropped over the curling hair where her thighs met.

Heat flared, deep inside, as if a tinderbox had been thrown into a furnace, a rush of fire running up her spine. His strong legs were against hers. His crinkled nest of hair and the soft pressure of his sex pushed against her buttocks. At each place where cold flesh met cold flesh—his to hers, hers to his—a white-hot flame leaped into being.

Her breath came fast, racing.

She had only to step forward to douse the fire, to reclaim the cold, dark night and the lonely moor where bairns are lost forever. She knew it clearly, the moment of decision. Her decision. This was a man. And an Englishman. There was no safety in his embrace. She should defy his warmth and walk away.

Yet moved to her soul by the intensity of longing, she dropped her damp head onto his shoulder and closed her eyes, letting her legs open a little where the silk brushed against her.

His hands stopped moving.

She reached back and wrapped her arms about his hips,

feeling the strong muscle and hard bone beneath.

For a moment he seemed suspended, his breath rasping hot in her ear, the sound of it blotting out the night. She pressed herself into him, seeking the heat and comfort of it, letting her hands move back over the swell of his buttocks, inviting.

The damp silk slithered to the ground.

Taking her head in both hands, he lifted her face and bent her body. His kiss was cold, cold. Icy lips pressing onto her mouth. She opened and breathed him in, and another flame flared. Instantly it became devouring, a conflagration. In the great cold universe, under the wide dark skies with the ghost trees circling like silent sentinels, blazed this one point of white-hot light—his mouth joined to hers. Sweetness, like spiced hot wine, flooded her tongue and she was bathed in fire.

He groaned, still kissing. His palms flared with warmth as he dropped his hands to her breasts. He cupped their weight as his thumbs flicked up over her nipples. Sensation pierced as he rolled them, hard, under his palm, then caressed again. Everywhere he touched became hot, leaping into flame. Bolts of heat spiked between her legs. She gasped for breath, arching back, offering herself.

He breathed in strongly, taking her kiss, taking her heat and her essence deep into himself. His tongue danced over hers. White-hot. Sweeter than melting honey. Her nipples stood stiff on swollen breasts and he cosseted them, flicking, teasing.

His skin glowed beneath her fingers. She marveled in the feel of it, questioning nothing, seeking that warmth. Pulsing against her buttocks, his *bod* had hardened, hot and strong, demanding. As his fingers tormented her she slipped one hand between their bodies and felt him. Smooth. Heat steaming from the shaft as his male essence leaped in her palm.

Her hand slipped lower, exploring the wonder of him, how he was made, how he was so different from her. The strange weight, and roundness, and vigor, rooting below the velvet shaft. She slid her fingers back up and caressed the rim, absorbing his startled, intaken breath in her mouth. His burning shaft leaped at her touch as her own knuckles pressed into her spine. The fire ached between her legs and ran licking over her skin. He slipped both hands over her belly, seizing her by the hips, and she turned in his arms to welcome him.

He said nothing as he laid her down in the cave made by the fallen oak. Under the overhang of the upended roots the ground was soft and dry, with the scent of mushrooms and soil, wholesome earthy smells. His discarded shirt made a clean bed for her back. The sky disappeared as he moved over her. Pitch darkness. Mixed with the tang of roots was his scent: clear, piercingly masculine. She wanted him to take her clean and hard, like an enemy. She wanted him to linger slow and deep, like a lover. Her eyes burned with unshed tears.

Kneeling, he cradled her head in both hands and stared down into her face for a moment. She couldn't see his features in the shadows, but she gazed up steadily. She knew he could not see her expression, could not fathom her thoughts. Reaching up, she touched his shoulder with her fingers, then ran her palm over his warm, hard chest. She had made her decision. She wouldn't have to fight him any longer. She would be free.

He stretched out beside her. She lay passive, open to him, feeling the length of his body pressed against hers and the hard throb of his sex. His hands moved and his mouth began to pleasure her. She tensed a little, but he touched and breathed slowly, caressing her hair.

"Catriona," he whispered. "Are you sure?"

The words slipped from her as if someone else spoke them. "I am sure."

His lips feathered gently over her jaw and chin. It was exquisite. An exquisite fire. She didn't know if she could stand it. She moaned aloud as his tongue trailed from her shoulder to her neck. Suddenly he suckled hard at the hollow of her throat. Shivers of fire streamed from the spot. She gasped, involuntarily sinking her nails into his arm. But then he kissed delicately below her ear, firing sensations so intense she thought she might melt. She heard his intaken breath, as if he laughed in delight, but swallowed it. She turned her face blindly, seeking him.

His tongue licked at the corner of her mouth and over the curve of her upper lip. Extravagant sensation blossomed and burned, until she sobbed with the power of it. Should she beg for mercy? *A Dhia,* for now she had given him permission, he was merciless! She opened her lips to moan, but he pressed his mouth over hers, swallowing her cries. He kissed her as Adam kissed Eve, until her lips swelled and pulsed with the pleasure.

As his mouth enthralled hers, his hands stroked the curve of her flank as if he found the very shape of her entrancing. His fingers spoke in secret tongues. Their message blossomed. She was beautiful to him! Beautiful to his touch. Beautiful as Deirdre to the High King, beautiful as the Swan Maidens raising their wings by the bright waters, beautiful as the Sea Women. His hands whispered of adoration, of honor, of devotion to her pleasure—and of his own depth of pleasure in her softness and curves.

In the black darkness, he was faceless, a dream lover, ultimate mate of her imagination. As if she awoke pinned by the incubus—demon lover of the night—she knew nothing but surrender. Yet it was only her own soul that caressed her so deeply, delving into her secret self, dark twin of her own longing.

His hands stroked over her breasts, trailing wonder. Her nipples rose hard as he rolled them between thumb and forefinger, spiking ecstasy through her blood. She thought she moaned. Her hands slid helplessly over his skin. She moved her legs around his, holding him to her in the darkness.

He tugged harder at her nipples, making her gasp, then he dropped his lips to them and nipped, suckling, then gently closing his teeth again. Sensation pierced to her core. She opened her legs and felt his hands slide down her flanks as his lips trailed over her belly, lingering to swirl his tongue at her navel, kissing ever more intimately until his

mouth parted her curls and touched her most secret self
with fire.

Surprise melted in the furnace.

She was moaning aloud. She writhed beneath him. Without mercy he buried his face between her legs, parting her
with his tongue, bringing all the flames he had fired in her
blood to this one white-hot center. She was aching and
swollen for him, her woman's moisture softening her for
his invasion. She would be free, if only he would penetrate
her! Her hands moved weakly, unable to grasp him, his
smooth muscles, the terrible beauty of a man, of all men
to their lovers, from the beginning of time.

The dark earth enclosed. Only their mingled breathing
rasped in the night. And at last he reared up above her and
she felt his arousal, throbbing against her swollen sex. His
bod stroked her trembling female flesh. Someone was sobbing. Only her, only her. Sobbing like the maiden tied to
the rock as the flame-breathing dragon comes to devour her.

This is what Fate had denied her, leaving her twenty-five
and alone and lost in darkness. Desperate, she opened herself, pulling her legs up out of the way, welcoming him.

Smooth, round, the tip of his rigid shaft touched her hot
flesh. She was laid bare to accept him, caressing the in-
vader. Fire thrilled in that secret female core. He rubbed
there for a moment, then entered, just a little. Exquisite
ripples of sensation pulsed from that molten center, deeply
tantalizing, promising paradise. Without knowing what she
did, she sank her nails into his buttocks. He thrust strongly,
plunging deep until he was buried in her flesh. Catriona
stiffened in shock and cried out.

Black silence swallowed her voice. She bit her lip, but
tears stood hot in her eyes at the sharp bite of pain.

Dominic hung rigid above her, unmoving. He kept still
until the burn at their joining dwindled to a dull ache, until
her panic at the fullness and stretching subsided a little. She
reached up and felt the columns of his arms. He was shaking. She realized she was clinging to him, sinking in her
nails, clutching him. Turning her head aside, she dropped
her hands and let go. Slowly, as if she were fragile chiffon,

he pulled away, carefully withdrawing. Then he rolled aside and left her, with the fire turned to agony.

She sat up, knowing there would be blood on them both. He was sitting with his knees drawn up, his head in his hands, at the edge of their tree-root cave. His body glimmered whitely.

"I'm sorry," she said.

"Bloody hell." He raked both hands through his silvered hair. "Oh, bloody, bloody hell."

"It's all right," she said. "I wanted you. I just didn't expect it to hurt so much."

He tipped his head back, staring at the stars. "For God's sake! You're—" He took a deep breath. "You *were* a virgin. Pray allow me a little consternation."

He reached for his dry shirt and, stepping out into the night, pulled it over his head. The moon had risen. The white fabric and his pale hair shone like a knight's polished armor.

"Tomorrow's sin was lust," she said quietly.

"Today's sin. It's after midnight. Today's sin. As if it matters. Oh, God, if I had known—" He turned back to face her. "I will marry you, of course."

Cold bit into her again. She grabbed her dry petticoat and put it on, before she stepped out of their cave and found her voice. It felt raw. "I will not marry you."

He picked up his jacket and wrapped it around her shoulders, an unthinking gesture of chivalry. "I thought—damnation! We shall marry as soon as we get to Scotland."

"Why? Is this your idea of gallantry? I *wanted* to lose my virginity. It is—it was—of no use to me."

"Don't be absurd." He seemed filled with contempt.

"You would not have taken me, if you had known? Why not? Why should I not choose my time and take a man into my body on my own terms?"

He bent and tugged on his damp trousers. "There is too much to say for us to continue this here. Damnation, there's so bloody much, I think I might suffocate under the choking weight of it all."

"What is there to say? You have won."

"*Won?* Dear God, have I misunderstood everything? I was so sure you were experienced." His laugh rang with bitterness. "I even thought you a mother."

She was genuinely puzzled. "Why?"

He shone silver against the dark forest, like a prince of Faerie. "I thought Andrew was your son, for I know damned well he isn't Harriet's. I could think of no other reason you would be willing to sacrifice so much for him. I thought Calum MacNorrin was your lover."

It was instinctive, her plea to Mary, Mother of God. "*A Mhuire!*"

Fiercely he thrust his feet into his boots. "Perhaps I even wanted to share pleasure with you for Calum's sake as much as my own, because I thought you mourned him as I did. Instead I find I have been used for your convenience. As a tool to rid you of your uncomfortable virginity."

Anger brought tears to her eyes. "Why not? You were happy to use me as a tool of your patronizing flirtation. It is the way you have used a great many women."

"No," he said. "It is the way they've used me."

She was crying. Silently. The tears ran salt into her mouth. The pain burned between her legs. Yet she could still feel the touch of his hands and his mouth on her body and the piercingly sweet pleasure of it.

He turned to her. "Catriona. For God's sake! This must wait. We are lost in Sherwood in the middle of the night, and someone out there in the dark wants our lives. I must get you to shelter. Then perhaps we can sort out this whole bloody mess."

"Did you so hate touching me?" she asked.

The moonlight shone full on his features. A dimple raced into his cheek as he grinned suddenly. "Oh, no. You were like ambrosia to me—until I broke your damned maidenhead. Put on your shoes."

She did so, without further remonstrance. "Where are we going?"

"Where we were headed before we were so rudely interrupted by those unlikely highwaymen. To the home of a friend of mine."

She straightened up and looked at him. "Is it far?"

"I don't think so. Can you walk comfortably?"

She didn't know, but she replied instantly. "Of course."

"Then let's go. Everything else can wait until morning. Though there is one thing I think you must tell me now: what the devil was Calum MacNorrin to you?"

Catriona glanced over the dark lake to the sleeping forest, then up at the sky to the star she had named for him. "Calum was my brother."

Seven

∽

SHE DID NOT complain. Highlanders knew how to walk. Dominic plunged north through the trees, sighting their way from the far-flung group of stars that pointed the way, ultimately, to Scotland. He had made no reply when she had admitted Calum was her brother, just taken her hand and walked.

They came out at last on a lane. It ran west of north, but Dominic strode along without hesitation, carrying her sodden dress. She ignored the ache between her legs and the strange emptiness in her heart. Wearing her torn petticoat and his jacket, her palm in his, she kept up.

The country opened out into rolling fields scattered with dark copses, a wash of ivory, gray, and black under the moon. A footpath branched off, running along the edge of one of these shadowed groups of trees, then across rolling parkland, finally to follow the north edge of a small lake. Away to her right, beyond overgrown gardens, Catriona saw the sleeping bulk of some great house, solid against the skyline.

The path turned into a well-beaten track. They came ever closer to the buildings, until they passed high walls which towered over her head and thrust them completely into shadows. Cutting around the edge of this great block of outbuildings, Catriona was confronted quite suddenly with the west face of the structure, gleaming in the moonlight.

She stopped in her tracks, pulling Dominic to a halt.

White spires and arches reached into the star-studded night. Gothic towers and three huge, gaping, empty church windows. Like teeth, broken edges of stone tracery fringed the massive central arch. To the right, stepped down from the church face and busy with medieval detail, the rest of the facade was stepped with bay windows and a fanciful arcade. Where the wall met the sky it was cut with battlements.

At the far south end, a long flight of stone steps marched up to a second-story entrance, like the guarded doorway of an ancient Highland keep. Beyond that lurked more buildings, roofs and chimneys clustered against the stars in random confusion.

"It is a ruin," she said at last. "A ruined abbey."

"Yes. Newstead Abbey, home of wicked lords. Come."

She followed him up the long flight of stairs and stood at his shoulder as he hammered at the door. It was a long wait, but at last a voice called though the heavy timber. "Who's there?"

"Dominic Wyndham, Mr. Murray. I have a lady with me. There has been an accident."

"Good Lord!"

Bolts clanged and the door was thrown back to release a blaze of light. A portly, dignified man with graying hair peered out at them, a lamp uplifted in one hand. A ruddy flush ran across bulbous nose and healthy cheeks. He was dressed in a dark jacket and pale yellow waistcoat, the clothes of an upper servant of some kind, obviously donned in some hurry.

"Major Wyndham? Good Lord! His lordship's from home, sir." He made no comment on their ragged appearance, though his eyes flickered from Catriona to Dominic and back.

"Yes, Murray, I know. May we come in?"

The man ushered them in though the doorway, then led the way into a great medieval hall. The lamplight flickered over a high arched ceiling and peeling plaster. The room was entirely without furniture.

"I have no guest rooms ready, sir," Murray said over his shoulder.

"Then perhaps we may use his lordship's private apartments?" Dominic asked. "One room will suffice."

Mr. Murray opened a door at the far end of the hall. "I will have the fire lit for you, sir, and refreshments procured."

"Murray," Dominic said. "You're a treasure, but a bed is our only requirement. We shall retire immediately."

Catriona stepped into the room. The contrast to the ruined hall they had come through was stunning: it was an entirely modern dining room. As she stood staring about the small chamber Mr. Murray disappeared through another exit.

"I don't understand," she said. "Whose home is this?"

Dominic sat down in a walnut chair. His pantaloons had dried on him, the fabric shrunk tight over his thighs. "A Scotsman's, as it happens: George Gordon, Lord Byron. Another man whose wife couldn't abide him."

She stared at an elaborate carved overmantel above the fireplace. Painted figures surrounded a bold coat of arms. Three heads in sixteenth-century hats stared down above it. The paint was peeling. "Lord Byron, the poet?"

"He's in Europe, but he'd be happy to lend us shelter. He's a generous man."

She felt awkward, lost. News of Byron's scandalous treatment of his wife, and his self-imposed exile as a result, had reached even the Highlands. "We are to share his bedchamber, but go without food?"

Dominic gazed idly at his boots. "Anything else would cause considerable inconvenience to Joe Murray, whom we just routed from his slumbers. As you saw, most of the place is uninhabitable. Byron used to practice with his pistols in that great hall we came through. When he first arrived here, it stored hay."

Catriona hugged his coat closer about her shoulders and said nothing, though she was ravenous for hot food.

There was a rap at the door and Joe Murray peered around it. "The bedchamber is ready, sir."

In silence they followed the servant through galleries and hallways and up a spiral staircase buried in the ancient abbey wall. When there was so much that needed saying, Catriona had no idea where to begin. She felt only numb. As Dominic exchanged a hushed conversation with Murray, she went ahead of them into Byron's bedchamber.

It was dominated by a canopied, dome-topped bed, a baron's coronet topping each post. Since it stood several feet off the ground, a set of wooden steps sat on the fitted carpet beside the bed. Compared with the echoing medieval spaces below, the space was both cozy and sumptuous— the bed hangings were a rich chintz with a pattern of gold-and-green Chinese pagodas—but the room was small.

"Thank God." Dominic came in and closed the door behind him. "A bed. In which we shall sleep like babes. I shan't touch you."

"You do not question—" She broke off and started again. "You are angry?"

He sat on the steps and tugged off his boots. "Anger is tomorrow's sin. We've already indulged today's, so let's use the rest of the night for simple sleep."

"You are angry," she stated.

He looked up at her. "Catriona, you have suffered a shock. The attack, the killings, the runaway carriage. You made love to me because of it. We shall discuss all the consequences in the morning. In the meantime please take off that wretched coat and get into this bed. We shall be warm. We shall sleep. You are safe. Nothing else matters until tomorrow."

She wanted to weep. The surprise of it burned away the tears before they began. Outside the window it was pitch night. Somewhere in the forest, perhaps men still hunted them with death in their hearts. She shivered.

"It's all right." Dominic came up to her and peeled his jacket away from her shoulders. Then he sat her on the bed and drew off her shoes. Her petticoat was filthy, torn and ragged, from their walk through the woods. Gently he lifted it over her head, turned down the bedcovers, and tucked her inside. In silence he snuffed the candles and undressed himself. She felt him slip into the bed with her.

Without words he pulled her to him, holding her in his arms until she fell asleep.

Her breathing feathered softly against his shoulder. She was warm, and naked, and infinitely desirable. He was fully aroused. The ferocity of his longing kept him awake, staring through the blackness at the dark lining of the bed canopy and berating himself for a bloody fool.

The child in Edinburgh was not hers. Calum MacNorrin had been her brother. He'd had everything wrong. She had been a virgin.

And he had ravished her, the sister of a man he had loved, taken her maidenhead under a dead tree. Dominic had no illusions about her willingness. She thought she'd been willing, but she hadn't known what she did. Only he did. He knew exactly what it meant to seduce a woman, and he had done so deliberately and without mercy—as he had promised when he first saw her.

She had been a virgin.

He had taken her—as he might any of those women in London—with an assumption of her experience and no care at all for the possibility of innocence.

With a soft moan, she turned over. He opened his arms and let go. Yet the curve of her bottom nestled against his thigh; her slim back begged for his palm. With a grim determination he turned away, cursing silently. What better punishment for his carelessness than this? To have her at his mercy and not act?

The thought of her lying open beneath him in the forest haunted him. He had wanted with the single-minded, blind determination of male desire to continue to plunge into that velvet bliss, to spill his seed into her yielding female warmth, to ignore the shock of her torn maidenhead. To

pull out and not consummate that desire had been the
bloody noblest thing he had ever done.

Yet he did not feel in the least noble. He wanted to slip
away into the dressing room and take care of the damned
ache in his groin himself. Deliberately, as a punishment, he
did not. He suffered the discomfort and the craving like the
original Augustinian priors of Newstead must have suffered
theirs, as an act of penance. Yet he could not take solace
in either holiness or prayer.

She had been a virgin.

Obviously he would marry her, although, thank God,
there was no chance of a child. But what the hell did he
have to offer her? A husband whose old enemies had
caught up with him and promised murder. To take his mind
from the demands of sex he tried to think about it. Why
the devil had Yarrow Fletcher suddenly decided to waylay
them in Sherwood, with death on his mind?

Birdsong awoke him. She slept still, her bedraggled hair
escaped from its plaits and spread over the pillow. Her upper lip curved like a petal. He wanted to kiss it. His body
urgently let him know quite how badly he wanted to kiss
it. Instead he dropped from the bed and strode into Byron's
dressing room, where Joe Murray had already laid out a
dressing gown and towels. With a grim smile, Dominic
shrugged into the gown and took up the towels. He ran
down through the labyrinth of stairs and passages to the
old cloisters. Next to the chapel was the high, vaulted passage that Byron had converted into a cold plunge bath.
Dominic threw off the robe and dived into the water. Ice-
cold shock parted over his head and enclosed him.

An hour later, bathed, shaved, and dressed in his own
newly washed and pressed garments—thanks to the indefatigable Joe Murray—he left the spare bedroom where he
had performed all these functions. He found her in the small
dining room. She was wearing her black dress, also washed
and pressed. Her hair was shining, once again coiled in its

neat plaits. In his calm, efficient manner, Murray had seen to everything. He had also seen to the hearty breakfast spread on the table.

Catriona looked up as Dominic came in. She seemed unchanged by their ordeal, but beauty shone in her eyes and lurked at the corners of her mouth. That she had become so inexpressibly lovely to him stirred a deep self-mockery. It was women who were supposed, inconveniently, to see a rose-colored view of the man after a single act of sex—even an aborted one.

"You slept well?" he asked.

"Chreach thu mi," she replied without blinking.

Dominic took a seat and helped himself to bread, meat, and eggs. "You have the advantage of me. Gaelic isn't a language I understand."

"Och, well then." Her dark head bent solemnly as she spread marmalade over a slice of toast. "Like stealing young birds from the nest, *creach* has the meaning of 'pillage' or 'plunder.' In English I might say, 'You have ruined me.' "

He flushed scarlet. It was so damnably unexpected and bizarre that he stared at her, refusing to hide the humiliating color. She turned the butter knife in her capable hand and glanced up at him. He could not quite read her expression; it was almost as if she were amused.

"We shall marry," he said at last.

"Why? Because I was virgin? Because you were the first? What sense does that make? You might have taken me without remorse, if only some other man had been there before you? My maidenhead was my possession. I decided to lose it."

A sharp anger shook him. "Most women consider their virginity a valuable commodity."

"Though a man loses his at the first opportunity, often when barely more than a boy. Then he has the effrontery to want a virgin bride."

He attacked his eggs with knife and fork. "It is different for men."

"Because a man can act in lust and still think himself a

gentleman? A woman must hide her desires, never act on what her body tells her, even if it is honest, even if it is right for her at that time. It was right for me last night. I wanted you. I wanted your body joined to mine. Only that. I do not regret it. Can you not understand?''

The eggs were fresh and tender, breaking under his knife like flowers. He clung to the illusion of normalcy, bracing himself to remain cool.

"You had come too close to death, so you turned to the act that makes new life. It was natural enough. But I had killed before. I was not in shock, as you were. I did not have to respond to you and the final responsibility was mine. I must in honor offer you my name. For God's sake, surely you see that?''

"*Dé tha cearr ort?* What is wrong with you? What if your first woman had demanded marriage because she had taken *your* virginity? Thinking I had known a man, you pursued me single-mindedly. You did not want to marry me then. Now you know I was virgin, you are wallowing in self-righteous regrets. Damn you and your noble sensibilities!''

"You were willing only because you were in shock.'' He dropped his fork with a clatter on his plate. The food tasted like dirt. "Unless you insist on believing me a monster, you must allow me a modicum of remorse. I was careless. I hurt you.''

"I did not realize it would pain me.'' She set down her knife and bit into her toast. "You must be large.''

He almost choked. Then he laughed from sheer surprise. "You have grounds for comparison?''

She stared past him, out of the window. The morning light shone on her severe bones, her blue eyes a stunning contrast to her pale skin. "Twice I have had a man close to my heart. Once when I was seventeen and once when I was one-and-twenty, but I do not have the knowledge to compare you with them.'' She looked directly at him. "They were the two men I would have married, but I had not touched them as I touched you last night.''

"Of course not." He couldn't quite keep the bitterness out of his voice. "They weren't rakes."

"They were men of honor. Yet they left me to die a virgin."

"What happened?"

"Vimiero and Ciudad Rodrigo."

Battles. 1808 and 1812. He pushed away from the table and stalked to the window. "They were soldiers," he said. "Highlanders. And they were both killed in the Peninsula." She had loved. She would have married, if either one of these men had come back alive. Instead the news had come, the lists of killed and wounded, and left her alone. Twice. There was nothing else to say but the mundane, appallingly inadequate inanity. "I am very sorry."

"Och, so am I, but that is not why I will not marry you. I won't marry you because you are a man of conceit and because I do not wish to marry. I do not wish to belong to any man, but especially to an English nobleman like you— a man in love with clothes and fashion, who lives in the night on the blood of others like a vampire. What future could we have?"

"I don't know." She had thought she was going to die. So she had decided to lose her virginity, coldly, in a calculated move, without passion. "I know damn all about you. You have lied to me ever since we met, ever since you involved me in your godforsaken schemes. Was Calum really your brother? Who the hell are you?"

She stood up, her back straight and her chin high. "My name is indeed Catriona. But I am not a Sinclair. My father was a MacNorrin and my mother, too. She was sister to the laird." Her voice rang with pride. "*Mac an Urrainn,* son of a remarkable man. I grew up with the laird, my uncle, in Dunachan, the castle in Glen Reulach—the Valley of Stars. Not that it matters, but we have chairs like these, and silver, and carpets fitted in the bedrooms. What did you think? That we all live in bothies?"

"Hardly. Calum had more learning and culture in his fingertip than most officers dream of. He let me know he had grown up with the pure blood of Glen Reulach in his veins. Indeed, his honor was downright prickly. If he were alive, no doubt he would stab me to the heart for what happened last night.''

"No doubt he would.'' She met his gaze squarely. "Or I could do it myself. When we were children Calum taught me as they taught him. The two-handed *claidheamh mór* was too heavy, but I know the dirk and pistol.''

"I noticed,'' he said. "Or at least, one of our assailants yesterday discovered your prowess for himself. I think, Catriona, you are going to have to tell me everything.''

"Outside,'' she said. "Under the sky, away from this paint and plaster. I will tell you outside.''

They left the dining room and walked down through the passageways into the grounds. The morning sun beat against the east wall of the abbey. In front of it lay the remains of a formal walled garden. Dominic watched Catriona as she stepped outside, the soft line of her shoulder, the swell of her breast. The memory of her sweet nakedness burned in his palms and blossomed on his tongue. He wanted her desperately and despised himself for it.

The garden was laid out in the geometric symmetry of the previous century, but the flowers grew untamed, as if the staff couldn't find time to take care of them. Unkempt lawns sloped down to a large rectangular pond. Beyond the flat water lay a tangled stand of trees, a dark backdrop to two distant white statues.

Catriona walked up to a large monument which dominated the garden closer to them. She read the inscription aloud: "Near this Spot are deposited the Remains of one who possessed Beauty without Vanity, Strength without Insolence, Courage without Ferocity, and all the Virtues of Man without his Vices. This Praise, which would be unmeaning Flattery inscribed over human Ashes, is but a just tribute to the Memory of Boatswain a Dog, who was born in Newfoundland May 1803 and died at Newstead November 18th 1808.''

"His portrait is in the house,'' Dominic said. "He was black and white. An excellent dog. Byron wants to be buried here with him.''

Catriona shaded her eyes from the sun. "Vanity, insolence, ferocity? Your friend Lord Byron does not think much of his own kind."

"Neither do you."

She turned to him suddenly, her color high. There was a bright glitter in her eyes, like unshed moisture. "The people of Glen Reulach are about to learn something of their own kind. Their livelihoods are all in the hands of the laird. That one man rules the entire glen. He holds the lease on every household, farm, and bothy. Though the clan has lived on the land since before Adam was, the people's lives are in his palm."

"I thought the laird was your uncle."

"He is dead. The acknowledged heir is a bairn named Thomas. His father was my other uncle, the old laird's younger brother. He fell from his horse and died. Wee Thomas is in the care of his mother, a redheaded Englishwoman named Mary. And Mary's fate and future, and the future of her little son—with all his inheritance and holdings— are controlled by her father, the Duke of Rutley."

The shock exploded in him like gunfire. "Rutley! Glen Reulach is in Rutley's hands? Oh, for God's sake! What about Andrew, the child in Edinburgh? Who the devil is he?"

"The old laird's son and the true heir, if I can prove it. The MacNorrin married an Englishwoman named Sarah, his second wife. His first wife was barren and died without children. It is the fashion now in the Highlands to take brides from the south. They bring English manners with them, and money. Andrew is Sarah's child."

"Then you would see Andrew displace Rutley's grandson?"

"I would. You must help me."

She stood against the stone base of a monument to a dog, the sun shining on her dark hair. She looked stubborn, her mouth set. She looked beautiful. He wanted to make her kiss him, not argue through all this family history.

"You expect me to get embroiled in this mess? Why the devil should it matter to me which baby inherits some obscure Highland estate? And why the *hell* did you tell me Andrew was Harriet's son?''

The stubborn set to her chin didn't change. "Sarah left Dunachan in 1814, the Victory Summer. She did not like the hills. She did not like living with an old man. She was English. She went to Edinburgh to live with the Souls of Charity. I believe she was carrying his child when she left, but she would not have known until later and she would not have told my uncle."

"Why not?"

"Two days after she left, he was struck down with apoplexy. When he recovered, he could not speak. He sat in his great chair and glared like a gargoyle beneath a dropped eyelid. When we asked him if we should send word to Sarah, he shook his head and roared like a bull. He wanted no communication with her and she offered none. He died last month without once letting us speak of her in front of him.''

Her emotion showed now in the quiver of her nostril, the little dip at the tip of her nose. Dominic tried to soften his voice. "How do you know Sarah had a child?"

"Confectioners came from Edinburgh to cook for the funeral, that is when I learned of it. One of them spoke of Sarah, the laird's wife, that she'd borne a child in March of 1815, that the child was with the Souls of Charity, that his name was Andrew. 'Born to trouble, poor lamb,' the woman said. 'He took his first breath as Napoleon seized Paris. They say March comes in like a lion. The bairn will know trials.' I went to find him, but when I arrived, Sarah had died. They said he was Harriet's."

"And what did my wife say?" *A baby born to trouble, like a changeling?*

"Harriet did not deny it, but I knew it wasn't true—the laddie was dark and blue-eyed."

He took a deep breath. "Not a blond angel, like Harriet—or myself."

Her eyes flashed. "You may scoff at your wife and her vocation, but the ladies did real work among the poor. Someone brought back a sickness and many of the Souls of Charity were ill. Sarah was dead. Harriet was dying. At the very end she told me she had papers—Sarah's diaries, other documents—proof of who Andrew really is. But only you, her husband, have legal claim to her things. They would not give them to me. Only you can prove Andrew is rightful heir to Glen Reulach."

As he stared at her and tried to make sense of the entire bizarre recitation, absurdity bubbled, a sudden release from the tension of days. "This what you have used me for? This is why I must come to Edinburgh? To fetch Harriet's papers, which are truly Sarah's papers, to prove my wife did not have a bastard, after all?"

She nodded.

"Why the hell didn't you tell me this to start with?"

"You would not have come. Unless you thought Andrew was your son, you would not have come."

The urge to laughter died, leaving nothing but a scathing sarcasm. "Because you knew, of course, I had no morals and no finer feelings, that simple justice to a stranger's child would not have moved me, that only an appeal to my baser nature would make me leave my depraved life in London."

She blushed. The color made her eyes brilliant. "That is what I thought."

He turned away, shading his gaze from the morning sun. "You will give me leave, perhaps, to think about all this?"

"Where are you going? We must go to Edinburgh."

Dominic pointed beyond the rectangular pond at the drift of trees behind the two white stone figures. "Those statues were brought here from Italy by the fifth Lord Byron. They are satyrs: woolly of thigh, but hopefully clear of head. A family. The mother and child are very rare, I believe. The spinney behind them is known as the Devil's Wood—a suitable place for me to make a decision."

He walked away rapidly, not looking back at her, down the terraces of the old formal garden, around the stagnant water, and through the rough grass at the base of the stat-ues. The mother satyr glanced down tenderly at her goat-legged child, holding him by the hand, their gazes locked forever in stone. He strode past her. The trees seemed to open up and embrace him as he stalked into the Devil's Wood.

∽

Catriona watched him go—tall, his hair shining golden in the sun—before she sank to the ground at the base of the monument to Boatswain and thrust her knuckles against her teeth. Her nurse had said it more than once. She could almost hear Magaidh speak, laughing, in Gaelic.

"Och, it is a smart wee bairn Catriona is, with her bonny black hair and blue eyes like a gentian. She'll not make many mistakes in life. But when she does, they'll be big ones."

She had done it extravagantly this time. Huge mistakes, one after another. The small details had gone perfectly. The large plan lay in ruins. He would not come now. Now she had told him the truth. He would go back to London. Glen Reulach would be lost. Without Dominic Wyndham, she could not get Harriet's papers. She could not claim Andrew. She could not see the rightful child in Dunachan, and the eagles would scream over the heads of Englishmen.

She closed her eyes and thought of that last, magnificent funeral. Her mother's brother, the old laird, laid to rest beneath a tall granite column, where his young brother, wee Thomas's father, had been buried only a few months before. The clan gathered from far and wide to witness the splendid display of pipes and feasting. Sugar confections from Edinburgh, and a woman who had also baked for the Souls of Charity.

"They have a bairn living with them," the woman had said, her eyes bright. "Born over a year ago. I asked about his mother. They said she was dead, but I can put two and two together. She was an Englishwoman. She arrived in 1814 carrying the child in her belly. I ken she was the wife of your laird who lies dead and buried now. The bairn's a bonny lad, dark-haired and blue-eyed, like you. Born to trouble, poor lamb . . ."

"My uncle's wife had a child?" Catriona had asked at last, breathless.

"Aye. Wee Andrew MacNorrin was born there, among all those women. Another Englishwoman cares for him and says he's her own son, but he's not. He's a pet for all the ladies. They'll none of them talk about his birth. But I ken well enough he was Sarah's child."

So Catriona had traveled south with the confectioners and gone to the Souls of Charity, not admitting who she was. She had met Harriet, Dominic's wife, who claimed Andrew was her own son. Two weeks later Harriet was also dead, victim of the contagion brought back from the slums and perhaps of her own unhealthy regimen. Dressed in silk and satin, the ladies ate mostly bread, or dainty confections, taken with tea. For safety, the housekeeper, Mrs. Mackay, had taken the child away with her into her own home. But he was a robust bairn. He showed no signs of sickness. Catriona could have stolen the child and taken him home into the Highlands with her.

But what use without proof of his identity? Without proof that her uncle had fathered him on Sarah, his own legitimate wife, before she ran away? Without proof that Andrew was Catriona's own cousin and cousin of that wee Thomas, Rutley's grandson? Without proof, Andrew could not take his place as true heir to a castle and a clan.

Only Dominic Wyndham could get that proof. Only the man to whom she had just given her virginity.

Should she promise to marry him to make him come to Edinburgh? She laughed, a little bitterly. As old Magaidh had said, she only made big mistakes. *Och-òn,* he was not known to be very good with wives!

Dominic walked blindly past the trees, the sun striking green-and-gold dapples on the grass. It was not a big spinney and beyond it lay the garden wall. He squatted with his back against the warm brick, his eyes closed. He had taken her virginity. It was insane to feel guilty, but he did.

Yet a cold fury rose in him like a tidal wave. She had used him. He expected the ladies of London to use him, but that was a mutual exchange. This had been nothing like that. He had made love to her as if she were truly a lover, openly, with passion, only to find she had cynically used him.

He ought to walk away. He ought to go back to London, back to Stansted and that foolish, idealistic project with his friend, which—in spite of Harriet's death—was all he had left: happiness for Stansted, at least.

If only Yarrow Fletcher had not just offered murder.

Dominic picked up a stick and scraped it over a bare patch of dirt.

He drew a small circle. Harriet. The heart of the whole problem. Like spokes on a hub, he scratched lines for the other women who had touched her life: Rosemary, Sarah, and Catriona. Two families interlinked, their lives meeting in Edinburgh. From Calum, he had learned something of the Scots side. From knowing Rutley and Stansted, and from what Catriona had just told him, he knew the rest.

Two family trees. Dominic sketched them in the dirt. The English branch, headed by the redheaded Duke of Rutley, with his two children: his daughter, Lady Mary, and his son and heir, Lord Stansted. Each married. Mary to a scion of Glen Reulach, who was dead. Stansted's dark-haired wife, Rosemary—who had stolen Harriet away with her—still lived with the Souls of Charity. Thus Stansted would produce no heir, so Mary's child Thomas was Rutley's only legitimate grandson.

Then the Scots: the blue-eyed, black-headed family of Glen Reulach. Three siblings: the old laird who had died, his sister with her two children—Calum and Catriona—and his young brother who had married Mary, linking the two families in the center, like ivy joining two ancient oaks. The old laird's wife, Sarah, had borne a child also, Andrew.

Dominic scratched a line from one child to the other. Andrew, true heir to the MacNorrin, and Thomas, Rutley's grandson, were cousins—the sons of two brothers and their two English wives. But only one of those English wives had a duke for a father. If Andrew were proved rightful heir to Glen Reulach, Thomas would lose that Scottish inheritance. Something Rutley would never allow, when little Thomas was all he was likely to leave of his own blood. The dukedom would be lost to Rutley's direct line if Stansted had no son, but the duke would make sure this one grandchild had everything he could gain for him.

So Rutley might care, but why did it matter so much to Catriona? Both little boys were her cousins. Why should it make so much difference?

There was only one person not linked to any of it by either blood or marriage: Harriet. Yet she lay at the center, the hub of the wheel. His poor, confused wife, who gave her loyalty only to other women. First Rosemary and then Sarah, the dead wife of a dead Scotsman. Harriet had taken charge of Sarah's papers and only Dominic could claim them. In one violent gesture he swept his boot across the diagrams he had drawn in the dirt. It was not his business.

But for a child.

Not his child, not Harriet's child, not even Catriona's child. But a little boy with blue eyes and dark hair, who had never known his father. *Poor lamb*. A little boy who had seen the women who cared for him die, one after another, from a contagion from the slums, and one of those women his mother. Andrew had no one. Dominic dropped his head in his hands.

He could not abandon the child.

Especially to Rutley. If Catriona proved Andrew's identity and the duke discovered the existence of this rival claim, how the devil would he react? Not kindly. Rutley would never stand by to witness the disinheriting of his only grandson in favor of Andrew.

In his mind's eye, he saw the yellow goat's eyes, and Rutley staring at him in St. James's.

If a Soul of Charity must die before her time, do you openly admit you would rather it were your own daughter-in-law, Rosemary, Lady Stansted?

If she does not come to her senses and do her duty, I would. Dominic could see the duke's smile, and the clever,

ruthless light in the yellow eyes. *But perhaps Rosemary
isn't fecund? Or perhaps it's my son who cannot keep up
with your supposed example, however hard he tries. And
yes, that is a pun. Good day, sir.*

He jerked back his head. What example? What the *hell*
had Rutley meant? Dominic had thought at the time it was
just a crude comment on his own rumored prowess with
women, but perhaps it was more. Had Rutley known there
was a child living with the Souls of Charity? And thought
it was Dominic's? No, worse. Known the boy was not
Dominic's son—suspected perhaps that the child said to be
Harriet's was Sarah's? He'd better send a warning with new
instructions to Mrs. Mackay, just in case. If a confectioner
could gossip to Catriona, then such tales could certainly
have reached the sharp ears of the duke.

With an oath, Dominic leaped to his feet. Catriona was
right. No one else, not even an English duke, could force
the Souls of Charity to give up Harriet's possessions, except
her husband. Which meant, for the sake of this stranger's
child—but to the detriment of Lord Stansted's little
nephew, Thomas, and thus to Dominic's consternation—
there was no escape.

At which thought, he leaned back against the wall, gazed
up at the blue sky, and began, quite helplessly, to laugh.

Catriona watched him walk back from the Devil's Wood.
She was sitting on the steps near the house. She felt defeated. He would not come. She would have to get back to
Edinburgh by herself, and somehow, by any means possible, get Sarah's papers. As for what had happened between
them at the lochan . . . The memory burned, hot and bright
for a moment. *Big mistakes?*

Dominic walked toward her, the sun shining golden on
his hair and skin. As he sprang up the terraces from the
pond, her heart turned in her breast like a salmon in a waterfall. He strode up to her, lithe and strong. His moss-green
gaze swept over her—secret, hidden, as he had looked the

first time she'd seen him—dangerous, as if he were drunk.

"It won't pain you anymore after that first time," he said. "So now we may enjoy to the full the culmination of our pleasure. I'm looking forward to it."

She blushed, furious. "What are you saying?"

He dropped down beside her. Not touching, but so close her blood caught fire at his scent. "I asked Joe Murray to find us a vehicle so we can continue our journey."

"What did you mean—our pleasure?"

"Oh, dear." He leaned back, stretching out his legs, casual in his male strength, like a wild animal. "Are you about to become coy, Catriona?"

She watched the play of sunlight on his long fingers. "You think so?"

He turned, looking up at her beneath his lashes. "You agreed to travel as my mistress. Last night—at your inspiration—that became a reality. Do you now balk at the idea that I intend to treat you accordingly? I'm used to the best whores in London. Don't you want to find out all the naughty things they taught me? The unnatural acts I practiced on Harriet?"

Green shone in his eyes like sunshine on grass, and the crease deepened in his cheek. "I fully intend to use all of those wicked, delicious little tricks on you."

Eight

CATRIONA TOOK A breath, yet the shaking deep in her bones didn't stop. "I do not blame you for being angry. It is our next sin. But there is an explanation you owe me: the attack on our coach. You know who it was, don't you?"

"I'm not angry," he said. "And that isn't an answer."

"To what question? That we continue as lovers? You wagered not for my body, but my heart, and that is still mine. You have not won." She stood up, filled with distress. "My maidenhead was mine to lose. My body is mine to give. I will not be browbeaten or coerced by you. I will not make any answer. Do you still tempt me? You do!" Catriona looked down at him, the lean lines of his face and body, the golden, sunny sheen to him. "Och, you tempt me! Leave it be! You will *never* win my heart."

He looked away, sunlight sliding across his jaw, shadowing the corner of his mouth. " 'Get thee behind me, Satan?' " The ironic edge was strong in his voice. "Don't worry. I'm not serious. I will take you to Edinburgh. You may keep your heart and what remains of your virtue. Our wager was foolish and we have paid the price."

"What do you mean?"

"This disorder between us. We made a mistake. But I imagine we can control our lusts for the next few days." Shadows leaped as the dimple indented his cheek. "After we reach Edinburgh and secure Sarah's papers, you may seduce me at your leisure. It will certainly amuse me to bed a cousin of Rutley's little grandson, Thomas.''

She saw it then, the lightness in him, the humor bending the corner of his lips. She didn't know what he laughed at, but it made her furious.

"Damn you!" she said, frantic now. "Damn you! It is a man *you* recognized who tried to kill us, who murdered your coachman, who hurt our horses. A man *you* knew, not me! *Your* enemy, not mine! Yet you talk of nothing but your desire and your greed for it!"

He glanced up at her. "Greed? The deadly sins *are* over-taking us, aren't they? Anger will be followed quickly enough by gluttony, when all this outrage gives way to indulgence. I assume Rutley offered to provide for you and you refused him?"

She nodded.

"The man who attacked us is Yarrow Fletcher. I knew him in the Peninsula."

She waited for him to go on, but he stood up and took her elbow. At his touch, she felt the burn and the longing, and despised herself.

"Our conveyance," he said, "should be here. As you have reminded me often enough, there is a child who awaits us in Edinburgh. Thanks to Yarrow Fletcher, we pursue a new strategy and damn your reputation. We shall travel fast and openly, then take shelter tonight in a place I guarantee to be safe. I will tell you what you want to know as we travel."

"Will this Fletcher follow?"

"I don't know. But he can hardly attack us on the turn-pike, unless he is more clever than I know him to be. On the other hand, there may be better brains than his behind all this. I know exactly what I would do, were I him." He grinned. "When we get to Nottingham, we'll find out."

"Nottingham? We left it behind yesterday!"

"So we did. But there is nowhere else to get transpor-tation."

They cantered away from Newstead in a pony cart. She

was grateful. She was grateful, in spite of her surging fear and uncertainty about this man, for his presence. He could have walked away, returned to London. His anger was justified enough. She had told him to his face she thought him dishonorable and a man without generosity. Yet how could she trust him? History showed clearly enough that trust in the English was often just another name for treason.

If she didn't suffer this vehement attraction for him, she wouldn't feel quite so desperate. He had brought her north. He had promised to come to Edinburgh. Very probably, he had saved her life. She was in his debt. Which made her desire impossible. To bed him in payment for his services was the act of a harlot. Couldn't he see she would never accept such terms? Yet the desire in her burned and festered, breaking her heart.

The cart yawed violently as an iron-shod wheel skipped over a rock in the road.

"Tell me about Yarrow Fletcher," she said. "Why did he attack us?"

"At that particular moment?" His lids narrowed over the moss-green eyes. "I have no idea. But we don't like each other."

"Where did you meet him?"

"In 1809 at Talavera. You know, of course, about the Peninsular campaign." There was no laughter in him now, though his voice remained light. "Portugal and Spain: that barren land where Wellington fought Napoleon's army for supremacy."

"I know." *Vimiero and Ciudad Rodrigo*. Portugal and Spain. Lands soaked in Highland blood.

"Talavera began with a night attack. We broke off at darkness, but sentries fired at phantoms all night. No one slept. The uproar started again at dawn, with cannon. The noise was indescribable. Within two hours the valley filled with corpses. The sun rose in the sky like a bloody brazier. Our weapons burned our hands. Sweat blinded the men. When the heat became intolerable, the generals called a truce to let both sides drink and bury the dead. For those few hours French and British mingled at the stream, talking and joking, sharing food.''

"You were very noble, then," Catriona said. "To help the enemy."

"Why not?" His profile was clear and sharp. "We didn't share any personal animosity. I drank wine with a French officer. He had only one arm. We talked about Paris, his wife and children. When the truce was called off at eleven, I shook his hand and wished him well. I meant it. Hours later I saw him again."

She spoke into the lengthening silence. "What happened?"

"He was wounded in his one arm, lying beside his dead horse. He had surrendered to one of our captains." His voice had become flat, as if it hurt to speak. "That French officer was no danger to us, poor bastard."

Dread built in her. "Tell me."

Dominic's face was stone. "Before I could reach them, our captain took the Frenchman's sword and used it for a little sadistic—" The pony jibbed. "I'm sorry, you don't need to know the details. It was one of the foulest things I have ever witnessed, and my introduction to Yarrow Fletcher."

Catriona shuddered, wrapping her arms about her body. "*A Mhuire!* Did Captain Fletcher know you had seen it?"

"I offered to kill him for it later. But Wellington got wind of our quarrel and stopped the fight. The Iron Duke forbids dueling. I was the only witness of what had happened and Fletcher accused me of having a private grudge against him."

"*Och-òn,*" she said. "When a man is wounded and down, he isn't the enemy, he's just a man, at least while there is any honor left." She watched the pony, the red shine in its coat, the wind blowing the brown mane, and her heart ached. "Could you do nothing?"

"Wellington knew I must have had good reason. Unfortunately for me, he let Fletcher know that."

"So it was not the end of it?"

"Shall we say Fletcher's career did not prosper and he

saw it as my fault? Yet I was gone a great deal doing reconnaissance work, so our paths didn't cross much. Then in 1811 I went to Russia. Just before I left, I found Fletcher trying to rape a Spanish woman, with a knife to her throat. I beat him within an inch of his life and I did it before several of his men, deliberately humiliating him. The men were on my side in the issue. No one reported it.''

The countryside sped by, wooded and green. The clear, bright morning was giving way to dark clouds and a rising wind. ''So Fletcher hates you?''

He laughed, a release of tension. ''Obviously. Yet I hadn't seen him again until he appeared in Sherwood yesterday.''

Chills raced down her spine. ''Why would he wait until now for revenge?''

He tugged the pony to the right. ''I only wish I knew.''

They had come out onto the main road to find it jammed with walkers, carts, and carriages, all traveling south. Instantly Dominic gave a ride to a woman carrying a large basket of cheeses. He let her gossip and chatter as they jolted along. It was Fair Day. Catriona didn't know whether to find comfort in the news or not. Would such a mob of people make it easier or more difficult for Yarrow Fletcher to find them?

They were backtracking several miles of yesterday's journey in the hope of finding a carriage in Nottingham. Yet would there be any horses to hire, or any seats on the stage? Or would they be stopped first by a man who would torture and kill a crippled Frenchman, and rape women? A man who held a virulent hatred for Major Dominic Wyndham?

She glanced at him. He had shed his dark mood as a snake sheds its skin. He was flirting openly with the farm wife, who laughed and blushed at him as her tongue rattled on. Another female stricken with the charms of a rake!

Nottingham rose before them at last, marching up its hill to the castle, the houses clustered in terraces. They made their way toward the marketplace, jostling along Clumber Street and Smithy Row. Sharp breezes raced up and down the streets, fluttering ribbons on bonnets, bowling scraps of paper. The town was packed.

"There's to be a big horse fair." The farm woman beamed at Dominic, her cheeks wrinkled like dried apples. "And races. And a balloon ascent with aerial acrobats. Aye, it's a grand day."

They stopped outside the inn where Dominic had promised to leave the pony cart. "Thanks to your presence, ma'am," he said with a wink.

"Ye're a pretty-mannered fellow, right enough!" The woman laughed as she leaned up to press a kiss on his lips. Dominic kissed back. "And a big, fine man! Your lady's lucky to have ye!" Chuckling, she disappeared into the crowd.

Catriona looked about nervously. There was no sign of Yarrow Fletcher in the milling throng. Perhaps all this hubbub would let them escape without notice? But with so many people, would there be a carriage for hire?

The wall outside the inn was plastered with notices. As Dominic tied the pony Catriona glanced at them. One print advertised races. Several gaudy notices hawked stockings and cheeses, Nottingham specialties. A drawing of a balloon, with two women suspended beneath it—apparently by their teeth—invited the populace to watch an ascent that morning. The teeth were visible, bared in a grimace, as if the artist had been fascinated by them.

"Ah!" Dominic glanced over her shoulder. "Sometimes we win a wager and sometimes we lose. Sadly, we have just lost this one."

She looked up at him in alarm. "What?"

He grinned. "To come into Nottingham was a risk, I admit, but devil if I saw much alternative." He pointed. "It's exactly what I would have done: enlist the whole damned town."

Catriona looked closer. It was hastily printed: NOTICE. A *horrid crime. Willful murder of an innocent coachman . . . hanging offense . . . reward offered . . . particular caution to be taken by any persons letting horses for hire.* The drawings were crude, but recognizable. The names and descriptions were their own: guilty lovers fleeing to Scotland.

Her heart contracted in fear. "*A Dhia!* You have led us into a trap!"

"The charges would not stand," Dominic said calmly. "Though we would be held, very probably, in jail until I could prove it. Thus we would not reach Edinburgh."

She looked about. As if a pall of dark smoke clouded the scene, the crowd seemed sinister. "It is also possible," Catriona said, "that we would be destroyed by a mob, particularly if there is someone to agitate them."

A man in a smock came out of the inn and gave them both a sharp glance, but a wagon turned in front of him. Dominic took Catriona's arm and casually moved her away. Another man shouted. A small group paused to read the notices, and a woman looked Dominic up and down. Of course he was a striking man, just as the description said. A man who would be noticed anywhere.

"Come on," Dominic whispered. "Discretion is the better part—"

He hurried her away down a side street. On every flat surface copies of the notice leaped out at her, her own face, filled with accusation, the portrayal of her dress and Dominic's clothes. A woman watched them go by, then called out. Her voice was lost in the crowd. But it was only a matter of time. They would be recognized and a dozen hands would seize them. If they met Fletcher or his men, they might die.

Dominic made two sharp turns into an alley lined with small shops. The dingy windows were thankfully free of paper notices. But the cobbles ended in a blank wall, apparently the back of a warehouse. It was a dead end. Fear and frustration choked her. What now? Back into that crowd, where men drinking too freely could turn merriment into mayhem in a moment?

"Adam and Little." Dominic read aloud the name above one of the shops. "Angels come in many disguises. In this case, purveyors of used apparel." He reached into his pocket and pressed coins into Catriona's palm. "Are you any good at charades?"

She stared at the gold, then glanced up at him. "You think a new dress and bonnet will prevent my being recognized?"

"It might."

"What about you?"

"I have always fancied a brown wig and a parson's hat." He pointed farther down the alley and grinned. "Hench and Brothers, specialists in theatrical outfits. How kind of our lady with the cheeses to tell me so much about Nottingham!"

"You foresaw this?" Catriona asked. "This is why you flirted? For information?"

Dominic laughed. "I always like an alternate plan. Get whatever makes you the least like that damned description. I'll meet you back here in fifteen minutes."

"And you paid her with flattery and kisses."

He raised a brow, grinning comically. "What use being a rake if you cannot charm women? But you may have both and demand payment from me." He bent and kissed her lightly, a mere touch of his mouth over hers.

She watched him walk away, confident, carefree. Her heart bounded in a crazy rhythm, like the rattle of a drummer. Her lips burned. She felt hot with anger. It was not over. What she had done in the forest had only made it worse. She had thought to assuage the hard knot in her heart, thought to shed the burden of being twenty-five and a virgin, thought to shake her fist at the fate that had left her so bereft. But instead the knot had tightened, like a vice. *Flattery and kisses.* It was not over. And to fall irrevocably in love with an Englishman would be a betrayal of her Highland blood.

Catriona lifted her chin and marched into the little shop. A small man beamed at her.

"I need a set of clothes," she said. "For my younger brother. He is about my height."

"And what is the occasion?"

"He has been ill and lost weight. He needs nothing special. A jacket, shirt—och, and boots. I see you have boots."

They selected shirts and boots, and rustled through stacks

of coats. She selected a loose-fitting blue jacket, suitable
for a young gentleman of modest means.

"Can you be sure it will fit him?" the man asked.

Catriona met his gaze evenly. "I could alter it if necessary. Yet I wish to surprise him. Do you have a room with
a needle and thread? I should pay you for your indulgence."

A minute later she was alone in a cramped back room,
obviously used for alterations. Thread, needles, shears,
scraps of fabric littered the rickety table. A small glass
flecked with age mirrored her face, mottling her skin. Her
blue eyes stared back above her mother's strong cheekbones. She wasn't pretty, but just once, in the dark, cold
forest, a man had found her beautiful and let his hands say
it.

As earlier he had let words say it. *A Mhuire,* they had
been precious enough, though he had meant none of it,
neither the words nor those lovely, speaking fingers.

She closed her eyes and put her hands on her coiled
braids. *As thick as thieves and as fine as a summer's day,
with all the colors of brandy and night, shot through with
moonlight and shadows like a blackbird's wing—*

And then he had used her desire against her.

This is a game women lose.

Biting back tears, she took up the shears.

Dominic came out of the interesting premises of Hench and
Brothers with the scent of glue and horsehair in his nostrils
and a small laugh on his lips. His legs were gaitered. A
round black hat sat firmly on a wig of brown hair. He had
done his best to assume a suitably pious expression when
he had admired the results in the mirror. He knew he looked
absurd and completely unrecognizable.

A youth lounged in the street beyond Adam and Little's
used-clothing shop. For a moment he thought he saw an
old friend, oddly diminished and made vulnerable, as he
might have looked before he had grown broad and strong

and become a soldier. But if so, it was the ghost of a man
who didn't exist—who had never existed—a younger
brother of Calum MacNorrin. Dominic stopped in shock
and took a breath. Before the breath was released, he knew
what she had done. A profound sorrow shook him and then
he was furious.

He strode down the cobbles. Catriona turned to face him,
her color high. The man's coat echoed her eyes, endlessly
blue like cobalt. She wore trousers. Her high shirt collar
cut close along the line of her jaw. As he came up to her
the flush deepened, running rose red into the short, savagely
cut curls—all that was left of her hair.

"Why the *devil* did you do it?"

She lifted her chin. "We can ride like this. We shan't
need a carriage. Only horses. A man and a boy—tutor and
pupil, perhaps."

He took her arm, letting his fingers score into the fabric.
"Are you mad? Such an offering was hardly necessary!"

"Why should you care?"

"You wantonly destroyed something radiant."

Her eyes glittered. "*A Dhia!* Perhaps I did it for a French
officer who died at Talavera, or for my great-uncles who
died the same way after Culloden."

"Don't try that! Even if it's true, it's only part of the
truth." He knew he was right. Her eyes revealed it: her
sacrifice and defiance were not for the fallen men of her
clan, nor a French officer she had never met. So he told
her the truth, even if it should wound both of them. "You
did it, damn you, to spite me."

She wrenched away and laughed. "*You!* You have a very
fine opinion of your importance. Why should I think of you,
if I cut my own hair?" She ran her fingers proudly over
the brutal curls. "I wanted a better ruse than a different
dress."

"Devil take it! You cut it because you thought I liked
it, which I did. You thought without your long hair I would
not find you lovely. You were wrong. Even like this, you
are lovely. Your very bones are beautiful."

Her chin lifted a little more. "You would speak so to a lad?"

He wanted to shock her. "Why not? Do you need me to prove it?"

Catriona laughed with clear defiance. "You would not dare! Mr. Adam might look from the doorway and see a parson kissing a boy!"

All reservations fled. His hands closed on her upper arms and he pulled her toward him. She tried to snarl at him, but her lips trembled.

Deliberately he let his voice snarl back. "I'm not sure what it says about me that I find that idea so intensely exciting. Or about you, that you so obviously feel the same way."

Her arms were soft beneath the boy's jacket. The skin of her cheek was fine and unblemished. Her trembling mouth ripened, red and moist. She looked infinitely female. Desire rose blindly as he closed his lips over hers.

He kissed her ruthlessly, demanding capitulation. She didn't fight. Instead she opened her mouth and kissed back—soft and sweet and hot beneath his lips. He heard himself groan, wanting her, wanting more. Her tongue met his without hesitation. He suckled on it, on her lips and mouth, and she returned the fire, thrust for thrust, bite for bite. Yet it was not surrender. Damn her! Damn her! It felt more like a declaration of war.

He pulled away, panting. Her eyes had dilated to black pits. Her mouth was swollen. Her breasts rose and fell visibly beneath the boy's shirt. A sudden madness of grief shook him, for the glorious darkness she had hacked away and for the wall of stone she had erected between them.

"At least learn to tie a cravat," he said, "if you want to be my catamite."

She looked lost. "What?"

"A boy lover. Like Ganymede, cupbearer to the gods. The ancient Greeks knew how to use a pretty boy. I wouldn't be the first tutor to impart such ancient skills to his pupil."

He had shocked her now. Her eyes were huge, their

depth of color emphasized around distended black pupils. "That is how people would see us?"

"I don't know what else they would think, if they witnessed what we just did."

She dropped her head suddenly, her cheeks burning, and bit her lip. Then she touched the clumsy knot at her throat. "This is not good enough for a lover of yours?"

"No boy of mine would appear in public in such an abomination. Stand still."

She stood for him, stiffly, as he untied the knot. He tried not to let his fingers stray, though they wanted to stroke delicately along her jaw, touch her throat and the corner of her ear. Her color mounted and her nostrils flared, but she would not meet his gaze.

"There." Her pulse throbbed beneath his fingers as he touched below her ear one last time, pulling the collar straight. "A passable job on such wretched linen and a noble exercise in self-control for both of us. Let's go."

They walked quickly down the alley, came back onto the main street, and pushed through the crowds. No one paid them any attention. They could probably hire horses and ride north without notice. To any passing stranger she did look like a boy. He took another deep breath and laughed.

She glanced up at him. "You see, no one is looking at us at all."

"The disguise is excellent."

"You do not mean it, but you are gracious to say so."

"Oh, I mean it. But my thoughts are not in the least gracious."

A short walk took them to the edge of town. As the farm wife had told him, the last building on the street was a livery and bait stable. A sign proclaimed it the premises of one J.E. SMITH, JOB MASTER: HORSES AND CARRIAGES LET ON HIRE. Beyond it the road ran into a large open field where crowds milled. Mounts stood in lines, or were trotted out for prospective buyers: the horse market.

Dominic mercilessly suppressed his vision of untying that damned cravat, then the buttons in her shirt and at the waist of her trousers, where he would not find a boy. For

God's sake, he had no interest of that kind in boys what-soever!

"Shall we hire animals from Mr. Smith and ride silently away, like Odysseus slipping from the Cyclops' cave?" he asked.

She knew that reference, at least: the myth of Odysseus, the wanderer, who had destroyed the one eye of the giant who had captured him, then escaped by clinging to the wool of his sheep. "On the bellies of the horses?" she asked. "With our would-be captor blinded?"

"So we hope."

The yard of Mr. Smith's establishment was reached through an archway. Before Dominic could stop her, Catriona marched in.

"He is blind," she said with confidence. "He is looking for a blond man and a woman, not a corrupt parson and his pupil."

Instantly he grasped her arm. He wanted to stroke her clipped hair in some kind of reparation and apologize. Too late! It was so much too late that he laughed. "Alas, Cyclops has two perfectly good eyes this time."

She followed his gaze, then to his immense surprise, she laughed, too. It was only slightly tinged with hysteria. "Like Yarrow Fletcher?"

Fletcher was standing in the yard. The only man in Nottingham who would know Dominic, even with wig and parson's hat. The only man who would know Catriona, even dressed as a boy. The man who planned to kill them. As they backed up, Fletcher yelled and started forward, his henchmen at his heels.

Dominic took a tight grip on Catriona's hand and ran, dodging through the crowds, past horses and wagons into the open field of the horse market.

The shout went up behind them. "The parson and the boy! Murderers! Seize them!"

Damnation and double damnation! Horses snorted and flattened their ears. The horse brokers' necks craned in their direction. Their way filled with heads and manes—and myriad gesticulating hands. Hands that would drag off his hat and wig, proving him an impostor. Hands that would tear at Catriona's coat and shirt, and discover the soft female flesh beneath. For this she had sacrificed her hair and, God help him, everything else? For him to lead her directly into capture and shattering humiliation, after bullying her with the threat of depravity?

Shouts and running feet closed in. A burly fellow in a check cap grabbed at Catriona as they raced past. Dominic landed one blow to the man's jaw and dropped him where he stood.

The field was packed: with horses; the crowds examining them; the pie men and peddlers hawking their wares. A small troop of mounted soldiers paraded on one side of the field: recruiters, no doubt.

"The horses," Catriona gasped at his side. "I can ride."

A string of draft horses was tied to both sides of a rope stretched between two trees. He dragged her around the brown and bay rumps, tails endlessly switching at flies, then dived into the space beneath the horses' heads, a cat's cradle of halter ropes. For a moment the massive legs and grass-sweet mouths formed a barrier against pursuit.

"These horses are like seawater to a thirsty man on a becalmed ship," he said, breathless, as they dodged along the rank and a nervous horse tried to pull back. "Not a drop to drink. Didn't you see the dragoons? If we stole mounts we'd be hunted down and torn apart like foxes. Anyway, these cart horses don't have much speed, though I thank God, now we're under their feet, that they're so gentle. We need a diversion."

He ducked out between two chestnut mares into open space, pulling her with him.

"That woman selling cheeses!" Catriona pointed. "Our farm wife, who told you about Nottingham!"

Confusion and pursuit snatched at their heels as they ran to the woman's pitch. She had just bent to retrieve a coin that had dropped to the ground. Dominic raced up to her and slipped his hands over her eyes.

"Well met, my sweet!" He dropped a kiss on her temple.

"I'm buying all your cheeses. Here." He released his hands and pressed coins into her palm.

The woman looked down and gasped. "That's enough to buy a thousand cheeses, sir!"

He kissed her quickly on the mouth. Her lips were dry and cracked. "But I'm buying your basket, too."

As the woman stood gasping he upended the basket. Cheeses scattered, rolling like toy carriage wheels into the feet of the crowd.

"Free cheese!" he shouted. "And for good measure, free gold!"

With a single sweeping gesture, he threw a handful of coins after the cheese. Within seconds a crowd of children were scrabbling after both cheese and money. Their parents followed. It was instant chaos. With a quick prayer to the gods of Olympus—who controlled the wind and the sports of throwing—Dominic threw the basket directly at Yarrow Fletcher. Athena smiled. The wicker landed squarely over head and shoulders, pinning the man's arms to his sides as it knocked him to the ground. Fletcher rolled and cursed, flailing his hands. Dominic grabbed again for Catriona's fingers and ran with her across the field.

Over the heads of the horses, the inflated balloon bulged like a huge pudding. Canvas and paper glittered with garlands and flags. Two men had been busy shoveling straw: one from a pile on the ground, the other standing in the basket beneath the balloon. He was tossing the fuel into a brazier to create an updraft of hot air. Two women, probably their wives, waited in bright pink tights to catch trailing ropes in their teeth and be hoisted up beneath the balloon to the delectation of the crowd.

Now all four were frozen as if in a tableau. Their necks craned toward the hubbub at the cheese stand. The crowd was breaking up like chaff before a wind and streaming back toward the promise of unearned wealth.

The farm woman shrieked at the top of her lungs. "Free cheese! Free coin! Come one, come all! Free gold, my lads!" She turned and shook her fist, laughing in Dominic's direction. "That was my mother's best basket! I'll not find another as good! Free gold, lads, free for anyone!''

The first balloon man dropped his pitchfork. Following the crowd, he ran past Dominic and Catriona, the two women in pink tights at his heels.

"I'm almost out of money." Dominic grinned. It might yet be possible! "Do you think I have enough to buy a bloody balloon?"

Catriona stopped, gasping and clutching at her side. "Not the balloon!"

"Why not? An excellent application of hot air, perfect for us. Come on!"

He dragged out his purse and threw it at the man left in the balloon, who caught it automatically, his mouth gaped open like a fish. Canvas strained and flapped ponderously above his head. The balloon had now lifted a foot or two off the ground, held down by ropes. Dominic grasped Catriona by the waist and tossed her in. An instant later he threw out the man. The fellow shouted, but he was still clutching Dominic's purse in both hands. The two women in pink tights looked back and shrieked.

The dragoons at the side of the field galloped toward the incipient riot. Yarrow Fletcher heaved the wicker off his head. His men shouted and thrust about with fists and sticks as they tried to push through the crowd. Dominic leaned over the side of the balloon basket and calmly cut one rope. The basket tipped, almost tossing them out. Catriona clung onto one of the supporting cables which held their perch to the great fabric monstrosity above their heads. He cut the opposite rope. The balloon lurched upward, leaping like a startled partridge, just as the soldiers reached them.

With her short black curls blowing about her head, Catriona shoveled more fuel into the open brazier. Hot air rushed into the towering globe above their heads. The wind picked up. Frantically they fed the flames with more straw, until the brazier roared like a furnace. Dominic threw his hat and wig into the fire. They burst into bright flames, fueled by glue.

The balloon soared.

The town dropped behind them and shrank to the size of

a toy. The soldiers and Fletcher's men, now mounting horses for a vain pursuit, milled like ants disturbed in the nest. The balloon floated silently northward across open fields.

"Thank God," Dominic said. "The wind's from the southwest."

Catriona leaned over the side of the basket. "Och, there is Sherwood—and Newstead!"

He glanced at her. Her nape seemed like a small child's. She was breathless, laughing. She turned to look at him with the balm of joy at the corners of her mouth, her eyes liquid with merriment. His heart turned over.

"If you don't want to land there, keep feeding our flames," he said.

The balloon dipped, the basket brushing treetops, breaking off small branches in a shower of leaves. Catriona frantically helped him toss more fuel into the brazier. The balloon lurched up once more.

The woods dropped behind. Apart from their own unceasing labor, it was a magically silent and majestic ride. Fields and villages passed like images in a dream. The countryside below them became flat and open. As Catriona worked to keep feeding the brazier Dominic took down a strange contraption that looked like a grappling hook. Perhaps it was some kind of anchor. He didn't know, but he knew they needed more fuel.

"What are you doing?" The glow of the brazier colored her shirt and turned her skin a rich honey. The cravat he had tied with such care had come loose, revealing a hint of her soft, feminine throat. Perhaps he was developing a taste for boys, after all!

"Fishing," he said. "It's something I like—fish and baskets."

He leaned over the side. The hook dragged across a series of ricks, where straw had been stacked in bundles. Laughing, he reeled in more fuel and threw out the last remaining coins from his pocket, hoping the farmer would find them scattered over the ground. He had nothing left now but the ugly clothes he stood up in.

The wind made no sound as they sailed with it, but it was getting stronger. The ground raced by. Trees bent and swayed. Their bulbous shadow danced in and out across the fields, winking at them as clouds slid over the sun.

"This is magic, like a nursery tale. We are flying! What would happen if we flew into that storm?" Catriona pointed north. Lightning flickered along the horizon.

"I have no idea," he replied. "But cold rain would surely crash us!"

It didn't rain. With a wind that filled the sails on the ships in the estuary, they soared over the broad valley of the Humber. Villages and farms, church spires and woods, raced beneath them like a multicolored carpet.

"When the first balloon landed outside Paris," he said, shoveling in more straw, "peasants attacked it with pitch-forks."

She wiped one arm across her forehead, leaving a smear of soot. "We shall land filthy and penniless among strang-ers. Will they attack us with pitchforks?"

"We'll find out. In the meantime this balloon will pre-vent us indulging in sloth, at least."

She laughed aloud—infinitely inviting. "Sloth sounds good right now."

He thrust in more fuel. Hard work was an excellent cure for anger. Too bad it wasn't equally effective for desire. "Sloth will drop us very quickly to the ground. How the hell do you suppose we land this thing?"

"We don't," she said. "We sail it all the way to Scot-land."

But the balloon didn't steer. They would be carried wherever the wind took them. Anyway, there was not enough straw, and fewer convenient stacks came within reach. Yet they kept afloat, sailing with the sucking wind as the storm retreated ahead of them. The spires and turrets of York, crowned by its ancient minster, passed by and dropped south. The countryside broke up into small green hills, crisscrossed with sparkling streams. Beyond the hills rose the barren heights of the North York Moors, where the sound of thunder growled like a mad dog. They were down to the last shreds of fuel.

Dominic threw out everything that wouldn't burn. He broke up flags and tore down bunting to add to the fire. He threw away the grappling hook and burned the ropes. Yet a small hill rushed up at them and the basket screeched over bushes. On the top of the rise the balloon skipped up for a moment, only to fall suddenly and drag the basket along the ground.

Catriona braced herself. Dominic struggled to change his balance so he could protect her from the inevitable crash, but she shook her head fiercely.

The wind howled, battering at the canvas. The balloon shook and billowed. With the wind boring into it, the colored fabric dragged them mercilessly over grass and rock. They tore sideways over a rough field, bouncing and jolting, scattering sheep. A stone wall raced toward them.

Dominic lunged at Catriona as the basket slammed into rock.

Too late.

Nine

WATER BEAT AND trickled, alternately rushing in spate, then dying away. Yet a fire crackled somewhere and she was warm and dry. Catriona opened her eyes. For a moment she thought she was back at Dunachan. The ceiling was vaulted, ancient; the window embrasures giant thumb-prints stamped in stone. Flames sprang in a vast fireplace, the mantel supported by Gothic griffins. She was inside a castle and in bed. It was raining outside. Spouts of water gushed past the window, then a scatter of drops trickled over the glass. There was wind behind it.

A man and woman stood framed in a stone doorway, talking softly.

They were not touching. Yet they seemed one, as if they were forever part of each other. The line of the man's shoulder, the tilt of the woman's head, spoke of a shared tenderness so profound Catriona wanted to weep.

She closed her eyes, gulping back sorrow. Boots strode away. Soft footsteps came to the bedside. A sweet, exotic scent enveloped her.

"You are awake?" the woman asked. "It is evening. You were knocked out, but you are safe now. Dominic is unharmed. You managed to come down on the edge of our estates. You are at Rivaulx. My name is Frances. My husband is the marquess."

Her mind heard a voice speaking in English about sin:
*The Marquess of Rivaulx. An old comrade. It's an ancient
Norman name, with an "x" that's not pronounced. And
yes, I covet his wife.*

"*Is farsaing do rìoghachd 's gur fial—*"

"I speak some strange languages," the woman said.
There was a soft laugh in her voice and a depth of compassion. "But not that one. Can you translate?"

"Extensive is thy domain and hospitable." Catriona
turned her face into the pillow. She had a headache. She
put her hand to it. Her hair was cut short. And then she
remembered everything.

"So what the devil are you up to?"

Dominic glanced up at the speaker. Nigel Arundham,
Marquess of Rivaulx, stood at the fireplace. A tall man with
black hair, Nigel still had all the feral power that had
marked him in Russia and Paris. Here, at Rivaulx Castle,
he had at last come home. The beautiful carpets and paintings, the Flemish tapestries and Russell globe, formed a
graceful gloss to the strong, stark bones of his medieval
stronghold, a bastion of security with the wild moor just
beyond. The marquess's ancestral home suited him.

Their balloon had brought Dominic and Catriona, like
homing pigeons, straight to their goal. But it had taken time
to get Catriona safely to Rivaulx Castle and to help Nigel
remove the wrecked balloon from the field of an irate tenant. Though the marquess had armies of servants, it had
seemed better to oversee it themselves.

"Do you want to tell me?" Nigel asked.

"Certainly." Dominic lounged back in his chair, dropping his gaze to the flames in the grate, deliberately flippant. "I am taking Catriona MacNorrin to Scotland in a
basket."

Nigel turned the Russell globe with one finger. "Your
companion in the breeches and blue coat? She just woke
up. Frances is with her. I'm sorry my wife insisted you stay

down here. Frances has her own ideas about things, as you know.''

"No, she's right. Catriona won't want to see my face first.''

"Why was she so interestingly dressed?''

The fire hissed whenever a stray raindrop found its way down the chimney. "That was her idea, not mine. It's a long tale involving orphaned waifs and, it appears, the Duke of Rutley.''

Long fingers stopped the globe dead. "Rutley? How?''

"One of the waifs in question is his grandson, Thomas. You remember Rutley's daughter, Lady Mary, married to a Scotsman named MacNorrin and recently widowed? She's Thomas's mother. Thus the child is in Rutley's control. Nevertheless, I intend to disinherit Thomas and replace him with another baby named Andrew. It's a little complicated.''

Nigel dropped into a chair opposite Dominic and stretched out his legs. "I can imagine,'' he said dryly. "Stansted's nephew! More than a little inconvenient at the moment. So how fares your project with Stansted? You know I think you are mad to pursue it.''

"Half London thinks I am mad. Strange to say, we finally made a successful attempt on the church steeple.'' He looked up, hearing the derision in his own voice. "Don't look so astonished. I await your congratulations.''

Nigel raised a brow. "You have them. A glorious wager, I assume?''

Dominic laughed. "It took months of scheming and enticement—like cajoling a nervous hound to come out of his kennel to bay at the moon. I had to get him pretty drunk, but he did it.''

"As I recall,'' Nigel said with a grin, "our redheaded friend is a questionable athlete.''

Wood crackled and spat in the fireplace. "Yet he's bloody brave. I made a rope from my shirt to assist him. Afterward he cast up his accounts.''

There was a certain sympathy hidden in the amusement in Nigel's gaze, more than he would ever admit to. His wife's influence, no doubt. "The steeple was the second condition, wasn't it?"

"Yes." Dominic narrowed his eyes, concentrating on the flames. It was a relief in a way to be able to discuss the whole absurd mess with a friend who would neither judge nor condemn. "As set by dear Rosemary, Lady Stansted, my dark nemesis."

"What about the first?"

"It's met only if Rosemary will allow that the center-piece at Lady Bingham's supper two months ago, with the pretty little cherubs of butter around the lake of red wine, counts as an ocean. Some of the butter was melting into the wine. By drinking it, Stansted rather disarranged her table. Needless to say, it was my idea. He was already foxed and he was sick again. Lady Bingham wasn't in the least amused, especially since I had not been invited."

Nigel exploded in laughter. "Oh, dear God! Were you thrown out?"

"Of course. A habit of mine." He grinned, though he didn't feel in the least amused either. "Alas, it's all ridic-ulous. The third condition is something which I can neither wager for, nor trick Stansted into doing. The conditions remain impossible."

"Because Rosemary still wants you."

Dominic flinched comically, a deliberately exaggerated shrug of the shoulders. "Merciless, as always? We're not spying on Napoleon any longer, my lord."

Nigel steepled his long fingers together. His eyes shone with wry mischief. "Old habits die hard. I'm just trying to get a grasp of the situation."

Dominic slouched back in his chair. "Rivaulx, you have the mind of a bloody machine."

"You told me that once before, in equally trying circum-stances."

He shot back friendly fire. "When I offered to ravish Frances on your hall table, as I remember."

Nigel's grin widened. "I hadn't yet married her, so it doesn't count. Anyway you didn't mean it. But there's something sad in it, Wyndham, that Rosemary should have accepted Stansted when she treasures this undying passion for you. *Does* she still harbor it?''

''Alas, she does. It was her reason for going to Scotland, of course. There has never been meaning in what she demanded I do about it. It's like that old fairy tale: I will only love you if you do the impossible: bring me a shirt without stitches, or water in a sieve. Or in this case, I will only stop loving you.''

''And Rosemary's control of Harriet is still absolute?''

The flames made fantastic patterns, alternately castles and forests, burning. ''It has all just become irrelevant. Harriet is dead.''

Nigel jerked upright. ''My dear fellow!''

''It's all right. I don't want to talk about that.''

''So how does this concern the young woman upstairs?'' Nigel asked gently.

Dominic was grateful his friend was astute enough to let Harriet's death go unremarked when asked. ''I don't know, except she brought me the news. I know only this: Yarrow Fletcher tried to kill us.''

There was a soft rustle and the faint scent of jasmine. Dominic looked up to see Frances, Nigel's wife. She closed the door and came in. ''Am I interrupting?''

The gold griffin ring of Rivaulx glinted as Nigel held out his hand. ''Of course not.''

Her walk was graceful enough to catch Dominic's breath for a moment. She had been trained in a harem in India for four years, before returning to England and becoming embroiled in the adventure in Paris which had led, in the end, to her marriage. It was a training guaranteed to render any man breathless. In addition, she was beautiful, honey hair and wide blue eyes. Frances was a hothouse flower, heady, perfect.

She came directly to Dominic and bent, kissing him on the cheek. ''Catriona has told me. I am very deeply sorry, dear friend. I see you and Nigel have agreed not to talk about it, but you will allow me to say that much, at least?'' She settled herself on the arm of her husband's chair and smiled.

Dominic put his fingers to the spot her lips had touched. Had he been in love with her? A little, certainly. No man could meet Frances and not be impressed. They had spent several weeks alone together when he had brought her back to England for Nigel after Waterloo: a time when he had still believed he could win Harriet back, before Rosemary made her conditions. Of course, they were weeks in which he had also believed his friend had cruelly used and abandoned Frances. So he had offered, from honor, to avenge her.

"Thank you for your forbearance, Lady Rivaulx. I am just remembering," he added wryly. "I offered to kill Nigel for you once. Did you know that?"

She laughed. Nigel had slipped an arm about her waist. Like flowing water, she fit her body against his. "No," Frances said. "But I'm glad you didn't succeed. I rather like him as a husband. So what is happening now? Who is Yarrow Fletcher?"

Yes, Frances was perfect, but perhaps the perfection of the orchid was not what he wanted. What about that less cultivated grace, a brave flash of beauty tossed in the fey wind off the mountains, like a harebell?

Dominic told her briefly about the attack on their carriage, while the truth sank in. He, not Nigel, was the man who—in a mad repudiation of honor—had promised heartless seduction to a virgin.

Then done it.

If Nigel knew that, would he demand a duel in his turn?

"So why have you committed yourself to this cause?" Nigel asked at last.

"That's easy to answer," Frances said. "Our friend Dominic cannot resist gallantry. He's a romantic, like Galahad. And he recognizes loss when he sees it."

Dominic stared at her. "Forgive me the language, Frances, but what the *devil* are you talking about?"

"I'm talking about Catriona MacNorrin, of course. She's a wounded creature."

"You think I have wounded her?" he asked starkly.

"Don't be so conceited. I don't imagine you're that important to her."

"No," he said, hiding his surge of dismay. "Of course not."

Frances leaned forward, completely serious. "Look, Dominic. She lost her parents when she was little. She lost her first sweetheart to Napoleon, then her second. She lost her brother at Waterloo. She lost her hair, which must have been lovely. Her whole life has been defined by loss. Her courage in the face of it is breathtaking. I fear what might happen if that bravery ever faltered. She has nothing else left. That's why you acted the gallant and took up her cause, you quixotic man. You couldn't refuse if you tried."

He sat silent for a moment, appalled. "Frances, with all due respect, you have no idea what I've done, nor intended to do."

She smiled, and spoke lightly. "If you deliberately wound Miss MacNorrin or bring her more loss, I think you would owe womankind a debt of honor. Then I should have to ask Nigel to kill you."

Nigel set his wife on her feet and stood up, though his arms remained about her. "For God's sake, Frances! Last year Dominic saved you for me. There's nothing he could do that would make me call him out."

She looked up at her husband. There was passion in it. "No, of course not. Now, let's make plans. How are we to get these two lost souls to Scotland, when we are supposed to leave for Paris in the morning?"

Catriona stared at her reflection in the mirror. The balloon had crashed. She had been knocked out. Apart from a slight headache, she felt fine. But she would never take down her hair for a man now. She had hacked it off in a self-destructive taunt at Fate. The sin of anger. Her one beauty, destroyed. What did it matter? The people of Glen Reulach would have to sacrifice their very roof trees if she did not succeed in her quest.

She moved restlessly to the window and gazed out at the rain. The woman he coveted had just left: Frances, who had married her marquess and loved him as part of her own soul. She hadn't had to say it; it was obvious in every breath. Frances was totally indifferent to Dominic's admiration. Did it make any difference?

"Any friend of Dominic's is welcome at Rivaulx," she had said. "When I met him he was the only real friend Nigel had left. It was a friendship that cost Dominic a great deal, I'm afraid. Would you like me to tell you about it?"

Catriona had met the other woman's eyes as if defying her to see that she cared at all. "If you wish."

Lady Rivaulx had given her one of her own robes and invited her to sit beside the fire, a simple gesture of hospitality that made Catriona think of home. "It was a matter of an old enemy of my husband's, a woman. She plotted both for Napoleon's success and, for personal reasons, to destroy Nigel. It began in Russia early in 1812, when Britain was trying to enlist the Tsar against Napoleon. Both Dominic and Nigel were British agents, you see."

Catriona sat down, smoothing the folds of the gown, annoyed that she felt nervous. "He told me he went to Russia in 1811. He had been under Wellington in the Peninsula as a reconnaissance officer."

"Dominic was sent to St. Petersburg that Christmas, where his talents could be put to even better use. He stayed into 1812 when he moved to Moscow and was joined there by Nigel. He went back to the Peninsula later. I don't know all his exploits. He doesn't talk much about it. But after Napoleon returned to France in March last year, he and Nigel worked together in Paris. I was there, too. It was a dangerous, feral undertaking."

The wavering firelight made the stone griffins seem alive. "You are trying to tell me Dominic was some kind of hero?"

"I know he is." Her smile was lovely. "If you said it to him, he'd deny it, of course. But he's very much a hero."

A hero. What she had come to find. And been disappointed. "When did you first meet him?"

"In London, before he left for France that April. He and another man went to Paris to gather information about Napoleon's plans. The woman, my husband's enemy, drugged and captured Dominic when he arrived, then kept him hidden. Part of her plan was to attack Nigel through his friends. She had Dominic beaten quite brutally on a daily basis."

The griffins seemed to leap, baring their claws, as Catriona startled and looked up. "*Beaten?* Why?"

"She told him it was because he wouldn't love her. Of course he knew it was because of Nigel. He never gave in. Dominic would have died rather than betray his friends. In fact, we all believed he was dead. This woman was a master spy who'd been double-crossing British agents for years— at different times both Nigel and Dominic had each been her lover."

Catriona bit back her distress. Would Dominic share a woman so freely with his friend? Like a mongrel dog, of no morals? "But Dominic was married!"

"Not when he had his affair with her, in 1812. That only lasted three weeks. When Nigel arrived in Russia, Dominic was sent back to London. He married Harriet as soon as he returned. Yet I have wondered if it was not a reaction against this Moscow woman's corruption: to marry a naive girl. Perhaps that's why his marriage was doomed."

Catriona closed her eyes. So he had gone from this evil woman's bed straight to Harriet? And demanded innocence join him in depravity? "I'm not sure why you're telling me this."

The other woman's voice was soft. "Because Dominic has been through a great deal. More than any man ought to face, and he has had to do it essentially alone."

Catriona looked up. "He told me he coveted you."

Frances laughed. "Yes, it is something of a joke between us. When I first met Dominic last year, I hadn't yet discovered I loved Nigel, and I didn't know Dominic was married. Harriet was living in Scotland, of course, but I should think that's why he and I didn't pursue an affair. I was willing. He was not."

She couldn't conceal her reaction. Frances was so obviously in love with her husband. "Even *you* were willing?"

"Oh, yes. I was trained as a professional courtesan and I thought Dominic would make an excellent protector. He's a very attractive man, after all. He let me down gently. He's very kind."

Distress beat at her. The pain in her head intensified, making her drop her face into her hands. *O, mo chràdhlot!* "You cannot know him well."

Frances was still, like water in a deep well. Her tone stayed steady and sincere. "I know him very well. While the armies clashed at Waterloo, Dominic was left for dead in a cellar in Paris. He was freed only after the news arrived of Wellington's triumph. Nigel had to stay in Paris, so Dominic brought me home to England. We were together for some weeks and I was ill. His face showed the marks of his torture, but he gave me a courtesy and consideration I shall always cherish. Not much later I married Nigel. Dominic has been a regular visitor here ever since."

The headache throbbed. "So you are all friends?"

"If he were in any way dishonorable, neither Nigel nor I would love him as we do."

"You don't know him." The pain came in waves, battering at her composure. "He is a madman."

"Everything he does, however random it might appear, is done with one aim: to win back his wife."

"I know that." Tears slid down her face. "But his wife is dead."

Frances put her arms about Catriona's shoulders. "Then he *will* be like a madman," she said slowly. "And he has made you pay for it, when tragedies of your own burden your heart. Would you like to tell me about them?"

❧

Catriona glanced at him over the supper table. It was late. Flickering candles danced in mirrors and dazzled from crystal chandeliers to cast Dominic in bronze.

She didn't want it to make a difference, but it did: that

Lord and Lady Rivaulx knew him only as kind and honorable. They were people of extraordinary gifts, compassionate, perceptive, not easily deceived. In spite of all that had happened, it made a difference. Just as the balloon ride made a difference. The inventiveness, and gallantry, and the care to pay their way so no working person would face financial loss. His laughter had soared like an archangel's as they sailed. It had been fun! Were heroes *fun* to be with?

Yet if Dominic Wyndham was a hero, he was also a fool. Like a knight sworn to the grail, he had devoted himself blindly to a lost cause. It was the height of romantic absurdity: *to win back his wife*. Harriet had hated him. He could never have won her back. Were all heroes fools?

As she was, against all her resolutions, to care?

Dominic and Lord Rivaulx were dressed formally, as if there were thirty guests rather than two. The borrowed evening wear suited him. Yet it made him seem remote, formidable, like a knight in armor, the cuirass made only of elegance. There was no hint of that slack, disorderly rake she had witnessed in London, or the gawky churchman who had hustled her through the horse fair. Easy, confident, he sipped a glass of red wine as he discussed their new plan with the marquess. Carriages had already been ordered for four o'clock the next morning.

She shifted restlessly in her chair and silk slid over her legs. The marchioness had loaned her a sari, a dress from India, and wrapped Catriona's shorn hair in a veil. The strange clothes felt soft, comfortable. The veil hid her tear-blotched face. It was as if she had landed for a moment in Tir-nan-Og, the Land of Youth, where everything was luxury. The table smiled with dishes she had never dreamed of, subtly spiced, delicious.

Her headache had gone. She was ravenous, as if she had never eaten before. While the men talked she tasted everything.

"But if Dominic and Catriona are to be our servants," Frances said, "how do we account for Catriona? An extra lady's maid would be noticed."

The golden moment of indulgence shattered. Catriona

snapped back to the seriousness of the planning. "I can remain a boy," she said. "I don't mind."

"You would have to share a room with another man at night." The marquess's dark eyes assessed her. "I would never order a single room for one manservant."

"She can stay with me." It was Dominic, smiling lazily, his green eyes shuttered. "I shall guard her like my own sister."

The marchioness frowned at him. "You don't have a sister."

Did they guess, this astute marquess and his wife? She had told Frances everything but this: that she had given herself to Dominic Wyndham in a forest. Did they know how much she desired him? Did they understand that she wanted this mad fool of a false hero as the moon desires the ocean—as the moon longs to see its own rippling reflection spread away across that watery vastness, only to slip into it at last and drown?

Yet to the ocean, of course, the moon's longing was laughable. And to the moon, doomed to fickleness, it was a longing never assuaged, one repeated every night to eternity.

To travel as a boy would thrust her constantly into his company. But what choice was there? Frances normally traveled with just two women. If she replaced one of them with a Scotswoman with cropped hair, it would be instantly noticed. But there was bound to be a gaggle of menservants. A new lad would attract no notice at all.

Catriona took a deep breath and helped herself to a peach, peeled, and spiced with something heady and sweet.

Dominic grinned at her. "Gluttony?"

"Why not?" she asked, the juice of the peach on her hands.

Frances smiled, her eyes kind beneath her perfect eyebrows. "Then we have a plan. Although married women are supposed to be responsible for propriety, I'm afraid my years in India rather destroyed my more English sensibilities. Anyway, I maintained a far worse deception with Nigel and I trust Dominic absolutely."

Lord Rivaulx stood up. Once again Catriona sensed that he and his wife were connected by an irrevocable bond. Nothing overt revealed it. They did not offer caresses in public, nor use endearments. It was just there, like sunshine and light, indivisible.

The marquess smiled at her. "No one would imagine we shelter fugitives among our servants. You will both disappear completely. Dominic will make sure you suffer no insult from the other men." He winked at his friend. "If he does not, he will answer to me."

Catriona leaned back in the carriage and stared at her buckled shoes. *A Mhuire!* What a misplaced trust the marquess had in Major Dominic Wyndham!

Her legs were encased in white stockings below old-fashioned knee breeches. Her new coat was full-skirted, heavy with silver braid. Her hair—less ragged since Lord Rivaulx had handed her to his barber—was hidden under a white wig. The powder smelled musty. It tickled. Dominic wore identical clothes: the livery of the marquess's servants, and their disguise. He sat next to her on the seat, his thigh crushed against hers, and ignored her. He was entertaining the four other men in the coach with a bawdy tale, defying her to blush and give herself away.

As they had planned the previous night, Frances and Nigel were taking them to Edinburgh, bringing mountains of baggage and a long train of staff. It was a surprisingly fast way to travel. The marquess could command the freshest horses, the best service. He and his wife would sail for Paris from Leith, the port just outside the Scottish capital. An odd itinerary, but no one would ever question the whims of a marquess. The two extra footmen, a tall man and a boy, were indistinguishable from the rest, crowded in with his genuine menservants. Dominic was keeping them in an uproar of laughter.

"The lad's blushing!" one of the footmen said suddenly.

"Aye." Dominic had coarsened his voice just a little.

"My young charge is wet behind the ears yet. We'll soon cure him of it, won't we, lads?"

The laughter redoubled.

To hide the fire in her cheeks, Catriona turned her head and gazed from the window. She hated the prickly wig and the hot smell of the other men, packed too close, their linen crumpled. Only Dominic seemed unruffled and cool. The faint scent of cedar and lavender drifted from his coat. Squeezing into the corner, she pulled her thigh away from his. Though he must now stay braced against the movement of the carriage, he allowed her that tiny space. She was as aware of it as she was of the Great Glen, dividing Scotland in a deep gash from sea to sea.

Raucous laughter beat at her ears as Dominic finished another ribald tale. The four footmen were convulsed with merriment: coarse, good-humored, the raillery of men with men when they thought no women were present. She had become invisible.

She saw what he was doing and how well it was working. She saw it and understood it, yet how dare he so casually take control of the plan? And how dare he deliberately burn her ears with such stories?

They stopped at Newcastle for the night. At the premier inn in town, the marquess ordered rooms for himself and his wife, and an entire set of rooms in the attics for his servants, where they would sleep two or three to a bed. Dominic ushered Catriona into a space under the eaves no bigger than a cupboard. There were, however, two narrow beds.

"Our accommodation," he said with a grin. "Warm, dry, and more than we deserve. Must I apologize for those dreadful jokes in the carriage?"

The neat wig framed his strong cheekbones. In contrast, his eyes were startlingly green, like burning copper. He did not look like a servant now. An echo of a lord of the previous century, he shone resplendent and deadly—like the painting of the MacNorrin at the time of the '45, her great-grandfather, with his plaid over his greatcoat and a sword at his hip.

She pulled off her wig and sat down on one of the cots. "I did not know until now how men really think about women."

Dominic snapped open buttons engraved with tiny griffins. The marquess marked his men as his property. Strangely, they seemed proud of it.

"Men try to hide vulnerability. No man tells another how much he loves his mother, or his wife."

"You were not talking about mothers, nor wives." The ceiling sloped sharply above the bed, like the overhang of a cliff. "Nor about love."

"No, we made coarse jokes about sex. It's not what women want to believe, but the male impulse is pretty basic. Most men are uncomfortable facing such a powerful force in any other way. So we talk crudely, with an emphasis on anatomy. I hoped you understood why it was necessary."

"I understood."

He shrugged out of the braided coat and hung it up. "But you are angry."

Was it anger, this pain, this desire to curl up and clutch her hands over her belly? "The fourth sin? We have already indulged it."

The waistcoat had been cut for a narrower man. It stretched across his shoulders like silver plating over the flank of a heraldic lion, revealing muscle and tension.

"Like gluttony last night? So only envy and sloth are left. And why not? We have nothing else to do. We are completely safe traveling like this."

Catriona rubbed her cuff over a mark on her white stocking. "I am not safe. You do not know it, but in spite of those indecent witticisms, you are betraying me."

He turned. "What the devil do you mean?"

She looked up at him. "You hover by me. You show me small courtesies. In the coach, you laid your leg along mine without bracing against the contact until I moved. The other men will suspect. Any talk, at public inns, at tollgates, could reach our enemies. It takes more than ribald tales to treat me like a lad."

He tore off the white wig and ran his hands through his hair. "Catriona, I played cat and mouse with Napoleon's spies for most of the war. For God's sake, trust me. I am a bloody professional at this. No one has any idea you are not what we claim: a boy in training to be a footman."

"Then those men won't object that you corrupt me?"

He unbuttoned the waistcoat and tossed it aside. His shirt gleamed faintly. Particles of dust danced in the last thin rays of sunlight struggling in through the window. "Of course not. They think you are willing. It doesn't occur to anyone you are female." He dropped to his cot and stretched out, disappearing into shadows. "The men suspect nothing, except my predilection for boys. Common enough, and since I am popular with them, they won't hold it against me."

She didn't know why it distressed her so much. She had enjoyed the masquerade in the balloon. Her breeches had freed her for those few hours, from cumbersome skirts, from her own memories. But this fabric felt rough against her thighs. "Why must there be such an interpretation? If you did not look at me so, no one would have to think such foul things."

"Do you think," he asked dryly, "that I *like* that? Yet it doesn't matter. They are believed about the roles we play, that's all."

"Why must those roles be as lovers?"

"Because the first rule of a deception is to keep to the truth as closely as possible. Nigel is too courteous to ask outright, but he knows. So does Frances. That's why they agreed to let you stay with me like this. So even now I must let it seem we are lovers, for you give yourself away, Catriona."

She leaped up. "What do you mean? How?"

"Like this." He reached out and took her wrist. With one powerful tug, he spun her onto the cot beside him. She landed in a heap, arms and legs sprawled, her breasts crushed against his chest. Immediately she wrenched away, twisting from his grasp. Dominic opened his hands and let go, his face lost behind the dancing motes. "A man would have punched me for that. Men attack. Women flee.''

"And boys?''

"Catamites sulk.''

"Och, do they?'' With her full strength she swung back and struck straight toward his face. He caught her fist easily in one hand, spun her beneath him, and pinned her to the bed. Catriona stared up at him, breathing hard. The sunbeam edged his hair with fire. "So how else are men different?''

"Apart from the obvious ways?'' He grinned down at her, shifting his weight a little so his body pressed intimately into hers. "Men know when they are aroused,'' he said softly. "Women only know they feel something. They aren't always sure what it is, so sometimes they call it anger or confusion.''

"*Diabhal*—'' But what she felt was neither anger nor confusion.

He rolled away and stood up. "Go to bed, Catriona. You are safe until we reach Edinburgh. Trust me. Nothing I do will betray you to Yarrow Fletcher.''

He bowed, a half smile dimpling his cheek, and reached down a hand to help her up. The lines of his arm and shoulder were lovely in the dusty light, his palm strong and inviting.

Ignoring it, she kicked out her legs, crossing them at the ankle like a man, and put her hands behind her head. "You are a grand teacher and a bully with it. I am a better catamite already for the lesson. I should not have tried to hit you.''

He dropped his hand. "But you are sulking very well.''

"*Och-òn*. I am glad you are so sure of your word. It is no problem to trust in your honor, Dominic Wyndham, is it?''

"No,'' he said. "It is not.''

Catriona stood up and went to the other cot. She shambled out of her jacket in a deliberate caricature of his casual male movements, then bent and kicked off her shoes, carelessly, as a boy would.

He stood, arms crossed over his chest, and watched her.

Her cravat came undone with a few hard tugs and she tossed it aside. She shed her waistcoat, deliberately stiffening her shoulders so her breasts thrust forward.

His knuckles turned white.

Defiance seized her, making her shake a little. "If you break faith, the marquess will kill you. Is he a better fighter than you?"

"Yes."

"Then I am safe, indeed."

She felt hot and clumsy. Her fingers fumbled at the griffin buttons on the breeches, but she scrambled them open and tugged down the blue fabric. Clad only in white shirt and linen underdrawers, she stood up and bent over to pull off her stockings.

His breath came faster, through nostrils flared like a stallion's.

The stockings did not want to roll, so—with fingers that felt like a stranger's—finally she wrenched them off.

"You will not touch me until Edinburgh," she said, staring at her bare feet. "Your corrupt wee laddie. What a splendid thing the English gentleman is!"

"Catriona." His voice was husky, tension palpable in the clipped words. "We are at a bloody impasse. You used me as you wished in Sherwood. Why should I want to repeat it? When I have you back in my bed, it will be on my terms, not yours—and for our mutual enjoyment."

"I did not suppose you wished to repeat it." She pulled her shirt over her head. The collar caught around her ears, leaving her naked body exposed. Cool air washed over her skin, raising goose bumps, yet her bare breasts felt hot and heavy and full. They swung unprotected as she wrestled with the shirt. At last the fabric pulled free and she threw it aside. She was nude from the waist up. She began to turn around. "You like lads better."

The door slammed.

Catriona stared at the battered wood. Her neck felt stripped without her hair. Her nipples stood hard and erect, proudly. He had fled! He had fled, before she was even half-undressed. So he did not have as much courage as she!

She sat down on the cot and wrapped her arms about her nakedness. A lump sat in her throat like the *urisk* in his cave, the lonely water fairy who seeks human company in vain. Why did she do this? To cry defiance at her loneliness? But she had always been lonely. She expected nothing different. And she would find no answers in the arms of an Englishman.

In Edinburgh there was a child. They should be there by midnight the next day. That was her purpose. Nothing else mattered. Once Dominic had the papers, she would never need to see him again.

Ten

∞

"YOU TAKE PRIDE in charming these footmen?" she asked.

They were together for a moment in the yard of an inn on the English border. Horses and carriages clattered on the cobbles. But she was aware only of him, her ruin. She had no idea where Dominic had spent the night. In the stables, possibly. Yet he had appeared in the morning relaxed and sleek, wig in place, coat brushed. No doubt the marquess had conspired to assist him.

"I was an officer," he said bluntly. "I can handle men."

She didn't know what drove her, what demon made her challenge him, even now. "The brother of a lord condescends to fool the servants. It seems a sorry kind of disdain to me. You would not be so cavalier were they to take such liberties with you."

"Catriona, what are you talking about?" The green eyes were moss dark.

She looked about at the inn yard, the hurrying ostlers, men bending their backs under the load of work, the lords and ladies stepping daintily past them. "I am talking about men from different worlds. Like leaves on a runnel they touch for a moment, but an oak and a birch leaf can never share a stem."

"They can share the same wood."

She glanced back at him. "Och, the Scots birch grows solitary enough these days, and the oak I speak of is English."

"I would like to think," Dominic said in her ear as the other footmen came out of the inn, "that you were sorry about that."

Catriona turned aside and climbed into the carriage. A few more hours and she would never see him again. She *would* rejoice in that!

They reached the small inn south of Edinburgh well after dark. With his tail of carriages and servants, the marquess had traveled for seventeen hours. The men staggered into the inn yard like drunkards. The maids yawned as they scrambled after them. Yet Dominic leaped onto the cobbles, lithe and light for a tall man. Like the marquess, he showed inexhaustible energy. From the corner of her eye, she saw Nigel help Frances from their coach, keeping her hand in his as he led her into the inn. The marquess moved with the ease of a dancer, but his wife was a reed to his wind, wine in his cup.

It hit hard enough to knock the breath from her. After gluttony, had she gone so directly to the sixth sin—envy, the most ignoble and burning of the seven sins? The sin that consumed the sinner. The sin that ate out the heart, yet still devoured long after the heart was a hollow shell. So this was the difference between envy and covetousness? She did not want the marquess for herself, but dear God, how she envied his wife! Envied the certainty and grace: that stillness in Frances, as if contentment lay so deep no surface wind could ruffle her—the certainty of a woman loved by the one man she loved in return more than life.

"It's all right," a voice said. "Come, lad, I'll catch you."

She looked down into Dominic's face. His features blurred. As tears burned and pricked she swayed with exhaustion, clutching the side of the door, afraid she would weep openly, making ugly noises, like a woman.

"The boy's asleep on his feet!" one of the footmen cried.

In spite of their load of boxes and fatigue, the other men laughed.

Dominic set down the bandbox he had picked up. "Never mind, lads! I'll carry him." Grasping her wrists, he tossed her bodily over his shoulder. "Turn your face into my coat," he whispered, "and kick a little."

The powder of his wig scattered over her as the tears broke and rolled. She sneezed. He shook her, not gently, and carried her into the inn. The laughter of the other men followed.

Dominic set her on the one bed jammed into the attic they were to share. He took off her wig and smoothed the damp hair from her forehead. She gulped, snuffling, hiding her face in the pillow.

"I know how it feels," he said. "I feel the same bloody way whenever I'm with them. Nigel and Frances are wild swans, mated for life. It's what everyone wants and rarely finds."

"It is not what everyone wants!" she said into the pillow. "There are more important things."

"Though I have never expected to find it, I'm damned if I see anything in this world more important than love, Catriona. Good night."

She sat up, ashamed to have revealed her weakness. Ashamed he had been forced to cover for her in front of the other men. Ashamed that without his quick thinking she would have revealed herself as female and broken their story. "Where are you going?"

He grinned. "Somewhere else for a bed. They say the maids at this inn are all whores."

☙

He slept crushed in Nigel's carriage. It had fur rugs. Rich fur. The fabulous fur of Russia. Something Nigel had brought back. Cursing as he tried to cram his long frame into the narrow coach, Dominic closed his eyes. The images came back, forcefully.

Voices rang clear: himself confronting Nigel in his London study in the spring of 1815, just over a year ago. *Since Catherine had been my lover before she was yours, I think I have the right to speak of her.*

And Nigel, striking back, had conjured that harsh memory of the brilliance and corruption of Moscow, and the brilliance and corruption of the woman they had both loved. *Frost clung to her hair like diamonds on flame*—the beautiful, wicked Princess Katerina. The woman who had changed him for life, and who had gone straight to Nigel's bed when Dominic left Russia.

Dominic had not resented it. But after Russia, after the splendor of Moscow and the knowing skills of a whore, he had come home and married Harriet. Of course, the engagement was long-standing. It had been impossible to break. Yet he had not wanted to back out. He had taken Harriet happily to the altar, trusting in her innocence and love, and willing to lay his heart at her feet.

So here he was, four years later, a widower, relict of a marriage that had never really existed. A marriage he had tried to resurrect in the tiny snatches of time left a soldier between battles—the awkward meetings on the few occasions he came home from France, from the Peninsula, and could come north to Edinburgh.

He did not think of Catherine often, though it was because of all those connections, all those threads going back to Russia, that he had been imprisoned in Paris that spring before Waterloo. Their enemies had threatened to kill Nigel, but only Dominic had been chained in a cellar and tortured. He turned over, banging his knee, and cursed once. In the morning they would reach Edinburgh and the house of the Souls of Charity—the end of Catriona's quest.

∽

It was a large house in Queen Street in Edinburgh New Town. The white facade gleamed like fresh snow in the bright morning sunshine. Dominic was no longer dressed as a footman. Not only was disguise unnecessary now, but only as her husband could he claim Harriet's belongings. He had bought clothes with money borrowed from Nigel, and gratefully washed the stench of powder from his hair and skin. In future, he thought wryly, he would make sure no footman of his ever wore wig or powder again.

He was shown into the same waiting room with the green-and-pink wallpaper and gilt chairs. The room where he had sat with Stansted on so many mornings in the Victory Summer of 1814—that break between the Peninsular campaign and the recall to duty before Waterloo.

Harriet had refused to see him, except once. Yet Rosemary had come into the room every day smiling, holding out her hand to her husband, while looking over her shoulder to see if Dominic cared. How splendid an absurdity that he had not learned until then why Rosemary had taken Harriet to Edinburgh to begin with! And that it had taken so long before they made the bargain that he'd hoped would, in the end, win back his wife. He had made it a habit, he thought wryly, to indulge in vain hopes.

Rosemary entered in a flurry of skirts. She was tall and dark, with the intensity of her Italian mother. She hadn't changed. The skin over her jaw and cheek was pale alabaster, a marked contrast to the red, expectant lips.

Dominic stood, holding his cane, and bowed.

Stansted's wife trembled with energy, her smile wonderful. "Dominic! At last! I can leave within the hour. It won't take me long—"

"Lady Stansted, I beg of you! I have not come for you."

The smile wavered. She stopped, facing him, her eyes searching his face. "What are you saying?"

He had dreaded this. "Just that. I have not come for you."

She turned and crossed the gracious room with its high ceilings to stand by one of the tall windows. "You don't know what I have sacrificed—what this moment has cost me! Oh, God! You spurn me?"

"We have been over this before," he said. "I have tried

to be as gentle as possible. I have a great deal of esteem for you, but I don't love you and never have. I never gave you any reason to believe otherwise.''

She sat down. Tears sprang suddenly. ''Because you loved Harriet.''

''I *wanted* to love her, Lady Stansted. She was my wife.''

The dark head bent as Rosemary looked down at her hands. ''You should never have married her.''

He tried to keep the mockery out of his voice. He failed. ''I realized that almost immediately.''

She looked up at him, her black eyes startling against the reddened lids. ''Yes, she loved me! Why can't you?''

He felt embarrassed. ''You think you're in love with me, but you don't even know me. I was in uniform. I had been involved in adventures that seemed glamorous to you. It was four years ago and we've met only occasionally since. You have married a fine man who'll be a duke one day. I wish to God you would forget this misplaced interest in me and give your husband a chance. Stansted is braver and better than you know.''

Dark ringlets tossed as she lifted her head. ''Ha! Is he?''

His throat was dry. He wanted, quite inappropriately, to laugh, but not because any of this was funny. ''He successfully climbed the church steeple and left his handkerchief tied to the spike at the top. It's a bit irrelevant to me now, I suppose, with Harriet dead. But you ought to know. He was afraid, but he did it anyway. In my estimation, that's the very definition of courage.''

Rosemary stood up, her breasts rising and falling. ''Did you come here to tell me that?''

''I also came for Harriet's things.''

She bit at her thumbnail like a child. ''You still care for her *things*? When she died, we packed everything in a trunk. I thought—I thought it might bring you, but why do you want them?''

Dominic stared at the little frieze of plaster leaves around the ceiling. The sooner this was over, the better. ''Well, first of all, I purchased most of her finery. Secondly, her papers and letters probably contain humiliating personal missives from me. Thirdly, anything she left is mine by law."

He didn't know what she was thinking, how she felt about the climb up the church spire, what she thought she had sacrificed. Rosemary had always been a mystery to him. She gazed up at him as if blind. "Even though she is dead you still think of her?"

"I'm sorry, Lady Stansted," he said. "If we could order our hearts, I would certainly have ordered mine to feel for you as you wish. But alas, it seems love is entirely random and strikes out of the blue, like lightning."

"But what about all the letters I've written you? Why can't you love me? Is all my loss in vain?" The brown eyes widened further as if in deep shock. "You're in love with someone else, aren't you?"

He began to deny it. But the thought struck him out of the blue, like lightning: *I am in love with someone else. My God! My God!*

"Dammit!" He didn't want it to sound so abrupt. "My feelings are not your concern, Lady Stansted. Now, will you please show me that trunk?"

"Why should I? Why should I help you? What will you give me if I do? Would you tell me you had looked at me at least once with lust or with longing? Would you kiss me?"

His shame was complete. "I can't. What the hell is a kiss without heart? Let me see the trunk."

She was a trapped doe. "For a kiss," she said. "With heart or without it."

Why was it so impossible to kiss her? She was passionate, attractive. What harm would it do? Yet he couldn't. He shook his head, hating this mutual humiliation.

I am in love with someone else. My God! My God! Catriona!

Yet love wasn't exactly an emotion he could trust!

He almost stumbled, remembering her tender breasts as she peeled off the boy's shirt; her shorn hair and the vulnerable, piercing shape of her head as she looked at him so defiantly in that lane in Nottingham; her stricken tears as she told him about her brother, Calum, whom she had loved; her cries under a cold moon as she gave him her virginity. Devil take it! Devil take his soul and his heart! He had done it again: fallen in love with a woman who despised him and wished him in hell!

The door banged open. Dominic looked up. Rosemary was studying his face, her hand on the doorknob. Without another word, she led the way from the room and along a corridor between white-painted doors. He followed blindly. At the end, a flight of stairs led down.

Beyond a small entryway, Rosemary unlocked the door to a storeroom. It was empty but for a small chest in the corner. Dull light filtered down from a tiny window that let onto an outside stairwell. She took another key from her belt and tossed it to him. Barely noticing, Dominic snatched the key from the air with one hand.

I am in love with someone else. "This is everything Harriet left?"

"Yes," Rosemary said. "Everything. Why would I want anything of hers? Help yourself. That door over there goes outside. You haven't won. Maybe you *have* proved you can't love me, but I won't go back to Stansted!"

"He climbed the steeple," Dominic said bluntly. "The rest is up to you. We had a bargain. Even though Harriet's dead, he lives, and you gave me your bloody word!"

She ran up the stairs, leaving him alone in the room. Dominic stared at the chest for a moment. He felt oddly disoriented. He had come all this way; survived lethal attack; experienced a balloon ride; loved Catriona Mac-Norrin—for this?

Rosemary had no reason to lie. This sad little trunk would contain everything. Harriet's pathetic little gloves and reticules. All the pretty toys she had demanded he buy for her, the things he had purchased even when he couldn't afford it. But presumably, somewhere in the frippery lay her papers—letters or diaries, perhaps—and the documents from Sarah that showed little Andrew to be heir to the

MacNorrin: papers that would free Catriona from needing him any longer.

The stone flagstones rang under his boots as he walked to the chest. He inserted the key, but it was already unlocked. With his senses screaming caution, he threw back the lid. Silks and lace, gloves and stockings, rioted together in a tangle of color. It looked as if a large mouse had made a nest in Harriet's clothes—or as if someone had been here before him.

Something moved. Dominic whirled about. The open mouth of a pistol barrel grinned at him from the doorway.

"You're too late, Major Wyndham," said the man holding the gun. "I already have her papers." He tapped his breast pocket, then waved his free hand toward Harriet's trunk. "You can have the trumpery, of course, if you wish."

Dominic closed the trunk and sat down on the lid, the key still gripped in his right hand. It cut into his palm. He wasn't armed. For God's sake, it was broad daylight in the heart of a city. His only concession to self-defense was his sword cane, which he had left leaning against the wall, not much use against a pistol or the man holding it.

"So your master has won." He opened his hand and let the key fall to the floor. It hit with a clink. "Did he also instruct you to kill me, Mr. Fletcher?"

Above the window to her right was a motto in gold paint. The paint had peeled, so the motto was no longer legible. The house stretched eight or ten stories above her head to finish against the sky in sharp roofs and jutting chimneys. Catriona walked through the narrow entry into the close. She had visited Mrs. Mackay here before Harriet died. Here she'd seen Andrew squalling in his nurse's arms at the indignity of being shown to a stranger, then his smiles when she'd produced a sweetmeat. Rosemary, Lady Stansted, had given her the money and suggested she buy something for Harriet's child—wee Andrew, with his bright blue eyes and thatch of black hair—truly the child, Catriona was sure, of the MacNorrin.

She went up a flight of stairs and knocked at the door. No one answered.

She knocked harder. Silence echoed about her. The bustle in the High Street was muffled by thick walls of ancient stone. To come into these Old Town closes was like a step back in time, a removal from the modern world. But the silence from the house felt far more eerie than that.

Catriona tried the knob.

The door pushed open under her hand, yawning wide on creaky hinges. The room beyond echoed of emptiness. She caught her breath and stepped inside. The hair stood up on the back of her neck.

"Is he in love with her?" Frances gazed out at the seabirds wheeling and crying over the docks at Leith.

Nigel grinned at his wife. "I hope so. She's a remarkable woman—and she looked wonderful in trousers. It's about time Dominic forgot Harriet and found himself a female who likes men."

She looked up. "Harriet didn't like men?"

He reached for her hand. "After Catherine, she must have seemed only innocent and shy. That was not exactly the case. I'll tell you about it later. Damnably, we must take this ship for Paris, so Dominic must sort out this entanglement for himself."

"Yes, I know," Frances said. "As we did."

He kissed the pad of her middle finger, letting his tongue linger, then kissed her on the mouth. Frances twined into his embrace like a vine.

"My orders?" Yarrow Fletcher looked at Dominic across the small storeroom. He cocked the pistol. "My orders were to delay your getting here and to secure your wife's effects before you did.''

Dominic leaned back, letting his spine rest against the wall. He stretched out his booted feet, quietly flexing muscles, as it sank in. *Your wife's effects!* ''So the attack in Sherwood was just a delaying tactic? It seemed damned lethal to me. My coachman and a couple of your hired thugs died.''

Fletcher shrugged. ''Irrelevant. An accident. They were fool enough to shoot each other.''

Dominic let his gaze wander over the stone walls and high window, assessing distances. ''So how the hell did you manage to persuade the Souls of Charity to give you access to this chest, when Lady Stansted guarded the key with at least her virtue, if not her life?''

Fletcher smiled. ''A bribe to a maid, a key stolen and replaced without being missed. Simple. You could have done it yourself.''

''Of course,'' Dominic said. ''Sadly, I loitered too long on the way. But then, this trunk is mine. Why should I think anyone else would want its contents? Did you find what you were looking for?''

It was a damned unpleasant smile. The smile Fletcher had worn when he had killed a French officer all those years ago in the Peninsula. ''What do you think?'' He tapped his pocket. ''It's all here, Major. What an insipid little whore your wife was, wasn't she? I must say I was touched to the heart by the love letters you—''

As Fletcher's hand touched his jacket again Dominic launched himself across the storeroom. He hit the other man in the gut. Fletcher grunted and doubled over, balance gone. The pistol clattered to the floor, skidding as Dominic kicked it aside, spinning as it encountered the key. He hit Fletcher one more time in the chin. The man's head snapped back, hitting the wall with a nasty thud. He slid, unconscious, to the floor.

Dominic propped him up and unbuttoned his jacket. He pulled out a bundle of papers and rapidly went through them. He looked briefly at his letters to Harriet. Should he at least be glad she had kept them? He tossed them on the floor. There were no documents written by Sarah Mac-Norrin, the old laird's young wife—absolutely nothing about little Andrew, nothing that said he was Sarah's baby, nothing that would save Glen Reulach from Rutley.

Dominic took out his tinderbox, struck a spark, and burned the little pile of letters. Throwing aside Harriet's clothes, he turned out the trunk, slit the linings, broke open the sides. Dry glue feathered away beneath his fingers, sifting to dust.

He found nothing.

And this was all Harriet had left; he believed Rosemary in that. So he had failed: failed Catriona, as in a different way he had failed Harriet. Fletcher must have ridden day and night like a demon to get here first. That delay at Rivaulx Castle while Catriona lay stunned was all that had made it possible. Even so, Fletcher could only just have arrived—not time enough to hide anything more than he had in his pockets, though time enough, of course, for any document's destruction.

Eventually Dominic left the scented gloves and the lace garters where they lay, and walked out into the streets of Edinburgh. Why the hell hadn't he ridden ahead the previous night and roused the Souls of Charity from their beds? Had he dreaded the encounter with Rosemary that much?

It was a long enough walk from the New Town, with its modern squares and crescents, to the Old Town. He paused for a moment to gaze across the deep valley, dry remainder of the Nor' Loch. The houses on the other side were living memories of a different and darker age, clustered beneath Edinburgh Castle. To his right Calton Hill rose steeply near the entrance of the road to Leith. Wind roared into Edinburgh off the sea, billowing the skirts of the ladies on the North Bridge like so much ship's canvas. Nigel and Frances would have embarked by now, sailing with the tide to Paris. Thank God for such friends! He knew Nigel had stretched his scheduling to the limit in order to come here at all. Then he had made Dominic an immediate and generous loan.

The North Bridge, arching over sheds and markets, led him to the High Street, the Royal Mile linking Edinburgh Castle with the old palace of Holyrood. Dominic turned toward the Canongate, past the displays of wares and the windows with their ancient mottoes. He ducked into the entry to the close where Catriona had gone to find Andrew and Mrs. Mackay—the address to which he had sent his gold and his instructions. He had failed to get proof of Andrew's identity, but at least he could salvage this much: he could save the child.

The bustle of the street died away. Dominic stopped. Dressed once again in boy's clothes, Catriona sat on a doorstep, staring at the ground. Her skull curved delicately beneath the cropped hair. She was holding her hat, turning it around and around in both hands. Something in the set of her shoulders spoke of profound dread. Yet at the sound of his step she looked up and her face flooded with hope.

"You have Sarah's papers?"

Damning his impotence in this, he shook his head. "There are no papers. I'm sorry."

For a moment he thought she would fold, there on the step, and collapse. The color drained from her face and her knuckles turned stark white on the hat brim. But with her stubborn courage she kept her back rigid and took a deep breath, leaning back against the door and closing her eyes. "Why not?"

Above them a window opened and a woman looked down. She cackled suddenly. "It's a braw laddie you make, hen, an' it's a braw laddie's come for ye!"

Still chalk white, her eyes burning like sapphires, Catriona glanced up at Dominic. "We can't talk out here. Come inside."

What would he have given at that moment to have brought different news? All his worldly goods? His bloody soul, for God's sake? Choking back silent curses, he followed her up a flight of stone stairs and into a small, dark parlor. It was empty, obviously disused, cold ashes in the grate. Snuffed candles had been set neatly together on a shelf in a corner.

So this was the shock that had already tested her courage: no fire; no nurse; no child.

The house lay silent, unless the creak of the door closing behind him was an echo of the devil's laughter.

So why had they left? Had word of danger to Andrew frightened the nurse away? Or had Mrs. Mackay had some other reason of her own? Dominic hadn't really thought Rutley would threaten the boy directly, but thank God he had written again, just as a contingency against this very thing. He propped himself on a pine table and forced control into his voice. "The child, where is he?"

Throwing her hat on the table, Catriona began to pace. "Andrew is gone."

"Where?"

She looked so damned fragile, yet her woman's thighs seductively filled the breeches. "North. Mrs. Mackay has gone home to Sutherland, where she was born—or so the neighbor says—and taken the child with her."

"Sutherland?"

Color came back to her cheeks as she walked. "Away north, several days' travel past Inverness and without roads."

So the sooner he got to Inverness the better—assuming Mrs. Mackay had done as he'd asked.

Catriona stopped and leaned her head on the edge of the window frame. She ran her fingers over the leading. "Why couldn't you get the papers?"

"There are no papers. I searched all of Harriet's things. If there ever was proof of the child's paternity, it is gone now." He had so wanted to return to her triumphant, not with his failure like dust in his hands, yet there was at least this small comfort. "Without the papers, Andrew is no threat at all to his cousin's inheritance. The child is safe, Catriona."

She was rigid. "How can you be sure?"

"Rutley's man was there first."

Once again she faced it with her rigid courage. "Rutley's man?"

"Yarrow Fletcher," he said, and realized how much of

his unease was pure fury. "I left him unconscious. But the attack in Sherwood wasn't just personal revenge against me, it was to prevent us reaching Edinburgh in time."

"So the duke does know about Andrew!"

"And now he's made sure Andrew can never inherit. If there were papers, Yarrow Fletcher destroyed them. He'll have sent word of his success to the duke, so neither Rutley nor his man is a threat any longer. All that remains is the child. Let's get to Sutherland."

"You!" Shaking with distress, she thrust her fist into the window frame. "I don't need you. It is only my quest now."

"Really?" The turn of her neck was achingly defenseless, the line of white skin and the delicate ear. "For Andrew's sake, wherever you go I shall follow. I'm damned if I see how you can stop me."

She gestured violently. "Och, you stubborn man! Let be! Let be! I am done with you!"

Like a rein on a rearing horse, something snapped in him. Rage flooded his mind. "*Done* with me! It's too late for that, Catriona."

In two strides he was at the window and had grasped her upper arm. He spun her to face him. Her cheeks were wet, tears running freely, blindly, spilling over her dark lashes, turning her nose pink.

He cupped her chin in both hands, not gently, forcing her to look at him. "You are not done with me, Catriona MacNorrin. There is far more between us now than this mad, blind quest. Why the hell do you deny it? Because you cannot deny this?"

He slipped one hand behind her head, sinking his fingers into the soft dark curls at her nape. The curve of her waist slipped under his other palm, piercingly desirable. Her lip curled. He dropped both hands to her bottom and pulled her into his body as he kissed her. She tasted of salt and grief and anger. Beneath the fabric of her breeches, female softness filled his palms. She didn't struggle or pull away. Instead, fiercely, she kissed back, her tears running into his

mouth. His anger burned away to leave nothing but desire—
a desire far more ardent than rage.

He released her and held her head cradled against his
shoulder. Her hair was soft against his mouth. "It's all
right. I will take this child as my own. He will be raised
as nephew to an earl. He'll want for nothing."

"But the glen—" she said.

"Does it matter so much?"

She pulled away. "It is all that matters. Damn you, Dominic Wyndham! You cannot understand."

"Is there not enough between us now for you to explain?
After all of it?" He chopped the air with his free hand.
"All the sins we have shared? Why the hell have you never
explained what's really going on?"

Using his handkerchief, she wiped her eyes and blew her
nose. "You are English and a rake and a gallant fool. If
there is danger, you will rush into it unheeding. If there is
tragedy, you can do nothing about it. There is no possible
future for us except heartbreak. I can manage better alone.
I don't want your help."

Damn her! Did Catriona really think she could dismiss
him like this? It was something he'd seen in her brother: a
seemingly intransigent romantic fatalism. At first it had
been almost unintelligible to his pragmatic Anglo-Saxon
mind. Yet Calum had shown him it was the wellspring that
gave Highlanders such splendid courage in the face of disaster and explained so much of their history.

Nevertheless, he was damned if he'd tell her what he'd
arranged with Mrs. Mackay! "What of my body?" he
asked bluntly. "Will you leave with your curiosity una-
bated? Don't you want to finish what we began in Sherwood?"

She tipped her chin and bit her lip before facing him
again. "How could you think I would want it now?"

"Because for all your duplicity, I think you are honest
in this. Desire has lain between us like a flame-breathing
dragon ever since we first met in London. If we're to part

now because of my failure, I would give you this one
thing—that you not leave here a virgin.''

She looked confused. "I am not a virgin now.''

He stroked wisps of hair back over her ear. The skin at
her temple felt warm, as smooth as her inner thigh. Desire
surged. Might he breathe fire?

He grinned, keeping his voice cool. "Yes, you are. Not
technically, but in your soul. You wanted to become a
woman. I couldn't give you the papers about Andrew, but
I can give you that. Now is your chance.''

"So you can bind me? So you can come with me into
the Highlands?'' She laughed shakily. "But you cannot
have both, Major Dominic Wyndham—my body and my
soul.'' She gestured to a door buried in the wall, then thrust
her hands in her pockets, leaning back against the wall like
a boy. "There is a wee bed through there. If we make love
in it, will you let me ride away from here alone?''

So it was still war, but desire flared, blotting out any
other concerns. "If you demand it.''

"And not follow?''

He deliberately caught her by the waist so she couldn't
pull away. "If you let me have my wicked way, if you
surrender to my desire, if you refuse me nothing, then you
have my word: I won't follow.''

Her nostrils flared. A dapple of color bloomed in her
neck and cheeks. Her eyes dilated. "Do you think you will
frighten me as you frightened Harriet? Do you think I am
scared of your corruption?''

The desire was thundering now. His groin pulsed with
pleasure. He had a clear vision of her nakedness, her round
breasts, the dark hair hiding her woman's moisture and
heat.

"I shall touch nowhere, do nothing, without your consent. But if you do not consent, then I shall follow you
north, find Andrew, claim him as Harriet's, and take him.''

"Very well.'' She thrust both hands through her short
hair. Her voice stabbed with bitterness. "If this is what it
comes to—I admit my weakness. I have never denied it.

Yes, we began something and we did not finish it. So show me what sin is like, unfettered by virtue, and may you have joy in it.''

He took her hand and kissed her tense knuckles, giving her a bow. ''Oh, I shall,'' he said. ''And so will you.''

Eleven

∞

THE DOOR CREAKED. In the small bedroom a feather bed nestled between its four posts. A scatter of plain rugs lay on the plank floor. The walls were paneled in dark wood. Yet rainbows crackled in the corners of her eyes. The ceiling was painted. Between the low beams ran a riot of stylized flowers and leaves, small creatures and birds, interwoven in a tapestry of paint. The beams rang with primary colors: red, yellow, blue, green.

Dominic glanced up and stopped. "Good Lord! We'll make love in a veritable garden. It's like the bower of Titania."

Catriona turned away and crossed to the bed. *Could she take this risk and survive it?* "Like the Fairy Queen, do I give myself to a monster?"

" 'A very gentle beast,' " he quoted with a smile, " 'and of a good conscience.' "

Her blood sang in her ears, the frantic ring of thunder overhead, of waves roaring into a cave. A fine sweat broke all over her skin. Desire burned between her legs like a fever. She wanted him. She had wanted him since London. Yet to deny him—and herself—had not been simply a matter of pride. Any future was impossible. Whatever the outcome over Andrew, any future for Catriona MacNorrin and Dominic Wyndham was impossible. They must part now, before it was too late and they both broke their hearts.

She had never meant their fragile connection to continue after Edinburgh. And now in this bed she could make sure it did not. He would keep his word. If they made love, he would not follow her. So this joining of flesh was the first and last time. The first, because that brief coupling in Sherwood had not been completed—as he'd said, in her soul she was still a virgin. The last, because she would leave him behind and continue on into the Far North alone. The Far North, where it was cold at night even in midsummer.

Whatever happened now, her future was cold. She could face it better, perhaps, as a woman. Surely it was no sin to take with her something of the vibrant physical heat of this man? A small kernel of warmth to hide away in her heart, a memory to sustain her in the years to come? As long as she made sure he went back to England, where he belonged, and left with his heart whole, thinking her merely ruthless and hard.

He was standing, apparently relaxed, by the window. His eyes glittered like green water, filled with shadows.

"Show me," she said. "Show me what you did to Harriet."

"What happened with Harriet has nothing to do with us."

"Does it not?" She choked down the high note of hysteria and began again. "I would know, nonetheless."

"To show me how brave you are?" He walked up to her. "I already know that."

Heat emanated from him in waves. "Do you? Do you think I have enough courage to endure your depravity?"

The painted ceiling capered behind his blond head. Dimples deeply cut his cheeks. He was achingly handsome, like the devil. "It was our wedding night," he said. "She sat on a stool and held out her arms to me."

"Like this?" Catriona hooked a small stool with one booted foot and dropped onto it, holding out her arms.

He took one of her hands and brought it to his mouth, palm up. A treacherous spike of flame ran down her arm to her breasts. The boy's shirt rubbed rough against their aching tips.

"Then I undressed her. Of course she was wearing an ivory silk gown, not a man's shirt and breeches." He began to kiss her fingers one at a time.

She snatched her hand away. "I have no silk gown with me."

To her surprise, he dropped to both knees and flung his hands wide. "Not for want of my trying," he said ruefully. "You left at least twenty such garments at Ralingcourt."

Suddenly she giggled. She knew it was sheer nerves. Her blood spun and eddied in her veins. Her nipples throbbed. The heat pooled between her thighs and made her legs weak. She had given herself to this man once. Why should this time make her so confused, even afraid?

"What I have will have to do, then," she said.

He caught both her hands in his and held them firmly. "You have exactly what I desire, Catriona, with my heart and soul. Don't be afraid, sweetheart. I know what I'm doing. I'm practiced at this. I promise you nothing but plea-sure. We have no ties other than this: I am male; you are female; we share a longing. It was easier for you in Sher-wood, because it was night and it happened unplanned."

Memory bloomed and flared—of his hands and mouth on her flesh, of her own voice moaning.

"Yet this is more honest," she said. "In daylight, eyes open, but I would not make a bastard."

"I guarantee there will be no child."

He released her hands and slipped his own to her knees. Gently he pushed them apart and moved between her thighs. In spite of the barrier of the breeches, she felt open to him, exposed. The pulse quickened between her legs. She grasped his shoulders as he bent forward and kissed her. His palms slipped to her hips and settled under her jacket, holding firmly. His mouth was gentle, moving softly, teasing.

Urgency flared. She ran her fingers into his hair, holding him as she twisted her mouth beneath his, opening her lips, letting him explore as deeply as he would. His tongue met

hers, dancing over the tip until sweetness flooded like burst
honeycomb. At last, he drew back for breath, laughing,
golden—*a bonny man.*

"Let's get these damned clothes off," he said.

Muscles flexed beneath his shirt as he shrugged out of
his jacket and waistcoat and flung them aside. Then he
grasped her boy's jacket by the collar and peeled it off her
shoulders, momentarily pinning her arms behind her back.

"I like that," he said, grinning.

She followed his gaze. Beneath her shirt her breasts jutted forward, the erect nipples like buttons. As she looked
at them they rose to stand harder yet. Fire flushed over her
skin. "I don't understand," she said. "They do that when
cold—"

He smiled like a cat given cream. "*And* when hot?"

With a yank, her jacket followed his. He peeled off his
shirt. She let her eyes feast on the broad planes of his chest
and shoulders, the ridged belly, the small man's nipples as
hard as her own. His skin stretched firmly over his muscles.
He was beautiful. Achingly beautiful. She touched his
chest. It was warm and smooth, with a soft sprinkling of
hair, golden, springing under her palm. He tossed the shirt
across the room.

"Yes," he said. "Touch me." She looked at him. He
bent his head and kissed her wrist. "As you would like me
to touch you."

Tentatively she trailed a forefinger to his nipple. It rose
harder and she snatched away her hand. He leaned forward
and kissed her again on the mouth, running his hands up
her back, carrying her shirt with them. Cool air teased as
the fabric tugged from her waistband. He broke the kiss.
The shirt pulled over her head, leaving her naked, like him,
from the waist up.

His hands lay lightly on her shoulders, holding her still
as he looked at her. He held her braced backward so her
breasts thrust up, entirely exposed to him. They felt heavy,
distended, surging up and down with her breathing. The
nipples were swollen and dark, jutting hard. Heat pulsed
and coursed in every vein. Yet he held her still and looked.

His green gaze was as calm as a summer ocean, and as deep.

Catriona bit her lip. As she watched her own breasts rise and fall, she saw the throbbing in the front of his breeches. He followed her gaze and watched, too. The moment stretched as if they both pulsed in rhythm: the silent, private song of the body.

Together they looked up. She knew she was blushing, fiercely, hotly. His smile had become secretive, impossible to read. Then slowly his hands slipped down. Down over her shoulders, over the upper swell of her breasts. His palms slid gently over the outer curves, his knuckles brushing the inside of her arms, until he held each breast cupped. Still gazing straight into her eyes, he moved his thumbs forward. Spikes of fire concentrated. A fierce, sweet pleasure, overwhelming in intensity. She gasped and groaned aloud, gripping his shoulders.

"You are lovely, Catriona," he said quietly. "Your veins dance like little fish."

The groan became a sob as he moved his thumbs again. An exquisite intensity of sensation. It built and built, radiating, sending shards of fire into her belly and her swollen, aching groin. He raised each breast as if weighing it, while his thumbs continued their tantalizing dance. The vehement throb between her legs pulsed harder, darker. She closed her knees against his hips, pulling him closer. He let go as her breasts crushed into his bare chest. She dropped her head on his shoulder, with a little half laugh.

"Och, you did not lie," she said.

He raised one hand to stroke her hair. "About the fish?"

"Not that, not that." She rocked back, so her breasts sprang free again, the hair on his chest tickling madly on their sensitized tips.

He rolled her left nipple between thumb and forefinger, pinching slightly.

"But that I know how to do this?" His voice was ragged.

The sensations peaked. "That! That! Och, you will—" She gasped and cried out as he did it to the other breast. "How many women have taught you?"

"Enough," he said, smiling. "They taught me this, too."

He dropped his head. His tongue swirled over her heated flesh. His lips nibbled and sucked, dancing to the tips then away again. Suddenly he took her right nipple completely into his mouth and suckled. He pulled and rolled the other, until the heat and throbbing between her legs flared white-hot. The melting began so deep she couldn't fathom it, but something in her soul melted, ringing with the wild rhythm of storm waves roaring up beneath sea cliffs and exploding in a cave. From that white-hot center the explosion roared through her, convulsing in exquisite pleasure. She fell forward into his arms, sobbing.

He picked her up as if she were dry straw and placed her on the bed. Rapidly he pulled off his boots, breeches, and smallclothes, then turned back to her, naked. Sweat finely beaded his chest and hairline. His erection jutted. His man's balls had pulled up so tight into his body they seemed a single round weight. As lovely as a god, he knelt on the bed beside her and kissed her eyelids, before taking her mouth again with his. Her lips caught fire, swelling. As he kissed her he tugged away what remained of her clothes.

Frantically she helped him, kicking off her shoes, lifting her hips as he wrenched off the breeches and linen underdrawers. At last, as naked as he, burning at her own boldness, she reached with one hand and caught his *bod* in her palm, smoothing the soft skin over the head.

He broke the kiss and reared up, head tipped back, eyes closed, as she tentatively stroked the shaft.

"It feels—" She broke off, confused, looking for words.

He opened his eyes and grinned at her. "Yes?"

"You like that?"

"Oh, yes!"

"It feels very strange," she said at last, unable to describe her awe at that hardness and velvet, the shape and weight of him, the alien maleness.

"It feels," he said, moving his own hand to guide hers, "wonderful." His shaft throbbed in her palm. At last he sucked in a torn breath. "Too wonderful. I want to share that wonder with you."

She was pinned to the bed. He stroked her body—long, tender caresses—until every muscle surrendered, until she lay soft and abandoned. Then his fingers rubbed gently over her downy nest of hair, concentrating her attention once again on that white-hot center. When his mouth followed, she cried out.

Naked and helpless, she was entirely in the power of a strong man—and this man had sent his innocent wife sobbing to her parents, in horror over his corruption. A shiver of cold ran beneath the flames, a spiral of apprehension mixed with her intensity of desire. Yet he fired her, bringing her to the ecstatic edge of delirium, then forcing her to plunge over into that dizzying free fall of rapture.

As his hard *bod* slid against her, she felt herself open to welcome him and the fear dissolved. This one time! This one time she would learn what it was to be a woman and hold nothing back. She had a rake for a teacher, a rake she would never see again. She was as safe as if they were both anonymous. This one time! Without consequences! Why deny anything?

He slipped inside easily. She concentrated, feeling him penetrate, deeper and deeper. The gentle, nudging pressure and stretching filled her with wonder. *I want to share that wonder with you.* Gently at first, he moved his hips against hers, until she responded, reaching to match his rhythm in long, slow strokes that fired ecstasy.

He lifted her in his arms as he rolled over, still joined to her, balancing her above him. She choked back her surprise and let him do it. With both hands on her hips he rocked her back and forth, so her hot woman's flesh pulsed up and down his shaft. She felt the deep, agonizing tickle and knew he held her there deliberately, on the edge of the precipice. Defiantly she worked to throw herself over again and did so. He laughed up at her, his eyes demon dark.

"How much," he panted, "do you want to experience?"

Catriona gazed down at him. She was trembling deep inside, weak with delight. "Everything! Is there more?"

"There is always more wickedness for lovers, if they both like, for fun. Turn around."

She began to move, but he held her down with both hands, still impaled. "You can turn around like this," he said softly.

Bravely, she did it, his shaft solid inside her hot flesh as she spiraled her body. He smoothed both hands over her bottom, stroking down with one finger to the heat where their bodies joined, then slipping the other hand over her belly to touch her moist flesh. The waves of pleasure raced and plunged, spiraling into a whirlpool of sensation.

"Ah, Catriona," he said. "It is fun, is it not, to be naughty? Shall we try more?"

He lifted her again, bodily, and set her before him on hands and knees. Still joined to her, he began to move in her once again, long and slow, while he rubbed his hands over her back and bottom, kneading. Weak with desire, she dropped her head onto the sheets so she was bent before him like a reed. She was totally unprotected now, her most intimate self helplessly displayed. Yet ripples of feeling flowed through her as he thrust. She moaned with the pleasure and heard him pant helplessly in rhythm. He was as defenseless, as carried away, as vulnerable as she!

With heart and soul she gave back to him, restraint abandoned, pulling with him, feeling the electric exchange from her most intimate self to his, like lightning sparking over the mountains. When the lightning gathered and struck, shudders overtook her. He exhaled helplessly, groaning. Yet he pulled back and the flood of his seed, like hot honey, washed onto her thigh. He bent forward to kiss her nape and wiped the moisture away with a fold of the sheet.

Only a rake, she thought madly, *could have controlled himself enough to prevent our making a child.*

Exhausted, she collapsed to the bed. He wrapped his arms about her, holding her close, her back nestled to his chest and his mouth against her hair. The ceiling reveled above them, leaves dancing with flowers, stylized lions lying down with curlicued, golden-horned lambs.

Ravished, she thought, wanting, insanely, to giggle.

"Ah, my love," he whispered in her ear. His voice was deep, purring. "I am yours forever."

She snuggled closer and pulled his arms tighter, feeling the long lines of his body tucked against her. "Och, you don't need to say such things. I don't want your flattery or your promises. I only wanted what we did. I liked it. Did you like it?"

He laughed, nuzzling her neck. "Oh, God. I liked it."

"But what," she asked sleepily, turning in his arms, "did you do with Harriet?"

"Little enough. I would not have danced such a dance with you, if you hadn't welcomed it. But then, you are unique in the world, Catriona."

She nestled into the crook of his arm, wrapped in his embrace, not caring if it was true or not. He reached with one hand and pulled the bedcovers over them. Her head neatly fit the curve of his shoulder. He held her completely enclosed.

"And now you will leave," she reminded him, valiantly shutting out the roar of dark wind rising in her soul. "Or break your word."

He kissed the top of her head. "And now I will leave."

There was a faint sound, a low rumble. Catriona stirred and flung out an arm. The rumble crystallized into a purr. Somewhere a cat murmured happiness. She moved her arm lazily. Small spurs of feathers pricked through from the mattress. She was warm. Her blood ran in sunny rivers of contentment. She opened her eyes and gazed at the ceiling. The bright colors ran together in a delirium of pleasure— her pleasure. The memory swirled in her like flames. Something thumped, soft and heavy.

Catriona sat up. Sunlight streamed in the open window. A large tabby cat on the windowsill looked at her from round green eyes, then leaped down to the floor.

"Well, puss. Where is he?"

She wrapped her arms about her knees as the cat jumped onto the bed to rub against her legs. Catriona ran her hand over its soft fur. Then, as the cat purred, she put her face to her knees and wept. He had left. She had demanded it. She wanted him gone. For the darkness ahead of her allowed no softness or sentiment, no place for a golden-haired Englishman who had a way with women.

The cat arched its back and leaped back to the floor.

"Are you offended, puss?" She rubbed her palm over her eyes. "By him or by me? Och, I don't weep often."

There was a dull click somewhere in the house, then a whirring of gears. The quiet shattered as a grandfather clock chimed the hour. One . . . two . . . three . . . four. *A Dhia!* Four o'clock! Had she slept away the whole day?

Catriona scrambled from the bed. Her clothes were folded neatly on a chair. On the table sat a jug of water and a washbasin. Near them lay a small bag. She lifted it. Coins. He had left money—and a folded sheet of paper. Deliberately she washed and dressed before reading it. Had he written a farewell? And was his message what he had promised when he had first challenged her in London?

Every day you will be besieged by a man who has a great deal more experience in the game than you do. I shall seduce you. You will fall in love and I shall break your heart. I guarantee it. What say you to that?

In love? Ah, she was a foolish, weak woman, after all! The cat curled itself into a ball and watched her with slitted eyes as she took up the paper. The long slanting sweeps of his pen formed only five sentences:

By the time you wake up, I shall have ridden ahead to Inverness.
Thus, as I promised, I shall not follow you.
In truth, I prefer to lead.
By sleeping so soundly you have allowed it.
Such is the price of the seventh sin: sloth.

Stunned, she read it twice, then tore the paper across and across until the shreds fell through her fingers to the floor. How could he? How *could* he? It was despicable. Her instinct in London had been correct. She should have taken out her little knife then and killed him.

In truth, I prefer to lead.

What the devil did he mean? If her heart had been in danger, even for a moment, he had just handed it back to her, whole and unscathed. *Fall in love?* She was as likely now to fall in love with Yarrow Fletcher!

Catriona thrust the money into her pocket. She was not too proud to take it. How did he plan to travel? If he hired horses in relays and rode through the long twilight, only stopping for the few hours of true darkness, he could theoretically move fast enough, but only if he took the longer road. The direct road, with its poor inns and steep climb over the Grampians, was sadly short of decent horses for hire. He would not find the roads, nor the accommodations, he had been used to in England. The public coaches were infrequent, and took three days and two nights on the road.

So how had he gone? How many hours' start did he have? The obstacles he would meet traveling into the Highlands would be there for her, too. Would he be in Inverness before her? Damn him! Would he find Andrew? And even if he tried, did he expect her to abandon her cause?

Inverness nestled against the south bank of a broad expanse of water, where the Beauly Firth narrowed before spilling into the Moray Firth and the North Sea. Dominic reined in his sorry mount and looked down at the town. The massed roofs, banked around a handful of spires, seemed almost forcefully French in appearance. In the rose glow of morning, the town shone salmon and pink, like a cluster of crab shells.

But this was not the tame countryside of France. Beyond the water the hills of Ross-shire swept away, rank upon rank, into a blue wilderness of mountains until the horizon merged with the sky. As if the rugged peaks spoke, an odd longing seized him by the throat. It was so unexpected, he immediately looked away again. Across the Firth gleamed the rich fields of the Black Isle. The long furrow of the Great Glen slashed away to his left. Behind him rose Drummossie Muir and the tragic battlefield of Culloden. This was Grant country.

During his Peninsular years, Dominic had known Colquhoun Grant, head of Wellington's intelligence. That brilliant mind and brave spirit had matured here. Somewhere east of Inverness lay the fine stone house where Colquhoun had grown up. To the north, the fertile glens and straths were home to Chisholms, Frasers, Rosses. And somewhere in those floating blue hills lay Glen Reulach, the Valley of Stars, ancestral home of the MacNorrins.

The guide who had given him all this information had just turned his pony and ridden away. With a wry smile, Dominic thought of his journey, hustled from farm to inn, over mountains and through streams, exchanging horses for ponies, ponies for nags, until he'd made the last stage on this run-down mare. He'd made similar journeys in Portugal and Spain—though here, so far north, the long twilight had allowed him to travel far into the night. So he had covered over one hundred and fifty miles in about twenty hours, even snatching a few hours of sleep in a friendly farmhouse on the way.

The one thing he had not allowed himself to think about was Catriona. Would she fly here, as he had done, on tracks and drove roads? If she did, she would have the advantage of him. She spoke the language.

Refusing to be denied, the memories flooded in. Her firm, young body—the taste and smell and feel of her—absorbing him into her warm flesh, encompassing him as if his entire body were a sexual organ, dissolving his very soul in ecstatic intensity.

The flush of heat and desire on her brow and breasts.

Her eyes bruised and dilated with passion.

Her swollen sex, milking him.

Her voice calling out in a tongue he didn't know.

He had brought her to her climax again and again, holding back his own, reveling in her pleasure. And in that superhuman effort of self-control, he had made sure he would not make a child.

The brown mane of the mare blurred. He rubbed one

hand over his face. In shock he wondered if he had been about to weep over a stubborn Scotswoman. Well, he could be equally stubborn. If she would find Andrew, she must come here. All roads to the north went through Inverness and across its old stone bridge with its seven arches. He surprised himself by laughing.

Seven deadly sins, seven arches.

How did a man make up for years of sin to win the virtuous heart of a woman? It had been the question of his life, but now he really meant it. An unpleasantly fickle thought. His fierce determination to win back Harriet seemed the delusion of a madman. For God's sake, if he had succeeded, how the hell would he and Harriet ever have made a marriage? Had all his anguish been only bruised pride? Couldn't he bear it that Harriet—of all women—had rejected him?

Dominic pressed his heels into the mare's insensitive sides and rode down into Inverness. There he found the right inn, hot water, hot food, and a boy he could pay to watch the bridge and the roads for him while he slept.

She traveled almost exactly in his footsteps. To her fury, the farmwives chattered of the big, blond-headed Englishman riding so boldly through the Grampians, like a hero of one of their own tales.

"A braw man," said one. "Gey bonny for a Sassenach."

"Nach ann aige a tha a' bhodhaig," the old woman in the corner added. "What a handsome body he has!"

The gold he had given her paid her way. Because she was at least four or five hours behind him, dark caught her out in the hills. She rolled in a blanket under a rock and snatched a handful of hours of ragged sleep. As soon as dawn came, she climbed back on her pony and rode on with the man she had paid to accompany her. Yet the pace exhausted her. For miles she let her pony walk, furious that it lost her time, yet knowing her strength was almost at an end.

She came down into Inverness in the early evening. The streets were busy. She rode her pony past the throngs out to enjoy the sweet air of the gloaming. To travel any farther would kill her. The people blurred as she came into the yard of the main inn. Laughter swelled as the door swung open for a moment. Some laird entertaining friends, no doubt. She swung down from her garran and stumbled, her head as heavy as lead.

"You look pickled," he said behind her, "like a herring. Come, there's nothing left now to be gained by bravery. Let me take care of you."

Catriona stood on the filthy cobbles and burst into tears.

Dominic carried her into the inn and up to his room, where he sat her on a small couch. He rang the bell for hot water. It was delivered immediately and poured into a bath.

"You are also almost as salty." He was testing the water after the servants had left. "Though the tang of the stable adds a refreshing piquancy."

He tugged off her boots and stripped off her boy's clothes. He lifted her without effort and put her in the tub. She didn't care that she was naked while he was fully clothed. She didn't care if this was somehow even more intimate than his lovemaking, though he scrubbed her back and limbs almost impersonally, without lust. She only knew it felt wonderful, like sun on her face after a rainstorm, and she no longer had the energy to object.

"Drop your head in the water. If I don't wash your hair, you'll get lice."

"I shall *not* get lice," she said then, rankled. "I just washed my hair."

One hand rubbed gently over her head. "That was an infinity of mountains ago, sweetheart. Those things in your hair may be springs of heather, but I don't want them in my bed."

"I shall not sleep in your bed."

"Yes, you will. Alone, if you like."

Defeated by exhaustion, she leaned her head back and let him massage soap into her hair. His fingers felt deft and certain, banishing the leaden headache. He poured clean water from a pitcher to rinse away the soap, then wrapped her head in a towel and rubbed. She felt like a kitten being bathed by its mother, pushed this way and that with a rough forbearance. In spite of her misgivings, she wanted to purr.

"There." He pulled off the towel and combed her damp hair back over her ears. "Almost human. Now you will eat soup, then sleep like a babe."

"Are you like this with all your mistresses?"

"My mistresses usually greet me already bathed, and certainly not with sprigs of wood in their coiffures." He rang the bell again. "They are *never* in need of soup."

She yawned. It felt huge, childlike, so she tried to stifle it. She looked up at him. "Och, then they're sorry creatures who subsist on air and weak tea. I'd like oatmeal and kippers for my breakfast, please. Perhaps you could order it?"

"Your wish is my command, ma'am. But soup first."

He helped her from the tub and dried her before wrapping her in a large, soft robe. When the inn servant knocked at the door, Dominic stepped out into the hallway for a moment. He came back with a bowl.

Because it was there, perhaps even because he had thought of it, she ate the soup. He sat in a chair and watched her in silence. What thoughts ran in the head of this crazy man? What did he really want, after all? Not just sex. He could have that with any of a thousand women, with a lot less trouble than he was taking with her. An answer to a challenge? A sop to pride? And why was she glad, after all, that he was here?

What a handsome body he has.

With that thought, the empty soup bowl slipped from her fingers. Vaguely, she heard it rattle on the floorboards.

∽

She awoke to the scent of hot bread and kippers. She was in the bed, alone.

"I shan't make it easy for you." His voice was lazy and sunny, like bees among heather. "But I will tell you this:

last night I tucked you between the sheets like an innocent slice of cheese in a bun.''

Catriona sat up, clutching the pillow to her breasts, and looked at him. Fully dressed, he was eating breakfast at the small table by the window. Something in his confidence unnerved her.

"You will not make it easy for *me*?" she said. "It is you who tricked me. *You* deserve punishment."

"I had my punishment last night. I slept on the couch." He grimaced slightly as he pulled apart his smoked fish with a fork. "And now I'm eating salted leather."

She laughed. "Then you ordered kippers, so you are in a generous mood. How will you not make it easy for me?"

He glanced up and grinned. "I'd have preferred to wake up this morning with you in my arms, your legs entwined with mine, and your hand on my sex."

"Ah. That does make it hard."

He almost choked. "Did you mean that as a pun?"

Color, absurdly, flooded her face. "Och, does it matter? What do you intend now? Now you deceived me in Edinburgh? Now you have shown both your carnality and your restraint?"

"My carnality?" He raised a brow. "We've established we're great lovers, Catriona. Lovers may quarrel, or pout, or play games, but they sleep together. From now on we sleep together. In order to do that, we travel together. Your adventure is my adventure—for now, at least, or until it is naturally over. Do you agree?"

"As we go north, people will know me. People in Inverness know me. Do I tell them all you're my lover?"

"You can remain my brother, if you like, for we don't travel north. Andrew's nurse hasn't taken him to Sutherland. She's gone west. Mrs. Mackay has a sister who married a Chisholm."

In shock, Catriona dropped the pillow. His gaze immediately riveted to her bare breasts. Not caring, she climbed from the bed and slipped into the robe. He dropped his eyes and poured tea for her.

Catriona took the cup and sat down opposite him at the

small table. "How do you know?" Ignoring her, he forked up a mouthful of kippers and chewed them. "*A Mhuire!* You crazy man! How do you know?"

He swallowed. "These kippers taste better than they look. She left me a message."

"A *message*!"

Sunlight gleamed on his blond hair as he leaned back, grinning. "Eat your breakfast. You gave me her address in London. I sent Mrs. Mackay money and persuasive instructions. The danger was always there that Rutley might get wind of our quest and try to seize the child. I told her to use her own discretion if she felt it politic to flee Edinburgh, but to leave me a message here if she did so."

"Here?"

"It wasn't hard to get the name of the best inn in Inverness."

Fury exploded from her. She leaped up and cursed him volubly in Gaelic before remembering he wouldn't understand a word—and worse, that he couldn't understand what a disaster this was. What little Andrew faced here in these mountains had nothing at all to do with him—an English popinjay—and she had tried, with every ounce of courage and determination she possessed, to save him from the distress of it. But if he was determined to involve himself, then so be it. At least, perhaps, he could carry witness back to London. Not that any of the witness, nor the supplications, nor the protests, had slowed the catastrophe happening in the glens.

Finally she sat down again. "Then in Edinburgh you already knew where Andrew had gone."

"No, I did not. I only knew there might be a message here. Yet I couldn't be sure Mrs. Mackay would trust me that far. Fortunately she was charmed by my literary style. Now I know where he's been taken. That's all."

"*A Dhia!* Why didn't you tell me?"

"Why the devil should I? You've told me nothing of what's really troubling you. Nothing of why Andrew's inheritance is so damned critical. You like to use me, Ca-

triona, but you don't trust me. I have accepted it. But why
the hell should I give my trust to you?''

"Och, you shouldn't! When could there ever be trust
between the Scots and the English? Go home!''

"I can't go home," he said. "We're lovers. Remember?''

Twelve

AN HOUR LATER they rode together over the toll bridge with the seven arches. Dominic had hired two stout Highland ponies at the inn. Women were washing clothes in the River Ness as they crossed it, laughing with each other, skirts hiked up above plump knees. Ladies and gentlemen strolled along broad stone walkways nearby. Some wore Highland dress, some the height of English fashion. Here and there Dominic noticed interesting combinations of the two. It all seemed prosperous and peaceful, with an unfamiliar depth of social tolerance, rich and poor mingling with apparent ease.

Only Catriona was not easy, her back rigid as she rode. Dominic watched and remembered that spine fluid, supple, bending beneath his hands. She wore a simple blue dress, claiming she could not appear as a boy among her own people. Displaying the white hem of her petticoat, she rode astride. Highland leather shoes over heavy wool stockings encased her feet. So she wouldn't be recognized by anyone who knew her, she wore a red shawl over her head. She enthralled him.

In a few hours she was leading the way along the banks of the River Beauly. The shallow water ran peat brown between its pebble banks. Rich fields filled the broad valley and the road passed through a series of small townships.

Yet it was not the tame landscape of England. Wooded mountain flanks folded down from the heights above Kilmorack. The roar of falls echoed from tumbling water nearby. They were heading into Chisholm and Fraser country.

He could almost feel her intense concentration. Dominic wanted to caress away her anxiety and sorrow, but he knew no way to reach her. He only knew they were riding closer and closer to something that distressed her and that to voice or act on his desire now would be the action of a blackguard.

"What do these hills mean to you?" he asked.

She stared straight ahead. "Longing."

"For what?"

The shawl dropped from her head. Sunlight spun copper and gloss in her hair.

"Not *for* anything. That's not even the right word. There's no real equivalent in English. It's the longing that's still with you, even though what you long for is in your hand. It's the longing for Tir-nan-Og, the mystical place beyond the setting sun, though we live already in the light of our own glen. It's that longing sweetly colored with melancholy, as if a drift of birdsong brought back a mother's lullaby half heard by a drowsy child—a longing for the things that already are, but can never quite fulfill the heart. You would not understand."

"I understand," he said. "It is, perhaps, how I longed for Harriet."

"But she left you," Catriona said. "You did not hold her in your hand. You were in love with a fantasy."

"Exactly."

She did not reply, so they rode on in silence. The roadside was thick with bluebells, violets, red campion. Broom blossomed bright lemon yellow on branches of deepest green. The tracery of trees along the river veiled stark red-and-gray cliffs. The colors leaped, more vivid than in England.

They stopped now and then at houses along the road, where she talked urgently in Gaelic with the people, mostly women and children. The children peeked shyly, but the women looked at him with suspicion, even resentment. Where two streams ran together they took the left-hand fork along the River Glass. Dominic focused his attention entirely on Catriona. What did she fear so intensely? And why was that fear mixed with such burning rage?

"We can eat soon," she said suddenly. "Any of the people will give us bread and cheese. I'd rather not stop at the Inn of Cannich, where someone could ask after us later."

He nodded acquiescence, though he doubted anyone would follow them into these remote glens. She led the way up a narrow track toward a lone house crouched against the hillside. Low-roofed byres stood beside it. Chickens cackled, scratching about in the dirt. A broad vegetable patch flourished near the front door. Flowers grew gaily among the carrots and potatoes. Dominic tied the ponies and looked at the stunning view across the glen as Catriona knocked on the door. A woman came out, spoke briefly, then beckoned them both inside.

Dominic ducked his head to step over the threshold. As his eyes adjusted to the dim light, a man rose from his seat by the fireplace and held out his hand. The man's eyes were bright blue, shining like periwinkles beneath thick white eyebrows. He was wearing a red-and-green kilt and black hose, but his blue waistcoat was cut from simple homemade stuff. It was impossible to guess his age. His hair was completely silver, yet he was vigorous and upright.

"Welcome to Strathglass, sir," he said in perfect English. "You will eat with us and take a wee dram?"

To his shame, Dominic knew he stared about him in amazement. He didn't know what he'd expected. From the outside the house had looked very much like a hovel. The walls were turf and rock, the thatch heather. Smoke curled from an open peat fire. Yet the simple room was neatly, even finely furnished. A dresser held ornate china and glassware, yet open shelves ran around the walls. On one side they held cheeses and kitchen tools; on the other, leather-bound books.

"You admire Latin poetry?" the old man asked in his soft, polite voice. "Perhaps you have read these?"

Not knowing quite what was happening, Dominic found himself sitting opposite Alexander Chisholm, sipping some very potent whisky and discussing the finer points of Catullus. Mr. Chisholm was both perceptive and well read. Dominic remembered some Highland soldiers who had once boarded with him in Plymouth for the Peninsula. They had sold their rations of grog for money to buy books.

The whisky and companionship wove a mellow spell in the dimly lit room. On campaign, Highland officers had always offered him excellent company, but they were usually the sons of landowning families with great houses. Why should he be surprised to find the same courtesy and culture in this remote glen? He asked Mr. Chisholm about Highland poetry and listened with real interest to the answers, entranced as the old man illustrated in Gaelic, his voice as liquid as a waterfall, then slipped easily to an English translation. *Our Highland songs are of wild things, the sea, and the heather. We don't joke about sin.*

Meanwhile Catriona talked earnestly in Gaelic with the woman, apparently Alexander's daughter.

"Och-òn," he heard her whisper once. *"Mo léireadh!"*

Dominic didn't know what it meant, but he knew it was a cry from the heart. His mellow mood shattered. Though he kept his concern from his host, poetry suddenly seemed of very little importance.

Yet an hour later, his belly full of excellent bread and cheese and his head singing from the whisky and words, Dominic rode on up the glen. He felt slightly bemused by Mr. Chisholm, a small tenant who was so completely a gentleman. Nothing like it had ever happened to him in England. Whenever he was invited into a tenant's house on his brother's estates, it was to bowing and scraping—a deference sometimes transformed into resentment when those humble men became soldiers.

Yet Alexander Chisholm had the dignity of a lord. It was impossible to imagine such a man tugging his forelock. Dominic realized with a small shock that more than their language had made the Highland regiments keep to themselves, and more than family pride had kept them aloof from the crimes that invited flogging. He had entered a culture, it seemed, where every man was a gentleman, however poor, however simple. Furthermore, it was a culture that felt no dishonor in poverty or simplicity. So what had the woman told Catriona that had caused her to cry out in such soul-wrenching anguish?

Catriona urged her pony to a fast trot. The landscape had opened out into rolling foothills. The great bulk of granite-topped peaks rose above them. There was a clear distinction between the cleared, planted valleys, bright green with new growth, and the rough pastures of the hills above, mantled in folds until snowcapped rock reached up to kiss the blue sky. The air was sharp. Airy birches and rowans clustered by foaming rills of white water. Scots pine clustered on the hillsides. An eagle shrieked. He saw a flash of gold on its wings as it turned against the sun.

"Foxes and eagles for the lambs!" Catriona said bitterly.

Her pony broke into a canter. They were following a track up a side glen now, heading—or so he assumed—for the township where Mrs. Mackay had taken Andrew. The beauty of the country broke over him like an ocean wave, making him breathless. He was more than a little foxed.

"How much further?" he asked as they rounded a hillock and came into a broad, sheltered crook in the hills. The peaks of the mountains rose rank upon rank above a small loch. Rocky reflections shimmered into fathomless depths. The silence was so profound it seemed crystalline, like glass.

"Here," Catriona said. Her voice broke. "Here!"

There was a small shift in the breeze. The smell of burning assaulted his nostrils. He looked away from the mountains. Spirals of smoke swam lazily in the summer air. The valley smoldered. With intense shock, he realized he was looking at ruined walls, their turf burning slowly. Not just one house, but an entire township, scattered along the glen, lay grotesquely broken. Homes, barns, kilns, garden walls, had all been torn down and set on fire.

A handful of crows rose flapping and croaking.

Catriona swung from her pony. She walked, head high, through the trampled remains of a vegetable patch into a tumble of stones and smoking peat. She turned to face Dominic. Wisps of gray smoke wreathed about her. Her cheeks streamed with tears.

"Here," she said again, waving both hands. "This is where Mrs. Mackay brought Andrew. But they have burned it."

Dominic stepped from his mount, stripped off its bridle, and left it to graze. He strode up to her and wrapped his arms about her shoulders. "Go ahead and cry," he said. "Whatever happened here, it warrants weeping."

He led her away at last to a pebble beach beside the loch, where he made her sit down. He took off his coat and wrapped it around her shoulders. With his handkerchief, dampened in the still water, he bathed her face. To get her to this pure spot, he had been forced to walk her through the ruins of gardens, the young cabbages trampled, the flowers smashed and destroyed. Crows squawked at him as they pecked at the remains of chickens, burned alive in their byre. Charred heaps of blackened straw had once been bee skeps. That profound, unnatural silence: no bees.

In Spain and Portugal, he had seen what armies roused to revenge or plunder could do to civilians. He had heard from Nigel what had happened when Napoleon invaded Russia. Man's inhumanity to man was something he thought he knew. But this seemed so incongruous and incredible Dominic was completely at a loss. It was peacetime, for God's sake, in Britain!

When he had helped Catriona over the last little wall, he had turned her head so she would not see the broken child's doll half-buried in the ruin, wooden arms and legs tossed awkwardly. The doll had stared at him from wide painted eyes, its chipped smile touchingly bright. Someone had flung it there and a horse had trampled it. What child had been carried weeping from this place, stripped not only of house and home, but of this small, well-loved friend?

He held Catriona steadily against his chest until the shudders subsided and her weeping stopped.

"You learned of this at Alexander Chisholm's house?" he asked gently at last.

She pulled away to sit upright. "His daughter told me—these people are all kin."

"Then he knew, too. Why did he say nothing of it to me?"

Her eyes were brilliantly blue in her tearstained face. "He would not have thought it polite to so trouble a guest."

The bright blue eyes under the white eyebrows. The gentle voice explaining poetry. And all the time the old man had knowledge of this? "Oh, God. Was anyone hurt here?"

Catriona shook her head. "Not this time. Yet two years ago, away north in Strathnaver, they burned William Chisholm's house with his wife's old mother inside. Her blankets were afire before she could be carried out. She died five days later."

"For God's sake, that's murder!" Dominic took a deep breath, fighting to control his surge of rage. "You're going to have to explain, Catriona. Who's doing the burning? Why?"

She stared out across the water. "The laird, or his factors."

"But Alexander told me Chisholms have lived in Strathglass more than five hundred years and their ancestors before them. It's their land, surely?"

"Their land?" She clenched her fists and her voice poured scorn. "And you English? In modern law this is all the land of the chief: *An Siosalach,* the Chisholm, William, the twenty-fourth of that name. It may once have belonged to the clansmen, but now they pay rent to the laird for their homes and farms. To them it is a gesture of respect. To him it's his income and there's not enough profit in it."

"Profit?"

"How do you suppose our Highland chiefs can afford to

live in London and dance the Strathspey in a Mayfair ball-room? Not from the rents of these farms. If instead he leases the whole strath to one tenant for sheep, he can command enough for luxury. The people are only in his way.''

He was incredulous. ''They can't pay enough rent?''

''Even when they offer more—and they would give their very souls to stay here in their own glens—the leases are sold away to Lowland herders and strangers. Sheep are less trouble to *An Siosalach* than caring about his people.''

''So entire townships are evicted and the houses burned? How long has this been going on?''

She picked up a handful of pebbles and threw them into the loch. From each small splash, ever-widening ripples ran out across the water, intersecting in intricate patterns. ''Since I was a child. It began here in Strathglass fifteen years ago, a little at a time. It is happening all over the Highlands: Gunns in Kildonan; Mackays in Strathnaver; Macdonnells in Glengarry. When the land is wanted for sheep, there is nowhere to put the clans except on ships to America or New Holland.''

''Can they pay for their passage?''

She shook her head. ''There is not so much cash in the Highlands. The people must sign their liberty away and be indentured into slavery.''

''The slave trade was abolished nine years ago!'' It came out with such rage, Dominic forced himself to stop for a moment and regain control. ''But what the devil happens when the price of wool drops and the people are all gone? They can't be brought back from halfway across the world.''

''Even if they could,'' she said, standing up and watching the ripples run away across the water, ''who would dry all their tears?''

''Why don't the people fight back?''

''*Fight back?*'' She spun toward him. ''How? With what? The young men have gone to fight wars for King George. The lairds have the law, the church, and the sheriffs with their constables on their side. We live in scattered, small populations, divided by wild country. Should we organize into armed rebellion? We saw the results of that after the '45. Though Archibald Dhu Macdonnell holds out now in Kinlochnevis with his seven sons and the broadsword his grandfather carried at Culloden, the days of the broadsword are gone. There is no fighting back.''

Gunns, Mackays, Macdonnells. The names of men he had known and fought beside. He felt sick. ''So those Highlanders at Vimiero and Ciudad Rodrigo and Waterloo, the men wearing the kilt for their king in India, when they come home—if they come home—they return to this: their homes burned, their parents and sweethearts transported? Dear God!''

She gave way at last to unalloyed bitterness, her voice sour and ragged. ''A sweet return for their bravery and service! You English lead a merry enough life in London dancing attendance on your fat Prince Regent, but in the Far North these are times when the very ocean weeps for tragedy. In the end who can fight against his laird—the chief of his clan, father of his people? The men of the Highlands have had their hearts broken. They will wrap their pride about their sorrow like a plaid, and emigrate rather than beg the laird for the mercy he owes his children.''

What she described sounded almost feudal. Why should men owe loyalty where their trust wasn't returned?

He stood up and stared back at the drifting coils of smoke. ''When did this happen?''

''Five days ago. Some of the people have fled over the mountains to take shelter in Fraser country. Andrew might be there.''

''And this is why we must find him? You fear Rutley wants maximum profit, so Glen Reulach will be cleared next? Why the hell didn't you explain all this to me before? Bloody hell! I had no idea how much was at stake. If I had known, perhaps we could have reached Edinburgh in time.''

''There was no reason to think Andrew would be taken away, or that your enemy could reach Edinburgh before us.'' The wheeling arc of mountains and sky framed her

white face and red-rimmed eyes. "What is any of it to you?
You are shallow, a Casanova, concerned only with pleasure
and women. You wanted to win back your wife, a silly
woman with nothing in her head but sanctimoniousness.
When I first saw you, it was to find you drunk and half-
naked, flushed with winning an empty wager. If you think
to help me any further in this, I don't want it."

"You *should* want it. For the sake of Glen Reulach, you
should take help wherever you find it. Your damned courage looks a lot like stubbornness to me. That same bloody
pride is both the gift and the curse of the Highlands. I'm
here, Catriona. I know how to fight. Use me."

"It might look like stubbornness, but how else can I
sustain my heart? You would weaken me, undermine me,
when I alone must face the results of what happens here.
For you, it is just an episode, a diversion before you go
back to London. For me, it is my very soul." She turned
away and bit her lip. "Why must you haunt me and dog
my steps?"

He caught her arm and forced her to face him. "Do I
haunt you? Good. I would ride in your dreams and bedevil
your waking hours. I would wear you down until I break
through that cold, dark shell of hurt and sorrow. You can
fight for Glen Reulach and for Andrew, and still allow
yourself a little happiness whenever the chance comes. Do
you think all this doesn't sear my heart, too? The world
offers us enough tragedy, Catriona, without immolating
ourselves on its altar. And besides, I love you."

She gazed up at him, trembling. "Och, you madman!
You do not love me!"

"I love you, Catriona. And though you don't know it,
you love me. We are bound together by fate and we're
going over those bloody mountains together."

He walked away before he tried to kiss her. The ponies
looked up. He caught and bridled them, then led them back
to the loch.

"Which way?" he asked.

She swung onto her pony and pointed toward a low

trough in the peaks to their north. "That way. And it will get dark and cold enough before we are through."

Their path led away from the burned township, up into the heather-clad heights. In a tangle of cow tracks and bright green patches stabbed with bog cotton, it disappeared. It was getting late, yet the pearly twilight cast long, soft shadows. They were up in the high pastures where the people had once grazed their black cattle. The pastures were empty now, but the white tide was coming: Lowland sheep.

Dominic was furious. An any point on their journey he could have saved a few hours, even a day. Then perhaps he would have arrived at the house of the Souls of Charity in time. Had there been proof of Andrew's parentage among Harriet's things and had Yarrow Fletcher destroyed it? Yet Catriona had been too proud to tell him the extent of the threat. He had not known, until he had seen the smoldering ruins above Strathglass, what fate awaited her home, while she had carried this burden alone.

Rolled in blankets brought from Inverness, they snatched a few hours of sleep in the bracken. With the thick wool between them, he held her in his arms, sharing warmth but not passion. Her hair smelled of peat smoke and heather. Her bent spine fit snugly against his chest and belly. She was soft and curved, female.

Desire fit as perfectly, but it was banked by tenderness. Deliberately Dominic held that balance. Much as he wanted her body, he wanted her soul more. Yet if she turned to him, or asked him—even silently—it would be a bellows to his forge, and he would burn away her sorrow in a blaze of ardor. She did not ask. She slept like a child, exhausted. So he breathed in the salt-and-smoke of her hair, and wondered why the hell he had ever wanted to win Harriet back. Because his pride was as stubborn as Catriona's?

She awoke to the weight of his arm around her waist. For a moment, a weak moment, she wanted to turn to him. She wanted to feel his pulsing life inside her body, here in the lonely hills. He groaned in his sleep and tightened his arm. It was wet. Catriona pushed it aside and sat up. Their blankets and clothes were sodden. The ponies were dark ghosts in the mist. The bracken and heather dripped. Clouds had come down in the night while they slept. Apart from her own breathing and the snuffling of their mounts, the silence was more profound than the grave. She glanced back at Dominic. His green eyes studied her.

"We are wet, beloved," he said. "How far to Andrew?"

She looked away to hide the sudden burn of her skin. If only he would not gaze at her like that! "Not far. But in this mist we'll be lost."

"So we sit here in the damp like mushrooms?"

She stood up, knotting her skirts so the hem was well clear of the ground, and picked up her blanket. "You can sit in the damp any way you wish. I shall go on."

He laughed. "Then I shall come, too. I've been lost all my life. Don't think the threat of these mountains will turn me aside from my purpose."

"To pester me? So stand up and kiss me," she said. "And have done. It is too wet for anything else."

He threw back his head and roared. The sound burst and echoed in the mist, a man's laughter, heartfelt.

Catriona squatted down and cuffed his arm with the back of her hand. "What is it, Dominic Wyndham? What is so funny?"

He caught her hand and kissed it, his breath returning in whoops. "I made love once in a lake . . . once beneath a waterfall . . . and several times in a bathtub, which is warmer though less spectacular. It's never too wet, dear heart, nor too cold, nor too hot, for that matter. It's just that we can't take the time now for lovemaking when the child needs us. If I kiss you, I must make love to you. So no kisses. No kisses, except this one."

He kissed her hand again, then released it. Catriona snatched back her burning palm, folding her fingers over it. She stalked up to the ponies and pulled the saddles and bridles from the heather. They were wet. The ponies were wet. Moisture beaded her world like spray from a wet dog. The only warm, dry place lay in the center of her palm where his lips had touched.

They led the ponies, since the danger of stumbling into a bog was too great for riding. Studying the land as it wreathed in and out of the mist, the slightly greater brightness that must mark the hidden sun, Catriona went on. Veiled somewhere out there were the brindled peaks of An Riabhachan, Sgurr na Lapaich, Scor na Diollaid. She had been given directions by Alexander Chisholm's daughter. But this was not her own country, and what would be a few hours over familiar mountains could be days of wandering for strangers.

Dominic said nothing and made no complaint, though she led him in and out of streams and through endless wastes of heather. Her legs began to tire and her stomach growled. They were lost in a trackless wilderness. Catriona plunged down into the next small glen knowing she was miles from her goal.

"Devil take it!"

The curse burst from him, then there was silence.

She spun about and peered back through the shifting mists. His pony neighed, shrilly. Catriona tried to backtrack. Like a giant's kiss something slurped, the sound of a bog, sucking. The fog swirled and parted like shredding spiderwebs. Dominic and his pony were mired knee-deep in a deceptive green snare. The pony lurched. The bog swallowed Dominic to his thighs. He closed his hands over the pony's eyes and spoke to it. The animal stood quiet, nostrils distended. Tugging off his jacket, Dominic tied it over the pony's head, crooning softly in its ear. They were both slowly sinking deeper. Fear clutched at her throat.

"Alas, ma'am," he said, formally bowing his head. "I have fallen victim to Will o' the Wisp. The pony objects. Do we have any rope?"

"Stay still," she said. "We have blankets."

She pulled her rolled blanket off the back of her saddle

and slashed it into strips with her knife. Tying them together, she fashioned a makeshift rope. In a few more minutes she found a stone to tie to the end. She threw it with all her strength. Dominic caught it one-handed.

Catriona tied her end of the rope about her pony's shoulders. She looked back. He had untied the stone and fastened it to his own blanket rope, secured around the pony's belly. "No, tie the rope to yourself!"

He grinned at her. "Then how the hell would we get the pony out?"

"We can't! You led him to his doom. Tie the rope to yourself!"

The mist dropped again, so she couldn't see what he was doing. His voice sounded hollow. "Just keep it taut."

Catriona urged her pony to lean into the makeshift rope, dropped her face to its rough mane, and prayed. Foolish Englishman! Why had she let him come with her into these mountains? Even Highlanders died out here sometimes among the treacherous bogs and cliffs. The rope shook and jerked, and her pony skittered sideways. She slapped its rump, forcing it to lean forward again.

Slurping and sucking echoed, the monstrous sound of the kelpie rising from its watery lair. Mired in green plants and black muck, Dominic burst out of the mist.

He leaned forward, hands on knees, as he took several deep breaths, then he gazed up at her beneath his lashes. He held something in one hand. He was grinning. "Leander, they say, swam the Hellespont. Byron proved it could indeed be done. Now neither hero nor poet can lay claim to the world's greatest feat of watery endeavor." He straightened up and laughed. "Behold, the new champion. Let's get my poor beast out of there, shall we?"

She stared at him. Her heart was pounding. She felt flushed and unsure. His cravat and shirt were gone. Black strands of peat webbed over his filthy naked chest. Even his hair was wet and matted. From the waist down he was entirely black, enameled with peat and mud—magnificent and wild, like the statues of the satyrs in Lord Byron's garden. The flush mounted, flooding into her blood. *A bonny man!* She had known him, taken him into her flesh. Ah, that such a man should have been her first lover!

The pony in the bog whinnied. A shudder shook Catriona's mount as it whinnied back. Dominic turned. He jerked something. "Now!" he shouted to Catriona. "Drive your pony forward with everything you have!"

She slapped its rump hard, and heard sucking, popping sounds from the bog behind her. The pony pulled. Dominic pulled. He had some kind of white rope in his hands. The wet muscles of his back flexed, graceful as a shoal of fish. His pony came scrabbling out of the bog to stand trembling and shaking on the heather.

"Well, old fellow," Dominic said, patting its neck. "Your time hasn't come yet, after all."

She looped her pony's halter rope over a bush and walked back to him.

"So." Her legs were shaking. "You made string from your cravat to jerk your jacket from its eyes. You made another rope from your shirt to tie to its halter rope. And with both you and my pony pulling, you have rescued him. But now you must face these hills wet and without a shirt."

"I was already wet," he said.

"This rope making is a hobby of yours. You did it in London."

Ignoring the filthy state of both himself and his jacket, he shrugged his arms into its sleeves. "Which endeavor stunk almost as badly as this." He leaned forward and kissed the pony's nose.

She knew she was crying. Angrily she brushed away the tears. "And you can't think of anything better to do than kiss the pony? Och, you're a fool!"

"The pony," he said, grinning, "is simpler to kiss."

She turned away to untie the rope, longing for his hands at her waist and his mouth pressed onto hers. Longing for him to seize her, there in the heather, like the insatiable satyr. He did not. They went on into the duplicitous mist without touching, without speaking, because that was her choice, and now his.

When she saw the flames through the fog, her heart leaped in fear. Was it too late? Was the factor burning here, as well? Surely they were still too high in the hills? This could not be Strath Farrar!

"What is it?" Dominic asked softly in her ear.

"He might ask instead," a man's voice said in the other, "*who* is it?"

Shadows wavered. Shapes moved. Five men had come silently out of the mist to surround them. Blond men, probably brothers, tall and well made, though she couldn't clearly make out their faces. One of them held his knife to Dominic's back. They wore green-and-blue kilts, with their plaids wrapped over their shoulders, and beads of water like diamonds on their bonnets. Dominic was braced, as if he were about to drop and take on five men with his bare hands.

"*Leig leis falbh,*" she said quickly. As soon as she spoke in Gaelic, the blade dropped. "Let him leave, before you shed blood between you. He is English and was a soldier, but he has no interest in stills. *C' ainm a tha ort?*"

" '*S mise Daibhidh Friseal,*" said the man who had first spoken.

"Do you not know me, David Fraser? Will you not speak English also for the sake of my companion?"

"Catriona MacNorrin? What are you doing here?"

"I seek Margaret Mackay and a small child she has with her. They left the burned township above Strathglass some days ago. Is she in Strath Farrar?" She dropped back to Gaelic and explained, quickly and simply, about Andrew, and why she had an Englishman with her. It was close enough to the truth.

Dominic smiled at the man who had apparently been about to knife him. "Do you wish me to go? I have no eyes for anything that doesn't concern me and am remarkably deaf when required. But I'd be grateful for a guide, unless you wish to find my bleached bones in the heather at some later date."

The man's grin wavered out of the mist. "Och, you would seem, from the grand look of you, to have come close to being bleached bones already." He thrust out his hand. "Alan Fraser, Major Wyndham."

Dominic shook it. "Well met, Alan Fraser. Weren't you with the Seventy-ninth in the Peninsula?"

"And a grand memory on you for an English officer." He turned to David. "Major Wyndham is as safe as I am, Davie. If he'll give his word to it."

"You have my word of honor," Dominic said immediately. "I'll report nothing of what I may see here."

Alan shrugged apologetically. "It's the still, ye ken. The revenue officers would like to have it and knock us over the head for their trouble."

The flames danced, beckoning through the mist. A small hut, tucked into an overhang of rock, and a manufactory for the making of illicit whisky. Minutes later they were inside the warm, dry hut. The Frasers gave them oatcakes, soft cheese, and whisky. Three of them went back out to tend the still, leaving Catriona and Dominic with Alan and David Fraser.

Dominic dripped with shreds of the bog. He leaned back on his bench and sipped his glass. As she had seen him in front of a London church, his jacket lay open over his naked chest, his shirt sacrificed for a hill pony. His taut skin glowed beneath its mantle of mire.

"Your whisky washes silken over the tongue and flows down the throat like smooth fire," he said with a wry grin. "There must be a good legal market for it. Why is the still hidden up here like this?"

"It is the taxes upon it," David replied. "We cannot compete with the Lowland whisky, which is not taxed like ours. Your government in Whitehall, Major Wyndham, wants to reduce the Highlands to a deer run and see the clans become wraiths, nothing but legends for a romance."

"It's your government, too, Mr. Fraser," Dominic said.

Alan snorted. "Aye, as it was our army! No offense, Major, but there's no one in London with a care for the Highlands. Our fine Scots gentry have tipped arse over nose in their scramble to become more English than—I would say King Geordie, but he's German! It was keeping that fine, fat Hanoverian stock on the throne began our slow death at Culloden. It's a leisurely strangulation, rather than a swift stabbing, ye ken, so we whistle about our business with the noose on our necks and tell ourselves it's a neck-cloth.''

''And speaking of neckcloths—'' David glanced over his glass at Dominic. ''Ye're not quite dressed for the hills, Major. Ye need boots that let the water out, like mine.'' He thrust out his feet, demonstrating how his soft leather footwear was deliberately slashed. ''The wool stockings keep your feet warm, then the wet doesna matter. Ye should wear the kilt like us. Wet trews will ruin your legs. Ye'll tire from it and the eagles will pick your bones soon enough.''

''Are you trying, very politely, to say my breeches are beyond repair, Mr. Fraser?'' Dominic ruefully glanced down at his legs. ''That my fine boots are ruined? That I'm about to contract an inflammation of the lungs? Miss MacNorrin has turned her dress into a kilt of a kind. Should I do the same?''

''If you'd not be knifed in the dark for a revenue man, perhaps you should,'' Alan said. ''Our mother will give you clothes before you head for the hills.''

Catriona leaned forward. ''Why the hills? Are Mrs. Mackay and the bairn not in Strath Farrar?''

David rubbed his long nose apologetically. ''Ye've a long journey ahead of ye, lass. Margaret Mackay left right before the burning. Ye'll not find out where, for she didna say. But I ken this: she's not in Strath Farrar. And the wee laddie's disappeared with her.''

Thirteen

❧

WATER WEPT OVER the mountain peaks. Dominic watched it glisten. Far above, an eagle soared golden into the suddenly blue heavens. Something moved in his heart, a yearning. *It's that longing sweetly colored with melancholy, as if a drift of birdsong brought back a mother's lullaby half heard by a drowsy child—a longing for the things that already are, but can never quite fulfill the heart.*

It had just rained, but his feet were warm in thick woolen stockings. Soft leather shoes let water in and out with equal felicity. He wore a blue bonnet on his dry head. His own jacket had been washed and pressed, and sat easily over a fresh shirt. A wrap of plaid served as cover against either rain or sun. Beneath it he wore a deep navy kilt, flashed with green and brown. Fine stripes—white, then red— made a bright contrast. He was supremely comfortable, thanks to the ministrations of Mrs. Fraser, mother of five fine sons.

When the mist had lifted, Alan and David had taken him and Catriona down to their mother's turf house. It sat in a small glen, part of the far-flung estates of the MacNorrin, owing allegiance to Dunachan Castle—and so now part of the inheritance of small Thomas MacNorrin, who was controlled by his grandfather. Dominic relived the scene in his mind. Goats bleated and chickens cackled by the door. His

English was just as unintelligible to Mrs. Fraser, for she spoke only Gaelic. Yet she made him welcome with the courtly manners of a duchess. After he'd dipped in the loch to wash away the remains of the bog, she'd produced the kilt.

Catriona translated. "It was her husband's. She would be honored for you to take it."

"I'll pay, of course," Dominic replied.

"You will not! Take it! Later you can offer her a kindness, but she is pleased for you to have it. Alan has told her he remembers you from Spain. He said he owed you. Is that true?"

He didn't want to talk about it. "I suppose so."

"Och, this is typical, is it not? There was some heroism between you, but you'll not mention it to each other, only talk about whisky and weather, as embarrassed as children. She lost two other sons there. Take her gift with a glad heart."

The women stepped outside. Goat kids cavorted in a pen in the corner as Alan Fraser demonstrated how to wear the Highland dress. Dominic went out to show Catriona, waiting in the sunshine watching the chickens. Mrs. Fraser laughed and nodded, and said something in Gaelic.

"What did she say?" Dominic asked.

Catriona flushed a little. "She says you have the legs and bottom on you for the kilt."

He grinned at her. "What kind of legs and bottom is that?"

Mrs. Fraser smiled and said something else.

Catriona's flush deepened. "She says you have long, strong legs and a wee, tight bottom like two buns, if you must know, and a goodly flat belly. It makes the kilt swing right."

"I don't look too bad, then, for an Englishman?"

Alan Fraser ducked out of the doorway and laughed. "Ye'll pass for one of us, Major, as long as you keep your Sassenach tongue between your teeth."

Dominic walked up and down in front of the small turf house, enjoying the free swing of the fabric against his thighs. "So this is why you Highlanders can outmarch all the English regiments?" He took a deep breath of the clear, bright air, wondering what on earth he could give in return. "Is your mother happy here? Is there anything she would like?"

Alan spoke to Mrs. Fraser, then translated her reply. "My mother says she is as happy as any woman in Scotland. She's in need of nothing."

Dominic glanced back at the poor hut, with its stone floor and homespun rugs. "Surely there is something she would like, something from England?"

Alan asked his mother again. She shook her head, laughing. Her Gaelic sounded like poetry.

Her son translated. "She says she has the red deer and the roe, the hare and ptarmigan and grouse. Trout and salmon leap in the river, pike and char swim in the loch. Berries grow wild for the picking, and she has her bees, goats, chickens, and garden. Only salt and sugar are wanting here, and we have that from Inverness."

"I'll send sugar," Dominic said. "And tea? Perhaps she would like tea?"

"Tea would be a kindness, Major," Alan said politely. "But truly, my mother wants for nothing."

Wants for nothing. As long as she had her home and her family.

He stared up at the eagle. A people who wanted for nothing, because they had all this: the peaks, the rivers, the rowan dropping its red berries over the salmon runs, wild roses blooming freely—and song. It was an ongoing counterpoint to the rustle of birds and the sough of the wind in the pines: women singing as they went about their work, men singing as they marched after their cattle in the hills.

Music traveled with these Highlanders like a shadow. He had heard the skirl of the pipes leading them into battle, seen exhausted regiments leap up, ready to fight, at the first breath from their pipe major's chanter. Now he saw something else: a people with nothing measurable in material assets, who paid dancing masters to come to their townships and measured their wealth in poetry. Yet their way of life

was doomed, because of sheep. Because the lairds didn't
know true riches when they already had it. And the one
thing Mrs. Fraser really needed—security in her home—
was the one thing he couldn't give.

He and Catriona had been on Margaret Mackay's trail
for four days. The ponies had been left behind at Mrs. Fraser's, since most of the tracks up here were just as fast on
foot. They had stopped at every township, cast a net of
inquiry through the hills and glens. They had slept in byres
and bothies and the small huts built near the high summer
pastures in the mountains. They had been made welcome
and found advice and hospitality. Yet Mrs. Mackay and the
child had vanished, as if dissolved into mist.

As guests of the Highland families, they always slept
apart. Dominic grinned a little bitterly to himself, not sure
what else he had expected. He only knew he had been
wanting to make love to Catriona for four days.

"You told me Highlanders don't value chastity," he had
said when this arrangement had first been made clear.

She had looked down, a small duck of the head like a
child caught out in a falsehood. "I meant only the wise
tolerance there is for young people who don't quite wait
for their wedding. It is something else entirely to sin openly
in a stranger's home."

So four days, devil take it, of noble self-restraint!

There was a small scatter of loose rocks. Catriona walked
over the rim of the rocky basin where he was sitting. Her
blue dress was belted up so the hem wouldn't get wet,
showing her strong shins and slender ankles.

Immediately his body stirred for her.

He took a deep breath and looked away. It would have
been easy enough to seduce her again, wrap her in his plaid
and lay her down—beneath a rowan tree, in the mossy,
sheltered nook beside a waterfall, in the bracken. It would
have been easy enough to let her act on her desire for him,
for she couldn't hide it. But he wanted more than that. He
wanted more than the gifts of her body, more than a seduction. He wanted to pursue a courtship, and he thought

perhaps that might mean beginning all over again—if he only knew how!

Dominic leaned back, lay his head among the mosses and tiny starlike flowers, and cursed himself. In all the years he had enjoyed the favors of women, it was the one thing he had never learned. He knew how to seduce, he knew how to surrender to a woman's seduction, but he didn't know how to woo and win a woman's soul. Even though myriad women claimed to have given their hearts to him, he had never been the seeker, even with Harriet.

"What are you thinking?" Catriona asked as she came up.

"Of you," he said.

She dropped down to sit beside him, the sun slipping over her short dark hair and casting shadows on the translucent skin of her cheek. "Och, the dragon that breathes flame between us? What a spice it adds to our travels! Besides that."

"Of Harriet, then. Do you think often of your lost loves?"

Color rushed into her face. She gazed fiercely at the blue mountains. "When I come upon you suddenly, dressed like that, I think of them. And I think for an Englishman to wear the kilt makes something of a mockery of it."

"Am I so comical, then?"

The color deepened. "Not comical, no."

"Tell me about them, Catriona, the men you would have married."

She pulled her knees up to her breasts. "What is there to tell? I was young. They were each handsome and gallant. I lost my heart easily, as a girl does. Twice. Ian Grant was the first. I hardly remember him, but that he was tall and brown-haired. He did not come back, that was all. William Urquhart was the second."

"Did he come back?"

Her eyes echoed the vast blue sky. "He returned holding the pieces of himself together only by willpower. A cannonball had taken his left leg and arm both, but a carpenter had made him a contraption of crutches. After traveling all that way, he laid down and died by the waterfall in Glen Reulach. I found him there. But he had not come back for me. He had not wanted me to see him so mangled. He came back for the Highlands, because he wanted his body to die where he was born. His soul, he said, had already died in him in Spain.''

Dominic looked at the soaring peaks, the ineffable peace of the hills. There was no place he loved that much, was there? He could have lain down and died in Spain, Russia, or France with equal indifference. ''I'm sorry,'' he said.

She glanced at him and smiled. ''I wept for the sadness of it, and for him and his mother, but not so much for my loss. I liked him, but I had no real passion for him. He had a grand stone house and was a suitable match. I would have married him because he could give me a home here. I have never admitted that before now. Don't be sorry.''

He was stunned by her honesty. Was he capable of ever looking at his own emotions so clearly? ''I am sorry for his death, for all the bloody waste of war. And for all the women left without their sons or lovers.''

''Is death sad?'' Catriona asked. ''I thought so once, when I was afraid of it.''

''You are not afraid to die?''

She lifted both hands and shaded her eyes, gazing up at the peaks. In the northern corries winter snow still lay like a drape of white linen. ''Why? Because we think death comes as a stranger?''

''How else could it come?''

''I think death is an old companion, dancing silently next to us from the day we are born, like our shadows. We think them reflections of us. So they are, but one day, if you look closely, you'll notice your shadow carries a sickle over his shoulder. He's always been with you, but because you know him now for the Grim Reaper, you are suddenly afraid. Yet it is only the same shadow you played games with as a bairn, shrinking and stretching in the changes of light, an old friend. I keep my fear for other things.''

''For sorrow and for suffering?''

''If you like.''

"Or for being torn away from these mountains and everything here that you love? What will happen if we fail to find Andrew, or cannot prove he's the heir?"

"Then Glen Reulach will be cleared and the people put on ships for Canada. I shall go with them and I am afraid of it. I am afraid the heart will die within me. I am afraid I don't have the courage to face a new life away from these mountains. There, is that honest enough for you?"

"It stuns me," he said.

"So what frightens you? You are not afraid of death, are you, Dominic Wyndham?"

Afraid of death? He was more afraid of this: Catriona's fierce attachment to this land. He had not thought enough about any of it. He believed he loved her, but he had assumed he could take her to England. So why did he want to court her? Why didn't he just accept this as another interlude, like so many in the past? Shouldn't he take all the physical pleasure he could from it while it lasted?

Yet he groped for the same honesty—to give back that same gift. "It's too easy to say we don't fear death when we're not facing it. In battle, the Grim Reaper is a trusted enough companion. The men make macabre jokes about him, shrugging off dread. But at the moment death threatens, you discover the body has its own will to survive." He took her hand. "The horror that grips your belly then helps to keep you alive. But there are other things I fear more."

"What are they?"

She had not taken her hand away. He looked at it, strong and capable. "Confinement. I'm afraid to ever again be locked in a cellar. You might say I'm afraid, in a way, of the dark." He laughed. "Only the dark of closed, human spaces—never the dark of night and stars. So now you know my weakness. What a weapon I have given you to use against me, Catriona MacNorrin!"

"Is this why you climb steeples?" she asked.

"Among other things. I also had a wager to win." He stretched out, listening to the bees and the soft whisper of wind from the far-off ocean. He stroked her fingers, one by one, feeling the strength in the square white bones. "We're sorry creatures, Catriona, you and I. But you won't have to leave for Canada. We shall find this child and restore him to his inheritance."

He watched her face, but he couldn't read it. She held steadily on to his hand, clinging to him as if he could make good on his empty promises and restore her world into her hands, bright and undamaged, with the threat of Lowland sheep gone. The dishonesty of that twisted in his gut. Little Andrew had been nothing but a name to him from the beginning. This child he sought was as much a chimera as the child he had buried: half-formed in his mind, then lost.

She turned her head suddenly and looked at him, pulling her hand away. "We cannot find him if his nurse deliberately hides him. We must go where Mrs. Mackay can find us. We must go to Glen Reulach."

"She won't go there, surely? It's under Rutley's control."

A small blush colored her cheeks. "When my uncle died, the duke gave me a free lease on Dunachan for a year—that and an allowance. I am his grandson's cousin, after all. I can stay at the castle as if it's my own home still. Mrs. Mackay might send a message there."

He sat up. "For God's sake! You cling to poverty when you could be living at Dunachan like a lady?"

A frown crossed her face, almost like anger. "Do you think I would take his charity when he intends to turn all the people from their homes?"

Mrs. Fraser gave them shelter again that night. Of course, once again they slept apart. Catriona made a bed with Mrs. Fraser, and Dominic with the barley and oats stored in the byre. The Fraser sons were away, with either their cattle or their whisky trade. Their mother—if she knew—apparently wasn't telling.

After the women went to bed, Dominic lay in the straw with his plaid wrapped about him and stared up at the rafters. Livestock breathed warmly in the black night. This wasn't the dark he feared. Deliberately he forced his mind back to those days in Paris—chained in a cellar, then the pain of light bursting like fireworks into his dilated eyes. The light had meant only one thing: savage beatings. He had never admitted to anyone, except Catriona, how afraid he had been. Death may seem a welcome friend, but pain, deliberately inflicted—and the helpless waiting for it— wasn't so easy to fit into a calm philosophy.

There was a noise outside. The door swung open. Light flashed over his face. Dominic rolled instantly out of its beam and threw his weight at the legs of the man who appeared there. The lantern crashed to the flagstones outside and went out. The man fell heavily, arms and legs sprawling.

"It's myself, Major! Alan Fraser! Dinna thrash me with that cursed thrawcock!"

"Dear God, man!" Dominic gave Alan his hand and helped him to his feet. "You'll forgive me? I was half-asleep."

Alan retrieved the doused lantern and struck another light. "Then I wouldn't want to fight you awake!"

Dominic looked down at the odd implement in his hand—a short hooked stick with a carved wooden handle. At least he hadn't pulled either pistol or knife. In that half-drowsing moment, he could have killed the other man.

Alan hung the light from a hook, before turning to face Dominic again. "Did ye find the bairn?"

Dominic shook his head. "I wonder sometimes if I have dreamed him. I'm hunting a child I've never seen."

"Och, he's no dream. But if the wee laddie is in truth Sarah MacNorrin's bairn and the rightful laird, ye'd better hurry. I have news you won't like. In the name of his own lassie's son, Rutley has already sent notice to Glen Reulach. There's to be a new factor and the people's leases are being sold off to Lowlanders."

"Have evictions begun?" Dominic asked sharply.

Alan Fraser looked him in the face, his blue eyes dark with rage and sorrow. "They'll begin as soon as the new factor arrives. Ye'll ken his name, Major. I remember him well enough.''

The wooden handle snapped in his hands. Dominic looked down at the broken tool. He didn't even know what it was for, but it was carefully carved, the loving work of someone in the family. ''Bloody hell!'' He held out the two pieces of wood. ''I'm sorry about this. I'll send another to your mother. I'll send a dozen, for God's sake.''

''Bugger the thrawcock,'' Alan said. ''I'll make her a new one. It is only a thing for making rope.''

''If you need rope, I'll make that for her, too. The factor, Rutley's man. It's Yarrow Fletcher?''

Alan nodded. ''Ye guessed then. What will you do now?''

''Take Catriona back to Inverness. I won't let her see him burn Glen Reulach. Don't tell her of this, Alan, I beg of you.''

Alan Fraser raised one blond brow. ''Do ye think ye can keep her from it? Then you're a better man with the lassies than me!''

''Where does it stand in Glen Reulach now?''

''If the people don't leave on their own, they'll be forced out. Yarrow Fletcher will take a pleasure in it, I fear. He wouldn't be the first factor to set the flames with his own hands. But it will not start without him.''

''So there's a little time yet.''

''Och, I imagine. Time enough for you to sleep this night and for me to be away with my brothers where I belong.''

Dominic woke with the cock's crow and strode down to the loch. He tried not to think about how Catriona would look at this moment, tousled by sleep in the box bed in the cottage. Dawn broke so early here that ice still nipped in the air. Thick dew lay like sugar on the grass. Dropping his plaid, he waded into the dark water. Liquid ice closed over his head, then sprayed rainbows about him as he surfaced. Bright birches and rowan clustered at the water's edge and on little islands out in the loch. Another cock crowed, shouting up the day, boasting the glory of the air and mountains, a golden summer morning poised on the edge of time.

"I imagine," he said aloud to the far peaks, "that it's grim enough here in the winter."

The mountains smiled back silently, not denying it.

He turned and began to stroke fast across the loch. *Remember! Remember who you are!* All this was only an episode for him, unreal, a momentary bluster on a foreign stage. He had a life in London. A life of political clubs and theaters and scientific meetings, burgeoning with the vibrant energy of the new century. There was peace in these hills, but the throng and flurry of the city was part of his identity. Why the hell did he think he was in love with a woman who wanted nothing but this, and just this? An alien, rural past, frozen forever like a fly in amber?

When he reached the opposite shore of the loch, he strode naked out of the water and sat on a rock, looking back at the cultivated side of the valley. A group of children ran up the path toward Mrs. Fraser's house. They hesitated there for a moment like a flock of sparrows, then skipped on up the glen to the next farmstead. The buildings seemed tiny, huddled in their gardens, her home little more than a hut, the outbuildings wretched. Who would have thought there were clean chintz curtains inside and a wealth of books! And that an elderly lady's prize possession was the pair of spectacles that enabled her to read.

Yet Mrs. Fraser churned her cream by pounding some wooden contraption up and down in an open bucket, for God's sake. Dominic had a very hazy idea of how butter might be made in a modern dairy, but he was sure it was with something more efficient than that. She even made her own rope. With the state of the roads, it wasn't surprising the nineteenth century had barely penetrated the Highlands. Perhaps if the people learned a little modern husbandry, they wouldn't be losing their farms to sheep!

God, what a cruel thought! He dropped his wet head in his hands for a moment.

He had fallen in love with a stranger from a strange land. He could not live here with her, and she would never return to England with him. No future together was possible. Should they not at least share each present moment to the fullest? Why the devil had he thought he owed her a courtship he didn't know how to perform, when he knew she couldn't return it? Why not give her what she so plainly wanted—a skilled, libertine lover, someone to offer her physical pleasure and comfort for a while? A rake, practiced in abandonment, who would leave her free when she no longer needed him?

The clatter of hooves rang across the loch. Dominic looked up. As if he watched toys, he saw a woman in a blue dress take a saddled horse from the barn. She rode away at a canter: Catriona, disappearing down the glen. Mrs. Fraser watched from her house door before retreating back out of sight.

He dived into the water and began to swim, knowing with every stroke that he couldn't catch up, that he didn't know the way, and that Mrs. Fraser with her Gaelic tongue couldn't tell him.

Lungs bursting, limbs on fire, Dominic tore from the water at last, wrapped himself in his plaid, and ran to the house. Mrs. Fraser opened the door and smiled at him, indicating the hot porridge steaming on the hob.

"Where has she gone?" he shouted.

The woman shook her head and made a soft, crooning noise as if soothing a baby or a madman. Of course, she couldn't understand him and shouting wouldn't help. Dominic leaned forward, took both her hands in his, and kissed them.

He ran from the house after the children he'd seen disappearing up the glen. He caught up with them at last, grouped about an older man in a black suit who looked up with a strange glint in his eye at the sight of damp nakedness, wrapped in nothing but a plaid, bearing down on him.

"You speak English?" Dominic yelled.

"And Latin and French, sir," the man replied politely. "I am schoolmaster here. How may I help you?"

"I need someone to translate for me with Mrs. Fraser. It's urgent!"

The schoolmaster tapped one of the children on the head, a boy of about ten. "Go with the gentleman, Jamie, and show him your English."

The boy grinned shyly, but ran back down the path with Dominic. "Are you English, sir?" he asked.

"To my shame, Jamie, I am."

"It *is* a shame," Jamie said seriously. "Everyone knows we are better folk than the English, but to look at you, I'd have thought you a Highlander."

"To look at me, your schoolmaster thought I was touched," Dominic replied.

They arrived at Mrs. Fraser's house. Jamie translated. The children had brought fresher news than Alan had delivered last night: the new factor, the Englishman Fletcher, had arrived at Glen Reulach yesterday in his gig. A group of women had taken his horse by the bridle, pulled him from his seat, turned out his pockets, torn up the eviction notices, and sent him away with a flea in his ear. The women had done it laughing. But Yarrow Fletcher was going back this very day with soldiers.

Dominic dressed, then stoically ate the porridge as he listened to all this. He had learned on enough campaigns to take care of his body, if he didn't want it to let him down at the critical moment.

"What does Miss MacNorrin hope to achieve?" he asked grimly between mouthfuls.

Jamie gabbled away and Mrs. Fraser replied in Gaelic. The boy duly translated. "She says the soldiers will no' attack women. So they'll block the road at the bridge and no' let the soldiers pass. Miss MacNorrin will speak for them, many of the women not having the English."

"Where are their menfolk?"

The double translation seemed excruciatingly slow. "Away up in the hills after the cattle. Yarrow Fletcher said if any of the people's livestock are found on his master's land, the men will be fined and the cattle taken. So they must hide the animals until it's all over. But a few of the lads will wear their mothers' dresses and join the women. It'll be a grand show.''

And the lairds have the law, the church, and the sheriffs with their constables on their side.

It would not be a grand show. If he could not prevent it, there would probably be bloodshed. Catriona would be in the midst of it, a ringleader, an obvious target for Yarrow Fletcher's rage.

He thanked the boy and asked him to thank Mrs. Fraser. Then he took the other pony from the barn and saddled it.

"Do you know where Alan Fraser is this morning?" he asked.

The boy shook his head, then asked Mrs. Fraser, who shook hers.

"Then can you tell me how to get to Glen Reulach?"

"Och, it's no' far," Jamie said. "I can tell you."

⚭

Three hours later, Dominic knew himself thoroughly lost. Endless wastes of small lakes dappled a moor. Ranks of higher peaks stretched away as far as he could see, brindled with patches of snow and stark, gray rock. A small wind blew at the wispy bog cotton and the harebells, only to move away through the reeds clustered by the lochans. Nothing moved in the landscape but a flock of sheep, bunched on the horizon with three dogs at their heels. Dominic turned his pony and rode straight for them.

One of the dogs looked at him as he rode up, then it sat down and wagged its tail. Just coming up the hill behind the flock was a small, wiry man in a cloth cap. He was riding a rough pony. At the sight of Dominic, he drew up.

"Good day, sir," Dominic said.

"Are ye English, then?" The shepherd scratched his chin. "I'd no' have thought it!" His accent was broad Lowland Scots.

"We're both strangers, I think?" Dominic said. "Is that Glen Reulach below us?"

The shepherd looked. "That's no' it. It's awa' yonder."

Dominic followed the pointing finger. Far away in the blue valley a road ran alongside a river, then branched into two glens. The farther was apparently Glen Reulach. As Dominic stared into the haze he thought he saw a flash of red and the bright glint of metal, moving slowly along the road.

"Will the sheep run?" he asked.

"If I tell it to the dogs, they will." The Lowland shepherd spat into the heather. "But I'm no' telling it."

"Oh, but I think you are," Dominic replied. "I have a pistol in this pocket, primed and ready. I'm a very good shot."

The man spat again. "Are you, then?"

Dominic pulled out his double-barreled pistol. "What do you wager I can split that tallest reed over there? A fair shot, wouldn't you say?"

The shepherd's face crumpled. "I'm no' much of a wagering man, sir!"

The explosion echoed like thunder across the moor. The reed collapsed, neatly bisected.

"If you don't tell the dogs right now to run these sheep straight down the brae and into the valley, I will split you like the reed, from throat to balls. I've no mind to see those soldiers reach Glen Reulach bridge. As you'll have noticed, I'm a bit touched, but I was once a soldier. Or maybe I'm very touched indeed." He brought the pistol around to bear on the man's chest. "I don't mind killing you at all."

The man's face turned green. "Ye *are* touched! Ye're mad!"

"The truest statement you've made yet. Shall we go?"

The shepherd whistled to the dogs. Instantly they darted ahead of the sheep and turned them. He whistled again. With Dominic at his heels, the shepherd hurtled his pony down the slope as the sheep poured, bleating, in a white tide over the lip of the valley.

The surefooted ponies danced over the rocks and heather, tearing after the bellowing sheep. Dominic laughed as if he were riding to hounds. One of the dogs barked and looked back at its master.

"Get on!" the shepherd shouted. "We've a madman wi' a pistol at our backs!"

As they reached the valley floor the scene unfolded before him like a play. With their shawls over their heads, a group of women waited at a small stone bridge over one branch of the river. They stood with arms linked and they were singing in Gaelic, almost as if this were a party. In their center, her head bare and the sun shining on her short black curls, Catriona blazed like an upright blue flame. He couldn't see her face, but he guessed she was both triumphant and crying, with the salt tears running into her singing mouth. Catriona, who was not afraid of death.

From the right, a company of soldiers marched jangling in step, red coats like bright splashes of rowan berries against the green hills. They carried their muskets over their shoulders and their gear banging on their backs as they strutted. Merely boys, too young to disobey orders to fix bayonets and charge a group of women. Boys who'd be too confused and upset about losing status to ever let those women face them down.

At the rear of the militia rode one sheriff's officer, a red-faced man who looked slightly the worse for drink. And next to him, Yarrow Fletcher—in a neat black coat and astride a tall bay—rode with a small group of other men, constables and local gentry. They looked around at the sound of running hooves.

Dominic rode close on the heels of the shepherd, close enough to jerk his pistol into the man's back.

"Stop here!" he said.

The man pulled up his pony and stopped, breathing hard. They were sheltered by a small group of trees perched on an outcrop of rock. Fletcher could see the sheep, but not the shepherds.

"We'll stop here in this nice little covert, while you have the dogs put those sheep to the bridge and block it, or I'll have your balls for my next game of billiards!"

The shepherd's hands trembled on the reins. He tried to whistle and failed. The sheep poured in a mass with the dogs running after them. In moments they would be across the road and onto the banks on the other side.

"My throat's tae dry, sir! I canna whistle!"

Dominic thrust a bottle of Alan Fraser's best malt whisky at the man. "Drink this and whistle to those dogs, or it's the last liquor you'll ever taste!"

The Lowland shepherd gulped the whisky and whistled. The dogs raced, black-and-white streaks. The sheep stopped running to mill about, bleating piteously, in front of the bridge, before pouring in a flood of wool toward the waiting MacNorrin women.

Catriona shouted something, then laughed. The women laughed with her. They tore off their shawls and waved them. The sheep surged back. The dogs charged again, pushing them back onto the bridge until the animals made a dense, crying mass between the low stone walls. The river was running in spate. No group of foot militia would want to wade it, and the handful of horsemen would never risk riding alone into the torrent.

The officer rode up and tried to flog at the sheep with his whip. The women flapped their shawls. The sheep only packed tighter, bawling. The dogs sat down and waited.

The shepherd took another gulp of whisky. "They'll no' shoot my dogs, sir?"

"Not if you'll work with me to save them. Go ahead and drink all of that, if you like," Dominic said. "It's good stuff."

He left the bottle with the man and crept silently up behind the small outcrop of rock. The officer had ridden back and was conferring with Yarrow Fletcher. The soldiers stood stiffly, like marionettes, in the sun. Sweat glistened on their faces and ran down into their leather stocks. The officer rode back to the soldiers and barked an order. One of the men stepped forward, saluted, and leveled his musket.

Dominic slipped back down the rocks and tore the whisky from the shepherd's mouth. "Whistle the dogs! Now!"

With a roar the ball sped from the soldier's musket barrel, but the dogs moved instantly. The bullet tore harmlessly into the road, sending up a spurt of soil. The women backed up a little, allowing the sheep to surge toward them. Frantic bleating resounded in the glen like a cacophony of dowagers at a ball.

Grabbing the shepherd by his collar, Dominic dragged him up onto the rocks. "Those lads couldn't shoot Napoleon if he was spread-eagled on a barn for target practice. Keep your dogs safe, but keep those sheep on the bridge. And between whistles, we'll keep moving. I've no desire to be their next target, and if you value your hide you'll stick close to me."

It became a dance. The dogs moved in and out. The women played their part. Dominic and the shepherd moved from rocks to trees, always whistling to the dogs from a new spot. The soldiers began to mill about as helplessly as the sheep. The red-faced officer rode back and forth, swearing and cursing. His horse began to sweat and prance. He sent some of the soldiers out in pairs in the direction of the last whistle, but he was obviously afraid to break ranks and let the entire body disperse to hunt for the multitude of shepherds who haunted the hillsides.

"Good lad," Dominic said with a grin as he watched him. "Keep the men together, make square to receive cavalry. There's no soldiers in the world better trained than yours, but no militia ever outwitted Highlanders in their own territory."

"Ye're English," the shepherd said.

Dominic laughed at him.

Suddenly, with a crack of his whip, Yarrow Fletcher set his horse into a canter. With the gentry, he rode away down the valley. The officer shouted hoarsely at his men, and the soldiers turned about as if they were on a parade ground. Another rasping yell and they fell into step. Moments later they were marching back down the road and away from Glen Reulach.

"You're a good man," Dominic said kindly to the Lowland shepherd. "Get your bloody sheep and get out of here. What's left of the whisky is yours. Here's a little gold for your trouble and more if you'll swear never to tell a soul about this.''

"Och, I'll no' tell. I'd look a bloody fool. But what about you, sir?'' the man asked, slurring the words. ''Ye're no' mad at me any longer?''

"I was never mad at you.'' Dominic gave the man a friendly cuff on the shoulder. ''But I am very mad at someone else.''

He left the shepherd and went back to his waiting pony. He rode alone through the flock of sheep, now being herded back up the braes by the dogs.

The women began to walk away up the glen, but one of them stopped and turned to look over her shoulder.

She waited patiently as he rode up, her hands folded in front of her blue dress.

"You are as persistent as a merry wee worker bee,'' Catriona said. ''King George's red-coated fellows were just here, but left again. You're on the wrong side. As an officer of his, shouldn't you go home with them?''

Fourteen

HER HEART WAS pounding. It had been pounding ever since she'd seen the sheriff's officer riding up the glen alongside the boys with their muskets, and the gentry with their whips and pistols. The pulse of fear was even stronger now, still dread, but mixed with a deeper anguish—this desperate new secret she must keep from Dominic Wyndham, even though it broke her. When she had tried to drive him away, he wouldn't leave. Now she couldn't bear it if he left.

He stopped his pony and looked down. The Highland bonnet sat rakishly on his blond head. The crease beside his mouth was set, his dimples gouged in stone.

"The kilt may be fine for stalking in these hills," he said. "But it's the very devil for horsemanship." He slipped to the ground and tossed his plaid over his shoulder. Turning his back, he ran the stirrups up and loosened his pony's girth. "King George's red-coated fellows are no laughing matter. What the hell do you think you're playing at?"

"I am not playing," she said to his broad shoulders and the swaying plaid. Gilt ringed his hair where it grew a little long at the back. "Though I would let these women laugh while they may."

"Fletcher will be back. He'll bring cavalry, if he must."

"For that he must ask the Lord Advocate, who'll not trust his men to attack us. It'll all be delayed. They'll not be back for a week. And they will not attack women."

He spun back to her, the tartan flowing about him. "For God's sake, Catriona. I know this man."

"Then what do you suggest?"

He looked away up the glen. A muscle twitched in his jaw. "We shall go to Inverness and make a case at law for delay—until Andrew can be found. It's what I should have done to start with."

So he would not give up! *A Dhia!* But she was so afraid! The fear wrapped icy fingers about her heart, forging a ceaseless hammering in her chest. "There is no case at law," she said. "We have no proof who fathered the bairn."

His eyes were ice green. "Then we bluff it out. Chicanery, not fact, is the very marrow of legal practice. Lawyers sharpen their teeth every day on falsehoods. We get horses and we go now to Inverness."

Catriona breathed in the masculine certainty and barely contained rage. She knew he was angry. She knew he was determined, that he would do this—or try to do it—and that now there was no hope at all for success.

"You do not control me, nor speak for me, nor think for me," she said. "Go to Inverness. I shall stay here."

"To march out and face down the militia with an apron?" He seized her by the arms. "Catriona, this is madness. There's real powder in those muskets. If you cannot save these people's homes, then why risk their lives?"

She gazed up into his face, meeting his anger with her own. "You think the MacNorrin women would not fight for their homes unless I led them? How little you know of the Highlands!"

Golden stubble glinted on his chin. Gray specks marked the green eyes like lichen, like storms over water. "I've been trying to learn. I've being trying to understand your contradictions and your stubbornness. I've been trying to court you, for God's sake."

Distress burst in her. "I have no time for you, for your

courtship and your seductions. Go back to England!"

"If I fight for your cause, I stay with you," he said grimly. "Would you turn me away, hungry and unshaven?"

She pulled from his grip, desperate, wanting him gone. Yet wanting him to take her in his arms. Wanting the blind comfort of a man's body. *Comfort?* There was little enough comfort left now!

"Och, come then, if you insist. Come back to Dunachan and get a hot meal. You can have a horse tomorrow. Tonight the people hold a *céilidh* to celebrate turning Yarrow Fletcher away."

"A *kaylee*? What's that?"

"A gathering. A party. Do you think we are wedded to sorrow?"

"We? No. I don't think that of the Frasers, or Alexander Chisholm, or any of the others who have shared their hearths and homes with me this past week." He glanced once again at the high peaks where the rocks wept moisture into the heather. "Only you are wedded to sorrow, Catriona."

"My two uncles. Unable, either of them, to hold on to life."

Catriona had come into the room.

In the paneled great hall of Dunachan Keep, he'd been gazing at a portrait of a young man and a boy. Above the young man's lace and silver, the painted eyes stared back, startlingly blue. The boy sat on a pony. He, too, stared with eyes like the sea. Behind them, the red bulk of the castle pinned the folds of the hills at the edge of shimmering water, where three tributary valleys snaked down from the heights into Loch Reulach.

Dominic looked around and felt his breath catch. It burst over him with stunning unexpectedness: a flashing impression of her wide blue eyes, the white skin of her throat, her lush body—not pretty, but a startling, rare beauty. She was wearing an evening gown of deep blue silk, high-waisted to emphasize her breasts. Her dark curls, caught in a blue ribbon, were brushed away from her forehead. Her eyes seemed huge. He had never seen her in anything but the ill-fitting clothes of a servant. *At home, I have dresses for Inverness.* She had dressed for dinner. For him? Desire moved in him like an uncurling dragon.

The keep had been invisible from the bridge where he had driven the sheep. Five miles later, past Achnadrochaid, the first MacNorrin township, it had burst into view: a handful of fanciful turrets clinging to massive walls of red stone, a frivolous afterthought, as if butterflies had landed on a hammer. Around the castle lay formal gardens; beyond them the outbuildings, stables and barns, and a small church.

The young man in the painting wore a red-and-blue plaid. The tartan Calum MacNorrin had worn.

"Bonny lads," Catriona said. "My two uncles—in spite of the difference in age, brothers. The wee lad grew up to wed Rutley's daughter, Lady Mary. The older, of course, became the laird. You would think he could have left a bevy of lads to inherit Glen Reulach, but both my uncles married Englishwomen with weak tea in their veins."

"It is not the fault of the English that Highland lairds turn their people from their homes."

"It is English law stops the slave trade, yet allows this." Catriona walked away to stare up at another portrait, a woman in pink satin, her skirts billowing. "My great-grandmother. She was twenty-two when Bonnie Prince Charlie kissed her hand before Culloden. Scots fought each other then, too. Perhaps it has always been our curse. We have never been able to unify against a threat."

"Your grandmother supported the Pretender?"

Shadows enveloped her. "Privately. She died when I was little, shortly after my own mother died."

She was wraithlike in the blue silk, an echo of the dying day, as if burning grief made her insubstantial, as if she had given up hope. Why? What had happened to rob Catriona of confidence? What was she not telling him now?

Or did the castle suck the blood from her veins? He wanted to breathe life into her.

Instead he turned back to study the two boys. "Who raised you?"

Her head tilted as she looked at him. "My nurse. There is no portrait of her. Other than Magaidh, it was a very male household when I was little. My uncle the laird mourned his first wife a long time. He did not notice me much."

"But you had Calum?"

"Och, what does an older brother really know of the heart of his little sister?"

It was a rare truth. He knew how much she had loved her older brother, but had Calum been merely tolerant, careless of that little girl's worship? He had been a splendid officer and a good friend. He had spoken of his home with passion, but he had never mentioned his sister. Dominic knew with sudden insight that Calum's love for Catriona, though real, had been casually given.

"You said he taught you to fight."

She moved restlessly and the light changed on her dress. His impression of fragility vanished. "He did. But he spent more time with our younger uncle. Your brother was much older, too. Did you play together?"

"Me and Jack? No! But I had friends, other family."

"Yet you have no roots. You belong nowhere!" It burst from her with passionate distress.

"You were lonely?" It seemed a revelation.

"Lonely? All Highlanders are lonely. It's in our blood." Catriona turned away, like a doe that flees the hunter, yet she laughed. "Dinner is ready, and after it, the *céilidh*."

∽

Dunachan exploded in merriment. Fiddles. Pipes. Flashing, energetic dancing. A free flow of whisky and fine food. The women brought their children and their babies. They had dressed in their finery: silver buckles, red shawls, red-and-blue plaids, red ribbons in their hair, white shoes and stockings of cotton. There was laughing and drinking. Although few young men were there, the old stone fortress rang with humor and good-fellowship.

Dominic watched Catriona laugh as she danced with a lad of perhaps twelve or thirteen. Any discernible vestige of that deep grief had disappeared. He watched her talk and smile with the women and dandle the babies. He watched her with an ache like an iceberg in his heart. He had offered her dresses. Not one had been as lovely as her own blue silk. A deep blue like the skies above the mountains long after the lingering sunset, just before the few stars came out in the never-night of the Far North at midsummer.

The evening lengthened. The children began, one by one, to fall asleep. The dancing and the wild music subsided. An old man played a slow, lingering tune on a violin. The people began to settle in small heaps about the walls. A woman stood up by herself and silence dropped over them all, as if a blanket were tucked about a child. The woman walked into the space in the center of the room. The violin fell quiet.

The woman began to sing.

Dominic was the only person in the room who could not understand the words. Yet the Gaelic wept and sighed, reaching into his soul. Her voice echoed in some minor key, haunting, speaking of something he couldn't name that once he'd lost. He was flooded with longing, the painful, bewildered longing of a lost child or a dying soldier. To his shame he felt tears prick at his eyelids. *Our Highland songs are of wild things, the sea, and the heather.*

Catriona had come to sit behind him. She spoke softly in his ear. "They will take turns now, those who are gifted. With a tune or a story or a poem. As our guest, you should offer the same."

He glanced up at her, at the soft curve of her breast and the glimmer of moisture in her blue eyes. "I can't sing."

"Och, you sorry creature," she said. "Anyone with a soul can sing."

There was another song, then a story. The tale reduced the entire crowd to hilarity. The next song involved them all in a rollicking chorus. But the poem that followed made the women sigh, and the children still awake turned their heads into their mother's breasts at the sound of the soft Gaelic words.

Dominic glanced inquiringly at Catriona.

"The teller is Iseabail MacNorrin," she whispered. "She is ninety-three and has the second sight."

"The second sight?"

"Visions foretelling the future. It is a gift she has. She also tells us our past, and in English if she likes." Catriona's gaze rested fondly on the old woman. "Her son taught her the English, but she likes to keep that tongue for cursing."

"What is this poem about?"

"It is a tale of the beginning of things, before Adam. I can translate."

Catriona's voice feathered into his ear as Iseabail spun the verses. "I will tell you of the four great cities of the first clans of the sky, the deathless people: Gorias, the city of jewels sparkling in the east; Fabias, sleeping under its one star to the north; Finias, tall with its shining towers before its fields to the south; Murias, city of hidden gardens by the great ocean in the west."

Dominic bent his head, listening, acutely aware of her scent and the warmth of her breath at his ear. Aware that every word carried another unspoken message: *You and I belong to different worlds. We have nothing in common. Go away, you mad fool, and leave me be! Do not give me your heart, mad fool! Not your heart!*

"When Adam was born, a great sigh went up as the children of the sky melted away like froth on a wave. Adam sent Eve to see what she could find. In Gorias, Eve found a flame of fire. She hid it in her heart. In Finias, she found a spear of white light and hid it in her mind. In the gathering night of Fabias, she found a star. She hid the night, and the star within the night, in her womb. But at Murias, by the shore in the west, she lifted a wave of the ocean and hid it in her blood."

Dominic knew himself utterly the outsider. If anyone in

the room looked at him, would they see the lost boy or the
dying soldier in his eyes? He closed them as Catriona's
voice went on.

"When she came back, Eve gave Adam the flame from
Gorias, and the spear of white light from Finias. She told
him of the star from Fabias, and that she would share that
star and that darkness with him. But when he asked what
she had found at Murias, she said she'd found nothing, and
Adam believed her. Thus to the end of time the salt sea
moves secretly in the blood of the children of Eve, and the
troubled surf agitates in their hearts, making them restless
as the wave and doomed to longing."

"She lied to him?" Dominic whispered.

Her breath feathered softly. "Women have always lied
to men. Should she have given him everything and kept
nothing for herself?"

Iseabail's voice stopped and the people applauded.

"And now it is your turn." Catriona brushed her hand
over his shoulder, a little push, though fire trailed from her
fingers. "If you would have me come to you tonight."

Shock shivered through him as hot blood flooded his
loins. Whisky glowed in his veins, too much of that smoky,
smooth elixir to think clearly or to deny her now. He
dropped his head to hide the rush of desire, but it came out
in the raggedness of his voice. "Why tonight? Will you
have me burn away your restless longing? Dive into your
salt sea?" He glanced up at her and was moved to the soul
by the desperate, heroic need in her eyes. If his touch could
assuage any of that deep-seated grief, she should have it.
"If you come to me, I shall be honored to welcome you,"
he said.

He walked to the center of the room and bowed. The
whisky curled in his belly. The peaty taste of it warmed
his mouth. His mind was blank. He didn't sing. He knew
no stories. He was damnably foxed.

"I'm not sure—" he began. "Alas, I don't speak
Gaelic." But then it came to him, the one poem he knew
by heart, written by a friend of his. Turning to gaze directly
at Catriona, he began. " 'She walks in beauty, like the

night . . .' '' A poem of Byron's, another Scot.

The applause broke around his ears as he walked back to his seat. It was only later that he realized he had recited a poem about innocence.

He had been given a room in one of the turrets. The view over the loch to the mountains took away his breath. The sky was deeply, velvety blue black. In the deeper, blacker waters of the loch, the stars' reflections glimmered like diamonds. *In the gathering night of Fabias, she found a star. She hid the night, and the star within the night, in her womb.*

He had left one candle burning. Its flame flickered over the ribbed ceiling. The furnishings were heavy and dark, unchanged since the sixteenth century. Light danced over the backs of his hands, braced against the window embrasure. He was naked but for the dressing gown belted at his waist. Naked, waiting for his lover.

Dear God, if only he weren't so foxed! He couldn't think clearly. He couldn't tell what honor demanded. He only knew the fierce flame of desire. But she did not come to him tonight in joy. She came in sorrow. Was it fair, or wise, or honest to act on that? Was it kind, or noble, or compassionate not to? And how could he tell when his groin had already made its own judgment?

The glow wavered. Silk rustled. Someone stepped softly into the room and closed the door.

"So after our starved and virtuous travels, our days of noble chastity in the hills, you wish to be my lover again?" he asked over his shoulder. "Tonight? In this tower above the star-filled water?"

"I wish it."

He turned from the window. Catriona stood with her fists clenched at her sides. The white swell of her breasts rose and fell rapidly. Color concentrated in two bright spots on her cheeks. Her lips were white. He knew she had come to

him only by calling on that frantic bravery, as if she knew
he might refuse to be used as her paramour.

"I am very foxed, Catriona. I shan't stop once we begin."

"If we begin, there will be no stopping." Her voice
trembled.

"If you want my body tonight, then from now on you
must be my mistress, as other mistresses."

"What does that mean?"

"I will not be at your beck and call. You will be at
mine."

Her eyes dropped. Then she took a deep breath and
looked up at him. "As long as we are together, I shall not
refuse you. Yours can be the beckoning and I will come to
your call. Here is my only condition: when we are parted,
you will never seek me, never send for me. You will not
trick me again with clever words as you did in Edinburgh.
Do you agree?"

He was unprepared for his sudden spurt of anger.
"*Parted?* We ought to define our bargain, or you cannot
visit the privy without me!"

"One hundred miles, then," she said. "If you go more
than one hundred miles from me, or I from you, we are
parted."

Rage and grief surged in him, uncontrolled. "Then I will
not trick you again, for we shall never again be over one
hundred miles apart. Oh, damnation! Come here and kiss
me, Catriona, before we both weep."

She came straight into his arms and her open mouth met
his. The dragon roared. He forgot everything, every con-
straint, as he burned his lips onto hers. With both hands he
took the blue silk by the shoulders and tugged. Buttons tore
away as her dress slithered to the ground. He shrugged out
of his dressing gown so he stood nude before her, his cock
springing strongly between them, the tip rubbing exqui-
sitely on the slick fabric of her shift.

Without restraint, unable to be subtle any longer, he
plundered, but she kissed back with the same intensity, her
salt tears maddening on his tongue. His fingers reveled in

the silk of her skin, her shoulders, her upper arms. Maddeningly, the lace edge of her shift kept her body from his questing hands, so he ripped it away. Her naked breasts fell ripe into his eager palms. Ah, dear God! She was so lovely!

He wasn't aware how he had carried her to the bed or how he had torn away her corset. He only knew he must possess her absolutely, without hindrance. And yet somewhere a small voice cried a warning. *Which of them would be bound for eternity if nothing were held back this time? Whose heart would be lost forever? Which of them would live to regret this mad bargain?*

He reared back and looked at her, his sex throbbing, his entire being pooled there. She lay white against the white sheets, clad only in her white stockings. Her hair and eyes seemed startling in contrast, like a painting. Her puckered nipples and the darkly springing hair covering her sex set fires in his groin. He ran his hands over her silk-clad legs, the trim ankles, her dimpled knees.

"This is what I asked for when I met you." He heard the rasp in his own voice. "Your naked thigh, soft with promise . . . your body surrendered for my pleasure . . . and yours. Catriona, there are layers of passion beyond what we have explored. Will you let me lead you there?"

"Let me," she said, her eyes like night with a star hidden in the darkness. "Let me know you as you have known me."

The ardor built, bright, towering. His balls drew tight against his body. "How?"

"Let me make love to you." She reached up and touched one finger to the head of his cock. Sensations shivered from the spot and a bead of moisture met her touch. "Like this. Let me kiss you here, like you kissed my sex. You are so splendid. So beautiful! Show me how a woman can do to a man what you did to me."

Desire pulsed. "With your mouth on me? Ah, God!"

"You would like it?"

He leaned forward and kissed her, suckling her tongue until her mouth blazed. She seemed possessed, kissing back with mad violence as if a vampire had drained her and left her grasping for another's life, more vibrant than hers. His heart turned over. He was pierced by compassion, but he couldn't deny her. Yet it meant trusting her, offering himself, vulnerable, naked.

At last he lifted his lips and breathed into her ear as he let his tongue trail along the sensitive earlobe. "I would like it."

She rocked him to the bed and knelt over him. He flung his hands wide, surrendering to her touch, his cock jutting boldly. Her hands rubbed over his chest and belly, over and over, as if she found him magnificent. She kissed lightly at his nipples, sending shivers of light to the base of his spine. Then, answering his leap of longing, she closed her fingers over his shaft. She kissed it lightly, tentatively, but he groaned aloud, throbbing in her mouth, unable to deny the exquisite sensations. Flames filled the room as they both caught fire. He reached to stroke her flank and the curve of her body. Her skin was hot, slick against his. As she suckled him he moaned, lost in a white-hot blaze of lust.

"Am I doing it right?" she whispered.

"Dear God! You cannot do it wrong!"

Her fingers tickled over his balls. "Then better? Can I do it better?"

"Flick your tongue," he said. "Under the rim. Ah! Ah! Yes, like that!"

It took all his control to retreat from the edge, to prolong the ecstasy, but at last—before it was too late—he lifted her away and kissed her full on the mouth. "My turn," he said. "My turn."

He pulled away to look at her. The mad, wild grief still burned in her eyes.

"Take me," she said. "Any way you like. Destroy me. I don't care."

"I am the one destroyed, Catriona. Do you think I can retreat from this?"

He suckled her until she cried out, then sank into her, into her velvety darkness, reaching for the night where the star had been hidden by Eve. Fierce, blazing, she reached back for him. Her fingers raked his back, her legs enclosed him. Slick with sweat, his skin melded with hers as he thrust over and over into the soft welcome of her body.

Were there skills? Were there expert techniques wise whores had taught him? Were there subtle pleasures? Not tonight. Not now. This was ferocious, devouring. He gave up his entire being for her frantic need, wrestling, howling like a warrior, desperate to bring her peace even if it brought him damnation. A night of combat, driven to the edge of delirium, draining him of soul and mind, and bringing him to a deeper passion than he had ever known.

He only knew how completely he was annihilated when his climax almost racked him before he could pull away. To his roaring shame and dismay, he lost any hope for subtlety, wrenching himself from her, unable to control the spasms that overwhelmed him, yet he was in time—barely. She shuddered beneath him, groaning and sobbing, and her nails drew blood.

With his eyes fixed on the single star he could see framed by the window, he held her for a long time while she slept like the dead.

He woke fully aroused—to brilliant sunshine, an empty bed, and a locked door. Dominic rattled the handle. No one answered. He hammered and called in vain for some time. Damn her! Damn her! The walls were thick solid stone. Is this what her loving had meant? That she could use his body, then bolt him in here like a prisoner! Stark naked, he crossed to the window and leaned out. Far away down the valley, beyond the finger of hills, a plume of smoke rose lazily into the summer morning. It mingled with the haze, a darker blue against the lavender of the far mountains. Another column of smoke rose beside it, blacker, denser.

The smoke billowed from the turn in the glen sheltering Achnadrochaid, the first MacNorrin township, the one they had passed the day before. He thrust his fist against the hard stone wall beside the window.

Had she known this last night while she ravished the soul
from his body? Was this what she hadn't told him? While
he slept away the morning, had she gone down to greet
with dread the expected news: *"Come quickly! They are
burning at Achnadrochaid!"*

Dominic swore loudly and inventively as he thrust on his
clothes, the now ragged shirt and the Fraser kilt. Taking
out his knife, he pulled the sheets and covers from the bed
and methodically began to rip them in strips. Surely Catriona knew what he would do? So why had she not plundered the room of its bedding? In moments he had one end
of the makeshift rope tied fast to a bar from the iron bed-
stead, which he jammed across the window opening, and
the other dropped down into space.

The sound came up from Achnadrochaid like the cry of
seagulls: the wail of women and children crying and shriek-
ing, and the hysterical barking of dogs. Beneath the din of
voices, a duller, more sinister sound turned the blood to ice
in his veins. The thud of batons and clubs striking flesh:
the soft, defenseless flesh of mothers and children, for the
men were still away in the hills. And Catriona, leaving him
sleeping, had gone to confront soldiers and sheriff's officers
with her apron.

Dominic scrambled along the side of the bluff above the
river. At last he could look down on the township. The
women had poured from their homes and tried to block the
road, as they had done the day before, but this time no
flock of sheep barred the way. Arms linked, some carrying
infants, they had stood in a body to protect their homes
from the militia. But this time the men had charged. The
women had wrapped their arms over their heads, or bent
their bodies over their children's. With the butts of their
muskets, with fists and boots, the soldiers were beating
them.

Bile rose in Dominic's throat. It was a mad frenzy, the
men's arms rising and falling like pistons. He had seen it

before: the mindless, vicious bloodlust of any frightened, angry group of men, ordered to punish what seemed just a stubborn insubordination and disregard for the law.

Some women fought back, but they had no weapons, while the soldiers used their muskets like clubs. An older woman went down under a flail of blows, her neat white kerchief ripped away, hanks of her hair torn from her head—Deirdre Fraser, whom he had met last night at Dunachan. A nailed boot crushed into her breast as another slammed into her temple. She fell limp.

Children screamed and ran crying. A boy of about ten tried to carry his little brother on his back while he dragged a small sister by the hand. The girl sobbed, her mouth open like a soft pink rose. Frantic, the boy rushed with his burdens into the roaring waters of the Reulach.

Meanwhile another group of men moved from house to house. As if they sowed fire, flames leaped and crackled into the heather-thatched roofs. Smoke poured from windows and doors and howled up flaming chimneys. Some of the women tried to pull their furniture from their homes, but many were too late. The books, the bits of fine china, the lovingly stitched chintz curtains, all the tools of everyday living became fuel for a roaring monster.

Mairead MacNorrin, eight months pregnant, who had flirted with him a little at the *céilidh,* had climbed from her byre onto the roof of her house. She lay spread-eagled on the peak, shouting defiance at the boys with the torches. Yarrow Fletcher rode up and lashed at her with a long whip. Dominic knew he shouted at her in English, of which she only understood a little, but the result was no different. Mairead slipped and a man caught her by the ankle. She fell heavily, crying out, as her house was set afire. Bent double over her swollen belly, coughing and choking, she stumbled away to collapse against the wall of her garden.

And somewhere in that vicious melee was Catriona.

He saw and registered all this as he tore down the brae past the burning township. Still clinging together, the children were spinning away down the foaming Reulach. Fighting through the freezing torrent, Dominic grabbed the older

boy and slung his little brother about his own neck. The
child clung there, his small fists locked painfully in Dominic's hair. The girl he managed to tuck under the other
arm. Wading through the icy water, he set them down by
a stand of pine trees.

"Stay here," he said. "Your mother will find you."

"They beat her," sobbed the older boy, his face a mask
of terror. "They kicked her in the breasts and tore her hair
and her dress. She is dead."

Dominic crouched down and looked the child in the face.
Thank God the lad spoke English! "No, no. Be brave. They
may have hurt her, but she will live. And until you know,
you must comfort your little brother and sister. Never lose
hope until you have all the facts."

The boy wiped at his nose and hugged the sobbing
younger children in his arms.

Dominic left them and ran back toward the flames.
Smoke poured heavily from the houses. Some women had
tried to flee among the buildings, but the soldiers pursued
them. Every bend brought him face-to-face with another
bloody, struggling group. He laid about with his fists and
the butt of his pistol.

"For God's sake!" he shouted. "They are *women*!"

It was like trying to hold back a torrent or a bolt of
lightning. The men had become mindless, a force of nature.
They didn't register his presence. A report cracked through
the air. The single shot of a pistol.

"Damnation!" He battled past a cluster of brawling
women and soldiers. Had Yarrow Fletcher just shot Catriona? As he ran he shouted. *"For God's sake! They are
women! They are unarmed!"*

He raced around the corner of the next house, to see
Yarrow Fletcher on horseback, just pocketing his pistol,
cursing.

A dog raced away, unhurt, though Fletcher's bullet had
just scored a track along the street. Not a woman, not Catriona. Thank God!

"Bloody curs! Clear the way!" Fletcher shouted.

"Leave the houses! You will all be arrested. The force of the law is behind me."

"No law for you, Yarrow Fletcher," called a firm, high-pitched voice. "No law for you! Ruin upon you! Destruction upon your house! No prison will keep you, nor gallows dangle you. No blade will pierce you, nor bullet harm you. No grave will hold you until high stones twist from their seats and every bell rings by itself to accuse you. A curse upon you, Yarrow Fletcher!"

It was Iseabail MacNorrin. An island of stillness, the old woman stood unmoving, her eyes open and calm as if seeing something that wasn't there. Against all his expectations, a shiver ran down Dominic's spine.

"You mad old witch!" Fletcher laughed and turned his horse. "Is that a curse? That I'll die in my bed?"

"You'll neither die in your bed, nor rest easy in it, Yarrow Fletcher," the old voice cried out. "A curse and a doom is upon you! Your grave is already dug, but no man will mark it."

Iseabail turned and walked away as the soldiers set fire to her house behind her. Her back was upright. The white linen cap on her snowy hair glimmered brightly as she disappeared through the thick smoke.

Still searching for Catriona, Dominic turned the corner of a cow byre and found himself trapped. The byre formed one side of a small pen. The house wall blocked the other side, and the back was the solid face of a rock outcrop. As he turned to escape, a group of soldiers burst around the side of the house and saw him.

"Fetch Mr. Fletcher!" The man's accent was North of England. He stalked slowly toward Dominic, musket leveled, as he spoke over his shoulder to his comrades. "We've one of their menfolk here. From the looks of him, I'd say he's been beating on our lads."

Dominic backed up to the byre wall and tossed aside his pistol. "Will you shoot me, sir?" he asked calmly. "In cold blood? I am unarmed."

"Your knife," the man said. "You fellows all carry knives in your socks. Throw it down and no funny business, or I'll blow you a new hole to fart through.''

Dominic pulled out his knife and tossed it down on the cobbles, then leaned back and raised his hands. If he dropped and feinted, the blade would still be within reach.

The man grinned. ''I have him now, lads. We'll take him in irons to the jail in Inverness.'' He spat, looking back at Dominic as the other soldiers left. ''You fellows don't like being locked up away from your precious mountains, do you?''

A horse's hooves clattered. ''Well, well!'' Yarrow Fletcher grinned down from his mount. ''Well done, Smith. You put in your thumb and pulled out a damned peach with this one.''

''Mr. Fletcher.'' Dominic coughed as the wind shifted and swept black smoke into his face. ''Isn't all this a little crude, even for you?''

Fletcher leaned forward in his saddle. ''I do my job, Mr. Wyndham. These people are trespassers. The land is not theirs. They have been sent notices to leave as the law requires. When they don't obey, we must evict them using any means necessary. They are the malefactors. Any of them offering resistance may be arrested and jailed. Smith is right. But I shan't put you with them in the Tolbooth. I have a black hole in mind for you. A private spot in Inverness. You'll like it.''

A black hole! The image yawned like the gates of hell. *Chained with his arms behind his back while he was mercilessly beaten. Left to die in the dark!*

''I'll love it,'' Dominic said. His voice sounded cool, even amused, but the panic pulsed just below the surface. ''Will you do the beating personally, or will you have this nice Liverpool laddie do it for you?''

Fletcher swung from his horse, his pistol cocked in his hand. ''You're so indifferent, Mr. Wyndham? Don't you believe me? You think there won't be enough evidence to hold you? What if the charge is murder?''

He swept up Dominic's pistol and knife from the cobbles. He thrust the pistol into his pocket, but as Smith stepped aside Yarrow Fletcher plunged Dominic's knife into the soldier's breast. Surprise flooded the coarse features as Smith dropped his musket. Clutching at the handle jutting from his chest, the soldier fell forward and collapsed.

Dominic didn't move. Fletcher still had his pistol, and, without question, wanted him dead. Yet he felt nausea as he choked back his fury.

"You are under arrest, Dominic Wyndham," Fletcher said triumphantly, "for the murder of this man, Smith. You are also a fugitive from a warrant in Nottingham. You will hang. But between now and that throttling, there will be a certain amount of unpleasant humiliation before I give you up to the mercies of the law."

"No doubt." The reflection of flames danced on the pistol barrel. It would not surprise him if Yarrow Fletcher first fired to maim: in the knee, perhaps, or the groin. He looked up at his enemy and smiled. "No one ever claimed death by hanging was dignified."

Fifteen

CATRIONA DRAGGED DEIRDRE Fraser out of the way of the horses. The older woman moaned.

"Be still," Catriona said gently in Gaelic. "Rest here. Your bairns are safe."

Deirdre's eyes fluttered open. "It is an evil day."

"Hush, hush, you brazen woman!" Catriona smiled at her. "There's many a militiaman, too, will limp home from this day's work."

The older woman closed her eyes and smiled back.

Catriona stood up. She had seen him. She had seen the flash of dark plaid and the glimmer of golden hair as he plunged into the stream after the children, to drag them out safely and leave them by the bank. She had seen him run like a dervish into the township. And last night, only last night, she had seen him naked and helpless in the grip of his ecstasy as he carried her with him to Tir-nan-Og, and let her forget, for a moment, all her troubles.

But—mad fool!—he was a soldier. He would fight. Dread grabbed at her heart. They would kill him. Why else had she been glad the MacNorrin men were away in the hills? For any menfolk who stood up to the brutal force of the law would simply have been massacred.

A shot rang out. Mairead's dog raced past. *A Dhia!* Had

someone put a musket ball into Dominic's brave, stubborn heart?

She ran back into the township. The women were bloody, their aprons and dresses and their neat, decent white caps, all torn and soiled. The uninjured ran away across the Reulach or up into the hills. Catriona choked on the roiling, thick black smoke and her own tears as Iseabail's voice cried through the roar of flames, cursing in English.

"No blade will pierce you, nor bullet harm you. No grave will hold you until high stones twist from their seats and every bell rings by itself to accuse you. A curse upon you, Yarrow Fletcher!"

Catriona dodged away behind a smoldering byre and fought for breath. If found here, she would be arrested. Yet she couldn't reach Dunachan now by the road without being seen, and Dominic was somewhere in the burning township inviting capture and imprisonment—his greatest fear.

Yarrow Fletcher said something nearby. Dominic's voice dropped like shards of ice into a furnace, cold but hissing.

"No doubt. No one ever claimed death by hanging was dignified."

Alive! Tears welled and burned. Devil take him and his damned English ways! She spun around the corner of the building and saw him—as vibrant as the sun, golden and strong. He was facing Yarrow Fletcher over a militiaman's dead body. Fletcher's pistol slowly lowered.

"You won't walk to the scaffold," Fletcher said, "at any rate."

Catriona screamed. *"Gonadh ort!"*

She picked up a loose cobblestone and threw. It hit Fletcher in the temple as he turned. He dropped like a stone. The gun fired harmlessly across the cobbles beside him.

Hot, choking tears fouled her throat. Nothing was quite in focus. "Come away, you foolish, foolish man. Ah, you are a lunatic!" She bent over, wrapping her head in her hands against the wall. She felt faint. "We must get you away into the hills. They will arrest you and have you hanged like a dog."

His voice spoke close to her ear, gentle, a little mocking. "I must get *you* away, before I myself wring your damned neck. What the hell were you shouting at Fletcher?"

She looked up into the infinite green of his eyes. "A witch's curse: a piercing pain on him!"

Dominic took her by both arms. He bent and kissed her, flaming hot, on the lips, then set her away again. "Iseabail cursed him, too, and made some quite extraordinary predictions about his death."

"I heard her," Catriona said. "They will come true."

"I'd much rather have heard he would hang for his crimes." He took her hand and laced her fingers through his. "You're in shock. Let's get the hell out of here."

He ran with her around the burning byre. They dodged into the cover of a thicket of trees and yellow broom. Blind, running only on instinct, she led him away up into the hills, until Achnadrochaid was no more than a smudge on the horizon.

"Is fhasa deagh ainm a chall na chosnadh," she said.

He lay on his back beside her. "It is hard enough for me to understand you when you speak in English, beloved."

She looked blankly at him and then she remembered. "It is easier to lose a good name than to gain one. You did not stab that soldier, did you?"

"No, Yarrow Fletcher did. But don't think I wouldn't have killed him if I'd had to."

"Och, you mad creature! You did not have to!"

"No. I'd have escaped Private Smith without taking his life."

"But now your name will be spread in infamy through Ross-shire. Soldiers will hunt you down for his murder. It will be more than the prison you must fear. It will be the scaffold."

"Hush," he said, pulling her down into the bracken. "Horsemen."

She lay beside him in the crackling brown of last year's

dead bracken with the young green fronds meeting over her head, intensely aware of his warmth beside her, remembering the taste and feel and smell of him in the starry tower at Dunachan. The thud of hooves came closer.

Between the bends of seed-studded young bracken she saw the glint of a stirrup iron, a bay's black legs and brown belly. The boot in the stirrup held a spur of steel. She clung to Dominic, barely breathing, until the horse moved away.

"We must hide for a bit," Dominic whispered.

"Follow me." Afraid to stand, she wriggled forward on her belly, slipping through the bracken bed until she came to the bank of a small stream. Rowans hung over the water. She knew every tree and rock of this place. Here she had played as a child. There she had once skinned her knee. Calum had taught her to draw her blade quickly and silently on the open patch of sward by the bend in the burn. Under the cover of the trees they were invisible to anyone moving above. She led Dominic up the stream bed, past the waterfall and the sudden rocky tumbles, away from pursuit.

"Here," she said at last. "We can hide here."

Dominic stopped and looked out across the flower-strewn meadow, then to the rocky cavity at her back. It was shielded with gorse unless approached just so. Yet from the cave's entrance he could see the stream and the meadow, with the high peaks mantled behind.

"Calum's cave?" he asked.

"Yes. Come away inside."

The floor was dry. Against one wall, dead bracken drifted in a soft brown pile. She bent to sweep it together, then spread her skirts over the prickly stems before she sat down, hugging her arms about her knees.

Dominic stood at the entrance and looked out. Scudding clouds put him alternately in sun and shadow, polishing his golden hair, then tarnishing it with rust. He was tall. His body gave the kilt swing and style, like a Highlander. She had to remind herself constantly that he was English and brother to an English lord. She had to remind herself not to reach for him, not to glory in that tall, lithe man's body.

"Why are mountains so sacred?" he asked quietly. " 'I

will lift up mine eyes unto the hills, from whence cometh my help.' What is it that makes us place heaven above the clouds? Which came first, do you suppose?''

''I don't know. We Gaels have magic places beyond the western seas, as well.''

''Magic, but not sacred. The gods of ancient Greece also lived on a mountain. Have all gods done so, from the beginning of time?''

''At the beginning of time there were no gods.''

He turned and grinned. ''Only mountains. I am a complete skeptic, Catriona, yet this seems a sacred place to me.''

The clouds raced faster, with a fey, cold wind behind them. She saw him shiver—his kilt was still wet from his dash into the stream. Thunder rolled somewhere, a giant clearing his throat.

''Am I forgiven?'' she asked, then bit her lip, wishing too late to leave the words unsaid.

With athletic grace he dropped down beside her, looking her in the eye. ''Forgiven? For what? For giving me the most passionate night of my life? Or for locking me in my room afterward to exclude me from catastrophe? Catriona, we shall find Andrew. We shall prove who he is. We shall save Glen Reulach from Rutley and Fletcher. Trust me.''

She looked away so he could not read her despair. The truth stirred in her, begging to be said. She could not. She could not tell him what she already knew. And for the keeping of that secret almost against her will, she felt a guilt that cried out for absolution. *Forgive me!* she wanted to say. *Forgive me, my love, for using you. Forgive me that I must then cast you aside. But if you knew the truth, you would leave now, and I need you—selfishly, basely, I need your warmth to save me from the ice in my heart—for at least a little while longer, before we are parted forever.*

She glanced up. ''But there is no proof and you cannot hunt for Andrew now. You are a wanted man. The charge will be murder again, and this time Fletcher will produce witnesses.''

He said nothing for a moment. He sat gazing out across

the meadow, watching the harebells dance in the strengthening breeze. "Those are impossibly delicate stems," he said.

"They are stronger than they look."

His eyes shone green, like the deceptive smile of the morass. "Are they?"

"Do not," she said, scrambling to her feet. "Do not look at me like that. I am just another woman. Like all those other mistresses you have enjoyed in London. Like the ladies of the town. There will never be anything between us but that. A fleeting attraction of the body. You must accept it!"

He looked away. "So you keep me to our bargain? Oh, God, I am mad to want you so damned much, even now. What the hell are you hiding from me, Catriona?"

The guilty flush burned across her skin. "Why do you ask?"

"I don't know, for I know it won't be answered. Catriona, if I beckon now, can you come to me?"

The burn deepened, firing into her blood, guilt fusing with desire. She wanted him to punish her. "Do we have anywhere left to go, after last night?"

Dimples danced in his cheeks as he looked up. "We have the other side of passion to explore, beloved. Where I would lead you now. Where I would have led you last night if you had not had other needs."

Treacherously the heat flooded between her legs as if she bloomed for him, opening like a flower. "I will keep my word. I shall not refuse you. Do you wish to lead me into depravity?"

He grinned. "What wickedness have we indulged that has been depraved?" He reached up and caught her hand. "No, sweetheart, I would lead you into tenderness. I would offer you succor. And if my heart is given with it, well, that's no part of the bargain, just largess."

"Do not give your heart," she said. "I don't want it."

"Ah, it was lost long ago. Don't let it worry you."

She tore her hand away and retreated into the cave. "It does worry me! Why must you do this? Come, I am willing to be your strumpet. Show me what it means!''

He leaped up and came after her. Catriona dodged him, wanting him to be angry, wanting him to degrade her and make her pay for her duplicity.

''Why do you ask that?''

Deliberately, frantically, she goaded him. ''You are the man all London whispers about, the man who sent his wife sobbing to her mother, the man taught by a wicked woman in Russia. Harriet told me in Edinburgh of her fear and horror at what you did to her on your wedding night. Corrupt, disgusting things. *Unspeakable acts—things too degrading ever to be described*—your own words. I am your mistress! Teach me everything! Show me what that means!''

He caught and held her, firmly, like a child. The tears rolled down her face as he held her against his warm chest.

''Not my words,'' he murmured in her ear. ''Harriet's words.''

The rage and despair seeped away. She clung to him, letting the tears dissolve her distress and knowing only that she was tired. Too tired to fight any longer. Tired enough to wilt. When she became quiet, he laid her down on his thick plaid, the bracken bed springy beneath it. Carefully he undressed her, kissing gently. His lips feathered on her knee, softly on her inner thigh, her belly, her right breast, her earlobe. It was a slow dance. Unable to fight it, she was ready long before he entered her. When his *bod* slid inside, she let out a long sigh.

''Teach me something new,'' she whispered, reveling in the gift of his gentleness. ''Something real.''

''Feel me.'' He lay quietly over her, not moving. ''Feel me inside you.''

She concentrated, lying still. His sex pulsed, throbbing in time with her heartbeat. ''Ah! Ah! I feel it! Can you do that deliberately? How?''

His chuckle rumbled against her ear. ''Easy. Practice.''

''Can I do it, too?''

''Try.''

He held still, braced above her on his strong arms while

she tried to contract her inner muscles. Sudden spasms gripped him hard. She felt him leap inside her in response. She laughed and tried again. It was more controlled this time, more of a caress.

He dropped his head and kissed her. He pumped slowly in and out. She practiced gripping him at each stroke. "*A Dhia! An fhearr leat so?*"

"Translate," he whispered.

She opened her eyes. "You like this better?"

He laughed, the laugh rumbling and shaking him so she felt it in her very bones. "There's no part of sex I don't like. Now, hush, give heed to every feeling and let us be lovers."

It built slowly in her this time, the openness, the profound depth of their exchange. A gift of tenderness, delicately expert. As if he were the sun, his warmth sank into her. Melting, blending, he reached deeply into her soul, undermining her defenses, dissolving her fears into liquid longings, like rivulets from thawing ice. Her spasms, when they came, rang so deeply she wanted to weep. She reached her arms about his cleanly muscled back and held him tightly into her body. It was the last time! The last time!

Silent, his expression focused, he waited for her to relax. Then he pulled away so they would not make a bastard child. His arms wrapped about her to hold her close. She lay still, listening to the thud of his heartbeat.

You will fall in love and I shall break your heart.

Ah, ah, but she had long been in love and her heart was already broken! If he did not escape to England, Yarrow Fletcher would see him hanged in Inverness and torture him in the dark first. So he must leave! And it would be more than a hundred miles would separate them, for nothing but the ships awaited her. Her fate lay across the western ocean, where she would not find the Land of Youth. Instead, she would be shattered.

A sudden gust whipped into the cave. Dominic sat up. He held his plaid about her as the cold air snapped at her naked skin. The temperature was plummeting, yet the sky was still blue.

"Dear God," he said. "It's snowing."

Wrapped in his warmth, she watched the air shiver and sparkle as snowflakes drifted past the mouth of the cave. In tiny silver drifts they wedged up against the flowers and the heather.

"It will melt as it lands," she said. "The ground is still warm."

Yet the wind shifted and the snowflakes flurried faster, coating the harebells until each blue bonnet bowed to the ground and the thin stems bent double. The snow glittered, half melting as it turned into glistening shards of ice.

He kissed the top of her head. "I only half believed Calum when he told me about this. That I should see it!"

"Och, it's not so strange a thing in these mountains. Ice and snow are ready enough to make lace caps for the bens whenever they feel they're getting too much sun."

"Like an old dame protecting her complexion?"

She snuggled closer, wanting his arm, if only for this short time, as her protection against the void. "If you like."

No more than half an inch, a frosting, lay on the ground when the snow stopped. Each crystal of ice glistened, winking rainbow colors as it slowly began to melt. One by one the harebells shed their burden of cold and sprang upright again as the colors glimmered in the sky, an echo of jeweled ice, arcing across the blue.

"Dear God, a rainbow!" His voice was reverent. "The promise of hope. I think I could love this land, Catriona."

Alarm shattered her pleasure. "You must go back to England! Go where it is safe! Yarrow Fletcher will arrest you and you will disappear into a hidden cellar."

"You deny hope? Can't we stay here in this cave forever?" His voice was soft, teasing.

"There is no forever for us. Why else have I tried to send you away? I shall leave, go to Canada."

"I could come with you."

"Och, you insane man! It is wilderness there. No, no. Go back to London, to your clubs and your women. I wouid not see you live in the wild like an animal, and have the heart broken within you."

He sat solid and unshakable beside her, holding her close. "Do you think me so wedded to my London life?"

It was the crux of it. She told him the simple truth. "I know what you are—brother to an English lord, used to all the whimsy and embellishment of civilization. You relish all that, don't you? Culture, learning, politics?"

"Yes," he said honestly.

"When we are forced to emigrate, the MacNorrins must carve new farms and new pastures out of a wilderness. Nothing but brutal toil awaits the men, with a rifle over the shoulder to guard against the Indians. There won't be time for much culture, even our own. Our books will be left behind and our learning. There won't be room for songs or for poetry. Our children will grow up like savages. What do you know of tilling soil and tending livestock?"

"Nothing. But you don't have to go. You can come to England with me."

"And let my clansmen be sent away to a new land without me? I could not be so disloyal."

"Well." He lifted her hand and kissed her fingers. "I understand loyalty. Let's not discuss the future. Let us kiss and say our good-byes."

"What? Are you leaving now?"

He smiled down at her. "Yarrow Fletcher has annoyed me. I'm going to Inverness to take care of him."

She wrenched away and faced him. "You cannot!"

"Trust me. Go back to Dunachan and give succor to the people of Achnadrochaid. You must be there in case Mrs. Mackay comes with Andrew. You must give a dry bed to Iseabail MacNorrin. You must take a bath and change into a new dress. If they come to question you, act the lady and deny you ever left the keep. If you are arrogant enough, they won't question it. After all, Rutley's daughter is your aunt."

She looked away to hide her face, in case she gave herself away. "They will accuse you of murder. You cannot go to Inverness."

"You cannot stop me." He stood and took up his

clothes, belting on the kilt and tossing the plaid over his shoulder.

Catriona scrambled into her dress and clutched at his sleeve. "Dominic, do not do this!"

The green eyes were implacable. "You would let Yarrow Fletcher tear these glens apart looking for me? You would see another township burned tomorrow and the next the day after that? You would see Glen Reulach swept clean of all human habitation by the end of the week, because I went into hiding?"

"The burning will happen anyway."

He took her by the arms, as if determined to make her agree. "Not immediately, not without Yarrow Fletcher. For God's sake, Catriona. The duke's desire for profit is one thing. Fletcher's yen for personal revenge is another. Rutley may have given orders for Glen Reulach to be leased for sheep walks, but this breakneck rush to destruction is Fletcher's. I can keep him in Inverness and buy the MacNorrins that much more time. It is something only I can do."

"You sacrifice yourself for nothing! If you are locked away, how does that help Glen Reulach?"

"I shall not be locked up."

"You will be if they catch you. There is a risk!"

He leaned forward to kiss her. "I'm good at risk. Catriona, time is the only hope for the glen. I have the one coin that can buy it."

She broke away, blinded by tears, unable to tell him the depth of her despair, the choking truth that he still didn't know. "Och, go then! Go to your destruction, you mad fool!"

He said nothing. He stood for a moment at the mouth of the cave to look up at Ben Wyvis dominating the far skyline. Then with a last wink, he turned to run away down the glen. He moved lightly, his kilt swinging, like a Highlander. *Long, strong legs and a wee, tight bottom like two buns, if you must know, and a goodly flat belly. It makes the kilt swing right.*

Ah, it made everything right—but that she had a duty

destined to keep them apart. She knew what he was and
loved him as he was. She would not allow him to destroy
himself by coming to the wilderness, where he would grow
to resent it and eventually to hate her.

∽

Dominic crept back to his rooms at the inn in Inverness at
night. Avoiding the toll bridge, he waded the Ness, then
dodged through the sleeping town to climb up to the window of his room. Excellent, his trunk from London had
arrived!

He ordered eggs for breakfast and made himself eat
them, though his stomach clutched with nerves. In spite of
his bravado, he wasn't sure this would work. He wasn't
sure he might not be cast into some black cellar to be tortured by Yarrow Fletcher. The fear clamored. The accusation against him in Nottingham could be backed by paid
witnesses—and the death of Smith? Several soldiers had
seen them together. They would have found Fletcher lying
unconscious by the soldier's dead body. The law would
draw the obvious conclusion.

He dropped his head in his hands, forcing himself to face
what was at stake. Two charges of murder, the last with
genuine onlookers. He was known in London as a libertine—*drunk and half-naked, profaning a church.* If it went
to trial, Fletcher would be sure to twist that into evidence
of a reckless and treacherous temperament. So a trial would
find him guilty, with the noose waiting. What mercy was
owed a man who wagered with sin, had corrupted his innocent wife, then knifed to death a member of the local
militia who had only been doing his duty?

And Yarrow Fletcher intended no mercy at all.

There was a rap on the door. Dominic opened it.

Alan Fraser pulled off his blue bonnet as he stepped into
the room. "I had your message. Ye were lucky. The lad
intercepted me on the road. I was to come to Inverness,
anyway."

"With whisky, I hope? You'll allow me a purchase?"

Dominic indicated a seat. ''You've had breakfast?''

''I have. I'll no' stay.'' Alan reached into his inner coat pockets and produced bottles. ''I have the whisky for you. It's grand stuff!''

Dominic smiled. ''It is that!'' He gave Alan the bundle containing kilt and plaid, all the trappings of his flight through the heather. ''You'll thank your mother for me? I'm afraid your father's kilt is a little the worse for wear.''

''Nothing that won't mend.'' Alan clapped him on the back and laughed. ''Ye'll transform back into a braw Sassenach, but it was grand to ken you as one of us.''

Catriona fled back to Dunachan, the strong keep of her ancestors, where MacNorrin Dhu had defied the Frasers in 1463, and where no MacNorrin other than a baby had the right to live any longer. Once the people were all cleared from the glen, the castle was to become a shooting lodge. Her wee cousin Thomas, the rightful heir, would maybe never live there. He'd be raised by his mother and grandfather as an Englishman, and his Highland inheritance would see the wind whistle through empty glens with nothing but the stalking red deer and the white sheep for inhabitants.

She didn't know if the frantic pain in her heart was only for that, or for the mad Englishman who had let her assuage her driving grief with his body. She knew he could not be exiled with her, as she knew in his wild gallantry he would suggest it. She could never agree. He must go back to England, where he belonged.

But first would Yarrow Fletcher imprison him in some secret cell? *A Dhia!* What did Dominic intend? *I am afraid to again be locked in a cellar. You might say I am afraid, in a way, of the dark.*

At Dunachan, she was distracted. Deirdre Fraser had been brought there, and several other women, with their bruises

and broken bones. Deirdre had slipped into unconscious-
ness and fever. Her three children waited at the knee of old
Iseabail MacNorrin and listened to stories and songs. Catriona made the great hall into an infirmary and the breakfast room into a nursery, and tended Deirdre herself—
fearing every day that a notice would arrive to evict all of
them. Yet Yarrow Fletcher did not return. The other townships gave shelter to the people of Achnadrochaid and went
about their business unmolested—except by dread.

Dread. Her daily companion. Dread over Yarrow
Fletcher.

*I can keep him in Inverness and buy the MacNorrins that
much more time. It is something only I can do.*

And she had thought he was not a hero! *A Mhuire!* What
sacrifice was he making now for the sake of strangers? *A
certain amount of unpleasant humiliation.* Fletcher intended
something much more diabolical than that! She lay awake
at night and shivered in the dark.

The next day Deirdre opened her eyes. She smiled at
Catriona *"A bheil Calum an seo?"*

"Calum died at Waterloo last year," Catriona said. "As
you well know, you silly woman."

"Och, of course," Deirdre replied in Gaelic. "I was
dreaming. It has all come back now. Alas, alas! Where are
the children?"

So Catriona was free. Free to leave Dunachan and go
after him. She dressed in her best habit and had a fine, tall
horse saddled with her sidesaddle. With a small tail of servants, she rode into Inverness like a queen.

Her heart hammering, sick with apprehension, she inquired at the inn where he had stayed.

"Och, ye've no' heard?" the innkeeper asked.

She turned her whip in her hands. "What? Major Wyndham was a friend of my brother's. Has he gone back to
England?"

"Not him! He has the town in an uproar. He came out
for his morning promenade two days ago and saw a notice,
like that one there."

He nodded his head toward a sheet of paper crumpled

on the counter. Catriona picked it up and read it.

"He is wanted for murder?" She was amazed her voice could stay so calm. "He has been masquerading as a Highlander and stabbed a militiaman?"

The innkeeper grinned. "It put him in a rare temper to see it! He ripped down that notice and went about town gathering the others. He took the whole lot to the fiscal and demanded an explanation. All the magistrates have been called together. They're having a hearing today at the Tolbooth. He insisted on it. It's become quite the attraction. The townspeople and tourists are all going. I thought you had come for the show."

"When?" she said.

He glanced at his watch. "Och, it'll be starting any minute."

With the fear like a madness in her mind, Catriona swept from the inn and made her way back down Castle Street. Before her lay the small town square, with the broken Market Cross and the Clachnacuddin, an ancient stone of almost mystic significance to the town's inhabitants. Behind them, the grim bulk of the Tolbooth sat squat beneath its tall steeple on the corner of Kirk and Bridge streets. She shuddered to see it—Inverness's ancient prison—sheltered behind its arcade. The walls inside were unpainted deal, the courtroom dirty and dim. A harsh stone gallery formed the prisoners' walk past the loathsome dark cells. Would Dominic yet lie incarcerated and forgotten in one of them?

The hearing was being conducted upstairs. The crowds parted and let her move close to the front of the room. The provost and magistrates were gathered at the bench, looking uncomfortable. The procurator fiscal, the prosecutor of crimes for the crown, stroked his lawyer's long jaw, completely bemused. A man strode back and forth before them all. Catriona stared in amazement. It was Dominic.

A vibrant, extravagantly cut jacket of blue superfine sent its high neck up about his ears. The points of his shirt collar, starched like boards, reached even higher. His cravat erupted in elaborate folds of stiff white linen beneath his chin. His trousers were some kind of knit fabric that revealed every muscle in his thighs. They were a pure, pale blue. An eminently impractical blue, which only a London dandy would ever consider and never outside the drawing room.

He had also done something to his hair. Trimmed it, certainly. But he had dressed it, dampened it with oil, perhaps, so it clustered about his ears in fanciful little curls. He was pale. Impossibly pale. She didn't know how he had managed it. He didn't look rugged and untamed. He was a popinjay, a London buck. The transformation was absolute.

Her giggle started somewhere deep inside, a wild mirth mingled with relief. He was alive! Not even imprisoned! Oh, how could he do this? He was wearing powder and rouge!

"You must see, my lords," he was saying, "that the accusations of this man are impossible!"

He gestured. With set face and hunched shoulders, Yarrow Fletcher sat on a chair at the side of the bench.

"Is it likely, I ask you?" Dominic's accent was impossibly clipped, very English and every inch the idle aristocrat. "Is it likely that I—brother to Lord Windrush—would careen about the countryside in Highland garb, murdering people I have never met? Not that I mean any disrespect to that dress. Indeed I admire it on a Highlander and esteem it on a soldier, but is it likely, my lords, that I should wear such a thing? I have a perfectly good wardrobe of my own." He sounded petulant. "Indeed, I take pains with my appearance. I did not come to the Highlands to be the butt of some wild joke perpetrated by this man."

Yarrow Fletcher stood up. "Any of a dozen witnesses saw you in kilt and stockings. You were the last one alone with Smith!"

Dominic turned. A long-handled quizzing glass appeared in his gloved hand. He peered through the single lens at Fletcher. "Did they? Then take me to jail and bring me to trial!" He shuddered convincingly and turned back to the bench. "Why do you not ask someone here, my lords? Someone independent, whose word you can trust?"

The leading men of Inverness obviously wished themselves elsewhere. The provost looked about the room. "Who saw this man in the hills?"

"I did." Alan Fraser stepped forward, proud and tall in his kilt. "And I'll tell you, my lords, he was dressed in a wet pair of English breeches when I met him, like a half-drowned dog, and he was gey miserable about it."

"You gave him a kilt." Fletcher turned to the magistrates, pointing. "It was a Fraser tartan Wyndham was wearing. This man must have given him a kilt."

"Then I'm a damned generous soul," Alan Fraser replied immediately. "I've only one kilt and plaid of my own. If I'd given it to this Englishman, I'd be bare-arsed myself today and creating a scandal among the ladies!"

A great shout of laughter rocked the room.

"Can you swear to us you did not wear Highland dress this last week?" the provost asked Dominic, mopping at his brow.

"Well, really." Dominic folded the quizzing glass and made a great show of checking his cuff after he had slipped the glass into his pocket. He apparently found a tiny fleck of dust. He flicked it away and gave the provost a tight, aggrieved smile. "Can you imagine it?"

"Then you did not murder the soldier at Achnadrochaid?" inquired the procurator fiscal, leaning forward suddenly. "Can you give us your oath?"

"I can and I will, sir. On my honor, I have murdered nobody. Good Lord! Is this how all English tourists are treated in the Highlands? If it is, I can see your inns and hostels must suffer for it."

Catriona hugged herself. One of the magistrates owned an inn.

Fletcher began to shout. "He does not answer—"

The provost silenced him with a gesture. "This is not a court of law, Mr. Fletcher. Major Wyndham has himself insisted on this hearing, hardly the action of a guilty man. We are here at his bequest to hear what he has to say. If you have evidence which is incontrovertible, you must place it before the procurator fiscal in the proper way at the proper time."

"I have a dozen witnesses who saw him at Achnadrochaid!" Fletcher yelled.

"Oh, I really believe I have had enough," Dominic said. "Bring out your witnesses, Mr. Fletcher, and let them swear under oath that with their own eyes they saw me strike down this poor man. Under oath, sir! They are honest soldiers. Will they think the ragged Highlander you have described seeing at Achnadrochaid is myself when they meet me face-to-face? I think not!"

"They will swear it! By the devil, they will swear it!"

Dominic raised a brow. "Really? How sure you are! I pray you will not think to offer them bribes. Wellington himself knows that you and I have a private quarrel. Bribes would be such excellent proof of it."

Oh, better and better! Catriona began suddenly to hope.

"You are on good terms with his grace?" one of the magistrates asked, obviously a little awed.

"I flatter myself Wellington is a personal friend." Dominic was almost haughty.

"I don't see," the procurator fiscal said, after leaning close to whisper in the provost's ear, "that testimony from any of Mr. Fletcher's witnesses could be trusted to be without taint in the circumstances."

Fletcher was almost foaming at the mouth. "I have witnesses! It was his knife, I tell you!"

The provost hammered on the tabletop. "If you do not sit down, Mr. Fletcher, and keep quiet, we shall have you evicted from this hearing! The knife found in Private Smith's body was a typical *sgain dhu*, not the likely possession of an English gentleman."

"There is the matter of the Nottinghamshire affair, as well," Fletcher said stubbornly after wiping his mouth with his handkerchief. "Are we to believe that the notices wanting Wyndham for the murder of his coachman are also a fabrication, a case of mistaken identity?"

The provost sighed, but he looked directly at Dominic. "Is there any truth to this, sir? Were you indeed in Sherwood on the specified date? And did your coachman die there in suspicious circumstances?"

Catriona swallowed hard. He had been there. The coachman had died. No one would believe the mad tale of what had really happened: the runaway coach ride, the bath in the icy lake—and what had happened afterward under the cold stars when he had first burned her with his pure fire. If Dominic admitted any of it, the coincidence would surely be too much? That both in Nottingham and Inverness he had been falsely accused of murder?

Dominic had not actually lied so far, any more than Alan Fraser had. She knew clearly he would not. If the right questions were asked and Dominic were forced to answer, he was bound to incriminate himself. In a court of law, he would have no chance. Only by forcing this hearing had he placed himself—for a moment—in command. Yet it was a hideous risk! If he left any suspicion in the procurator fiscal's mind, charges would be brought and the trial would follow. Fletcher could pack the court with testimony, some real, some false, and see Dominic hang yet.

"Well, sir?" the provost asked. "Were the authorities in Nottingham similarly deceived by a rogue who looks something like you?"

"Oh, I say!" It was a new voice from the back of the room. "What date was that?"

Everyone turned to crane their necks. A young man pushed forward. Catriona tried to place him. Yes! He had been in London when she had first seen Dominic at the church door, after he had climbed the steeple. The young man had been wearing a pink cutaway coat.

He nodded to Dominic and bowed to the magistrates. "Lord Lescombe, at your service. I happen to know the answer and freely give my oath it is true. On that particular day Major Wyndham was still in St. James's. I had cause to go to his rooms concerning a small wager between us, only to discover he was ill. His man was quite concerned. Lord Stansted, the Duke of Rutley's son and a particular friend of Major Wyndham's, confirmed it. Anyone in London can vouch for the fact and I will happily swear to it, on my honor!"

"Were you ill on that day?" the provost asked Dominic.

Dominic took out his quizzing glass again and stared at a painting on the wall—a stag, framed by rugged rock. "As I remember, I felt a considerable shortness of breath, then was chilled to my bones and taken with shivers. Later I was wild with an unquenchable flame in the blood. Quite delirious. That is a very fine painting, my lords."

Catriona hid her face. She thought she might choke.

Fletcher grimaced. "This is a farrago of nonsense! Wyndham was in Nottingham the next day."

"Then I *am* a fast traveler! And how did I leave there?" Dominic asked.

"In a balloon," Fletcher said.

Another burst of laughter rocked the room.

"Goodness," Dominic replied. "How marvelous!"

"I believe we are wasting our time." The provost leaned forward and spoke sternly to Yarrow Fletcher. "I am sure you have intended to serve only the public interest, sir. But you must agree we have a clear case of mistaken identity here. Lord Lescombe could have no possible motive for deceiving us. Indeed, he is personally known to me as a man of unimpeachable honor. And he would obviously be supported by Lord Stansted, were he here. By all means, keep searching the hills for your miscreant, but I believe we must remove Major Wyndham's name from suspicion."

Fletcher shook with rage. He stood and pointed his finger at Dominic. "I have not been allowed to speak. I have not brought my witnesses—"

The voice of authority snapped from the bench. "Mr. Fletcher! An end, if you please! We have already suffered enough embarrassment that notices were put out in Inverness calling for the arrest of an earl's brother, visiting from England. Let us lay this matter to rest."

"I think not." Dominic walked up to Fletcher. He towered over him. Beneath the colorful disguise, he seemed all the more dangerous. "My good name has been publicly besmirched. You will apologize, I trust, sir?"

Fletcher bridled like a mad dog. "Damn your eyes, I will not!"

Dominic sighed. Peeling off his exquisite white glove, he slapped Fletcher hard across the face.

"Then I must seek satisfaction. Perhaps your friends would like to call on mine at their earliest convenience?"

Sixteen

∽

"WILL YOU WALK with me, Miss MacNorrin?" he asked.

She seemed dazed, standing at the side of the room. He had known she was there, watched her from the corner of his eye, seen her smile light her face for a moment, like sun on bright water, as she realized what he was doing. But at the mention of a duel all that laughter had died, leaving her seemingly lost.

The crowd had broken apart and was streaming away. Fletcher had stormed out. The provost had shaken Dominic's hand and apologized that a friend of the Duke of Wellington had been put to any small trouble in Inverness—and then warned him, privately.

Her hat held an eagle's feather. She was beautiful, splendid, a Valkyrie—her Viking ancestors clear in her wide blue gaze. A fashionable riding habit, the train pinned up in elegant folds at the hip, hugged the curves of her breasts.

He spoke to her again, as if they were strangers. "I knew your brother, madam. I'm glad to make your acquaintance."

She looked up at him with eyes like jewels. "It is all a madness. If you fight a duel, you cannot win."

"I have to do it, whether I win or not," he replied.

"Fletcher will try to kill you and you cannot kill him!"

He took her elbow and guided her from the room. "You think not?"

"I know not. Iseabail said he would not die from blade nor bullet. I heard her."

Castle Street was crowded. Glances turned to follow them as they walked back to the inn. "You really believe that? She also said something about stones being twisted and bells ringing by themselves."

"It will come true. She has the second sight. It doesn't lie."

He stopped for a moment, keeping her out of the way of a passing carriage. "Curses and visions?"

She seemed vulnerable beneath her stubbornness, as if she would collapse if she relaxed. "Och, I know it is not easy to accept. Part of me doesn't accept it either. But I have seen such prophecies come true in the Highlands before. Fletcher will not die in a duel."

"Then let me set your mind at rest. I don't intend to kill him, much as I'd like to. If I do, I'll answer to valid murder charges, after all. The provost kindly warned me. A jury rarely convicts when a gentleman dies in a trial of honor, but under the circumstances, when the suspicion has already been planted that I might be casually homicidal—"

Her hands clenched. Sunlight moved over her clear jaw as she quickly moved her head. "So I am right! *Och-òn!* Why did you challenge him?"

He grinned, wanting to reassure her. "To give Fletcher something to worry about. Something to keep him occupied in town so he can't go back to Glen Reulach. Even something to torment him a little. I shall do some very public practicing with sword and pistols."

She glanced back, obviously alarmed. "You are not skilled already?"

He raised her hand and kissed it. "Very skilled. That's why I shall practice in public and let the rumors of my prowess get about. How fares it in the glen?"

"It goes hard with the families burned out. Where will they go now, except to the ships? But Deirdre is well enough and the bairns are with her at Dunachan. Mairead

MacNorrin went to her sister's, further up the glen, but the walk was too much for her after the shock of losing her home. She has a wee daughter now, too small, but bonny and bawling, though the birth came so early.''

Mairead MacNorrin, eight months pregnant, who had flirted with him a little at the *céilidh*. His burning rage at Yarrow Fletcher—whom he must fight, but not kill—almost choked him. If the rest of the glen was cleared, this fragile new life would never survive. So he made a promise to himself: if this child died, Fletcher would not see one more dawn, even if it sent Dominic Wyndham to the gallows.

They resumed walking, weaving through the strollers and the shoppers in town for the day.

Catriona paced beside him in silence. When they reached the yard of the inn, she turned to him suddenly. "How can I persuade you? You must not risk this duel!"

Her back was stiff, her chin tilted. He wanted to soothe the tight lines of her mouth. "It will buy us time, Catriona."

"Time will not help," she said, her voice breaking. "It is hopeless."

Dear God, if he could only save her home for her—though she would never make room in her life for him, even if he did!

"It is far from hopeless." He tried to fill his voice with conviction. "There is something I haven't told you, because I wasn't sure it would work. I sent out a network of messages for Mrs. Mackay. Alan and Davie Fraser helped. If she is anywhere in the Highlands, she will be found. I also appealed to Rosemary, Lady Stansted, for help. She owes me a favor, I think. And who knows? Perhaps Mrs. Mackay has sent word to the Souls of Charity. We shall find Andrew soon, Catriona. Then all we need is the proof of who he is."

"I already have proof enough of who he is not." She turned away. "We cannot save the glen."

"Why not?" It was sharper than he intended. Faces

turned to look at them. He wanted to enfold her. "Come," he said. "We must go in."

Her eyes filled with distress and an odd defiance as she shook her head. "You don't know! I learned when I arrived back at Dunachan. Sarah's body was brought there from Edinburgh. The women who laid her out for her coffin made particular note of it, because they had a concern in the matter. I was wrong. It has all been wrong from the beginning. Sarah never bore the laird a child, a true heir. She could not have. She is buried in the kirkyard beside my uncle, her husband, but there is no mistake: Sarah died a virgin."

The shock resonated in long slow waves like an earthquake. He tried desperately to control it, but the distress broke in his voice. "Then who the *devil* is Andrew's mother?"

Her defiance intensified, in the tilt of her head, her tight shoulders. "I don't know. Not Sarah's, that is all. So Thomas is rightful heir, indeed, and Glen Reulach is Rutley's to dispose of."

The waves gathered, long swells approaching the shore. "You knew this when we lay together in Calum's cave, and at the *céilidh,* and the day before at the bridge? You knew our cause was hopeless then? You knew it when I arrived in Glen Reulach? But you didn't tell me?"

She smoothed her fingers over her throat, looking away. "I made you help me for nothing. There never were any papers. You were never even remotely involved. There was a child living with the Souls of Charity, but how could the confectioners have known whose child? That woman in Edinburgh guessed wrong. The bairn is not Harriet's son, nor Sarah's son. We have been chasing a fantasy. Andrew's true parentage doesn't matter now."

The ferocity welled up in him, uncontrolled, the surge breaking in spume over rocks. He thought he heard a child's high scream as the waves swept him away to sea. "It matters to *him*. If we find this lost child and no one claims him, I'll provide for him, Catriona. Take that comfort, at least!"

She shrugged with pure bravado. "Och, comfort is your gift, is it not, you strange man? So what happened with Harriet? Why did she hate you? There is nothing depraved or cruel in your soul, is there? You are kind. Lady Rivaulx—your friend Frances—said you were a kind man. I should have believed her."

"You should have trusted me with this." The breath hissed between his teeth. It hammered at him: Lord Stansted's nephew, the child Thomas, was indeed the rightful heir. So after everything they had gone through, Glen Reulach could never be wrested from Rutley's control. Catriona had known it as soon as she arrived back at Dunachan. She had known it when she made love to him in a tower. Why the devil had she kept this, too, to herself? Did she think he would abandon her? "How dare you tell me that in one breath, then in the next that you knew something this important and didn't share it?"

That defiant tilt was back. It infuriated him. "You have the order of my breathing wrong."

He seized her by both shoulders. He wanted to shake her. Why couldn't she trust him? "Dammit! You know bloody well what I mean!"

"I know indeed." She stood rigid in his hands. It took a damned heavy dose of self-control to release her. "I don't care. How can I care? Can't you see what is important? I don't matter. You don't matter. There is nothing left now to save the glen."

You don't matter. His rage died, like the breaker running back in froth over sand, dissipated in bubbles of white foam.

"Oh, damnation!" he said. "This is a bloody tragedy."

"So it is, after all, the ships," she said. "We will go with dignity and courage. Though the heart break, MacNorrins will populate that new world and conquer it. Our children's children will think it their own place and forget the old ways. In a few generations it will not matter to them that the wind cries lonely over Ben Wyvis and the curlews call into an empty place. There will be no echo in their dreams that the ruins of the old homes became dens for rabbits and a foothold for willowherb. *Cha till mi tuil-leadh.*'' Her eyes were the blue of far horizons. ''I shall return no more.''

''Do you still forbid me to come with you?''

''You are English,'' she said. ''You are brother to an earl. You have a contribution to make to English civilization. You have a duty to your country.''

''—until Jack has a son and I am no longer heir.''

''What would you do in the wilderness? You are in love with argument and gaming. You like politics and learning and culture. You aren't a farm laborer or a woodsman. Can you live the rest of your life without ever seeing another library, another play, another great work of art? Admit it! Tell me I am right!''

''For God's sake, you make me sound like a dilettante! I have been a soldier. I have not the skills of your countrymen, but I can learn. I'm quite capable of hard work.''

''Of course,'' she said with a hint of sarcasm. ''You are a fine, strong man.''

''I love you. Do you think that counts for nothing?''

''Will your love be enough for the wasteland? Look at you! This would not be just another adventure. *Cha till mi tuilleadh.* Forever. Do you think the Indians will be impressed to see you dressed like that?''

The blue jacket and trousers, flamboyantly overstated, and deliberately chosen for effect. Dear God, as if that mattered! But there was no breaking her or convincing her, and a small voice whispered, the persistent message he could not ignore: *She is right! If you go, you will come to resent it, resent her, and finally, irrevocably break her heart. Is love really enough?*

''You are not a village woman, Catriona,'' he said. ''You grew up in a castle. You're a lady, for God's sake! Come to England with me.''

''And abandon the clan to their fate? I will not! So it is over between us! Now you know about Andrew, why must you stay? Why must you fight this duel with Fletcher?''

''For Iseabail and for Mairead and for Deirdre,'' he said. ''And because Yarrow Fletcher would even try to kill a pet dog. Surely a Highlander understands vengeance?''

She was bright, burning brightly with a pure fury. ''Don't you know he will trick you? Don't you know it won't be a fair fight? That there is bound to be treachery? Don't you know that while you don't intend his death, he intends yours? *A Mhuire!* Is death what you want?''

''I know what I want,'' he said forcefully. ''I want to call on our bargain. I want to make love to you again. These clothes that so offend you, I intend you to take off each garment—slowly. You will unbutton my jacket, peel off my damned trousers. Once I am naked, I will take you into my bed, giving, giving, until your blood burns and your lungs pant for air—until you cry out at last and forget for one moment that you think you are doomed.''

She was consumed, flaring like a charge set to gunpowder. ''Do not try to coerce or threaten me! And never, never try to tempt me! You stay because you intend to steal the child. You intend to take Andrew, because your own bairn died.''

''For God's sake! Do you hold that against me?''

''He is my charge, not yours. I will wait here in Inverness for him. And indeed we have a bargain, and indeed I will not be forsworn. Should you beckon, I will take off your jacket and your trousers and let your naked body take mine, if that is what you demand. But will you make me live here openly as your mistress?''

It was a rigid wall of defiance, as if they had shared nothing, given each other nothing. ''Devil take it! You know I will not,'' he said. ''But you won't turn me aside from my purpose, nor make me leave by denying our desire. What resources do you have?''

The rage visibly died in her. She trembled as if she might fall. ''Resources?''

''Money. Blunt. How will you pay for a room?''

''I will manage.''

''Oh, good God! Take my room. Here's the key. Go on. Take it! I will find another.''

She took the key, her fingers icy against his, before turning away to enter the inn. Dominic watched her go. She was a fire running through grassland, sometimes merely smoking, sometimes raging fingers of flame. *The men of the Highlands have had their hearts broken. They will wrap their pride about their sorrow like a plaid, and emigrate rather than beg the laird for the mercy he owes his children.*

She did not stay in Inverness now because of Andrew. She stayed because of him, to try to drive him away, because she feared for his safety. And from some deep well, she yet found the strength—even when she must deny the needs of her own body—to do it. A worthy woman to love. What the hell comfort would that be in the long years ahead without her? For if he abandoned his country, he also abandoned his duty. Never before in his life had duty and love made such entirely opposite demands.

"Well, good Lord," a voice said behind him. "They said I'd find you here. I hear you're in need of a trustworthy second for a duel?"

It was a moment of dislocation, almost of madness, before he regained control. Dominic spun about. With a guileless grin breaking across his freckled face, his hair tufted like red hawk's down, Lord Stansted—son and heir to the Duke of Rutley—had just descended from a carriage to stand in the inn yard.

Dominic buried his distress and anger, making sure he seemed nothing but urbane, and stretched out his hand. "I don't know who the hell told you that, but yes, if you'd like to act as one of my seconds, hail fellow, well met!"

Stansted's grin widened. "It's the *on dit* of the day, you damned rogue! I heard it as soon as I arrived in Inverness. You're to fight a duel with one Yarrow Fletcher, a man generally disliked, and it would be seen as a public service if you were to dispatch him."

"I shan't dispatch him," Dominic replied. "You'd better come in and I'll tell you about it. But first, what the devil are you doing here?"

A shadow flitted across the freckles as Stansted frowned. "Oh, that!" He looked away, obviously embarrassed. "Well, after you left London, I thought I'd go to Edinburgh to see Rosemary, if you must know. But when I got there, she was nowhere to be found. My wife has left the Souls of Charity. They thought she'd come north.''

"Oh, God." It was a mad laughter that welled in him. "You're trying to be noble and forbearing? You thought Rosemary might be with me, didn't you?"

"Well." Stansted looked uncomfortable. "She isn't?"

"I have no idea where she is, dear friend. Rosemary is certainly not here, so you don't need to fight a duel with me of your own."

"Then thank God for that!" The grin returned, but the unease beneath the bravado was obvious. "Dear fellow, forgive my asking—but are you really wearing powder and rouge? And what the devil have you done to your hair?"

∞

She ought to have gone back to the glen and prepared herself for exile. She could not. If Andrew was brought to Inverness, she must be there, though the poor bairn was innocent of involvement in her troubles. Catriona could picture him as she had seen him in Edinburgh, a black-browed changeling full of a passion too great for his tiny body. Whose child was he? Why did his mother not acknowledge him? Was he merely the bairn of a woman who had died, an orphan taken in off the streets? And did he have no one in the world but his nurse?

Nor could she leave Dominic, the mad Englishman who seemed ready to welcome death at Fletcher's hand and would not be moved from his purpose. She could not leave, but neither could she live with him and share his bed.

All of his things had been removed from his room, yet his essence lingered there, tormenting her. She craved his warmth and strength. She craved his body and his dry wit. Yet she denied him. She denied herself his caresses and his passion, for they could never give her now what she wanted.

Now he knew how she had deceived him, had she convinced him he could not travel with her into exile? But of course the possibility remained of one last encounter—a gentleman and his paramour, to be abandoned when the time came according to the well-understood rules of the demimonde. He would undoubtedly give her parting gifts that she could sell to buy her passage and supplies for her new life. It was the way English gentlemen enjoyed their mistresses: civilized, experienced, with cynicism.

The bargain she had accepted meant that if he asked, she must go to his bed. She was a coward to rely on his honor so he would not ask. But she moved in a void as unreal as a dream, as unreal as the stories of the creatures who shed their skins to become men. Whether seal, bear, or wild bull, as the fur slipped away the man revealed could seduce any mortal maiden. With the blinding beauty of his animal nature and his pure man's body, he would entrap her in nights of ecstatic intensity. But seal, bear, or wild bull, he always returned to the sea or the forests or the hills, and left the maiden stripped of her soul and pining away for her lost enchantment.

Catriona knew she was slowly bleeding to death inside, like a willow tree gored by a bull. Her sap ran away, her bark was torn asunder, and the leaves withered on her in a brutal, early autumn. She would pine away for her lost enchantment.

Och, it is a smart wee bairn Catriona is, with her bonny black hair and blue eyes like a gentian. She'll not make many mistakes in life. But when she does, they'll be big ones.

She had made the one mistake she could never atone for.

I shall seduce you. You will fall in love and I shall break your heart. I guarantee it.

She was seduced. She was in love. Her heart was broken.

Yet his plan worked. In the morning, he fenced with Lord Stansted in a vacant patch of land beyond the cattle market, laughing as he teased Stansted into wilder and wilder thrusts, deliberately displaying his prowess and strength, like a lion that yawns. Stansted played along, parrying and feinting, panting affably in a good-natured show of friendship. A crowd gathered to watch and applaud.

That afternoon Dominic purchased a pair of dueling pieces and began to practice with them. Catriona stood to one side and craved the profound devotion that came over him as he gave himself up to his weapons. The blade had been an extension of his arm, taut muscle and piercing beauty of movement. The pistol barrel grew straight from his concentrated gaze, sending the ball lethally to the center of the target.

By evening Yarrow Fletcher's seconds had arrived stiff-faced to arrange the details of the duel with Lord Stansted and Alan Fraser, who were acting for Dominic. It would take place on the Wednesday coming, at dawn. Fletcher would agree to Dominic's one demand, that they duel openly on the strand down by the Moray Firth, with a boat waiting so the winner could escape safely away. In return, Dominic would agree to Fletcher's choice of weapon: swords.

All Inverness knew of it. As by the next morning, all Inverness learned of the prophecy that old Iseabail Mac-Norrin had made about Yarrow Fletcher.

Ruin upon you! Destruction upon your house! No prison will keep you, nor gallows dangle you. No blade will pierce you, nor bullet harm you. No grave will hold you until high stones twist from their seats and every bell rings by itself to accuse you. A curse upon you, Yarrow Fletcher! Your grave is already dug, but no man will mark it.

Catriona didn't know what it meant. Only that she and most of Ross-shire now believed Fletcher could not die— or even be wounded—in a duel. So Fletcher would feel invincible as he aimed to kill.

One morning she cried out in her sleep and woke sweating. She had dreamed of his death, that Dominic lay wounded and helpless under Yarrow Fletcher's blade, while the tip of that fatal sword carved bloody tracks over his beautiful body.

"Die like a dog," Fletcher had said in the dream. "Or

do you beg me for mercy you will never receive?''

Catriona climbed from the bed and stared blindly from
the window, not seeing the clustered rooftops of Inverness
with the spire of the Tolbooth jutting above the houses,
heedless of the tall masts of the ships on the Firth beyond.
She had once thought she was brave. She had once thought
she could outwit this Englishman. Twice before in her
lonely twenty-five years, she had thought she had loved and
it had ended in death.

Ancient superstitions stirred in her blood. *No blade will
pierce you!* How could she go to Dominic now and tell him
she believed such powerful dreams might also be pro-
phetic? How could she poison his confidence with her
doubts and maybe help to bring about what she most
feared? So she must stay away from him and trust to his
honor that he would not call on her now to fulfill their mad
bargain.

Yet while Dominic charmed the town with his displays
of swordsmanship and Fletcher sweated, Glen Reulach lay
unmolested.

His plan worked.

∞

She met him only once face-to-face in the hallway outside
her room. He stopped and leaned back, his eyes dark. The
drumbeat of desire pounded. A silent reverberation shook
the very air between them.

''Dear God,'' he said wryly. ''You have no idea what it
takes not to call on our bargain.''

''I have every idea.'' The words came out breathy,
choked. She cleared her throat and began again, desperately. ''Promise to give up this duel, then come to me tonight. I will welcome you.''

He jerked as if tugged by a string, spinning away from
the wall. ''I don't trade lovemaking for money, Catriona.
Such a promise would be bloody base coinage.''

''It is an offer made in bright yellow gold and all the
more precious for the cost of it to me!''

His hand reached as if he couldn't stop himself. His elegant fingers brushed her cheek. "I will not beckon you on such terms, though the longing destroys both of us." He smiled. "We're a bloody stubborn pair, aren't we?"

"You are determined on this duel?"

"In spite of Iseabail and her prophecies, in spite of what I know about Yarrow Fletcher, I am. Would you have me run away now with my tail between my legs?"

She took a deep breath. Her very soul burned at the touch of his fingertips, her mouth filled with yearning, her body melted in flame. "*Och-òn,* I would not have you deny your own integrity, Dominic Wyndham. *Air sgàth t'urraim agus t' fhacail*—out of respect for your word and your honor—I shall coerce you no more." The desire pooled, weakening, making her legs buckle. She looked down. "Come to me, if you wish, without conditions."

His thumb brushed the corner of her mouth. "Don't break my heart. There are always conditions. Until I have destroyed this one man, I cannot fulfill mine. But the temptation will beat me to my damned knees, if I don't leave now."

He spun about and disappeared into his own room. Catriona blindly pushed open the door to her chamber and collapsed on the bed. Of all the games lovers can play, she thought wildly, denial is the worst!

"Bloody unusual," Stansted complained. "Who the hell duels with swords any longer?"

"The French." Dominic looked at him and laughed.

The town snoozed and sauntered in the long twilight. Couples strolled slowly toward the Ladies' Walk. Seagulls flew silently over their heads, like the ghosts of drowned sailors. He and Stansted were the only men who strode with purpose and direction down the long streets. The duke's son carried a leather case containing two matched rapiers.

"An unusual choice," Dominic continued. "But easier to wound with, less likely to kill—except deliberately, of

course. Fletcher is polishing his style with a Parisian fencing master, I hear. I'd love to see it, though I have witnessed his prowess with a blade before.''

The freckled face tipped up as a seagull cried overhead.
''Have you? When?''

He suppressed the foul memory and grinned. ''It doesn't
matter.''

Stansted said nothing for a moment. When he began
again, the strain was obvious in his voice. ''Listen, Wyndham, I do understand about Rosemary and you—''

''Your wife was never my lover, Stansted. Believe it.''

The duke's son blushed. ''I do! I would never think you
had so little honor. To lie with the wife of a friend? It's
unthinkable!''

''Though when you first arrived, you were thinking it.''

''Well, she wanted you, even when she let me—''

Dominic grinned. ''Let you *what,* sir?''

The blush became furious. ''We did consummate our
marriage, you know, and quite often. Even in Edinburgh,
in the Victory Summer, when you were there.''

He didn't want to hear the details, but he was amazed
by this. ''Good God! You damned dark horse! And I
thought myself the devil with women.''

''I love her,'' Stansted said. ''I think she wants to love
me, but her feelings for you are an obsession. She can't
help herself. That's why I thought she might have followed
you here. And if you had succumbed—I know it wouldn't
have been deliberate, but such things happen, don't they?
She's very passionate.''

''Stansted, put your mind at rest, for God's sake. Rosemary is indeed passionate. She's also lovely, intelligent,
and a little unhinged. But I would not have succumbed!''

They were approaching the inn. Catriona was there, the
focus and heart of his longing. She would be asleep, perhaps. Exhausted by her cares, curled up in what had been
his bed, with her hair dark on the pillow, her graceful limbs
relaxed at last. Dominic craved her. The craving beat at his
defenses, undermined his determination. Yet if he could not
burn away her sorrow, he would only consume her. Then

they would part seared and injured, with love charred to ashes. What choices remained when duty warred against desire?

"But I am worried about Rosemary," Stansted said. "Where the devil has she gone?"

They had come into the inn yard. "She'll take care of herself. Your wife is a remarkable woman. Now, if you don't mind, I have Yarrow Fletcher to face in the morning. I need my sleep."

"Major Wyndham?" A lad held out a slip of paper.

Dominic rapidly read the contents before handing it to his friend.

"Nairn?" Stansted asked. "Where's that?"

"About fifteen miles along the coast. We shall have to go."

"Now?" The duke's son set the rapier case down by the wall. He ran both hands through his red hair. "Fifteen miles? I thought you needed your sleep."

"I do. But this counts more."

"What if it's a trap?"

Dominic grinned. "I'm sure it's a trap. We'll go anyway."

They hired horses from the inn and set off. The town hummed behind them, sparking odd drifts of human sound out to the seashore. It was hard riding with the sunset glow streaming and the approaching night opalescent as a pearl over the North Sea ahead. The open moor lying between Strath Nairn and the Moray Firth bulked to their right—the heights where Bonnie Prince Charlie had led his Highlanders to destruction over seventy years before. A little brook gurgled through the stones on the shore's edge, emptying its laughter into the Firth. Far away across the water, the humped outline of the Black Isle dreamed and drifted under a roseate sky. Dominic felt absurdly alive, preternaturally alert, as if he saw the hills and the water for the first time. Each blade of grass quivered. A wash of sea air crept over his face like a caress.

A trap. At some point it was bound to spring.

If the trap sprung and he died out here on this seashore, he would never see Catriona again. Would it be better to let her mourn briefly and then find a new love in a new world? What vain hope made him think he could sway her with passion? And what respect could he have for her, if he did? Whether he left for Canada or she came to England, their sin—that one of them had so violated duty and honor—would destroy love in the end and turn it all to bitterness. So he had forced himself to stay out of her bed.

For her sake, he knew he should have left Scotland long before. But he couldn't bear to do it, and he couldn't shirk this encounter with Yarrow Fletcher, even if the man was destined never to be harmed by a blade. In the morning they would meet here and put Iseabail's powers of prophecy to the test. He didn't intend to die, he didn't want to die, but if he did, would that free Catriona to face her future more easily?

The horses cantered on. By the time they reached Nairn, the remaining day had bled away into darkness. The small inn was squat and square, its stone walls brooding. Dominic swung down and knocked at the door. It opened at last to reveal the white face of a woman. She held a large dog by the collar. The dog snarled.

"I have come in answer to a message," Dominic said. "Is Mrs. Mackay within?"

"There's no one of that name here, sir." The woman peered back over her shoulder and called out. "Geordie! Is there any Mrs. Mackay with us, or anywhere hereabouts?"

The negative answer came shouted back. Dominic showed her the slip of paper and insisted.

"Och, it's some kind of mistake, sir," she said. "That's our address, but no one here wrote that."

"And is there a child here?" he asked. "Black-haired, about fifteen months old?"

"Well, there was, sir, now I come to think of it. A lad with a woman. Och, is that the bairn you're after? It was earlier this morning, sir, when they passed this way and they did not stop here more than an hour. I never knew their names. Mackay, is it?''

"Do you know where they came from, or where they were going?''

"I don't, sir, on my honor. I'm surprised anyone should have noticed enough to send you that letter.''

He bowed deeply and apologized for disturbing her so late.

"It isn't a trap?'' Stansted asked as he handed him his reins.

Dominic mounted. "No, it's a wild-goose chase. Leading nowhere, like the scent of last month's fox. We had better go back to bed. After all, I have a duel to fight in the morning.''

It was slower returning—walking, sometimes trotting— through the short night. The hair prickled at the back of Dominic's neck, a premonition. Had Fletcher written the note, as he'd suspected? Why? To make him ride thirty miles the night before their affair of honor just to tire him out? To remind him that Fletcher had visited the Souls of Charity and knew of Andrew and Mrs. Mackay, and was also on the child's trail? But why the devil would this lost child matter to Fletcher, now the truth was known about the little boy's birth?

Inverness lay ahead, the jagged ruins of the castle jutting above the rooftops. The town lay in deep silence, the horses' hooves resounding hollowly as they passed through a small grove of pines. The feeling of premonition came stronger, a sense that the world was ready to spin out of kilter. Even the tired horses seemed nervous, blowing, and edging sideways at shadows. Stansted's horse minced as if the road were made of eggshells, frangible and translucent as porcelain.

Dominic corrected his mount again as it tossed its head. Why the *hell* had Fletcher sent them on a cold trail to Nairn? Simply to remove him and Stansted from Inverness—for God knew what purposes? They had been gone

for over three hours. Oh, dear God, not Catriona! He
glanced over his shoulder.

"Stansted—"

A blow to the chest knocked the air from his lungs. As
his horse skidded away beneath him he saw Stansted
plucked back by an invisible giant. The duke's son called
out once before landing heavily. Reins flying like kite
strings, the horses started away, only to be stopped and
caught by men who materialized instantly from the darkness.

Dominic hit the road and rolled. For God's sake! The
oldest ambush in the book! A rope stretched at the right
height to cut a horseman from his mount. He regained his
feet, knife in hand, but it was too late.

A familiar hawk-chested figure blocked the road. Like a
peacock's tail, a group of ragged Highlanders spread behind
him. Stansted, on hands and knees, had his back to them
and was struggling to rise. He seemed dazed. Without further warning, one of the men stepped up and brought his
fist hard into the side of the red hair. Stansted dropped like
an anchor, drifting, weaving for a moment, only to hit hard
at the end as his head met the ground.

"You did not find the child?" Yarrow Fletcher asked.
"How sad! Of course, he's not there."

Dominic sheathed his knife. He was vastly outnumbered.
"But you know where he is."

"I don't really care." Fletcher smiled, his face grotesque
in the shadows, as he stared down at Stansted. "My condolences on your friend. An awkward thing for me, since
I work for his father, but he cannot be allowed to interfere."

"Are we to fight now?" Dominic asked. "The duel is
not until morning."

Fletcher's head snapped up like a carriage step. "The
duel? Oh, yes. The event where I will turn up and you will
not. You will be revealed to the world as the coward you
are."

"You're not concerned about all these witnesses?"
Dominic indicated the Highlanders.

"Ha! Not one of them speaks English. They don't understand anything we're saying. They only know we have a private quarrel. In reality you will be my guest in the nice dark cellar I have prepared. I do, indeed, have blades there, and pistols—though the gun is a little crude for the subtleties I have in mind. Have you liked being a thorn in my side?"

"If I'd had things as I like," Dominic replied, "I'd have been a bayonet in your heart."

"Because you have no imagination. What waits for you is the entire rosebush. The petals to fill your throat and the roots to fill your gut, with a twist of thorns to reach into every sinew and muscle. You will scream, Wyndham. You will scream."

"And my corpse?" Dominic asked. "What will you do with that? Shall I be dumped in an alley? I hope you won't put it where women or children could find the results. I imagine they'll be gruesome."

"By God," Fletcher said. "You do like to play it cold!"

"Like a fish." Dominic grinned to cover the icy shaking deep in his belly. "Who will be blamed?"

"Blamed? Why?"

"I mean, sir, that when my mangled remains are discovered—whether tossed in the midden or floating in the Firth—someone will be accused of murder. I was last seen with poor Lord Stansted." He nodded to the red head lying quiet on the cobbles. "I don't imagine Rutley would want his only son implicated."

Fletcher grinned. "Yes, you tupped his wife, didn't you? Pretty dark-haired Lady Rosemary. She was so concerned about you in Edinburgh. So he even has a motive. Don't worry! A couple of the lads will take him back to the inn. They'll claim they found him drunk and make a fuss about it. Stansted will have his alibi."

"So who will not?"

"In your charmed circle?" Fletcher was picking at his nails with the tip of his knife. "Your lover, for one: Catriona MacNorrin."

The effort to control his rage, not to launch himself at

Yarrow Fletcher, made his muscles hurt. He could probably
reach the man and do him serious damage before his body-
guard rescued him, but then he would not learn what he
had done with Catriona.

"Poor, deluded girl," he said. "Is she still loyal to me?"

Fletcher folded the knife and slipped it away. "I don't
know. She'll be found in a wretched state, blade in hand,
by your body. She may not be hanged, of course, when it's
seen what you did to her. You are known for perverted
tastes, aren't you? Yet Catriona MacNorrin will have suffered outrages. She'll be hurt. No doubt she'll bleed. The
damage may even be permanent. If she's found to be out
of her mind with the horror, what court would convict her
for murdering her attacker? Any good lawyer could claim
self-defense—not that I imagine she can afford a good lawyer."

Bile rose in Dominic's throat. His knife would slide in
easily and Fletcher would be dead. But what if the man,
insane and desperate, already had Catriona? What if she
was bound and hidden, never to be found? Hidden where
she would starve to death in the dark and think he had
abandoned her?

So he kept his arms at his sides as Fletcher nodded to
the Highlanders. They closed in with fists to pummel him
to his knees—broken men from broken clans, who would
do even this to earn a little bread.

They dragged him, bleeding and bruised, through the
sleeping streets of Inverness into the small, mean alleys.
Dominic let his muscles relax, saving his strength. Stansted
had been picked up and carried away.

He saw only glimpses of his surroundings between the
swinging plaids of his captors, until they hauled him into
a courtyard. Dark shadows shifted as light flickered from a
lamp burning somewhere. The flagstones beneath his feet
were uneven, the rough walls at each side tall and devoid
of windows—warehouses, perhaps. A square stone well-
house squatted in the center of the yard. The men dropped
him there and stepped back as Fletcher came up. Dominic
fell to the flagstones, his skin on fire, and laughed.

Fletcher kicked. It sent a shaft of flame through his ribs. "Don't you want to know where she is?"

Light blazed as a man with brown hair went about lighting torches.

Dominic braced his back against the well and stared up into the face of a fiend. "Does it matter what I want?"

"She is here," Fletcher said. "She is going to watch."

The handle cranked, creaking as the chain rattled and the bucket came up. Dominic thought for one crazy instant she was imprisoned down there with the algae in the damp, sloshing darkness. But with a guard at each elbow, Catriona came out of the warehouse upright and proud. Her hands were bound behind her, but she was obviously unharmed.

Dominic had just lifted his face to the sky and thanked God, when a bucketful of cold water doused his face and shoulders. He gasped, unable to repress shivers. Fletcher stepped away. One of the Highlanders remained standing over him with a knife at his throat.

"*A Dhia!*" Catriona spoke rapidly in Gaelic to the men surrounding Dominic. One of them began to remonstrate in the same language. She cursed at him and nodded to Fletcher, talking fast.

"Tell them I have money in England," Dominic said. Water and slime trickled into his mouth. He wiped it away. "I can be left here. That doesn't matter. But all my gold is theirs if they take you to safety right now."

"Och, hush!" She smiled at him, ghostlike in the shifting darkness. "It is you I am buying to freedom!"

"No secret bargain will be made with these men, madam." Yarrow Fletcher indicated the small brown-haired man. "Harris will translate to me every word said in your uncouth language."

She tilted her head, like a queen. "Indeed! Yet these are men from the west with their own ideas of honor. They understand revenge in a personal quarrel, but they won't do anything that seems evil to them."

"For God's sake!" Dominic looked up at the brown-haired man, Harris. "Pray, translate for me, sir. There is gold for them all—and for you—if Miss MacNorrin is

taken to safety now! They were contracted to bring only
me to Yarrow Fletcher. No promise will be broken.''

Harris shrugged, but one of the Highlanders came up and
took the brown-haired man by the elbow. They started
speaking in Gaelic.

"No bargains!" Fletcher hissed. "Give them their blunt
and let them leave as we arranged. Nothing else concerns
them now."

Another of the Highlanders stepped forward, his hand on
the hilt of his knife, his native language rolling and lilting
from his tongue. Catriona spoke again quickly, arguing,
pleading. The Highlander answered. He sounded implacable.

Harris listened, then turned to Fletcher. "The woman
demands they release Wyndham without further damage.
She offers herself to remain as your captive. This man refuses, since they have a bond with you. Instead, they will
see you match your enemy in fair fight. If you win, they
will leave and you may do as you will with the prisoners.
If you lose, they both go free."

"No fight can be fair," Catriona said. "Major Wyndham
is injured."

"They have heard the prophecy and don't believe you
can be harmed," Harris explained to Fletcher, ignoring her.
"But they'd have Wyndham given his chance to defy his
fate. The woman won't be allowed to leave until it is over."

"Devil take all of you!" Fletcher spat. "Does my money
and our agreement mean nothing!"

"Och, be careful, Mr. Fletcher," Catriona said. "We
might offend the pride of these men with further talk of
gold. Their word and honor means more, even now!"

The knife blade pricked his neck, then withdrew. The
uneven stone of the well dug into his back as Dominic
shrugged out of his wet jacket. "Damnation! Mr. Harris,
pray beg this man to take her away now! Leave me here
with Fletcher, devil take it, with one hand tied behind my
back, if you will. But get Miss MacNorrin away. None of
this concerns her."

Harris spoke again with the Highlanders, then shook his

brown head. "These men will see the fight, sir. They won't let her leave and she won't go."

Oh, God! Oh, God! Could he win? If he did not—he felt sick—Catriona had no idea what she faced. Yet, in spite of the prophecy and the beating, he had a damned good chance! Fletcher might be expert with a blade, but Dominic knew he was better.

Fletcher stalked away across the yard. "Fair fight?" He laughed. "Very well. Bring the rapiers!"

The Highlander standing over him stepped aside. Light shimmered and slid as Fletcher tried his blade, whipping the air, then picked up the other. Dominic grasped the wooden upright supporting the pulley and began to stand, every muscle protesting. Strings of green slime trickled over his face. He wiped them away, his right hand on the rough wood.

"So we're to fight our duel?" He tried to make the words light, nonchalant, to hide his deep blaze of hope. "Don't I get a blade, too?"

Something darted, dazzling him, and pain exploded in his hand—exquisite, as if a red-hot hammer pounded into his palm, breaking bone, pulverizing flesh. Gritting his teeth so he wouldn't cry out, he looked at the wooden post. Fletcher had just pinioned his right hand to it with the tip of one rapier.

"Your blade, sir!" Fletcher said. "Shall be begin?"

He stalked away, laughing, then turned and presented.

Dominic clenched his jaw as he wrenched out the sword with his left hand. In a reflex, he hugged his right fist to his chest for a moment, holding his thumb hard over the spurting blood. His hand sizzled as if burning. It took an effort of will to wrap his handkerchief around his wounded palm and tie it there with his teeth. The cloth instantly soaked with blood. He was strongly right-handed. How the hell was he going to fight now?

The other men moved away, leaving a clear field of view. Catriona sat on a bench between two burly Highlanders. Something white drifted in the air near her head. A sweet scent came to him suddenly, a bizarre contrast to the foul

well water soaking his chest and back. A rosebush! She sat
near a rambling rose, its petals like lace.

Fletcher began to pace, stalking up and down before
Dominic. His eyes glittered. There was a new madness
about him. His laugh was frenzied. His hawk chest had
visibly expanded. It was a crazy confidence, even for an
excellent swordsman who faced a crippled opponent.

"So we shall duel like gentlemen," Fletcher said. "Why
not? I should like to see you sweat before we indulge the
final humiliations. You may beg me for mercy, if you like.
You can even try to win, but remember: I cannot be
harmed!"

Without warning, he spun and lunged.

Dominic ducked to one side. He could fence a little left-
handed, but not against a master, not against a man who
had made a study of French swordsmanship. His right hand,
bundled in cloth, hung useless, stabbing heat up his arm,
clouding his brain with agony. Yet Dominic still allowed
hope to bloom. Because without hope he was doomed and
Catriona with him.

Fletcher lunged again. Dominic met the thrust clumsily
and twisted away. "I hope you have made peace with your
Maker, Mr. Fletcher?"

"Why?" Fletcher reached and slashed a button from
Dominic's shirt. "No blade will kill me. The old witch said
so."

"It was a curse, not a benediction."

Fletcher strutted away, letting Dominic regain balance.
He flexed his thin shoulders and smiled secretively. "My
skin cannot be pierced, Major Wyndham. I am invulnera-
ble. You are not. And what if one blade has been poisoned?"

Seventeen

FOR A WHILE Dominic parried easily. Fletcher was just playing with him, wearing him down. The man was obviously mad, but he was indeed superb with a sword. The Highlanders watched, determined not to interfere. What did they see? Or understand? Nothing of what had been said, obviously. They stood like spectators at a Greek tragedy, fixated by the conflict, yet knowing the outcome was predestined.

He wanted, in crazy defiance, to sing or shout. Yet his lungs burned, his shirt stuck to his wet back, he probably had a broken rib, and he was fencing left-handed. His flaming right palm screamed for his attention. *Even if you survive this,* it clamored, *I will be forever useless. You will be crippled, or die helplessly from wound fever. Your right hand, Dominic Wyndham! He has destroyed your right hand!*

Shutting out the voice, he tried to concentrate. Why poison? Obviously because a clean death from a simple sword thrust was not enough. So a slow-acting poison, then. One wrong move, one scratch, and it would start working in his veins.

"Why poison?" He spun away as Fletcher's blade hissed past his ear. "Can you resist telling me?"

"Just a drug to make you helpless." Fletcher followed

through with a series of rapid thrusts. "Enough to make you obey. Your judgment will be suspended, but you will know everything you do."

Steel clashed, screeching. Dominic dropped back, feinting and parrying, losing ground as Fletcher pushed harder.

He was a mouse trilling defiance at a cat. "I thought it was a dark cellar waiting and your doing things to me."

Fletcher grinned like a dead carp on a fishmonger's slab. "That comes afterward. Did you think I or my men would violate your harlot? Oh, no, Dominic Wyndham. You will do it. Once we have satisfied these treacherous Highlanders with our nice swordplay, they will leave and we shall be alone. By then you will be bleeding here and there, and the drug will be corrupting your heart and seducing your soul. For an hour or so you will do everything I want and laugh as you do it."

Dominic took his chance and thrust hard under Fletcher's guard. His blade rang, sending shocks up his arm, as Fletcher met it. For a moment the men embraced, hilts locked together.

"There is no such drug."

"Then risk it, fool!" Fletcher twisted his hand until the hilt of his sword dug into Dominic's fingers. "She will be restrained. We'll tie her, you and I, to that bench. Does she think she knows all the secrets of the body? She has never imagined the things you'll do to her, willingly, because you won't be able to help yourself. You will plumb the depths of your desire, Dominic Wyndham. Her screams won't stop you. And then your turn will come. After the drug wears off, *you* will experience the pleasures of my fleshly tastes. You will beg me to die soon enough."

"What the hell," Dominic asked softly, ignoring the pain, "do you think you know about my desire?"

They broke apart and Dominic dodged around the well. Fletcher came after him, deliberately making him duck and sidestep. More buttons rattled away. The rapier whistled as it flicked at the wet sleeve of his shirt, opening a long gash from shoulder to wrist. His bare skin lay exposed, the chill air raising the hair on his forearm.

He could not win. He could not even break Fletcher's guard. Dominic was tired and his painful right hand rang a death knell. His left shoulder and arm began to burn, then to drag. His blade felt clumsy, moving slowly. But Fletcher's rapier was always there, fresh, accurate, cutting away more fabric, stripping him without—as yet—touching flesh. He knew it was deliberate, that at any moment Fletcher could lunge and sink his blade, or slice and cut him open, forcing him to yield. Then the Highlanders would leave. Harris would tie Catriona. The torture would begin.

His breath came hard. Shadows leaped and wavered, delivering monsters and phantasms in the gloomy corners of the yard. Catriona sat tethered under the white rosebush like a princess from myth. Dominic slipped on the wet flagstones. As he dropped to one knee he saw the Grim Reaper, quite clearly, smiling from the darkness. She had been right. There was no fear for his own demise now. Death was merely an old friend. But rather than let Catriona face a madman's sadism, he would sink his own blade in her heart and let her die instantly in her bower of roses. Although first he would fight to the end.

He twisted and regained his feet. Fletcher came after him, dancing. His sword skipped and sparkled. Dominic raised his own blade crudely, blocking, defending, with no hope now of going on the attack. He let Fletcher drive him. White shreds of his shirt trailed and broke away, exposing his cold, wet body to the air. He fought in intense concentration. *There! Now, there! Now, come after me, you madman! Like this! And this!*

The bucket sat where Fletcher had dropped it. The chain looped over the side of the well, shining dully in the darkness. At the foot of the wall, a small dark bundle of cloth lurked: his wet jacket. Circling, eluding, Dominic worked steadily toward it. Fletcher, grinning widely, followed. His blade sliced through the darkness, ringing destruction, until Dominic's shirt fell entirely away. As the tip of Fletcher's rapier drew back Dominic threw his own blade with all the strength he had left.

It clattered, steel singing, against the house wall.
Fletcher's gaze followed for a split second. Dominic
dropped, grabbed his jacket, and threw. The wet fabric hit
Fletcher in the face. The well chain fell hard and cruel into
both hands as Dominic pulled. Screeching, the windlass
spun, unreeling chain, and agony shot fire through his shattered palm.

Blinded, Fletcher stumbled against the chain. He
wrenched the jacket from his head with his left hand and
yelled. Raising his sword to his shoulder, he drew back to
lunge with the point. Dominic wrenched the chain so it hit
Fletcher across the chest. Fletcher dropped, trying to dodge,
but the chain caught his sword arm and pinned it back
against the wooden post. Dominic yanked. Blood spilled
from his makeshift bandage, splattering over the flagstones,
but the poisoned rapier dropped to the ground.

He bent and grasped it by the hilt. Pain doubled him,
sick and dizzy. The red stain ran onto his breeches where
his right hand lay curled in a reflex retraction. He didn't
know if he could stand straight or if he could lift the
weapon. He didn't know if he believed in the drug. Yet if
it was true, one scratch might be enough to disable Fletcher.
Mad voices began to clamor in his head: *no blade will
pierce you, nor bullet harm you.* He tried to force himself
upright, laboring to lift the sword.

The color had fled Fletcher's face, but he laughed as he
leaped up onto the edge of the well wall. He grabbed the
bucket by the handle.

"Try to strike me! Do it! You cannot! The old witch was
right. Meet your doom, Dominic Wyndham!"

Chain clattered. The bucket wavered as Fletcher hoisted
it up to cudgel the heavy wood onto Dominic's bent head.

And he could not stand. Or move. Or save himself.

Fletcher's rapier clinked from Dominic's hand onto the
flagstones.

A cavalry charge roared in his ears. The ground shook.
With a great rending and groaning, slates cracked on the
rooftops. Chimneys cried out, tumbling stones. Dominic
fell to his knees, his balance shredded. The light from the

torches flared and jigged, throwing wild shadows. The pain in his right hand blazed, knocking him to the flagstones.

Had he been cut and not known it? Was this the poison?

He looked through the rocking dark for Catriona. Rose petals rained down on her like snow. She swayed on her feet, alarm—a primeval panic—plain on her face, and their gazes locked.

Forgive me, my love, he wanted to say. *I was wrong. I am too late. Fletcher has won and I have not killed you first!*

In the next moment all the bells of Inverness began to ring out together, and madly, Dominic began to laugh.

Fletcher had half fallen, suspended over the open well shaft. He dropped the bucket into the water and grabbed the shaking post with both hands. The chain jerked and rattled as it pulled itself back into the well.

"The bells!" Fletcher cried. "The bloody bells!"

"No grave will hold you until high stones twist from their seats and every bell rings by itself to accuse you. A curse upon you, Yarrow Fletcher!" It was Catriona, shouting above the clatter of falling stones, the rose petals whirling about her.

The ground rippled, the flagstones bucking like colts, as the iron links clanked away into darkness. Fletcher kicked out and tried to reach for a higher support, but his ankle caught the chain. His foot snapped from the low wall and he screamed. The chain jerked him, pulling his legs into darkness, audibly snapping bone. One hand slipped, the fingers splayed for a moment. Frantically Fletcher grasped, but his fingertips slid off the spinning windlass.

"Save me!" he cried, his mouth soft and open, appallingly defenseless. "Save me!"

"For Private Smith, for my coachman, for a French officer in the Peninsula, for a township burned out and made homeless, for the sake of a baby born too soon, for the sake of what you planned for Catriona, I'll damn you, instead!" Dominic grimaced at the waves of pain from his torn hand. "Anyway, I can't bloody move."

Fletcher's other hand slipped. With palms tearing at the

chain he disappeared into the well. Above him the well-house crumbled, wooden posts buckling, pitching windlass, slate, and stone into the void.

The bells rang, carillons pealing into the night sky. Dominic looked up once at the dancing stars. As the world went black an old voice cried out. *"You'll neither die in your bed, nor rest easy in it, Yarrow Fletcher. A curse and a doom is upon you! Your grave is already dug, but no man will mark it."*

He woke up in his bed in the inn. No one else was in the room. The world appeared to have spun safely back onto its axis. Dominic sat up. He was bruised and his ribs throbbed, tender to touch. They were bound with clean linen. His right palm was bandaged, but the drumbeat of pain played merry hell with his breathing. Ignoring that, he tried to move his fingers and failed. Had the tendons been severed? If he lost the use of his right hand, what bloody help would he be to Catriona in the wilderness? For that was his temptation: to abandon his duty, his homeland, his natural vocation, and go with her. The words leaped into definition. *Your right hand, Dominic Wyndham!*

He forced himself not to dwell on it. Someone had washed him and put him in a nightshirt. He touched his head with his left hand. Even his hair was clean. Someone had washed and dried it while he lay helpless. Damnation! How the hell long had he slept?

He dropped his head back to the pillow and stared at the ceiling, willing Catriona to come to him.

She came in at last, almost shyly.

"You are awake?"

The plaster was cracked into a tiny mosaic, like a spiderweb. He was careful to strip any emotion from his voice. "Obviously. How much damage did it do to the town?"

She came closer, standing near enough to allow a hint of her scent. Desire leaped in him. He ignored it.

"The earthquake? Och, some. The Tolbooth steeple is

twisted several feet from the top. Large numbers of stones were tossed from the chimneys. They say the bells rang for a full minute as their towers shook. It was a grand peal. The people came running out of the houses in their nightclothes, but no one was killed.''

He glanced at her. Her expression was stoic, the tilt of her jaw beautiful. "Except Yarrow Fletcher?"

"The wellhouse cracked and sent stones after him. He is drowned. I am glad for it. Is that a sin? The wellhouse caved in, burying him."

"So it took a bloody act of nature to kill the bastard? Devil take it, I'm glad, too! Are Iseabail's prophecies usually fulfilled so dramatically?"

"Sometimes." She looked nervously at her hands. "But you might have bested him without it, with your dishonorable tricks."

Dominic stretched, then immediately regretted it. "Dishonorable? Don't you think, under the circumstances, that even the strictest code of honor allowed any means necessary?"

"I did not mean that." She sat down in a chair by the bed. "Lord Stansted said you received a message."

"He is unharmed, I trust?"

"His head is sore and he was a wee bit confused for a while. He slept through the earthquake. He has gone to tell the authorities Fletcher fell down the well, so the man will not be reported missing and searched for. Nothing will be said about the fight, although I told him. The message was about Andrew and Mrs. Mackay, wasn't it?"

"They had been in Nairn, but left before we got there."

"And you did not think, did you, to warn me or tell me where you had gone?"

"Should I have?" He did not mean it to sound so sharp.

"When I cut my hair, you told me I had wantonly destroyed something radiant. You were angry for it." Her voice was tight—with anguish or anger? "I have admired the bonny shape of your hands. You did not think to be careful? To expect ambush?"

"I paid for that omission."

Her chin jerked up. "As I did. Harris and Fletcher came and dragged me from my bed. I was blindfolded and taken to that place. It was a dark moment for me, until I was brought out and saw the Highlanders."

The apology he owed her was too great to give. "What happened to them?"

"They have gone west, home. Though their homes are long gone and only the seashore is waiting."

"Did you bathe me, wash my hair?"

She blushed. It surprised him. "I did. You had slime in it. You had better sleep."

She rose to leave.

"Catriona—"

"What?"

Dominic turned to the wall. "Go. It doesn't matter."

"Och, you stubborn man!" Her smile was unsure, even now. "The doctor tells me you are lucky. Your hand is swollen rigid, but you should get some use back. He cannot tell how much. It will take time. There will be damage, scarring. I am very sorry for it."

Nauseous, hurting, he knew now he was hanging on by a thread. *Your right hand, Dominic Wyndham! How can you go to the wilderness now?* "Are you?"

She patted the bedclothes, a gesture awkward with tenderness. "I am. I have enjoyed that hand on my skin."

∞

Dominic forced himself out of bed. He dressed, tying his cravat clumsily with one hand, and rang the bell. A maid brought breakfast. After he had eaten, the doctor came and replaced the bandage. Dominic made himself watch, with the same self-discipline he had used struggling with his cravat. He studied the torn mess in his palm and shuddered. *I have enjoyed that hand on my skin.*

The doctor left without offering more than platitudes, and Dominic walked into the corridor. Catriona's room was two doors down, Stansted's just beyond that. At the end of the corridor lay a communal drawing room for the use of the inn's guests. An odd sound rang from its open doorway: a squeal, followed by laughter.

Dominic strode down the passage and pushed the door wide. A small boy laughed in Catriona's arms. Dark hair curled on the toddler's round head. His little baby dress bunched over chubby arms and legs. The blue eyes gazed with a familiar artlessness. The small chin and fragile neck were equally recognizable. The child turned to stare at Dominic and his baby laugh died for a moment, giving way to an uncertain, trembling smile.

Oh, God! The child who had been a pet at the house of the Souls of Charity and haunted his dreams! Not Harriet's. Not Catriona's. Not Sarah's. The child of the one other lady who might have reason to hide her baby's existence from his father. Were earthquakes easier to deal with than this?

A motherly woman with her hands folded in front of her stood next to Catriona and beamed. The woman still wore her cloak. Obviously she had just arrived, bringing the child.

"Well," Dominic said. "Mrs. Mackay? I am pleased to make your acquaintance, ma'am."

"Boban," the child said, pointing at Dominic.

" *'S mise Anndra,"* Mrs. Mackay corrected. She wore a neat white kerchief over her hair, like the ones the women wore in Glen Reulach.

"Hello, Andrew," Dominic said, still digesting this new truth. "Would you like a cake?"

"Och, it is not his mealtime, Major Wyndham," Mrs. Mackay said.

Dominic waved everyone to a chair, then pulled the bell for service. "No, it is not mine either. But his mother will be coming soon, won't she? I think we should celebrate, just a little, don't you?"

"Cake," mouthed Andrew, and laughed.

∞

Catriona watched them, the child and the man. Her heart vibrated suddenly with longing, like a drum skin. Andrew had cake crumbs on his rosebud upper lip. His fingers were sticky. Dominic held the bairn on his lap as adhesive little fingers strayed onto his cravat and over the perfect cut of his trousers. He was making up games with his left hand to amuse the child. Andrew grabbed and giggled with absolute trust.

Mrs. Mackay sat respectfully to one side of the room and drank her tea without comment. At last the black eyelashes drooped over the periwinkle eyes. Dominic let Andrew lie back in the crook of his arm until the child fell asleep with the absolute abandon of the very young.

"I don't understand," Catriona said. "You said his mother would come?"

The dimples raced into his cheeks. "Didn't you guess? You were with him for some time. How could you have thought him a MacNorrin? Doesn't he look English to you?"

The child's eyelashes swept in deep curves over his round pink cheeks. His upper lip lifted to show a glimpse of milky teeth. "Indeed, he does. But I thought that was the influence from Sarah's family."

"Sarah and Rosemary were cousins." Mrs. Mackay rose and lifted the child from Dominic's arms.

"Sarah and *Rosemary*?" She felt bewildered.

"We may tell her, Mrs. Mackay?"

"I see you have guessed it all, Major Wyndham," the nurse said.

Dominic laughed softly. "You saw what you wanted to see, Catriona. Now that might be a typical fault of yours!"

And suddenly it all fell into place, though she still could not be entirely sure. "I have many faults, but I lived there in Edinburgh. How could I not have noticed if his real mother was present?"

Mrs. Mackay rocked gently, Andrew's dark head on her breast. "She made sure you would not, ma'am. As everyone was sworn to secrecy when he was born. It was not hard to maintain the deception. A house full of ladies and only one bairn. His mother paid for my wee house in Edinburgh. She sent me away—"

"Why *then*?" Dominic asked. "At that precise moment?"

"Because you were coming, sir," Mrs. Mackay said. "It was her love for yourself made her refuse to openly acknowledge the bairn to start with. It is for yourself she wanted the secret kept. But she loves the boy, Major Wyndham. She loves her son. Do not mistake that."

Catriona registered this privately, hiding the knowledge away somewhere deep inside. *Her love for yourself.* Andrew had been sent away to hide him from Dominic! The implications began to ripple, flowing away in wide circles.

He stretched out his long legs and idly traced patterns on the edge of the table beside him. "So why did you cooperate with my instructions, as well?"

"Och, I saw no harm in it. The more protectors the better."

Dominic looked up and smiled. "Except her husband, who should have had the care of him?"

Mrs. Mackay seemed a little indignant. "Indeed, he does not know the child exists."

Catriona leaned forward to interrupt. She couldn't help herself. "And who is that?"

The light from the window, the still bright day, gleamed on his hair like melting butter, this blond man like an Anglo-Saxon king. She saw the fine lines drawn at the corner of his mouth and knew his hand pained him. "I'm sorry Andrew is not your uncle's child, Catriona."

"Then whose?" she said. "Tell me!"

"Born to trouble, indeed, poor lamb!" Dominic said. "He has his father's eyes and features, and his mother's stubbornness and midnight hair. It is his mother in him that makes him frown like a black-browed kelpie, his father that allows him to accept strangers without prejudice. Surely you have guessed?" He met her gaze and smiled, the dimples cutting deep. "Andrew will be a duke one day. His mother is Rosemary, Lady Stansted, so he will eventually inherit the title of Rutley. Quite a burden of importance for such a tiny soul, isn't it?"

Rosemary—who had sent money and sweetmeats to the

child. It fit, now she had this knowledge and was not
blinded by her own hopes. All those little hints and eva-
sions. It all fit. "But why would Lady Stansted hide her
own bairn?"

He looked faintly uncomfortable. "She didn't want her
husband to know. And Rutley would have forced her to
return with the child to London. Oh, Lord! I suppose I owe
you the bloody truth. I imagine she didn't want *me* to
know—"

"Why did you matter?" There was a knock at the door.
Catriona ignored it. "Why didn't she want you to know?
What was Lady Stansted's child to you?"

The door opened. Catriona turned to see the slim, dark
figure of a woman hesitating on the threshold, a woman she
thought she had known quite well, a woman who had deceived them all. Dominic stood up and bowed.

"If Dominic had known I had a child, heir to Rutley,"
Rosemary, Lady Stansted said quietly, "then he would
never have loved me." Her gaze locked with Dominic's
and she flushed. "I prayed you would come for me after
Harriet died. I waited years for it to happen. If you had
known about Andrew—that I was a mother—you would
never have taken me for your mistress, would you?"

Mrs. Mackay hefted the sleeping child to one shoulder.
"I'll need to put the bairn down, Lady Stansted."

Rosemary crossed the room and touched her baby on the
cheek. Her face softened. "I have a chamber." She waved
her hand. "It's along there. The maid will show you."

Dominic walked to the fireplace, his wounded hand
clenched in a fist on his chest. "So you sent Andrew from
Edinburgh before I arrived, in case I recognized him for
your child?"

Lady Stansted watched as her baby was carried from the
room. Her eyes filled with tears. "Mrs. Mackay took him
first to Strath Glass. Since then she has been hiding him in
a house I rented in Strathspey. When I received your message and knew you were searching for him, I arranged to
meet her in Nairn. We would have been here yesterday
evening, but I thought Andrew looked tired, so we stopped

for the night. It was dreadful. There was an earthquake. Things fell off their shelves, frightening him and making him cry. We started slowly this morning.''

With his left hand, Dominic handed her his handkerchief. ''You are safe now.'' He grinned, reassuring. ''Why on earth did you let your son have a Highland nurse? He'll be the first Duke of Rutley to speak Gaelic, I imagine. You had better go after him and see he's not still frightened, after all that cavorting about in strange places.''

Catriona turned to Dominic as soon as the dark woman had left.

''Rosemary was in love with you?''

He leaned back against the cold fireplace. ''For years. We met at a ball once, when I was back in England between campaigns. I was already engaged to marry Harriet. But Rosemary is very attractive and I'm sure I was flattered. Perhaps I unwittingly encouraged her, though I didn't intend it.''

Something hammered in her blood, a ringing distress. ''So what you told me when we first met was the truth. You have been breaking hearts all your life?''

The stiff points of his shirt framed his face. He seemed calm, watching her intently. ''If you want to put it that way. Some women find a uniform irresistible. And then when I acquired a reputation—''

''For vice?''

There was the merest hesitation before he replied. ''Yes. After Harriet ran away. You would think I'd have been shunned by the fair sex, wouldn't you? Instead I was pursued, waylaid, hounded down. Usually it wasn't hard to submit.'' He paced to the window and looked out. ''Female curiosity is a powerful sin.''

''Perhaps we should add it to the list,'' she said. ''The eighth sin. I have suffered from it. When I came to London, I was curious, too. Like all the rest.''

He spun instantly to face her. "*Not* like all the rest, Catriona!"

She looked down to avoid the fire in his eyes. "Then it is my turn to be flattered. It doesn't matter." Tears pricked, hot and painful. "I think you should go back to London, Dominic Wyndham, and take your friends and their bairn with you."

He was rigid, his face white. "Andrew is not my son, Catriona. Rosemary has taken no one to her bed but her husband. Lord Stansted was there, in Edinburgh, that Victory Summer when the child was conceived. Rosemary and I were never lovers. For God's sake! Do you think I would have so betrayed my friend?"

Was it only for this, her distress? Or that what she had known was now finally proved—Andrew could not save the glen—and so now they must finally be parted?

She swallowed her feelings and lifted her head. "Indeed, I believe you. But if Andrew is Lord Stansted's son, both children are Rutley's grandsons: Thomas inherits Glen Reulach, Andrew the dukedom. It is what I have dreaded. Fletcher's death changes nothing. Rutley will appoint a new factor and the glen will be cleared. I have wasted your time."

"I wish the hell you would trust me," he said. "I haven't given up yet."

Pain stabbed at her. He must leave! Instead, like a knight errant in legend, he would destroy himself in a vain and impossible quest to change the inevitable. Glen Reulach would die. Any future together was doomed. Why wouldn't he accept it and leave, when she no longer had the strength left to be with him?

"Trust you? To do what?"

"I don't know!" His voice gentled, but his frustration was obvious. "I have some ideas—things that might work."

"In this? Can you change the tide of history? I saw it when I came to England. Steam engines and factories and mills, their fires lighting up the skies like the mouth of hell. The future will rip apart the old ways like bairns tearing up a rotten sheet. The Highlands alone belong to the past and this new century will destroy us.''

He leaned his left hand on the mantel, his back stiff, as if it took conscious effort to stay upright. ''Is there nothing will content you, but that the old life stay the same?''

''Why not? But these hills will echo to nothing but the call of sheep and the crack of a sportsman's gun. You are part of the new time, Dominic Wyndham, and part of that class who will come here to the empty glens to shoot grouse. Go away and leave us be.''

The color had drained from his face. His eyes burned, green as glass. ''I shall,'' he said. ''But first there is the matter of Lord and Lady Stansted and Andrew. They are a family—or will be.''

She felt shredded, like a kerchief torn apart by a wind. ''But it was you, was it not, who prevented that family from forming? Because you cannot help yourself. Because you are a magnet for women. Even the wife of your friend, you charmed her like a creature from a fairy tale, leaving her ensorcelled and pining.''

''I suppose I did.''

His left hand clutched at the mantel, then slipped, as he crumpled to the floor.

The blood had soaked through his bandage, staining his cuff. Catriona tugged out her handkerchief and bound it tightly about his palm, holding the pressure until the bleeding stopped. Then she fetched a cushion from a chair and tucked it under his head, his silky blond hair soft on her fingers. She had washed his golden head and dried it with towels, all the time weeping over him. Now she had railed at him when he was ill, because she didn't know how else to set him free.

He lay, arms outflung, as abandoned as a child. The pure bones of his face echoed the bewitching beauty of the heroes of myth. He had enchanted her, this mad Englishman, and left a sore hurt in her heart to take with her to the New World.

She put her arms around his shoulders and laid her head on his chest, hearing his heart beat in the ancient rhythm of the sea. Senselessly, she wept into his coat, dampening the front of his shirt, and berated herself for a foolish woman.

There was a small noise in the doorway.

Catriona looked up to see Rosemary hovering there. She wiped her eyes and laughed, sitting back on her heels. "Och, it is a hard thing to be a woman and have such men about, is it not?"

"He fainted?" Rosemary came farther into the room, her brow contracted—like a black kelpie, Catriona thought suddenly. Oh, why had she not guessed it to start with?

"He will be all right. It is a long tale, not worth the telling. I will ring the bell and have him carried back to his bed."

Rosemary glanced down at Dominic. Her eyelashes glittered. "I took my husband to my bed imagining it was him. I thought he would come for me yet, though he pined like a mooncalf over poor little Harriet. It was not until he came to Edinburgh this last time to get Harriet's things that I knew he would never love me. All my longing and my scheming were in vain. And then it died in me, quite suddenly. I do not crave him any longer, this troublesome Dominic Wyndham. Do you believe that?"

She seemed fragile. Catriona scrambled to her feet and helped the other woman to a chair. "Love is mad. It is hard to tell the heart to love wisely. Yet Andrew is Lord Stansted's son, isn't he?"

Rosemary looked up at her and clasped Catriona's hand. "Oh, yes. And Dominic never encouraged me, or led me to believe he would waver. In fact, he tried to make me go back to Stansted. We made a bargain. That is, when he pressed me to do it, I made him agree to a bargain. I was mad, wasn't I?"

Catriona sat down beside her. "I cannot tell without knowing the terms."

"It was quite simple," Rosemary said. "I had the idea from a story. I told Dominic I would not go back to my husband unless Stansted drank a whole lake, climbed a church steeple, and gave me a son. Of course, I should have known Dominic would bring the first two things about. And the son-making I had already done myself, in a moment of weakness, though I was sure he would never find out.''

''Because—I think—you love your husband, after all, Lady Stansted?''

''I don't know, but I made a child with him and I thought then he was—'' She broke off. ''Dominic told me in Edinburgh that Stansted had fulfilled the other two conditions. The lake was an artificial one at Lady Bingham's, but the climb up the spire was real enough. To think my husband should be so brave!''

That wild climb up the church steeple—when she had first seen him—had been for this? Not an entirely empty, drunken gesture, after all. ''I saw it,'' Catriona said. ''It was a very tall steeple.''

Rosemary looked away. ''I was blinded, I think, by Dominic's splendor. He was a secret intelligence officer in the war. Did you know that? And he's so handsome, like a god. Every woman in London wants him, but such men don't make good husbands or fathers, do they? And even as lovers, they are fickle. I was mad.''

Dominic lay like a sleeping child, breathing quietly. Not the kind of man to make a good husband: a rake, crippled, perhaps, in his right hand. *And even as lovers, they are fickle.*

''Why did Major Wyndham care to get involved in saving your marriage?'' Catriona asked. ''If he did not love you, what was it to him?''

Rosemary stood up and smoothed the skirts of her fashionable walking dress. ''Because as long as I was in Edinburgh, Harriet would not leave. Dominic believed if I returned to my husband, Harriet would return to him. It was foolish—insane—of him. She would never have done it.''

''Why did you marry Lord Stansted, when you loved someone else?''

The dark eyes looked at Catriona with an almost pitying derision. ''English ladies of our class don't wed for love. Only by marrying could I expect Dominic to take me as his lover. He would never have considered me as long as I was virgin.''

Dominic groaned and stirred a little. Rosemary instantly fled the room. Catriona went to Dominic and knelt beside him. It was all an unfathomable mystery to her, these English aristocrats with their mad games of the heart. How had she—a sensible woman of the Highlands—ever thought she could win, when her opponent was such a master of artifice?

His lids fluttered open and he gazed at her through narrowed lashes. ''I fainted? Good God! How humiliating! I heard your voices as if you were talking in a well. Rosemary told you about our bargain?'' He rolled entirely onto his back, nursing his wounded hand in the palm of the other.

Catriona nodded. If only she could nurse her wounded heart in the palm of her own hand as easily!

''Tragedy and comedy are often bedfellows,'' he said. ''To take Harriet with her to Scotland was a masterful strategy—brilliantly conceived! Of course, it forced me to see Rosemary, have dealings with her, even agree to her crazy conditions to try to make her return to her husband.''

''Rosemary ran away because she loved you. She took Harriet with her to prevent any chance to mend your own marriage.''

She saw him fight to control laughter, the defiant laughter that masked whatever lay deeper and had so little to do with mirth. ''Yes. Rosemary stole Harriet away because she thought she loved me. I'm not sure if she knew how thoroughly that fit with Harriet's own desires.''

Eighteen

DOMINIC WAS HELPED back to his bed. By nightfall he had a small fever. Catriona hovered, unable—in spite of her knowledge and her resolutions—to leave while he was in danger. Meanwhile the word of Fletcher's death would wing its way to Rutley, who would send a new factor and begin the clearances again. So whether Dominic Wyndham lived or died, crippled or whole, Catriona MacNorrin must leave with her clan for Canada and never see him again. Yet how could she visit him in his room—torment to both of them?

Was it even worse torment to watch two other people fall in love? Stansted and Rosemary were together, with Andrew. It was obvious their marriage was being mended, stitch by stitch, and that Rosemary was plying the needle. Stansted had been speechless when he first returned to the inn, his freckles flooding with color, his red hair thrust in tufts as he ran his fingers through it.

"Rosemary? Thank God!"

Andrew frowned at him, then giggled.

"This is *Boban,* your father," Mrs. Mackay said. "Tell him who you are: *'S mise Anndra.''*

"*Dra!''* Andrew held out his chubby arms.

With an awkward tenderness, Lord Stansted played with his little son for most of the day. Rosemary allowed them

to get to know one another. When the bairn was taken away
by Mrs. Mackay for his nap, Stansted met his wife's eyes
and took her back to his room. They came out later arm in
arm, talking quietly. It was even possible, Catriona thought,
that Rosemary had asked her husband for forgiveness. Yet
Stansted had already forgiven, for the sake of his black-
browed son who had the Rutley chin and his wife's dark
color. He was even prepared to offer love and Rosemary
to take it. So wee Andrew had found a berth from his wandering and would have a home of his own at last.

But then the bairn had turned out to be English. It was
only the Highlanders who were to be forced from their
homes and doomed to wander.

The next morning, the doctor said Dominic was out of danger. Catriona questioned the man closely.

"Och, I believe he will regain the use of it," the doctor
said. "It's muscle torn and a bone cracked, but the tendons
are whole. If he'll rest it and not use the hand at all, it
should knit well enough. But it will always be weaker than
it was." He picked up his hat and cane, his bag tucked
under one arm. At the door he turned and smiled at her.
"Not that it matters much, does it, for a gentleman? He
doesn't need that kind of physical strength in his hands."

So even if she weakened, even if she gave in to her
wailing temptation, he could not endure the breaking of a
new life in the wilderness. *He doesn't need that kind of
physical strength.*

She found herself walking the streets of Inverness, looking at the damage from the earthquake: the Tolbooth spire
wrenched from its moorings; the broken chimneys. The
cracked slates and stones had already been cleared from the
streets. Inverness would be mended, but it, too, would never
be the same again.

Never the same again. She had ventured to England on
her great quest and failed. She had lost. Once again, she
had lost. The sky began to weep a soft mist in sympathy,

which made her laugh, if a little bitterly, to herself. It was one of the faults of the Highlands to make everything into a story. If the real world were not poetic enough, why not interpret reality to match the needs of the myth? Yet this rain was real, though it fit her mood so perfectly. *These are times when the very ocean weeps for tragedy.*

She walked as far as the docks and stared at the tall ships, their masts and rigging a cat's cradle against the gray sky. Soon, soon, the proud Highlanders of Glen Reulach, the men who had fought all over the world for King George, the women who had sometimes gone with them, would sell themselves into servitude to buy passage to another world. Should she stay here in an empty glen, because she had been born in a castle, or flee to comfort in England? Catriona came back into the inn yard knowing she must sever this last tie, once and for all. She must cut this Englishman—finally and completely—out of her heart, and try, if she could, to let him cut her out of his.

A coach stood on the cobbles. A chaise and pair, hired with job horses from the inn. He was standing by the doorway, the damp mist darkening his blond hair. His right arm, with the hand in a splint, was strapped in a sling to his chest. He saw her and smiled.

"I've been waiting for you. You see, you have your wish. I'm going back to England."

Shock rocked her as if the earthquake set all the bells to ringing once again. She felt faint. "This very night? You are not fit to travel!"

Dominic glanced away, dismissive. "Nonsense. There's nothing more I can do here. Anyway, I can't stand to watch Stansted and Rosemary making sheep's eyes at each other."

The light rain shimmered and puddled on the cobbles. "It is what you worked to accomplish."

"Yes. And it's done, so I'll leave."

He seemed very broad in his caped greatcoat. The shoulders were soaking through with the rain, coming down harder now. "Then it is more than a hundred miles will separate us!" Immediately she wished the words unsaid.

He looked back at her, his eyes filled with shadows and green mosses. "I remember. I promised. I will never seek you, nor send for you. But for God's sake, do not give up hope, Catriona!"

She wanted to give him something, some gift to take with him at this parting. There was no gift left, but this one. She lifted her chin and met his gaze. "Then I will hope, for your sake," she said, though it meant a falsehood. Who could hope when faced with their doom?

He stepped closer and reached out with his left hand. His long fingers cradled her ear, his palm warm against her cheek, a gesture so tender it melted her bones. His eyes were soft, filled with longing, but his voice was almost angry.

"Why the *hell* did we waste any time? Even an eye blink? Why didn't we spend every bloody moment together? For lovers we shared so damned little! I can count on the fingers of one hand the times you entranced me with the gifts of your body. Love is so rare and precious in this world, Catriona. When it comes your way again, promise me this: you will take it in both hands and grasp it. You'll never let go."

Tears spilled, burning her eyes. "It will not come my way again."

His gaze searched her face, lingering on her lips. His fingers slipped down to caress her neck, the thumb brushing the side of her mouth. She closed her eyes and gave in for just a moment, letting her cheek rest in his hand.

"I cannot kiss you good-bye," he said. "It would destroy my resolve."

She smiled, blinking back the tears. "Och, go then, Dominic Wyndham, and remember me kindly. For I cannot kiss you either. You were a bonny man for any woman to take for her first lover. I do not regret it. Find a lass who is worthy of that gift and marry her."

"Dear God!" An odd quirk bent the corner of his mouth. "I want no more wedding nights. Especially with virgins! In my experience, it's a dreadful combination."

Madly, longing to put her arms about him—just once,

just this once more—she laughed and stepped back. "Well, then," she said. "You have saved me from that, at least."

Before he could reply, Catriona turned and walked into the inn. She heard the carriage creak as Dominic climbed inside. Faint, she leaned into the paneled wall of the hallway.

Don't think of him! Do not! Do not! Do not! Go back to Glen Reulach—to Deirdre, and Mairead, and Iseabail. Your life is with them, forever. And you have the glen to say good-bye to, and Dunachan, and Calum's cave, and the waterfall where William Urquhart died. All your history and your childhood must be left behind now. What does it matter that you leave behind your heart and your virginity with a man who has a different destiny?

Wheels rolled on the cobbles, a grating of iron and stone, as he was taken out of her life forever. *Cha till mi tuilleadh.*

∞

The journey was hell. Plain, unadulterated hell. The jolting of the carriage sent shards of hot pain through his hand and the fever came back. Yet he instructed his drivers to travel day and night, leaving the Far North a mere memory, like a poem of Valhalla. As he slept and woke, in a kind of delirium, he saw visions of Catriona, walking through the halls of Odin. Her eagle feather jutted, proclaiming pride and defiance: the sins, God help him, of the Highlands.

Stansted and Rosemary would travel south more slowly, bringing their son and his Highland nurse. Sometimes when Dominic slept, they wandered, too, in fields of spears and poppies, blooming red like the spilled blood of dead warriors. Sometimes they walked along an infinite beach of white shells while little Andrew toddled, laughing and weeping, his black hair turned to gold and his nurse taking him away, always away, across a vast ocean. Somewhere beyond that western horizon was the land of Tir-nan-Og, the Land of Youth, where Catriona would stay young in his memory forever.

Yet he had achieved this, at least. He had brought Rosemary back to her husband, even though the original motivation for it was gone. Harriet was gone. She no longer invaded his dreams.

When he arrived in London, he had to be helped up to his rooms. Still unsteady on his feet, the next morning he shaved and dressed with great care. His man looked at him with barely veiled concern as he handed him a freshly starched cravat. Dominic surveyed the results in the mirror. A London buck, in the first stare of fashion, gazed haughtily back. Were it not for the faint shadow around his eyes and the fresh linen sling for his right hand, no one would think he had ever been away, ever indulged in a dream of the Highlands.

He walked out into the streets, suddenly aware of the smell of coal smoke and horse droppings, the press of humanity. He had never much noticed it before. Holding himself together with a deliberate effort of will, he arrived at the duke's imposing town house and sent his card up to the Duke of Rutley.

"I will inquire, sir." The prim servant bowed and disappeared upstairs. Minutes later he indicated the door. "His grace is not at home, Major Wyndham."

"Then I shall wait." Dominic sat down gratefully in a fragile gilt chair in the hallway. The servant looked embarrassed. Dominic leaned back and closed his eyes. "Yes, it's a social fiction. His grace is busy and does not wish to see me. I am aware of that. But pray tell the duke I will see him, whether he wishes it or not. I have news he will want to hear."

The servant disappeared, his powdered head bobbing white in the dim corridor.

He was kept waiting, of course. It was close to an hour before he was shown up to Rutley's study and faced the yellow goat eyes across an expanse of walnut desk.

"What possible cause can you offer for this intrusion, Wyndham?" the duke asked.

"I rely on your forbearance, your grace," Dominic replied. "You wish to see me, though you don't know it. I am sensible that—in payment for my transgression—you expect me to stand on this charming Turkey carpet throughout our interview, but I must further beg your indulgence."

He crossed the room to a light ornamental chair. Carrying it in his left hand, he put it down in front of the duke's desk and sat. It took an effort to stay upright. Without the chair, he thought he might have fallen.

"Your debauchery catches up with you, I see." Rutley steepled his hands together, resting his long chin on his fingertips. "Are you completely foxed, sir?"

"Sadly, I am completely sober." Dominic smiled. His right hand had begun to throb again.

The duke was relaxed, confident. "I assume from your injury you have met with an accident?"

"It was not an accident, your grace."

"Go on, sir," the duke said. "I believe I might enjoy this. Yarrow Fletcher?"

"Did you tell him to attempt the murder of women and children in your name?"

Rutley sat absolutely still, but his nostrils dilated. "Good God, sir! What the devil are you implying?"

Dominic looked at him, the faint trace of powder on the aging skin, the assurance and self-control of absolute power. "I thought not. Indeed, I was certain of it. It is, after all, inconceivable that a peer of this realm should have ordered such mayhem. As for my injury, alas, Mr. Fletcher and I had an old quarrel. You could not have known. I'm afraid he vastly exceeded your grace's orders. Fortunately he is dead, so he cannot impugn your reputation any longer."

An element of tension seeped away. "You are a clever man, Major Wyndham. Pray tell me what Fletcher has done."

Dominic told him, briefly. He didn't mention Catriona. It didn't matter whether Fletcher's actions were based on the duke's orders or not. Rutley must always be beyond reproach.

"So he pursued a personal vendetta against me, with regrettable consequences," Dominic finished.

Rutley leaned back. "Why are you here, Major Wyndham?"

"There was also the matter of the child. Your grace is aware, of course, that a mystery child lived with the Souls of Charity where Lady Stansted was residing. I do hope you did not believe—as some ignorant servants had gossiped—that this child was a rival to your grandson, Thomas, for his Scottish inheritance. I can assure your grace that Andrew is no blood relative of the MacNorrins."

"Can you?" The duke was interested now, hiding that interest behind closed eyelids. "Then I was mistaken to have Fletcher inquire about him?"

Such an innocent explanation! Dominic grinned. "Oh, no, your grace. You were entirely right. I trust it will please you to know that this mystery child is also your grandson."

The silence was exquisite. A shiver passed over the duke's face. "Explain yourself, Wyndham!"

"His name is Andrew. He is the legitimate child of your son, Lord Stansted, and his wife, Lady Rosemary, who are at this moment, reconciled, bringing the boy back to London."

Slowly the lids lifted to expose the saffron eyes. As Rutley stared at Dominic the yellow began to shine, melting into pure gold. "*Rosemary's* child?"

"Indeed, and Lord Stansted is unquestionably his father. The title of Rutley is thus secure to the next generation."

With remarkable restraint, the duke stood and paced across the room. He stared blindly at his bookcase for a while. When he returned to his desk, a faint trace of moisture marked the powder on his cheek. "Am I to conclude, sir, that you played some part in this discovery and this reconciliation?"

Dominic grinned innocently up at one of the most astute and selfish faces in London. "Your grace must ask his son when he returns. But he brings a baby boy, which is all that matters."

"By God, sir! You're a bloody dark horse! What do you want from me for bringing this news? What damned favor do you ask? Out with it, sir!"

It took more effort than he expected, but Dominic rose to leave. "I beg no favor, except your grace's forgiveness for Lady Stansted." He leaned his left hand on the chair back, feeling the pulse of the returning fever ringing up his arm. "By the way, the child is charming. Handsome, sound, and intelligent. A credit to your house. Of course, he has a Highland nurse. She has taught him some of her barbarous tongue." He grinned. "You will have to root that out."

Rutley sat down at his desk, folding his hands. "That may not matter, sir, since his cousin Thomas's inheritance involves that very region. The language may prove a useful skill, perhaps, when Andrew and Thomas go hunting together and wish to understand their gamekeepers."

The shrewd old fox! Dominic laughed, though the fever made him dizzy. "The land is good for more than just game, of course. I assume you wish to bring your daughter's son a respectable income from his estates in Glen Reulach?"

"His future wealth is in sheep—it has been proved so all over the North." The duke's eyes narrowed. "I am aware of your acquaintance with Miss Catriona MacNorrin, Thomas's cousin. I have allowed her to stay at Dunachan for the present. Did she tell you I had also offered her a home here in England when the people are cleared from Glen Reulach? I am not in the habit of leaving dependent female relatives in want."

Trust Catriona to have left unsaid something else this important! "She was too proud to accept your charity?"

"She wrote me instead an impassioned appeal for her clansmen and refused to leave them to their fate. Did you think to make some vain plea for the ragged inhabitants of that wilderness? They are fortunate to go to better land overseas, and if Miss MacNorrin is determined to join them, I shall not interfere. I trust you did not think news of my son's baby would soften my heart on the matter?"

Dominic let go of the chair and concentrated on reaching the side table. Some bottles sat there: French brandy, a selection of port. "On the contrary, your grace. It is only right to exact the most profit possible from Thomas's Highland estates. But I did think you might like to toast little Andrew's health.''

The duke watched him, the yellow eyes darkened to amber, and said nothing.

Dominic reached into his pocket and brought out a small bottle. He poured a measure into two crystal glasses, the peaty fragrance summoning poignant memories.

''This is the local drink.'' For God's sake, was he about to pass out? ''They call it *uisge-beatha,* the water of life.'' Concentrating hard on each step, he walked over to the duke and gave him a glass. ''To Andrew!''

Light sparked from the glasses as they were lifted. Dominic washed the whisky over his tongue. The smooth liquor spread balm through his veins. He watched Rutley close his eyes, savoring this new flavor. Pray God, it would be enough!

There was a discreet rap at the door. The duke looked up, annoyance plain on his features. ''Come,'' he said.

A powdered footman stepped into the room. ''A gentleman is here for Major Wyndham, your grace, a matter of absolute urgency. He will not be denied.''

''For me?'' The whisky sent a bolt of heat to his stomach, but cleared his head. Dominic smiled as a man pushed into the room behind the footman.

''Your grace, a thousand pardons!'' the man said, bowing deeply. ''Major Wyndham? My lord, I beg you will come at once.''

My lord? Why the devil should his family's man of business make such an elementary mistake? Dominic shook his head. The fever seemed to have reached his heart, making it pound too fast. The patterns on the Turkey carpet began to swim together. It was a relief to drop to his knees, and a heady delight to bury his face in the swirling colored wool that some Rutley ancestor had brought back from his Grand Tour. His glass spilled. Peat and smoke enveloped him in memory.

∽

A slight noise disturbed the gorse at the entrance to Calum's cave, a twig snapping, a brush of yellow bloom. Catriona glanced up. A man in a navy-and-green kilt stared down at her, tall and blond. For a moment she felt faint, though she knew it could not be him. She looked away, counting her breaths as she had counted the days since he had left—fourteen, fifteen, sixteen . . . The far peaks seemed to be dreaming. Would they dream like this forever, even after the people who loved them were gone?

She had bound him with a promise. No English gentleman would go back on his word, solemnly given. In that he was indeed like a Highlander. How could she hope he was forsworn and had come for her—in violation of honor and his word? If he did so, he would damage something vital and fundamental to what she loved in him. She could not allow that. She could not hope he would ever come here to her now. In the next instant reality swung back into focus as the man spoke in Gaelic.

It was Alan Fraser with the sun at his back.

"Catriona MacNorrin? I have bonny news. Ye'll not fathom it."

He dropped to sit beside her. As the light struck his face she saw he was grinning widely.

"You will tell me, then, Alan Fraser." She forced herself to mention the name that haunted her, knowing of nothing else that could make Alan so happy. "Is it good news of Dominic Wyndham? Perhaps he is engaged to an English-woman?"

Alan took her hand and squeezed it. "Och, nothing so feckless! There is news of him, but first there is something else and I will not delay the telling of it. We have a letter from Rutley, and I see Major Wyndham's hand in the matter. Now, be glad, Catriona. He has given you—all of us— our dearest wish."

She searched his face, her heart racing. "Our dearest wish? How?"

"Here," Alan said. "Read it."

Her hands shook as she unfolded the paper. It was heavy,

best quality, with a bloodred wax seal. When she reached the end, the lines of writing blurred.

"Och, it is no cause for weeping!" she said at last, and burst into tears.

Alan put his arm awkwardly about her shoulders and hugged her to his broad chest. "It is himself has brought it about, isn't it? Why else should Rutley change his mind on it?"

"It says here his grace sees more profit for his grandson this way!" She laughed, gulping back tears. "A partner puts up capital and you are appointed the new factor. Well, Alan Fraser, it's good fortune for you to work for an English duke!"

Alan kissed the top of her head. "The law is being changed, ye ken, to allow the free market of whisky, and the duty reduced."

"The law is being changed?"

"Well, these dukes and lords make the law to their liking—especially when they see money in it. It's braw news for the glen to build a legal still instead of a sheep walk. Though our new distillery must be licensed by the magistrate."

Tears mingled with sudden laughter. "With a duke applying for the license in the name of his daughter's son, wee Thomas MacNorrin, it'll not be the magistrates in Inverness will be denying him!"

Alan nodded, his voice muffled in her hair. "It will be a year or so, but we'll have a new industry for Ross-shire and then Glen Reulach malt whisky will be famous in the kingdom. It will take folk from the glen to run the distillery and their farms to produce the barley. No sheep! No ships! No ships, Catriona!"

"And what will all you smugglers do?" she teased. "If your trade is to become legal?"

"I don't imagine we shall do all of it within the law, lass!" He grinned. "And there's still the salt to carry from the West until the legal distilleries are operating."

"Why do you think Dominic had a hand in this?" Yet she knew he had. He had told her not to give up hope! Had this been his plan? Was this why he had left so abruptly?

"Well, how else would the duke have savored the pure taste of our malt, colored by the golden glow of the grain and perfumed by the peat water from the hills? I gave Dominic Wyndham a grand supply to take with him to England. I imagine he drank the duke's health in it!"

She dropped her head to her knees for a moment, ringing with a wild happiness that made her dizzy and weak. *A Dhia!* Not to give up hope!

As if to give voice to her feelings, echoing across the hills she heard the skirl of the pipes. Pipe Major Murchadh MacNorrin—who had played Highlanders to glory all across the Peninsula; who had made sure Calum died with the sound of his homeland in his ears at Waterloo—was fingering the rant of victory. The men could stay home now, the cattle could be driven back into their summer pastures, the houses at Achnadrochaid could be rebuilt. No one would have to leave Glen Reulach.

"How did he do it?" she asked at last. "How did Dominic have such influence with the duke?"

"Och, I imagine it is the golden tongue on him. Yet there's other news," Alan said. "He has risen in the world. We'll not see him here again, running through the heather in his plaid."

Of course not. Of course not. He would not break his word and come to her, even now. Yet Alan couldn't know of that pact. "Will he not?"

"His brother John died gey sudden, an apoplexy. They took the news to him at Rutley's and he fainted clear away on the rug. Dominic Wyndham is an English earl, Catriona, Lord Windrush in his own right. So he has the gold now. Who else would have suggested a partnership to the duke? It's a grand finish, is it not?"

An earl! Standing up, she reached both hands to the heavens before she whirled about to face Alan. Her laughter rang near the edge of hysteria and made her gulp. While Dominic had placed her future in her hands, like a shining gift, his own destiny had caught up with him and snatched all his own choices away.

He had become an earl—with political duties and a seat
in the House of Lords—with estates in England and retain-
ers and tenants of his own—with a widowed sister-in-law
to care for—with a place fixed in that English world of
power and privilege—with every tie and every obligation
to keep him in London, where the theaters and clubs and
women would ensnare him. He was Lord Windrush. And
suddenly, no doubt, one of the most eligible bachelors in
the realm. What use would he have now for Scotland—
except this last gesture, because he was a man of morals
and compassion who would not see the MacNorrins burned
from their homes and enslaved in Canada?

"Ah, Alan," she said. "It is certainly a finish."

His blond brow contracted for a moment. "I ken you
loved him. What lassie would not love the man?" He stood
up, tall and strong, handsome in his kilt, and stared out at
the peaks. "Yet you belong here. I would see you in a fine
stone house to call your own and your own bairns to croon
over. I would see you with a husband at your fireside and
your own folk about you. To be mistress to an English
earl—who has had so many mistresses—would break your
heart for loss, Catriona, and ravage your very soul. I say it
because it is the truth. For all that the fate of the Highlands
is irrevocably tied now to the fate of England. For all that
I love him like a brother and the man once saved my life."

"Tell me about that," she said, knowing he was right,
yet grasping at anything to stop time in its tracks.

"It was not much, not really. In battle, with death all
about us, all soldiers look out for each other. But he was
an officer and English. Too often they stayed away from
the Highland regiments, except to send us to the front of
the fighting. I had been knocked dizzy and left for dead.
The enemy was advancing when I came to my senses and
tried to stand up."

"They were firing?"

"Volleys. All the while shouting that gibberish: '*Vive
l'Empereur!*' The tramp of their feet shook the bloody
ground. Dominic Wyndham rode his mount into the teeth
of their fire and grabbed me by my plaid. He got me over

his horse's withers and took me out of there. The bullets whistled about us like a hailstorm. He risked himself to save me. I'm not surprised you fell in love with such a man. Can you believe that?''

She reached out and touched his arm. ''Yes, Alan Fraser, I believe it. As I believe he is a hero.''

''But he'll not be back in Inverness. We cannot expect it. He'll not come drinking with us now in Glen Reulach, or sleep ever again in my mother's byre. It is a grand memory we'll have of the man and that's all.''

Here is my only condition: when we are parted, you will never seek me, never send for me. You will not trick me again with clever words as you did in Edinburgh.

''You are right.'' Catriona tipped her head and studied the glory of the far peaks. Tears ran freely, smarting. ''He will not be back. His destiny now lies far apart from ours.''

Unless . . . unless she could find a whole new kind of courage, one without pride, one that laid her soul open to a bitter, bitter wounding. Though she must find it, for self-immolation—if it robbed him also—was only another name for cowardice now.

Alan made an awkward gesture, of tenderness, of sympathy. ''Och, Catriona MacNorrin. How can an English earl have time for the likes of us? For all that we carry the blood of kings in our veins, will he think us noble enough? It is a great gulf of wealth and status between you now, with himself an earl and you dependent on Rutley's charity. If you go to him, will he offer for you from duty or from pity? How could you bear it? There is a Highland lad who will love you right here. Marry me, lass, and have done.''

So she must give Alan his due, out of kindness and honor. Catriona faced the risks and made her decision, though it put their future in the hands of the Englishman they both loved. Whatever it cost her, she would go to Dominic. She would give him the pen and let him write the last verse, though it must indeed be free from any taint of duty or charity or obligation.

She smiled at Alan and offered her hand, for he had just given her the means. ''When you know I love another? And when your love also is for him? Then there must be one more bargain, and this time between you and me," she said. *"Ged 's fhada an duan ruigear a cheann."*

Though the song is long, its end will be reached.

Nineteen

SHE WAS ALWAYS there.

Sometimes in the corner of the room, her hair as rich as blackbirds' wings, flowing to her hips. It flowed on like a river, over her round white breasts, curling at her soft waist, running away in a black flood across the floor. Sometimes she floated gravely over the bed, her Viking eyes fierce, a small frown creasing her forehead. He wanted to smooth away the frown, run his fingers over her face.

He lifted his hand to touch her.

His hand was gone.

He registered it without much surprise or sense of loss. He knew he was forbidden to touch her. He knew he deserved punishment.

But always, always, she was there.

She sang songs of Valhalla.

"By God!" his brother's voice said. "What songs?"

"I don't know, Jack." *Not Valhalla!* He grinned, knowing it was a foolish gesture of bravado. *My hand is gone?* "She sings in Gaelic. Shall I hear it forever? Songs sung by a woman I have lost, in a language I don't know—"

"Foolish boy," Jack said. "You were always a fool, Dominic Wyndham. Always a fool."

But I love her. The words remained silent. He gazed into

his brother's face and tried to say it again, but Jack dissolved into smoke.

He was left with nothing but the throb of pain.

"Remove the ring first," a voice said. "Always save any rings."

Jack was walking along a narrow path of light which arched across the night sky. Stars bloomed suddenly in the darkness, like white flowers, like snow. A little boy stood lost on the path, his hair a golden halo, a burst of celandine petals, a sunbeam. He was crying.

"I'm coming for you!" Dominic shouted. "You shall have the stars for toys and the moon for a playfellow. Don't cry!"

"The earl's delirious," someone said. "We must take more blood."

∽

It was a quick crossing. Six hours after the French coast disappeared, the white cliffs of Dover smiled a welcome. A small group of servants waited with the carriages for Lord and Lady Rivaulx.

"What news?" Nigel asked them as he came up, Frances on his arm.

The marquess and his wife listened carefully to an efficient summation of recent political events, estate business, then all the latest gossip.

"There is one more thing, my lord," his secretary added. "John Wyndham died suddenly—apoplexy. Major Dominic Wyndham is Lord Windrush now, but he has been gravely ill these three weeks past. They say he neglected an injury to his hand. The wound became inflamed. The doctors feared for his life. I'm afraid no more details are known."

Frances looked up sharply. Her fingers closed more tightly on her husband's sleeve. "The new earl is out of danger now?"

"I believe so, your ladyship. Lord Windrush should be out of his sickbed by the time you reach London."

∽

The invitation slid away to the floor. Dominic grimaced. Remarkable how a title and fortune had made him so suddenly acceptable to society, in spite of fingers that would not entirely close.

His secretary picked up the dropped paper. "If you would allow me, my lord?"

He smiled patiently at Jack's faithful servant—inherited with the title, the money, the houses, and the land—a man he had known since childhood. "I need the practice, James. The doctors say I must try to use it. But go ahead."

James flicked open the invitation, startlingly white in the candlelight. "Lady Mulleigh gives a select dinner on the nineteenth to introduce her daughter into company. How shall I reply?"

Dominic tried to flex the stiff fingers, massaging the scar. Still there. He had not lost everything. Just Catriona. "Don't you think it unseemly for me to court the daughter, when I have already bedded the mother and cuckolded the father?" He laughed. "I'm damned if I'll go to her ladyship's dinner."

Pain began to throb again—not with fever this time, thank God—but with the exquisite agony of scarred muscle forced to move. They had not gone ahead with the amputation. Somehow, he had healed. Thank God for small mercies!

James gazed imperturbably at the desk. "I shall send your lordship's regrets. And this next one?"

Why the devil hadn't James just taken care of all this in these last weeks: the condolences, followed in appallingly rapid succession by the invitations? There had already been enough today of estate papers and urgent financial matters. He'd spent interminable hours closeted with the family man of business. It had begun while he still lay in bed and only intensified as soon as he was up. Why the hell deal so immediately with these bloody social obligations?

Dominic stood up, stalked to the door, and threw it open. "Decline them all. It's been a hellishly long day. I retreat to the library to get drunk. And forbid visitors, for God's sake.''

He slammed the door behind him and stopped.

A tall man was just handing hat and cane to a footman, his dark hair shadowed in the hall mirror. He turned and raised a brow. ''Am I included in that order?''

''For God's sake!'' Dominic grinned and walked up to the visitor with his hand outstretched. ''Not unless you refuse to get drunk with me. When the devil did you get back from Paris?''

''This morning,'' said Nigel, Marquess of Rivaulx. ''May I shake hands?''

''If you don't grip too hard. Come into the library and I'll tell you all about it.''

The black eyebrows winged together. ''You are well enough?''

''God, I hope so, though I feel remarkably like wrung-out washing. I finally rose from my sickbed this morning.''

Nigel walked with him into the library. ''I heard something of it from Stansted. I just saw him. You've been raving, he tells me, and seeing visions.''

Dominic poured two measures of Glen Reulach malt whisky.

''Try this,'' he said dryly. ''Enough to give any man visions.''

Candlelight flickered, reflected in the tall windows. The two men sat comfortably in large leather chairs. Nigel offered his condolences over Jack's sudden death. Dominic, without any sense of hypocrisy, accepted them. He was not glad his brother was dead.

''So surely you aren't completely indifferent to both title and fortune?'' Nigel asked.

Dominic shrugged. ''It gave me one more weapon with Rutley. Otherwise the earldom only weighs me down. I'm drowned in duties and obligations.''

''You sound as if you've been robbed.''

''I have—of a brother and of what matters more now he's gone: time.''

''Yet you persuaded Rutley to invest in a distillery?''

Nigel sipped his malt whisky. "This is remarkably good."

"In exchange for my promise to vote with him on certain issues to come before Parliament. It was before I became really ill, amidst the chaos of first receiving the news about Jack. Fortunately the duke demanded nothing to outrage my conscience. He was feeling pretty mellow at the time. Stansted and his wife are reconciled and have a son. The boy's name is Andrew—did he tell you? There's every reason to expect they'll have more children, though Stansted may not father all of them."

Nigel leaned back, savoring the heady aroma of his drink. "Isn't that a bit cynical, even for you?"

Dominic slowly flexed his hand. "I hope I am wrong. If Rosemary ever publicly humiliates him, I'll wring her pretty neck. Yet Stansted is so indulgent, I'm not sure he'd notice."

Nigel watched the stiff fingers without comment. No doubt he guessed—or had dragged out of Stansted—how Dominic had driven himself in his first days as an earl and the price he had paid. "As I remember, Rosemary was a spoiled, selfish, romantic child, like almost every other debutante. There's no reason she won't settle down to become the very model of virtuous domesticity."

"I'll drink to that." The whisky burned down to his belly, leaving a comforting trail of warmth. "Though virtuous domesticity is your domain, not mine. Honestly, I wish they could be as happy as you and Frances. Your marriage is a rare treasure, Nigel, and I'm jealous as hell."

Nigel smiled, a little quizzically. "You never show it—at least, not in a way to make Frances uncomfortable."

"I have admirable self-control."

"You have rotten self-control. Shall I trespass and test it? You may throw me out, if you like. What about your own domestic felicity?"

Dominic tried to stay calm, let nothing into his voice but humor. "If anyone but you were so damned impertinent, I'd run him through on the spot, except I'm no longer much good with a blade."

"I've been trying to avoid alluding to it. What happened?"

"A duel with bad odds, but a successful outcome. Don't worry, it was worth it."

Nigel swallowed the last of his whisky and set the glass aside. "But you neglected the injury to pursue your self-appointed task with Rutley. Thus you developed an inflammation and fever. Stansted tells me you were lucky not to lose the arm. He had to argue with the surgeon over it."

"Good God, I don't remember that—I thought I had already lost it. But I was rather busy hallucinating visions of children and beautiful women."

"Rosemary and little Andrew?" Nigel grinned. "I saw him, as a matter of fact, with his nurse. A handsome child. I understand Stansted also brought his sister here with her small son, Thomas MacNorrin. I suppose Lady Mary thought her son should see the man who'd interfered so resolutely with his inheritance."

Dominic closed his eyes. A little boy, staring at him from strangely familiar eyes, and crying. Little Thomas, Catriona's cousin. Another baby to haunt the edges of his being, removed from his concern before he'd even known him.

"Why the devil bring a small child into a sickroom and frighten him?"

"From what Stansted said, I don't think he was frightened. The child was crying, apparently, but only for milk. Was his mother the beautiful woman? Lady Mary is rather striking. Yet I admit I had the feeling Stansted was hiding something, though he's not usually much of a dissembler."

Dominic almost prevaricated. Easy enough—not even an untruth—not to mention her. But he opened his eyes to see that Nigel had leaned back, pressing for nothing, just offering a confidential ear.

He stood and gathered the glasses. "I saw visions of Catriona."

Nigel gazed up blandly. "Frances and I rather thought you would marry her. Surely she didn't refuse you?"

Dominic set down the glasses on the side table. He ran

a finger over the neck of the whisky bottle. He had once overheard Frances when she first refused Nigel: *It is not because I don't love you, but because I do.* The shared memory hung between them for a moment.

"I didn't ask," he said at last. "It would have been too cruel a question at the time."

"Would it?" Nigel was treading carefully.

Dominic heard it with sour amusement. "The easy answer is that she has a passion for the place she was born. It lies so deep, it defines her very soul. I envy it. It gives her a rootedness I'll never know. You might feel something very similar for Rivaulx, but this is absolute. She won't leave the Highlands. And my duty is here in London. Like you, I'm a bloody peer. Damnable, isn't it?"

"Why don't you ask her?"

Amber fire swirled as he filled the glasses. His hand shook. "Because I gave her my solemn word that if I left— if I went further than a hundred miles from her—I would never return or contact her again."

Nigel's voice stayed deceptively calm. "What the devil possessed you to do that?"

Definitely time to sit, before he fell like a damned tree. Dominic handed Nigel his refilled glass and walked carefully back to his chair. His blood felt watered, like bad wine. "It doesn't matter. I live every day regretting it. I'm not sure love is something we should bargain over."

"It's a sacrilege, of course, like bartering with God."

He sank gratefully into the leather embrace. "You forget I'm practiced in impiety. From the day I met Catriona I tried to bind her with bargains, one after another. I put love in a balance and tried to haggle for terms. I'm paying a more than adequate price for it. But I gave her my word."

"Won't she come to you?"

Dominic looked up to meet the penetrating gaze and laughed. "Do you like to do this? That would be an incredible hazard for her, physically, spiritually. It would be an enormity to her to admit she loves an Englishman. Why the devil should she risk it?"

"I gather she is very proud."

"It's all she has to keep her demons at bay. I can't quite explain it. It's far more honorable, deeper, than simple pride. She won't come here, to this house—the bloody house of an English earl, for God's sake—where I first insulted and threatened her, where—for all she knows—I have already installed other mistresses. She'd die first."

"Because you took her maidenhead, didn't you?" The quiet voice echoed in the shadowed spaces of the room. "You deliberately seduced and abandoned her."

Dominic flung back his head and stretched out his legs. His right hand moved awkwardly. "Another turn of the screw? She and I talked often enough about sin—I tormented her with the idea of it. Yet the sin was all mine. I wanted to break her pride and her heart. Perhaps instead she broke mine."

"So, like King Henry after he ordered the murder of Thomas à Becket, you do a daily penance in pain." Nigel set down his glass and stood up.

Narrowing his eyes, Dominic gazed up at his friend. "You wish to be my confessor? I admit and repent all my sins. But there are some more deadly than the seven I originally planned to defy. A greater sin is to hedge love with conditions."

"Frances teaches me daily that love is the only bridge over the impossible. If Catriona hears how ill you've been—"

Dominic smiled. "If she came now out of pity, I should reject her. In fact, she has probably married a kinsman by now. And you can't honorably fight a duel with a crippled man to avenge her, though I'll stand up, if you insist, and let you dispatch me."

"God, what an easy way out that would be, wouldn't it?" Nigel walked away.

Dominic tried to force his stubborn fingers about his glass. It almost slipped. He had to rescue it with his left hand, a very small humiliation, but one he was getting used to. "It's what I wanted to do, when I thought you'd similarly betrayed Frances. Of course, I was wrong and you would be in the right. What punishment do you suggest?"

At the door Nigel stopped and turned to look at Dominic. "I'm neither priest nor confessor. I'm only your friend. The solution is for you to find. Yet I'd be damned disappointed to see you wallow in self-pity and drink, instead."

"The remarkable thing about this whisky is it never leaves a hangover." He grinned with the bravado he'd tried to show his dead brother. *Songs sung by a woman I have lost, in a language I don't know—* "Thank you for coming, Nigel. I deserve all your chastisement. It's all right. I'll do my duty by the earldom. I shan't shoot myself."

"I didn't think for a moment that you would." Nigel allowed the ghost of a smile. "I'm glad to see you have at last found something to live for, but I'm bloody annoyed to see you still have so little faith in love."

The Marquess of Rivaulx bowed once and left the room.

He sent the servants to bed. The spines of an infinite number of volumes winked and stared above his head. The house stretched about him, a vast, silent expanse. The Earl of Windrush's town house. There was also the huge country seat, properties in Norfolk and Derbyshire, and Ralingcourt. No, not Ralingcourt any longer, thank God. Dominic smiled. Fatigue sat like a malaise in his veins. He really ought to go to bed. The great ceremonial four-poster awaited him in what had been Jack's chamber.

The hallway breathed quiet. The stairs stretched away into an infinite emptiness, lit only by two braces of candles. Dominic took the candles in his left hand and went up into the darkness. At the top of the stairs he stopped to catch his breath, cursing his weak, stiff muscles, wasted by illness and bloodletting.

A door clicked open, flooding light into the corridor.

"Lord Windrush?" Catriona folded her hands, fixing him with that intense harebell gaze. Her hair had grown, just enough to brush up and catch with pins.

It was a moment of absolute disorientation. Speechless for a moment, he set the candles on the hall table, before

he should drop them and set fire to the house. He wanted
to kneel at her feet. "Catriona? Words break in my mouth.
I have seen visions of you."

She didn't move, only looked away with that maddening
tilt to her chin. The floor seemed to spin. He must hang
on! He must! For if he stepped forward and touched her—
If he felt her curves slip softly beneath his hands—
If his fingers traced her pliant back, her swelling hips—
If he breathed in her scent—
And she didn't want him, crippled?

"How—?" The scar throbbed in his palm. "What the
devil are you doing here?"

She glanced back, a tremble of uncertainty on her lips.
"I have been staying with Lord and Lady Stansted. I came
every day to see you. But you were delirious. You didn't
know me. And then you had more important business."

"Oh, I knew you. I just didn't think you were real." It
broke about him like a thunderstorm: she didn't trust—even
now—that nothing was more important to him than she
was, even if, still, any future for them was impossible? He
thought his fingers might crush the wooden carving on the
top of the newel post. Anguish shivered in his voice. "For
God's sake! You've been here all along? Why the devil did
no one tell me?"

"I told them not to."

It battered at him. "And they all agreed? You all conspired? Even Stansted? Even my own staff? Even Nigel,
for God's sake!"

"Lord Rivaulx didn't know." Stubborn light flashed in
her eyes. "Why do you stand there and browbeat me over
details? How else could I have done it? You don't think it
has cost me to come here? That there wasn't humiliation
for me when Lord Stansted persuaded your servants to let
me have this room tonight without telling you? Should I
have confronted you when you were ill? Don't question
it!"

"So you let me think you a vision? Oh, dear God!"

The Viking eyes blazed. "Och, I am real enough." She
stepped forward, holding out her hands. "You are a mad-

man to talk like this. You must lie down. Let me help you out of your jacket and shoes.''

These clothes that so offend you, I intend you to take off each garment—slowly. You will unbutton my jacket, peel off my damned trousers. Once I am naked, I will take you into my bed, giving, giving, until your blood burns and your lungs pant for air—until you cry out at last and forget for one moment that you think you are doomed.

It was all wrong! He had done everything wrong! ''I want to make love to you one more time,'' he whispered. ''But I don't think I'm strong enough.''

''*One* more time? Well then,'' she said, the passion still resolute in her voice. ''Even dying on your feet, you are a rake and a scoundrel. What if my hand in marriage has been requested by another man? And what if I have accepted him?''

The breath stopped, frozen in his lungs, trapped in his throat, chained behind his teeth. ''Marriage! To whom?''

''Och, he is an excellent man. Any woman would be glad to take him as husband.''

They will wrap their pride about their sorrow like a plaid.

''Then I wish you every happiness,'' he said.

''You are ill.'' Her eyes glittered with unshed tears. ''And cannot tell happiness from sorrow. Come, let me help you to bed, foolish man, before you fall.''

He dreamed again of that pathway through the sky. The MacNorrins walked steadily away into the west, a sparkling mist of stardust about their feet. As he watched them go, sick with longing, he searched for Catriona and couldn't find her. Somewhere in the mist he heard a child crying, too far away to comfort.

The rattle of curtains startled him awake. His valet was there to oversee the morning ritual: bath, shave, correct dress for the day. Catriona had brought him to this bed last night. She had helped him out of his coat and boots. She

had left him alone. He was confronted with his greatest
wish and his greatest fear: she had come; she would marry
someone else.

He came down to the breakfast room to find her sitting
at the table, buttering toast. Her nape shone white above an
ivory muslin dress. She was lovely in the morning light,
even the dull light of London. *She would marry someone
else.*

Dominic paused in the doorway and watched the deft
turn of her wrist. "So you aren't a dream," he said.

She spoke without looking at him. "I am not. Did you
dream?"

He pushed forward and poured himself tea. He made
himself carry the cup in his right hand. Hot liquid spilled
as he set it clumsily on the table, staining the white cloth.

"I dream like a lotus eater. Why did you come, Catriona?"

She looked up, her blue eyes guileless. "Did you think
we would not be grateful in Glen Reulach? That no one
would come to say thank you?"

He sat down. The hot tea sent a tiny waver of steam into
the air. "I don't expect thanks."

Her lids dropped as she studied her plate. "Not even for
Ralingcourt?"

He wanted that stark Highland beauty. He wanted to see
it melt into sunshine. He wanted to spend his days with her
in a flower-strewn land of always-summer, without responsibilities, without the cruel intrusions of reality.

"Ralingcourt was the only property unentailed," he said.
"So I was able to trade it. It was no sacrifice."

"You gave Ralingcourt—the house, the farms, all of it—
to wee Thomas MacNorrin, in trade for some high mountain land above Glen Reulach, worth only a fraction of it.
Why? The Duke of Rutley must have thought he bargained
with a simpleton."

"Windrush can afford the loss. Will Rutley's grandson
be raised with any care for his Highland estates? The duke
has charge of his education. Little Thomas will go to Dunachan only to play: to hunt or fish or dress up in a mockery

of his ancestors. What the hell will happen to the glen when the boy reaches his majority?''

''So you have given him a great house in England.''

He stirred his tea, so he wouldn't have to watch her. ''That and the distillery should bring him ample wealth. Meanwhile I own the high summer pastures above Glen Reulach, so the grazing can never be let for Lowland sheep. There will be no more clearances. The MacNorrins can control their own mountains.''

''And you think,'' she said, beginning to butter another morsel of toast, ''I should not have come to say thank you?''

The spoon clattered angrily against his cup. ''Not if that is all you came for! Is it?''

She said nothing for a moment, though the toast crumbled under her fingers. Then she looked up and met his gaze. ''There is the matter of my marriage.''

He took a deep breath, determined to keep bitterness out of his voice and knowing he would fail. ''Shall I pretend not to care? Shall I ask after the groom and offer felicitations?''

The knife met her plate with a small click. ''You did last night.''

What if he took her now by the arms and kissed her? Could she deny him then? ''It was shock. I tried to retreat behind pride. I have very little of that left any longer. Who is the man?''

''Alan Fraser.''

A good man, one of her own. Dear God! Could Alan make her happy? Did he love her? Did he know she had been loved and abandoned by an English rake? ''You accepted him?''

She sat in silence, laying her hands flat on the table and staring at them.

''With one condition,'' she said at last.

Dominic leaped to his feet. His stiff fingers brushed his cup and sent it ringing onto the table, spilling tea. ''Dear God! Haven't we learned a bloody thing? Will there always be contingencies?''

Her head flew back, her eyes blazing. ''What is it to you,
then, what bargains I make?''

The scalding splash burned his skin. He plunged his hand
into a pitcher of water. ''What, indeed! I admit I have never
before objected to any of my mistresses marrying as they
chose—when I was through with them!''

Her palm hung poised over the cloth, as if she were cast
in marble. Small, quick breaths made the buttons rise and
fall over her breasts. A deep crimson spot grew on each
pale cheekbone, spreading over the white skin like a sunrise.

''Because that is how it is for an English aristocrat! Who
makes conditions now? You cannot renounce your duty
here—I would not ask it, nor expect it. But that does not
keep me from you.''

He stalked away, drying the water from his hand with a
napkin, before he tried to touch her and made a worse fool
of himself. ''Doesn't it? Isn't this why you would wed
Alan—to stay in the Highlands?''

She looked away. ''It is *you* who would keep us apart,
now you're a lord!''

The napkin landed on the side table and crumpled like
white petals. ''Lord Windrush! God, how empty that is!
But there are countless souls dependent on that title. Besides the staff of the houses and estates, the farmers and
tenants, Jack had a network of investments, business
schemes. All of them have fallen into my care, like a
damned great ship. A careless hand at the tiller now and
hundreds of innocent people could find their livelihoods
ruined, their children hungry. It's not a responsibility I
asked for, nor wanted. I would renounce it if I could.''

She put one hand over her eyes. ''You have a seat in the
House of Lords. You can influence law, commerce, fi-
nance—the future of Britain and Europe. You can change
the tariffs on whisky and the regulations on distilleries. You
can save countless children, countless livelihoods. Can you
deny that you want it? Are you incapable of being honest
with me?''

He spun about, staring at her fragile shoulders under the

white muslin. "By God! I have always been honest with you. It is you who have hidden and concealed and refused to trust. From the day we met you kept secrets. Bloody hell! You have never been open with me."

Her other hand joined its fellow, her fingers crossed over her forehead. Her voice cracked like breaking ice. "I could not be when Glen Reulach hung in the balance. How could I have trusted you, an Englishman, when you bullied and coerced me from the beginning? So when I could not drive you away, I used you for my own needs. I used your strength and your kindness. I would not be a burden to you now, when the debt is all from me to you. I don't come to you in need. But why can't you believe everything has changed now? And why do you try to tell me you do not love being an earl and the power of it!"

"By God, Catriona, of course there's a certain seduction in it! But do you think I want it? For myself, I would renounce all of it"—he waved his hand about the room—"—the title, the fortune, the responsibilities, if it would bring you to me."

"But you cannot." She sat rigid at the table. Wisps of dark hair curled at her cheek, escaping the pins. "And you should not. I said I would not expect it. I would not take you from your destiny—the life that lets you fulfill your talents, the life here in London that you love."

He wanted to break china, take the water pitcher and see it crack in a thousand shards of crystal through the window. Instead he closed his left hand on the back of a side chair and leaned there, refusing to sit even if he fell first.

"I would still do it," he said. "But all the remaining property is entailed with the title. My own capital is invested in the distillery in Glen Reulach, the income of which I have promised to Rutley for Thomas for the first ten years. If I renounce the earldom, I can offer you only a pauper—and a crippled one, at that." He stopped her with a gesture as she began to speak. "I don't say that from self-pity! It is merely a fact. I was an officer. I have sold out. I have no other trade. How can I ask you to marry me? I might support myself gaming, but how could I subject a wife and children to such an existence?''

She dropped her hands and opened her eyes. The blue shone warm and bright, like gentians in sunshine. She let out a long breath. ''You should ask the wife. She might not mind—except for your sake. Indeed, she would never let you live with her in Scotland on the dregs of Rutley's charity. She would not let you sacrifice your very soul for her—deny your destiny and your honor. You are right in that.''

''So you offer us no future? I am pinned here in London and you in the Far North? My destiny is to be my curse? I would give up everything to marry you, but even that will not resolve it. Then thank God the earldom dies with me!''

''You are still beset, Dominic Wyndham,'' she said fiercely. ''Still trying to drive a mad bargain with fate. Would it not occur to you that I can bend as much as you can, that I am the one free in this, that a decision in it could be mine? Allow me my own contrition. Why do you think you deserve pain? I am as guilty as you. Is there any sin I have not been party to? Are you the only one who can make sacrifices?''

He spun about and the chair fell, clattering back against the wall. ''What do you mean?''

''I am more artless in this than you are. I came here because of you. Because of what lies between us. Because the longing is on me for you. Because I have denied myself and denied myself, until I am sick with the denying.'' Moisture glistened on her eyelashes. ''Do you think I would not humble myself for you? Strip away all my pride and vainglory? Do you think I cannot be honest? I would take you willingly, Dominic Wyndham. I would take you as you are, with everything that makes you—with your English title, and your own stubborn pride, and your damaged hand—all of it!''

His right hand began to throb. He clenched it into a semblance of a fist. ''I will not be loved from pity.''

She leaped up, dragging both hands over the tablecloth. ''*Pity!* Stubborn fool! *A Dhia!* I do not *pity* you! You have not changed—you are still a gallant, reckless hero, determined on the dragon even in the face of its withering fire! Why can't you trust me to love you enough?''

He felt frozen, pinned at the window. "Enough for what?"

"To live with you in London, in England—in a gutter, if must be—though there is no need for that. What if I should also like the theater and politics and the meetings on science?''

He picked up the fallen chair and straddled it, dropping his forehead against the back rail. Hope began to surge—a dishonorable, selfish hope. It terrified him. "I'm afraid you would die, like a tree cut from its roots.''

She raised both hands. The cloth, bunched in her fists, slid across the table. As if blind, she let go and twisted to face him, but the hanging cloth caught against her skirts. As she moved, the entire breakfast service—plates, silver, glasses, the remains of the toast, the spilled teacup—moved with her.

"Is that all that keeps you from me now? That you think I cannot leave the Highlands, even for you?''

His fingers clenched on the chair back. "You said the heart would die within you, that you did not have the courage to face a new life away from your mountains.''

The tablecloth kept sliding. The toast toppled. The water pitcher rolled over and flooded a plate of fruit.

"It was true then, when I thought the parting from Ross-shire would be forever. Now I know something else. The restless wave of the sea is in my blood, so the longing is always on me.'' She thrust both fists against her breast. "But I carry those hills *here*! In my heart! I do not always have to live where I can see them, as long as I know Achnadrochaid is still there and the black cattle still graze by the sheilings. If I can share my life with you, I shan't die like a tree. Can you understand? How could I have known that the history of my people might have taught me the wrong lesson? What is love of place without human love? What is my home without the man of my heart? It is *you*

I pine for. *You* are my roots and my life, and I cannot live without you."

"Then why the hell have you promised to marry Alan?" He stood, took the chair, and threw it hard at the window. Muntins splintered, chair legs fractured, in a burst of breaking glass. "I can make no more bargains, only offer you my heart. To what ruin will you force me? I have shredded my pride. I will happily throw my honor into the balance. But I cannot betray Alan Fraser and live!"

The cloth slipped in a final rush, a waterfall of damask and silverware. Gold-rimmed plates hit the floor and fissured. Glasses broke into shards. Cups shattered.

"Neither can I, nor would I." Her smile shone like a rainbow, magical, making him breathless. "My heart is yours, not Alan's, for all that you are an Englishman and it has been a great thing for me to admit that I love you. You can have your life here in London and you can have me, if only you would ask."

China and glass crunched under his boots as he walked up to her and took her in his arms. He clung to her, buffeted by a whirlwind, afraid he would break like the window, yet desire leaped in him, as if sap raced and trees burst in minutes into leaf. If he kissed her, he knew how she would respond, with that blaze of ardor, a roar of dry timber. Yet he wanted to offer her something far more profound now.

There was a rattle somewhere—in the corridor. The sound of footsteps.

"The footman!" She froze against him. "He has come to clear the table."

"The bloody table is already cleared. Devil take the footman!"

He pulled away from her and strode to the door. The key clicked in the lock as he turned it. He dropped his head back and closed his eyes. "You said once I was wicked. Perhaps it is true. I put virtue into the scales with sin and demanded your heart as the price—" It was a pain like a wound. It felled him, forcing him to sink to both knees. "I love you more than my own soul. I admit I didn't want to—even when you faced such total devastation with so much courage. I was filled with pride and arrogance and vanity. You have taught me what matters and what it is to really love, but I am still a wretched Englishman. Can you love me as I am, with all my sins? Would you even uproot yourself from the Highlands for my sake? Catriona, will you marry me?''

"Why else do you think I am here?'' Her pure voice rang like a bell. "Gladly. Proudly. I will marry you.''

Twenty

CATRIONA WAS THE wrack of the storm, flung up on a far beach as the tide ebbed. Her legs shook, but she went to him and put her arms about his shoulders.

She studied his bent head, the turn of the ear, the golden strands she loved at his temple. "Alan Fraser offered only from gallantry. I could not have loved him—when I have already gifted my heart, long ago, to you—and he knew it. But he asked out of honor. So I could neither refuse it, nor accept it. Instead, I told him I would have him in a month, unless you asked me before he had his answer."

"A month? From when? Dear God! When is it over?"

The tears spilled as she laughed. "Och, today! The month is over today. If you want to marry me, my lord, it is lucky you had my answer when you did."

"But why? Why did you agree to such a thing?"

"How else could I have come here, now you are an earl? I was afraid of your sense of duty, of your kindness, that you would feel some obligation. I could not risk your offering for me on such terms. If we are to marry, it must be as equals, because we know we cannot live apart. I know that now."

He bent his forehead to touch the back of her hand. "What will we tell Alan?"

"To find himself another lassie. He had an obligation he

believed he must fulfill, that is all. He loves you. He felt he owed it to you that I was not seen to be abandoned.''

Dominic looked up. His expression was perfectly blank for a moment. ''Dear God!''

''Why do you still kneel?'' She wiped the moisture from her cheek with one palm. ''The offer of marriage is done and accepted.''

''What the hell kind of idiot tries to propose amidst the wreckage of china? Tries to win a wife by railing at her and breaking things? Should I not kneel a little longer in penance?''

''The penance is done. Yours and mine.'' She glanced at the broken window and the ruin of their breakfast table. Noise from the town rattled into the room. ''We have spilled tea on the carpet.''

He grinned. ''Yes, but this carpet is mine.''

''Your knees will get sore.''

He sat back on his heels. The dimples cut deep. Then he sprawled unceremoniously on the floor, lying flat on his back, flinging his arms wide. Laughter welled up from some deep core, cleansing and splendid. His breath came in whoops, rocking him. He roared and thundered with mirth.

''My whole bloody body is sore,'' he said at last, still gasping. ''Every damned muscle complains and I'm weak as a kitten.''

''Then I'm sorry for it.'' She leaned over him. Moss-green eyes grinned back. Her heart melted like hot honey. ''For I would fain have the tom cat, not the kitten, in my bed.''

He sat up and caught her hand, pulling her down. ''Not until we're married. Though I assure you the strength is returning to the parts that count.''

She glanced down. ''Och, you stubborn man. You would have that go to waste?''

He took her face in both hands. ''Though I burn alive for you, I can control my desire. I want us to wait.''

The scar in his right palm tickled her cheek. She turned

her head and kissed it. "I have already been your mistress. Why should we wait?"

"Because it is the best way to celebrate our marriage."

The smallest voice whispered warning. She tried to ignore it. "I thought you were not so well enamored of wedding nights."

"I want a real wedding night with you. Call it superstition, if you like. I am afraid that if I sin again, I will yet destroy this and somehow still lose you. I think I must prove to myself I can wait. Though there is one thing I would do again: on our wedding night, too, I would like us to make a child."

It was a strange three weeks, both unreal and intense. They would be married in Glen Reulach with Deirdre and Mairead as matrons of honor and Alan and David Fraser as groom's men. Dominic had known and understood immediately. Though she would have willingly married him in London, the ceremony would feel more sacred to her with the snowcapped bens as witness.

But first the new earl must wrap up his most urgent business enough to leave London. So Catriona moved in with Nigel and Frances in the Rivaulx town house, an elegant manor in its own grounds off Piccadilly. The marquess and his wife spent hours in their music room. They both played with extraordinary skill. She listened, entranced, to strange, exotic melodies and watched the interplay of harmony between the players.

"Russian or Indian?" Dominic asked as he came in one day. "Good God, can't you play something civilized and tame like one of those marching songs the men used to sing in the Peninsula?"

Everyone laughed. He came courting every day—as if they had never met, never suffered together, never loved. It made her feel almost shy. To begin again from scratch, to talk about ordinary things, to joke and laugh—and find she still loved him. Her heart turned over whenever he arrived and her blood dissolved in a hot flood of desire.

Yet, though she saw the longing in his eyes and returned it with her own, he did no more than kiss her. When the kiss flamed and burned, he pulled away, laughing and dropping his head to her shoulder for a moment.

"I am determined not to give in," he said gravely, though the dimples marked his cheeks. "We must not sin in Lord and Lady Rivaulx's town house, must we? Not when they're going to witness our wedding."

He took her with him into London, to the museums and galleries and parks. It was overwhelming, huge, noisy. Yet at Dominic's side, she enjoyed it—that wealth of history and commerce and science. Perhaps it was best for the Highlands, too, to welcome this new century, as long as it did not mean their complete destruction.

They planned their future. The Season in London, while Parliament sat. A cottage to be built near Calum's cave above Glen Reulach for the endless blue days of summer. A circuit, spring and autumn, through the other properties of the earldom, and a network of trustworthy agents. So she would have her bright summers in the Highlands and she would have all her days with him. Was it too perfect to be real?

Lord and Lady Stansted brought Andrew and Mrs. Mackay. Dominic crouched on the carpet and played with the child. Andrew laughed and thumped the new earl with his round fists. Catriona studied Rosemary and hoped she was happy with her husband and child.

As they rose to go Rosemary stopped beside Catriona. "Yes," she said quietly in her ear. "I am happy. And I am happy for you and Dominic. Take care of him, won't you?"

Catriona smiled and agreed. There would be no more games between them. They would never again bargain about love. He was healing. Every day he was stronger. Every day his fingers were a little less stiff. He made her laugh. With that mad wit, he caught her unawares and made her laugh. Yet in spite of his brave, light heart, he was weighed down with business and the illness was not long behind him. And she thought there was still a concern in him that he hadn't shared, and that worried and fretted at her.

When he was stronger, she must ask, before they took vows and bound themselves forever. After all, what had he said? *I want no more wedding nights!*

And she feared that—whatever they had promised, whatever they had learned—he might be too proud to tell her what troubled him yet, leaving a canker of distrust to eat away at their happiness.

At last the journey north began, in a rainstorm, and she still hadn't asked. She was to go on ahead of him. It was to be a true Highland wedding. Contracts had been drawn up and delivered, sent back and forth to Inverness from London, but there were other arrangements to be made. She would travel with Nigel and Frances, and the phalanx of servants and maids suitable for a marquess and his wife—and the future Lady Windrush.

"I trust you to arrange everything in Glen Reulach," Dominic said. "I must stop in Derbyshire for a few days." He grinned. "But I'll be there for our wedding. I promise."

Sick with love, she leaned from the carriage window and kissed him, water soaking her shoulders and hair, big drops running onto his face. His mouth was wet and chill, but as they touched she thought their lips might sizzle and steam like a kettle.

"I'll keep you to that promise, Lord Windrush. If you do not come, I'll set Iseabail MacNorrin to rain curses on your bright head."

He laughed and waved, the rain beating over his tall frame, until he was out of sight.

There was a chaos of business, demanding, gnawing, like a dog at a bone. Dominic worked day and night, wanting it all to be done. Wanting to be free for a perfect honeymoon with Catriona. It was hell to be parted, yet he savored the depth of his happiness. A miracle had happened. He must strive to be worthy of it.

Yet the delays seemed interminable. He arrived in Inverness a day and a half after he'd planned. When his carriage pulled up at Dunachan it was close to midnight and his wedding was the next morning. The sounds of revelry poured out into the courtyard through open doors. He walked into the great hall and was blinded by candles. Dominic stood blinking for a moment, before myriad hands reached out to shake his, and a chorus of voices, young and old, pressed about him.

"Ciamar a tha sibh?" "Welcome, Lord Windrush!" *"Seo Dominic Bàn!"* *"An tusa a tha ann?"*

"I am very well," he said, laughing and pressing palms. "Thank you. Thanks to all of you!"

"I almost thought for a moment you had changed your mind," a dry voice said in his ear. "And planned to leave me waiting at the altar."

He spun about and swept her into his arms. *"A Chatriona!"*

Applause broke about them as he kissed her. Only later did he realize he'd addressed her in her own tongue.

He entered the church to the wild tumult of bagpipes. Alan and Davie Fraser walked beside him, striding in their navy-and-green kilts. He was vaguely aware of Nigel and Frances among the throng of Highlanders—familiar faces from their quest across the heather. Yet when Catriona came in with her two women, he saw nothing but her face. He barely heard the ceremony. He only smiled into the blue depths of her eyes and let his heart speak his vows. So why the devil should he think there was still something concealed behind that Viking gaze? A small tremor of doubt? A secret fear?

A Chatriona, keep nothing from me now!

They came out to the deafening roar of pistols fired into the air. A whole cow and sheep had been roasted for the wedding feast. *Uisge-beatha* flowed freely in toast after toast. A good-natured brawl broke out when the cake was broken and the company fought for the pieces. Pipe and fiddle struck up the dance. Blazing with whisky, Dominic led Catriona onto the floor.

"I don't even know what happens next," he whispered in her ear. "I have no house of my own here. Besides, I'm as foxed as a lord."

"Och, you *are* a lord." Color shone bright on her white skin. "But drunk or sober, the company will take us to the barn. Bride and groom are not allowed the first night in a house. They'll undress us and wish us well."

He spun her through the turn of the dance. "Why the barn?"

She ducked her head, not meeting his eyes. "I suppose it is a grand place for fertility!"

As she said it Catriona trembled. A tremor rippled through her, a wave of longing and excitement deep in the blood.

She was spun in dance after dance. Lord Rivaulx danced with her, as did Alan Fraser. From the corner of her eye she saw Dominic with Frances, and then with Mairead MacNorrin, recovered now and living in her house—rebuilt in Achnadrochaid—with her healthy new bairn.

"I'm gey glad for you, Catriona MacNorrin," Alan said, red-faced from drink. "It's a grand man ye're marrying."

A grand man. At last, she was hustled with him out into the cool night air. A full moon rode high over the peaks. In the loft in the great barn beside Dunachan, the women had prepared them a bed—a nest of feather mattresses in the sweet green hay. While the women undressed her and slipped a silk nightgown over her head, she heard the jokes and guffaws of the men, stripping Dominic. It was a bawdy, good-humored roughness. *The male impulse is pretty basic. Most men are uncomfortable facing such a powerful force in any other way. So we talk crudely, with an emphasis on anatomy.*

At last the women moved apart. Surrounded by the tall, kilted Highlanders, nude but for a plaid thrown over one shoulder, in the glow of the lantern Dominic was a god. She remembered with sudden vividness how she had first seen him—strength, ease and indifference, rugged and untamed—his naked flesh mitered with muscle. As his jacket had done then, the toss of tartan emphasized it, his masculine nakedness.

They were married. One until death.

Though there is one thing I would do again: on our wedding night, too, I would like us to make a child. He had spent a wedding night once before, and Harriet had run home hysterical to her mother the next day. Why? Why? *A Dhia!* Was that what he could not tell her?

She closed her eyes, remembering. *His smile was charming, sending a deep dimple into his cheek. Yet his eyes remained guarded, dark, like moss under a waterfall and hiding as many secrets. What on earth was she going to do now?*

"God bless you," said the chorus of voices.

The women moved away, gathering their bleary, laughing menfolk and herding them out of the barn. She was alone with her new husband. He didn't move, just stood in the golden lamplight and smiled at her.

"That bed," he said gently, "reminds me of the tale of the princess and the pea. Is it a test to see if we have royal blood?"

"All MacNorrins have royal blood," she replied.

"*A Chatriona!* I am three sheets to the wind. I don't want to be foxed when I bed my royal bride."

The fine silk nightgown brushed seductively against her legs. Her heart hammered. She tried to bury the tiny trickle of fear behind bravado. "Foolish man. You will not be sober until morning. What do you suggest?"

He moved suddenly and looked out of the window. "The moon is brilliant. Come here and look."

Her legs shook, but she walked up to him and stood at his shoulder. White light poured over the mountains and washed into the loch. Peaks, trees, water, outlined in silver, shining and glistening like the great cities of the first clans of the sky.

"In the gathering night in the gardens of Fabias, she found a star," he said softly. *"She hid the night and the star in her womb."* His fingers brushed her cheek, sending ripples of heat and apprehension down her spine. "Let us make a child up there in those hills."

She looked up at him in a confusion of longing and doubt. "Where?"

He strode away to their clothes, left in the corner. He rustled through them until he found her shoes and his boots.

"Come," he said. "We're going to Calum's cave. Perhaps, by the time we get there, I'll be sober."

∞

It was a strange moonlit flight through a silent, shimmering world. He led her higher, ever higher, into the mountains. The sound of rushing water echoed like a pulse of tiny bells. The air flowed sweet with honey and wildflowers. Warm and cool breezes ran on a fey whim over her skin under a moon like a pearl. The white silk nightgown whispered over her hips and thighs, caressing. Her own arm shone silver as her golden man led her by the hand.

She was enchanted. The wave of the ocean from the shore at Murias moved in her blood. Slick, the seals lifted their black heads from the white sea foam, and the bears in their brown fur rumbled in the woods. The wild bull panted and pawed the ground before taking his maiden bride and carrying her away into the mystic lands of the north.

At the mouth of the cave, he stopped and wrapped the quilt he'd been carrying about her shoulders. "What is it?" he asked. "We are married. Nothing must ever again come between us. But there is still something, isn't there?"

She sat down, hugging the quilt, staring out at the silver mountains and the meadow strewn with white flowers like stars and knew she must trust him. Now, forever, she must always trust him.

"I should have asked long ago. I was cowardly. I was afraid. I thought something in it might part us. But you are right. It is the not knowing that sits in my mind like a kelpie, black mouth gaping.''

The plaid moved in a dark river as he sat beside her. "What do you want to ask?"

She shook her head. "It is not that I believe evil of you—"

"Ask me, Catriona. We have expiated all the sins. Now our virtue depends on our honesty and trust. Be honest. Trust me. I love you.''

She dropped her face to her knees. "What timing I have," she said with a little laugh. "To marry you first!"

He took her hand and kissed her fingers. His mouth was hot and soft, caressing the sensitive pads. "There is nothing I would hide from you. Ask.''

Why did it take so much courage? More than it had taken to face him in London? More than it had taken to fight off a highwayman? She lifted her head. "There is something you have hidden, and though it is nothing to me, I must know it.''

"Ah," he said. "What happened with Harriet?"

"She said such bitter things in Edinburgh. How could you frighten her so much?''

For a moment he sat silent, the moonlight cutting his profile from stone.

"Very well," he said at last. "Only pride kept me from telling you the truth long ago. In essence, Harriet and I were strangers. I had been years in the Peninsula and Russia. I had been fighting. I had been seared by corruption. I thought she embodied purity, the perfect, innocent English lady. Yet we didn't have much of a courtship. I had never tried to kiss her, never touched her—until our wedding night.''

Courage. Courage. "At Ralingcourt. In ivory silk," she said.

"She held out her arms to me and asked me to kiss her. I planned to be gentle and careful, but she laughed at me and said she had been kissed before. Then she pulled down her nightdress and asked me to touch her breasts. She said she liked that.''

The fear moved, like a small current underwater. "*Och-òn,* she had known a lover?"

"It might not have mattered—I thought I loved her that much. It didn't even occur to me to blame her. After all, I'd known enough lovers. I thought she'd made a mistake with a boy, perhaps, when she was young. So I let her lead me, touching her where she wanted to be touched, kissing her as she wanted to be kissed. I was in a frenzy of desire. It was even a relief to think she wasn't virgin and wouldn't have pain."

"She did not touch you back?"

He looked around, surprised. "What? No. She just wanted caresses and kisses—intimate ones. She climaxed several times. So I thought she was ready when I took her to the bed. I was as desperate as a boy, I think, and blind with love. Nothing else occurred to me except that she'd known some other man."

"She had not?"

His hair shone pure gilt. "I didn't hesitate—but she was a virgin, after all. I tried to be gentle and give her pleasure. When she didn't respond, I was afraid she might be sore. Yet I wanted to consummate our marriage, so I hurried to my own climax. That's when she hit me and screamed that I'd ruined her. You see, she wasn't a virgin—at least, she was only a virgin with men."

The fear coiled, twisting in an eddy, but it was only for Dominic. "What do you mean?"

He dropped his bright head in his hands. "It all came out, through that long, bitter night. She said I revolted her—everything about my body—she thought me grotesque. She hated the penetration. She hated that part of me—she called me ugly, repulsive. She railed and wept—said I was loathsome and nauseating. I couldn't understand, until at last she stood up and explained. She said it with an odd satisfaction: she had been seduced by her governess—another woman—and that's what Harriet liked and expected."

Her heart broke for him. "Like Sappho of Lesbos?"

"Good God," he said dryly. "You had a damned eclectic education!"

She put her hand on his. "There is a grand classics library at Dunachan. Why didn't Harriet tell you to stop?"

He closed his fingers around her palm. "I think it was pure shock. She hadn't known how a man was built. That's why she seemed willing and why I misunderstood so completely. She had only wanted the stroking and the suckling and her own pleasure, but even that she said she would rather get from her maid. When I told her we might have made a child, she became hysterical. She hadn't known how it was done. She didn't want children."

Catriona clasped his hand to her breast. "*Obh, obh,* so that was the degradation she said you had forced upon her—the natural love of a man! So why did she marry you?"

"Because she didn't want Rosemary to have me."

It made sense. Little looks she had noticed and not understood in Edinburgh, some of the things Harriet had said when she lay dying. "She was in love with Lady Stansted?"

"Incredible, isn't it? Poor Harriet! Even after Rosemary took her away to Edinburgh, Harriet's desires weren't fulfilled. Rosemary didn't have that kind of interest in other women. It was a triangle that doomed everyone to misery."

"How could you think you could ever win Harriet back?"

He carried her hand to his lips and kissed it. "It was a challenge to my pride. I thought—always—that with one more chance, I could win her over, show her that she could love a man, after all. I was a fool."

"Yet you could tell no one the truth. How could you have explained? To her parents? To anyone? *A Mhuire!* I'm so sorry, Dominic."

He laughed. "No, it was my fault. After Russia, I pursued a nonsensical idea about purity. I took her reticence in our brief courtship for ladylike sensibility. A mistake."

She snuggled closer to him. "You are like me. You don't make many mistakes, but when you do, they are big ones."

"Then I hope when I get things right, they are just as absolutely and grandly right—like marrying you."

The happiness exploded in her, a shower of sparks, *absolutely and grandly right*. Indeed, indeed, she had done the right thing!

As if he saw the change in her, he laughed again—a different laugh, one of pure content. Their eyes met and heat flared, sending a flood of warmth over her skin.

"Then let us go inside for our wedding night and make ourselves a baby," he said.

"Whether he is golden like you," Catriona replied, "or black like me, no bairn ever had such a grand father."

He stood up. Without another word he swung her into his arms and carried her over the threshold of the cave. The pile of bracken was still there, dark in the shadows. Dominic made a bed of the quilt and his plaid—sliding the tartan fabric from his naked body. Catriona stood in her silk nightgown in the beam of moonlight flooding in at the cave entrance where he had set her down. He was magnificent to her, beautiful, wondrous, her hero. She would make sure, always, always, that he knew it. She would tell him daily, with words and with her body, that she rejoiced in him and loved him. She would make him bairns, a whole family.

He turned to face her, smiling. "We need your gown for a sheet."

Och, it was foolish to blush when she was melted with desire for him and proud in his love, but as she pulled the white silk over her head, she blushed. He stepped up to her and wrapped his arms about her naked body, his arousal thrust grandly between them, and the fire roared.

Warm in the bed of cotton and bracken, with silk and wool over and under them, they made love—an exchange, delicate, yet ferocious. He worshiped her slowly with hands and tongue, bringing her into a delirium of ecstasy. She adored him back, her hands on his resilient skin and limber muscles, touching, marveling at how he was made. His dauntless back and round buttocks. The delectable swell of shoulder and corded arm. The silk of golden hair and the rough, strong jaw—an enchantment of touch and scent and texture, profoundly male, profoundly glorious.

He entered her with fierce, strong tenderness and spared

her nothing, plunging her into torrents of flame. She opened herself, thrusting her hips against his, holding his body against hers, biting blindly at his shoulder. Panting, in a delirium of joy, she surrendered her soul—*giving, giving, until your blood burns and your lungs pant for air!*

He swung her above him. She looked down at his shadowed face, his head tilted back and his teeth white in the darkness. Moved, pierced, she dropped forward and fastened her mouth over his, breathing in his breath, mingling peat and smoke and honey on his tongue.

Skin slick with passion, he rolled her beneath him again, still kissing, still joined to her. As they thrust together his eyes opened and smiled down into hers. Catriona gazed up into the dark, secret depths—her soul reaching for the mystery at the heart of his life—as he carried her with him over a path across the sky and the dark exploded with stars.

She cried out, convulsing against him, her arms and legs taut, clutching at his body. *"A Dhominic! Tha m'anam a' snàmh an ceò!"*

The convulsions rippled away as the sea surged in her and his seed spilled at the mouth of her receptive womb. Spent, exhausted, she gazed up at the face of her hero. "I love you!" she whispered. "I love you, my heart, and I am lost, lost."

Oh, Dominic! My soul swims in mist!

"Hush, hush!" He gathered her in his arms and cradled her against his chest, pulling the quilt over their moist, satiated bodies, enfolding her in comfort. "We have created a life for a new soul, Catriona. Our child." His breath was warm, brushing in smiles over her cheek. "And who knows, it might be a girl—"

Author's Note

∞

IT'S THE STRANGEST things in this story that are true—the earthquake, the change in whisky laws, the belief in second sight, the description of Byron's home at Newstead. Yet if you look at a map of Easter Ross, you won't find Glen Reulach. I inserted an imaginary fold of hills and glens between Strath Farrar and Strathconan to make a setting for Dunachan Castle. As a Ross myself, I hope the people there will forgive me.

As far as I know, there never was a clan named Mac-Norrin. Incidentally, in Gaelic, where *mac* means "son," the women of the clan take the feminine form of the surname beginning with *nic,* meaning daughter. I let them all be known as "MacNorrin" only to avoid confusion.

The clearances, however, were real and I exaggerated nothing. Across the Highlands for more than fifty years, the people were driven away from their ancestral homes—often with vicious cruelty—to make way for sheep. Every incident described by Catriona in Kildonan, Strathnaver, Glengarry, and Kinlochnevis is genuine. With the exception of Iseabail's curse, every detail of the burning of Achnadrochaid—including the beating of the women—happened at various times and places. In reality women were maimed and killed trying in vain to defend their homes.

My descriptions of the people and their lives grew from careful research. Regency travelers were universally impressed by the culture and courtesy they met in the Highlands. The haunted glens admired today for their wild scenery were not always empty. In Glen Cannich, above Strath Glass—where the glen is now flooded by a hydro-electric dam—there is a small monument to the vanished Chisholms.

Though I moved its timing slightly to fit my story, the earthquake took place on Tuesday, August 13, 1816. The *Inverness Journal* reported a "universal shaking of the houses, the rattling of the slates and the tremendous crash of large stones which were precipitated with violence from many of the chimney tops." The bells rang for a minute, and "the beautiful spire attached to the Jail was at the distance of several feet from the top, completely rent and twisted several inches round." Although not much is left of Regency Inverness, that spire still stands guard over the town.

Whisky, and the growth of the necessary grain, was an important part of Highland economy and culture. Yet at the beginning of 1816, Highland whisky was subject to a higher duty than English or Irish liquor, and regulations on the size of stills made profitable legal manufacture impossible. In March, an Inverness distiller was ruined when the Exchequer prohibited the export of spirits to the Lowlands. Smuggling boomed. The situation was debated in Parliament that summer and the laws changed, so by the end of 1817, the Inverness newspaper describes the establishment of legal distilleries in Ross-shire.

The "second sight" was still commonly talked of when my father was a child. I'm a skeptic myself—but I wasn't there!

I hope you enjoyed meeting Dominic and Catriona, and were moved by the passions that lay behind their story. Dominic's previous adventures are told in *Illusion,* the story of Frances and Nigel (Berkley, September 1998). I love to hear from readers and may be reached at P.O. Box 197, Ridgway, CO 81432-0197. A stamped, self-addressed long envelope is much appreciated if you'd like a reply.

For more information, visit my web page at
http://www.jeanrossewing.com